KU-033-730

The Hardy Boys Mysteries

The Clue in the Embers
What Happened at Midnight
The Sinister Signpost

Franklin W. Dixon

This edition produced exclusively for Bookmart by
Armada, an imprint of HarperCollins Children's Books,
part of HarperCollins Publishers Ltd 1991

The Hardy Boys is a trademark of
the Stratemeyer Syndicate, registered in the
United States Patent and Trademark Office.

Printed and bound in Great Britain by
HarperCollins Book Manufacturing Ltd, Glasgow

Contents

The Clue in the Embers
5

What Happened at Midnight
161

The Sinister Signpost
313

The Clue in the Embers

The Clue in the Embers was first published in a single volume
in the U.S. in 1963 by Grosset & Dunlap, Inc.
First published in the U.K. in 1972 by
William Collins Sons & Co. Ltd.

Copyright © 1963 by Grosset & Dunlap, Inc.

·1· *A Strange Inheritance*

THE shrill ringing of the Hardy telephone greeted Frank and Joe as they swung into the driveway after a midsummer ball practice at the Bayport High playing fields.

"Hurry!" Mrs Hardy called a moment later. "It's the third time Tony Prito has phoned this morning!"

"Must be an important message," said blond, seventeen-year-old Joe to his brother Frank, dark-haired and a year older. "Be right there, Mom!"

Clearing the porch steps in two strides, Joe hurried in to the phone. "Hello, Tony. What's up?"

Tony's voice was serious. "How would you and Frank like to see some shrunken heads?"

"See *what!*" Joe gasped.

"Six shrunken human heads!"

"Where are they?"

Tony replied excitedly, "I've inherited a lot of mysterious curios from my uncle Roberto. He had a shop full of them in New York when he died. The shipment, including the shrunken heads, will arrive at the Bayport station at one-twenty."

"Wait till I tell Frank!" Joe exclaimed, and promised that the Hardys would be at the Prito house by one o'clock. "We'll help you load the crates."

"I may need you fellows for more than loading

7

crates," Tony remarked, his voice grave again. "Tell you when you get here."

Joe hurried outside and relayed to Frank the story of the strange shipment. His brother's eyebrows lifted. "No wonder Tony phoned three times," Frank observed as he followed his brother into the house. "This sounds as though we might have run smack into another mystery."

"Time for lunch!" Mrs Hardy told them as they walked into the kitchen. Then the slender, attractive woman asked, "What's this about a mystery?" The boys told her briefly what Tony had said.

Mrs Hardy smiled. "You're both just like your dad."

Fenton Hardy, the boys' father, an internationally famous detective, had served many years with the New York City police force. Later, he had settled in Bayport, a bustling seaport of fifty thousand inhabitants. From his big stone house at the corner of Elm and High streets he carried on a highly successful career as a private investigator, but he liked nothing better than working with his two sons, solving mysteries.

"Shall we call Chet and ask him to come along to help carry crates?" Joe asked. "He needs the exercise."

Chet Morton was the Hardys' chubby pal who often went along with them to follow up clues. He lived on a farm about a mile from Bayport.

Frank shook his head. "Better not take the time. If Tony's as worried as he seems to be, we'd better eat and get over there as quickly as possible. It's almost one o'clock now."

Within ten minutes the boys were on their way to Tony's house. They found their friend sitting on the front steps. One of the Prito Construction Company's large trucks was parked at the kerb. Tony wore an anxious look as he waved to the Hardys.

"What's this all about?" Frank asked, as they hurried up the path.

Tony's expression relaxed a little. "Some inheritance, eh?" he said. "All kinds of weird stories connected with the curios. But I'm puzzled why anyone would want to buy the collection without examining it to see what it's worth."

"What!" Joe exclaimed.

Reaching into his sports shirt pocket, Tony pulled out a telegram and showed it to the boys.

Signed with the single name *Valez*, the message was an offer to buy unseen, for two hundred dollars, the entire collection of curios.

"This arrived yesterday," Tony explained. "And you notice that Valez, whoever he is, says he's going to phone this afternoon and make arrangements for picking up the stuff."

Suspicious, the Hardys glanced at each other. The man certainly was not giving Tony much time to consider the offer. Frank suggested at once that the collection might be worth much more than two hundred dollars.

"Sure," said Joe. "I wouldn't take his offer."

"Right," Frank continued. "Valez is too eager to make a deal. And he doesn't present even one credential. Besides, I think he has a nerve to assume you're going to sell him the curios before you've had a chance to have them valued."

"Do you have a list of all the curios, Tony?" Joe asked.

"No, not a complete one," Tony replied, "but this letter from the estate's executor, a bank in New York City, mentions some of the items." From a pocket he removed a long, folded envelope. The boys scanned the paragraph that told of the curios.

"Look!" Joe exclaimed. "You even have some Moorish scimitars!"

"What about them?" Tony asked.

Frank, who had done some research in connection with a case, explained that a scimitar is a crescent-shaped sabre used originally by Moorish horsemen, and as late as the Wars of Napoleon. Made of fine Damascus steel, often with guards of gold set with precious stones, these antique weapons are rare and valuable.

"And here!" Frank continued. "The letter mentions the South American shrunken heads you told Joe about on the phone!"

These heads, or *tsanstas*, the letter explained, in spite of laws against their sale or barter in both Peru and Ecuador, have a considerable value in the souvenir market.

The savage Andean Indians used to take the heads of their enemies in local warfare. After the removal of the skull from the severed head, the rest was reduced by boiling to the size of a man's fist. The eyes and lips were pinned and laced, and the interior treated with hot stones and sand. With the use of a local herb, the hair remained long and kept its original lustre.

"Pretty barbaric," Tony remarked.

"I don't suppose these heads are as valuable as many of the other objects," Frank said. "But you shouldn't sell a single item until you've had a chance to find out the value of the collection."

Tony agreed.

"We'd better get started for the station," Joe urged. "The train's just about due."

Tony slipped the telegram back into his pocket along with the letter. The trio started off.

Brr-r-r-ing! The phone in the Prito hallway rang shrilly.

"Maybe it's Valez!" Tony exclaimed.

The Hardys followed their friend into the hallway and Tony picked up the phone. As he listened, his jaw tightened. For several seconds the three boys stood still while the high-pitched voice on the line chattered without a break. Tony nodded to indicate that the caller was Valez.

"No!" Tony said abruptly. "Thank you just the same."

Valez's voice grew louder and angry. Then it stopped.

"I'm sorry," Tony said firmly. "I can't accept your offer."

The Hardys heard Valez snap one more remark at Tony. An awkward silence followed. Then Tony hung up.

"What did he say?" the Hardys asked eagerly.

"Valez threatened me," Tony replied. "He said, 'You'll be sorry for this.' And he's right here in Bayport!"

"Wow!" Joe exploded. "We'd better get down to the station. Valez might try to pull a fast one."

"I'm sure glad that you fellows are along," Tony said nervously, as the trio dashed out of the house.

The train was not yet in sight when the boys arrived at the station. The usual small crowd of idlers and station employees bustled about or stared up the track to watch for the incoming freight train.

Glancing quickly round the platform, the boys saw no one who resembled what they thought Valez might look like. Most of the faces were familiar and the others were those of teenagers.

"Here she comes!" a youngster cried, as the whistle blew before it roared into the station area and ground to a stop.

The boys' hearts beat excitedly in anticipation as they watched the freight agent run his cart to a boxcar. The door opened. Crates and cartons were quickly lifted out.

Joe whistled loudly. "Wow! Some haul, Tony!" he exclaimed as box after box, some with strange foreign-looking markings, was piled high on to the cart. The boys watched alertly out of the corner of their eyes for any unusual action or the sudden appearance of any particularly interested persons.

"Okay, Tony!" the agent said, and handed him the bill of lading to be signed.

Without losing a moment, the three boys pulled the cart to the truck and started loading the cases on to it. Working feverishly to finish the job so that they could get home and examine the curios, the boys were glad to have the help of two acquaintances from the platform crowd.

As Joe lifted the last case on to the truck, he said quietly, "Frank, you sit up front with Tony. I'd better stay back here as lookout."

"Okay," his brother agreed and jumped into the cab. Tony climbed to the driver's seat and started the engine.

Sitting atop one of the cases in the open back of the truck, Joe commanded a good view of the station and the public square. "Still no sign of action from Valez," he thought. "I wonder if the whole business was just a hoax."

As they turned into the tree-lined avenue two blocks from Tony's house, Frank slid back the glass in the rear of the cab and said, "This job turned out to be a lot easier than I expected."

Joe was just about to answer when his eye caught sight of an arrowhead-like missile streaking through the air directly towards him!

•2• *A Stolen Curio*

SEEING the missile whizzing towards him, Joe ducked, but he felt a stinging blow on his right arm, which he had flung up to protect himself.

"Stop the truck!" Joe yelled to Tony. "Get that fellow!" He pointed to a man who had dodged from behind a tree and was running away from them at top speed.

The air brakes gripped and the vehicle lurched to a halt. The cab door was flung open by Frank, who raced towards a wooded stretch beyond the sidewalk.

"That fellow has a blowgun!" he called. Frank pursued the assailant into woods at the back of the houses and disappeared.

Meanwhile, Tony eased the truck to the edge of the road. Leaving the engine idling, he slid back the window behind him to see what had happened to Joe.

"Something hit you?" he asked.

"Yes, Tony." Joe showed him a small arrowhead. A tiny paper had been glued to the base of it. Without examining either the arrowhead or the paper, Joe thrust them into a trouser pocket. Asking Tony to guard the truck, he too dashed off in search of his assailant.

Joe sprinted a hundred yards into the woods. Struggling through a stretch of thicket, he called, "Frank! Where are you?"

"Over here!" Frank was standing near a wire fence that bounded two closely spaced factories.

"The blowgun guy jumped the fence," Frank panted, "and ran between the buildings. Never catch him now." Both boys paused to catch their breath.

"We'd better hurry back to the truck," Joe suggested. "This attack might have been just a ruse to get us away from it."

Suddenly they heard the noise of someone crashing through the underbrush towards them. They wondered if it was an accomplice of Joe's attacker, also armed with a blowgun.

"Duck behind this tree!" Frank whispered.

A moment later the figure of Tony Prito appeared in the nearest clearing.

"Tony!" Frank called softly.

Their friend approached the Hardys, a smile of relief on his face. "I just couldn't sit in that truck any longer worrying about you guys. I took the ignition key and lit out after you. Guess I shouldn't have left the truck, though."

The trio ran back towards the street. "Did you get a good look at the man?" Tony asked.

"Not too good," Frank replied. "He's short, thin, dark-complexioned, and has a small moustache."

Joe frowned. "How old do you think he is?"

"I'd say about forty, and a very wiry guy. You should have seen him vault that fence."

To the boys' relief, they found the shipment intact in the truck.

"Joe, you'd better sit up front with us," Tony said. "We can't afford to let that man take another pot shot at you. You might not be so lucky the next time."

Once inside the cab, the boys examined the arrowhead which was made of lead, and the paper which had covered the base of the missile. A message was written on the paper in a scrawled and barely legible script. The pencilled words warned Tony not to dispose of the curios.

"Gosh, what's a fellow supposed to do?" Tony complained. "First Valez threatens me if I don't sell the stuff, and now this guy tells me not to or I'll get in trouble!"

"I'll bet Valez is responsible for both threats," said Joe. "Maybe he has a reason for wanting to confuse you."

"How can we be sure that this warning was fired by Valez?" Frank asked. "There's a good chance that someone else is after the curios, too."

"You mean some enemy of Valez?" Tony asked as he started the truck.

"Possibly," Frank replied.

"At any rate," Joe commented, "we have a full-fledged mystery on our hands."

"You can say that again," Frank agreed.

Tony turned the truck into the driveway of his home and stopped at the rear. He suggested that they carry the cartons and crates of curios into the garage.

"We'll unpack them here," he said, "and carry the articles a few at a time into the house."

By the time they finished, the cases filled the place. The last box to go in was the set of four valuable Damascus steel scimitars.

"Tony," said Frank, "I'm not so sure the garage is

the best place for your curios. Wouldn't they be safer in your cellar?"

"I have an idea," replied Tony. "Why don't I ask the new Howard Museum to take care of them? Maybe I'll give the museum some of them and ask Mr Scath to store the rest for me in return."

"Good idea," said Frank. "I know the stuff will be a lot safer there than in your garage or cellar."

While the Hardys guarded the shipment, Tony went indoors and phoned Mr Scath, the curator.

"Well, now, I don't know quite what to say, Tony," Mr Scath said in reply to the request. "I remember well your uncle Roberto and his shop in New York. He was a delightful and interesting man, and if I remember correctly he was quite absent-minded at times. I liked him very much. But I can't believe that your shipment would include anything of value to our museum."

"But couldn't you at least—?" Tony began.

"I know just what you're going to ask, Tony," Mr Scath interrupted. "Yes. We'll store the curios for you temporarily."

"Swell." Tony explained how urgently he wanted the articles to be protected.

"The museum is open late tonight," said the curator. "I suggest that you bring your curios round about nine o'clock, after closing time. There won't be anybody in the building and I'll have a chance to look at them."

As Tony stepped into the yard he was startled to see a man tiptoeing along the side of the garage and listening. He was short and wore a felt hat pulled low.

Involuntarily Tony yelled. The intruder took off like a streak of lightning. Tony chased the man down the block, but he ran between two houses to another street and escaped in a car.

When Tony told his story to the Hardys, the brothers were worried. "That guy means business!" Joe declared. "We'd better keep a lookout." The boys took turns keeping watch as they inspected the curios.

As time passed, one thing became certain: the collection was worth much more than two hundred dollars.

"Do you realize what time it is?" Frank asked hours later. "Almost six-thirty. Boy, we'd better eat."

"My folks won't be home for dinner," Tony said, "so why don't you call up your house and tell your mother you'll eat here."

"Great idea!" Joe said. "I'll phone."

The boys took their time over the delicious meal and were deep in conversation when suddenly Frank interrupted. "Sh-h!" he warned.

"What's the matter?" Tony asked.

"I heard a noise coming from the garage!"

The boys dashed outside. Seeing that the garage doors were still padlocked, they ran round to the rear. The window was open!

"Careful!" Tony cried, as Joe leaped on to the ledge and climbed in.

Tony opened the lock and entered the garage with Frank. There was no one inside but Joe.

"One of the scimitars is missing!" Frank exclaimed. Only three of the Moorish swords remained in the rack.

Frank and Joe made a frantic search through the neighbourhood but found no trace of the burglar. In disgust they retraced their steps to Tony's house and reported their failure to him.

"Trouble's afoot," said Tony. "Let's wash the dishes and then load the truck before something else happens!"

During the clatter of washing the dishes, the sound

of the doorbell stopped the boys short. Could this be another uninvited visitor?

The tension was broken when Tony opened the door. The caller was the boys' chubby friend, Chet Morton.

"Did I just miss a meal?" Chet chuckled when Frank appeared, still holding a dish towel.

"Yes." Frank laughed. "You missed a meal, but you're just in time to help us load about twenty crates on to Tony's truck."

Chet groaned and slumped into a chair. "Okay," he said. "I walked right into your trap. I'll carry the little ones." Then he added, "But tell me what this is all about."

After giving him a brief resumé, the boys started the job. As darkness began to settle over Bayport, Tony confided to Frank that he thought they should not try to carry out the plan without police protection.

"After what happened today," Frank agreed, "I guess you're right. As a matter of fact, Chief Collig will be at headquarters now. He doesn't go off duty until late in the evening."

Tony phoned and told the chief what had taken place during the day.

"Land sakes, boy," the good-natured officer boomed, "you should've called on us long before now."

Tony estimated that the truck would be loaded by nine-fifteen.

"I'll come out there myself," the chief said. "And I'll bring along a little assistance, even though we shouldn't need it with athletic fellows like you and Chet Morton along!"

With the yard floodlights beamed on them, the four boys worked quickly to have the truck loaded before the arrival of the Bayport police escort.

"Here they come!" Joe called, as Tony swung the last packing case into position.

A squad car, carrying Chief Collig and a patrolman, followed by a motorcycle, pulled up to the kerb. The men waited for the boys to climb on to the truck. Tony switched off the floodlights, ran across the yard, and climbed up behind the wheel. All four boys sat in the big cab.

"Anyone who tries to stop us this time will get a hot reception," Tony remarked as he backed the truck into the street.

With the motorcycle shooting ahead into lead position, and the patrol car in the rear, the convoy started its trek along the dark streets towards the museum.

· 3 · *Fire in the Mummy Case*

THE tree-lined road to the museum, also an approach to the Bayport airfield, ran through one of the loneliest outlying sections of the town. In the long stretches between street lamps, the road was in almost total darkness. The thick foliage of the trees kept the light within a small radius of each pole.

"I'd hate to be walking along here with a blowgun blower in hiding," Chet said. "It's mighty eerie out this way." He shivered.

At that moment the motorcycle swung to the right and entered the curving, dimly lighted driveway of the ivy-covered museum. As the truck followed, all eyes searched the shrubbery that surrounded the building. But there was no sign of anyone lying in wait.

The massive door of the building creaked open and the slender figure of the curator appeared. Mr Scath hurried down the steps and greeted the boys, then told them to move the crates into the basement.

"Let's step on it!" Tony urged. "The sooner we get this stuff behind that door, the better I'll feel."

As the boys lugged the boxes from the truck, Chief Collig and his men kept an alert watch for Tony's enemies. For fifteen minutes the tense operation continued. Finally, Tony picked up the last crate and called to Chief Collig that the job was finished. After the crate had been placed in the basement, the boys went outside to thank the police official and patrolmen for their help.

The genial chief smiled. "In case you run into any further trouble, call me," he said.

Blinking a signal to the motorcycle officer to follow, he headed back towards town. Mr Scath then bolted the big door, and he and the boys went to the basement to unpack the curios and put them on shelves there.

The curator's eyes flashed with excitement when he finished listing the objects. "I can hardly wait for morning to make a more careful study of these pieces!" he exclaimed. "I can tell you right now I'd like to exhibit these unusual musical instruments with our present collection. Tony, there are some real treasures in this shipment. No wonder some unscrupulous persons are trying to get them."

Tony gulped. "Guess I didn't appreciate what I was getting," he said.

Relieved to know that his inheritance was safe at last

in the museum, Tony assured Mr Scath that he and the Hardys would come over whenever the curator was ready to talk about the curios.

"Of course there will be some items that don't amount to anything," Mr Scath added. "Things like this box, for instance."

For a moment the curator fingered an object that looked like an ordinary cigarette box; it was about four inches long and was made of dark wood. He was just about to toss it into a wastepaper-basket when Frank stopped him.

"If you please, Mr Scath, I'd like to keep this box," he said. "That is, if Tony doesn't want it."

"Help yourself," Tony replied, and Mr Scath handed the object to Frank.

Joe looked at his brother. What did he have in mind? Then Joe recalled one of their father's admonitions: Never throw away any possible evidence where a mystery is concerned.

The curator walked to the storage-room door, and beckoned the boys to precede him. He then locked the door. Frank went ahead, leading the way up the stairs. His footsteps echoed through the main hall. Instinctively he stepped lightly.

"Stop!" Joe whispered suddenly, grabbing his brother's arm from behind. "Did you hear a sound from the other side of the hall?"

"I'm not sure," Frank said softly, gazing towards the room where a mummy and several sarcophagi were on display.

"Listen!" Joe insisted, thrusting his arm out to stop the group. There was no sound.

"Mr Scath," Joe continued in a whisper, "is anybody working in this building?"

"No," the curator assured him. "We're the only ones here."

"Sh-h!" Joe warned.

A sharp scraping noise came from the mummy room. A muffled sound followed.

As Mr Scath switched on all the hall lights, the Hardys, Chet, and Tony ran towards the room where ancient Egyptian treasures were exhibited. Frank stopped at the opening, clicked the switch, and quickly surveyed the pillared room. There was no sign of an intruder among the sarcophagi, one of which held a body three thousand years dead.

"There must be someone in the museum!" Mr Scath whispered nervously. "One of you inspect the balconies upstairs. The rest search this floor!"

Chet Morton, nearest to the spiral steps that led from the main hall to the balconies, gripped the iron rail and started up. But he did not relish the job. Frank and Joe dashed to the left of the Egyptian Room. Mr Scath and Tony headed through the middle of the hall.

"What a spooky place!" Joe exclaimed in hushed tones to his brother, as he looked into an open sarcophagus and saw the painted face of the mummy which lay in an inner coffin made of cedar.

"Don't worry about the spooks!" Frank replied. "I expect to see a blowgun pop out from behind one of those columns!"

Moving stealthily along the outer passage, the brothers reached the other end of the room without catching sight of any intruder. As they headed towards the centre aisle to join the curator, Frank stopped abruptly.

"Do you smell smoke?" he asked, sniffing.

"I sure do," Joe answered, alarmed.

A strong odour of smoke soon filled their nostrils. It was hard to tell where it came from, but both boys dashed among the sarcophagi to locate its source.

"Here it is!" Joe cried out a moment later. "Mr Scath, Frank—come here quick!"

As the curator appeared in the aisle, followed by Frank and Tony, Joe pointed to a slightly opened, ornately designed sarcophagus. Grey-white smoke was pouring from it.

"Give me a hand!" Mr Scath cried. "Lift up the cover!"

The boys got their shoulders against the heavy lid and forced it farther upwards. The smoke thinned into a column, exposing, atop the coffin inside, a cone-shaped pile of embers!

Frank peeled off his polo shirt and smothered the glow that remained in the embers.

"Whoever made this fire must still be in the building!" Mr Scath warned. "No one could get in or out of here without the keys that I have in my pocket. That means someone must have hidden in here before nine o'clock."

"Say!" Joe exclaimed. "Wonder if Chet's found out anything." He called out, but there was no reply from the balcony.

"We'll search the entire building for the intruder," Mr Scath said grimly. "He can't get away. We'll start in the basement."

The Hardys, worried about Chet's failure to answer, decided that one of them should run up to the balcony to check on what might have happened to their friend.

"I'll go," Frank volunteered. "Joe, you help Mr Scath and Tony." Frank headed for the same staircase that Chet had taken.

As the others were about to start for the basement, Mr Scath decided first to remove the embers from the sarcophagus. "There's too much danger of their containing a scattered spark or two. Wait here."

The curator got a small shovel and an empty metal waste-paper basket from his office and returned to the sarcophagus. He was about to drop the ashes into the basket when Joe suddenly interrupted.

"Mr Scath, I'd like to take the ashes to our lab to study them."

"Certainly," the curator agreed. "Mighty good idea." He had heard of the modern, fully equipped, crime-detection laboratory that the Hardys had set up on the first floor of their garage.

Joe got a museum specimen envelope and the curator carefully poured a large sample of the ashes and charred remains into it. Joe sealed the envelope and slipped it into his pocket.

"Now let's find the intruder!" Mr Scath urged, and the trio headed for the basement.

Suddenly, from the balcony, came a crash and a blood-curdling shriek!

·4· Skylight Escape

ELECTRIFIED by the piercing outcry from upstairs, Joe and Tony dashed up the spiral stairs, with Mr Scath following as quickly as he could.

Frank had already reached Chet, who admitted yelling. He said he had not heard Joe calling him before. "B-but I sure w-wish I had," added Chet, sagging against the balcony railing opposite the entrance to the American Indian gallery. His face was white and he trembled as he started to explain.

"W-when I got to this spot," he began, "I looked in and saw that figure s-start to move!" He pointed to the tall statue of a Cherokee chieftain that now lay across the passageway.

"How did it get there?" Frank asked.

"It walked, yes, walked, and then it swayed a couple of times before it toppled over," Chet replied.

Mr Scath, reaching the top of the stairs, said, "Calm yourself, Chet. We've had trouble with that figure before. It's off centre. Needs to be balanced."

"B-but what made it walk?" Chet quavered.

The curator's eyes opened wide as a thought struck him. He said the figure could not walk. Probably the intruder had moved it!

"You almost caught him, Chet," Joe remarked.

Chet looked crestfallen at the lost opportunity. Through his being tricked, the stranger had been able to escape. Chet was as indignant now as he had been frightened earlier. "Let's keep looking," he urged, "and find that guy!"

The search for the unknown person continued for half an hour. Methodically the group went from top to bottom of the museum, without finding a trace of the intruder. There were no windows on the ground floor and those on the first were locked.

"How about the skylight?" Frank suggested.

"There's just the one in the prints gallery on the top floor," Mr Scath answered. "I never thought of that. It's not fitted with a special lock!"

Frank went up to the second floor and looked at the skylight. The glass frame was in its properly closed position. But the hasp hung downwards! It was unlocked!

"The intruder went across the roof and down the ivy vines," Frank decided. "A clean getaway!"

The young sleuth returned to the first floor and told Mr Scath of his discovery. The curator explained that the skylight was checked every evening at closing time, so the intruder definitely had hidden in the museum before it closed.

"Boys, we've done all we can. You'd better get some sleep," Mr Scath said. "We can discuss this mystery at another time."

"In the meantime, we may discover something of value about the ashes in this package," Joe added.

After Frank climbed up and locked the skylight, the group headed for the ground floor. Mr Scath asked if Tony would mind following his car in the truck. "With all the odd things going on round here tonight, I don't feel much like driving home alone."

Joe offered to ride with the curator. Tony would follow. The car moved slowly along the drive and turned into the highway.

Its two passengers rode for a couple of blocks in silence. Then Joe remembered the arrowhead that had been fired at him from the blowgun earlier in the day. It was still in his pocket. He brought it out.

"Mr Scath," Joe said, holding the arrowhead in the light from the dashboard, "do you know what country this is from?"

The curator stopped the car and picked up the object from Joe's palm. He looked at it carefully. "Hm-m. It's not North American," Mr Scath said slowly, "and it's not like any I've ever seen before."

"Where would you guess it's from?" Joe prodded.

"That's hard to say," Mr Scath replied. Chuckling, he added, "I wouldn't want to pull a boner in front of a famous young detective."

Joe laughed and slipped the arrowhead back into his pocket. After getting out at Mr Scath's home, Joe stepped up into the truck. Chet was taken home first, then the Hardys.

"See you soon, Tony," Frank called. "Let us know if you hear from Valez again."

The brothers hurried upstairs to their bedroom. Frank stood lost in thought.

Joe eyed him a moment, then remarked, "For a fellow who's been on the go since nine o'clock yesterday morning you don't seem very sleepy." He had noticed that Frank was inspecting the envelope containing the charred remains of the coffin fire.

"I'm not," Frank replied. "Guess I can't sleep until we've made an analysis of these ashes and charred bits. I'm pretty sure it's wood, but I'd like to know what kind."

"Let's try not to wake up Mother," Joe warned. "She'll think we've lost our minds working this late."

The boys removed their shoes, put on moccasins, and headed for their garage laboratory.

"Set up the microtome," Frank suggested. "I'll get the photomicrograph ready."

Joe shook out the contents of the envelope and selected one of the firmer tiny charred pieces. He clamped this in place on the microtome. Then, running a finely honed knife blade delicately through it, Joe cut off a section.

"What thickness?" Joe asked.

"About two thousandths of an inch," Frank replied. Working carefully, Joe cut other tissue-thin sections from several angles, letting them drop on to a glass slide. In a few moments Frank had prepared several photomicrographs of them, showing distinct wood grains.

"Now we'll see what was burning in the sarcophagus," Frank said quietly as he prepared to project the first lantern slide on to the screen in the darkened room.

The enlarged curves in the picture revealed clear patterns. Frank compared them with a chart in an encyclopedia.

"The grain matches the mahogany," he said. The boys examined the pattern again and compared it with further angle shots. "It's Central American mahogany!" Frank concluded.

"Now why would—?" Joe began.

"Just a minute," Frank interrupted thoughtfully. "How about the name Valez?"

"Sounds Spanish enough to have some possible connection," Joe agreed.

"And we know that the missile is not North American," Frank added. "The first thing we do tomorrow is airmail that arrowhead to Dad's friend, Mr Hopewell, in Chicago. He'll be able to identify it. He's a specialist in primitive weapons."

Storing the packet of ashes and the lantern slides in their small safe, the boys returned to the house and tiptoed up to their bedroom.

"I'd like to get up early to work on this mystery," Frank said drowsily.

"Me too." Joe set the alarm for six and switched off the light. A few moments later both boys were sleeping soundly.

"Gosh," Joe exclaimed, when he heard the rasping buzz of the alarm, "I feel as though I'd just gone to bed!"

"You did practically," Frank muttered as he sat upright and blinked.

Then both boys dropped back on their pillows and fell asleep again. It was eight o'clock when they again awoke and the brothers grinned sheepishly.

"Mm, I smell bacon and eggs!" Joe said, and got out of bed in a hurry.

"What are you boys up to now?" Aunt Gertrude asked them as she passed the crisp bacon and honey buns.

They gave an account of the curios, the missile, the chase, and the events at the museum.

Breakfast was almost over when the telephone rang.

"Wonder who's calling," Mrs Hardy said.

"Might be Fenton," Aunt Gertrude suggested.

"Or Mr Scath," Frank said.

"I'll get it," Joe offered, pushing back his chair. He disappeared into the hallway.

"Hello," Joe said cheerily.

"Hello, Joe," replied the excited voice of Tony Prito. "Valez has just phoned again!"

"What did he say?"

"Joe, he threatened you and Frank!"

·5· *Missing Valuables*

"FRANK and I are being threatened by Valez!" Joe cried. "Why, Tony?"

"Valez says that you're interfering with my selling him the collection. I told him you had nothing to do with it. I wouldn't sell it, anyway. Boy, was he mad!

Threatened to make me give him whatever he wanted and said if you fellows didn't keep out of it he'd get you too!"

"How in the world does Valez know Frank and me?" Joe asked.

"I don't know," Tony replied, "but he called you 'those Hardy boys.'"

When Frank heard the threat a few minutes later, he began to speculate on what action they should take next to learn more about Valez.

"Now listen to me," Aunt Gertrude interrupted. "You'd better pay attention to that warning. There's just no sense in waiting until danger's right on top of you. If I were your parents—"

The front-door bell sounded and the lecture ended. As Frank started for the front of the house Joe followed, grinning.

Frank opened the front door. A tall, broad-shouldered stranger with red hair, who appeared to be a merchant seaman, was standing on the porch. Several tattoo marks covered his thick, bared forearms. As he took a step forward, the boys, suspecting that he might be an agent of Valez, braced themselves in the doorway and eyed the visitor.

"Good morning," Frank said politely. "What can we do for you?"

"You're the Hardy boys?"

"Yes."

A broad smile creased the young man's face. Awkwardly he fingered his crew cut. Then he extended a sun-tanned hand to the brothers.

"My name is Wortman," he began in a voice that seemed no less friendly than his handshake. "I've been lookin' for you for some time."

Joe asked the man to come into the house. "Don't mind if I do," Wortman replied. "It's quite a walk from the Bayport station."

This answer puzzled the boys. They had guessed from his clothing that he had come from some ship docked at Bayport.

"Did you arrive here this morning?" Joe asked, as they entered the living-room and he swung a chair round for the caller.

"Yes, I came from New York on the sleeper," the man replied.

"You came all that way just to see us, Mr Wortman?" Joe asked incredulously.

"Well, indirectly," Wortman began. "But first, let's quit this 'Mister' stuff. My name's Willie and that's what you're to call me."

"Okay, Willie." Joe smiled. "I still want to know why you'd travel all the way here from New York just to see us."

Wortman explained that he was an able-bodied seaman on a freighter plying to Central and South America. At the mention of these last words Joe and Frank exchanged glances.

Wortman, noticing their sudden interest, asked, "Anything unusual about a fellow shippin' to South America?"

"Oh, no," Joe replied hastily. "Nothing at all."

"Well," Wortman continued, "my ship docked in New York last week. After I was paid off, I went to visit an old shopkeeper friend of mine—a man named Roberto Prito."

"Prito!" Frank repeated. The name had startled him, but he restrained himself from showing this.

"Yes," Wortman went on. "But my friend had died

and his shop was locked tight. I sure felt bad—he was a good pal." After a pause the seaman continued. "I was disappointed, too, because I'd hoped to pick up two medallions there—one the size of a half dollar, the other somewhat larger.

"I heard from a neighbour of Roberto's that a large shipment of objects from the shop had been sent to Tony Prito here in Bayport. Figuring the medallions might been have in the shipment, I came on out. I went to Tony's house as soon as I got off the train. He says he's pretty sure they're not in the collection. Tony had to take the truck out on a rush job for his dad, so he advised me to come here and talk to you about them."

"Did these two medallions belong to you?" Frank asked.

"Yes," Wortman replied. "I got them from a buddy of mine who has since been killed. A short time ago, when I was broke, I pawned them with Roberto."

"And you were trying to buy them back?" Frank asked.

"Y-yes." His halting reply puzzled the brothers. Wortman went on, "I guess I may be a bit foolish about goin' to such trouble to locate them. They're really of no value to anyone else. I'd just like to get hold of them for the sake of sentiment—something to remember my friend by."

"Can you tell us more about their appearance?" Frank asked.

Wortman explained that the medallions were made of some kind of cheap metal, and had a design of curving lines. In addition, the larger one had a fake opal set in it, while the other had the word *Texichapi* inscribed on it.

"What does that mean?" Joe asked.

"I don't know," the seaman answered.

"You must understand," Frank said, "that even if we do find them, we wouldn't have the authority to hand over the medallions to you immediately. We'd have to return them to Tony, then you'd have to make arrangements with him."

"That's fair enough," the visitor replied.

Wortman rose from his chair, and after thanking the boys, started for the door. Suddenly he stopped.

"There's one other thing," he said. "I was told by a man in a seaport down on the Gulf that there's a curse connected with these medallions."

"A curse!" Joe exclaimed.

"The man told me that trouble will come to anyone who sells these objects," Wortman explained. "That's the real reason why I want to get them back."

The boys drove Wortman to the station and watched him board the train for New York, then they returned home to finish their breakfast. They reviewed for their mother and aunt in careful detail the whole story Wortman had told them.

"How much of it was trumped up?" Joe asked his brother.

"Surely the part about the curse," Frank replied. "I believe Willie's imagination got the better of him at that stage. But for the rest, it sounds real enough."

"Do you think that there is any connection between these medallions and the episode at the museum—the intruder and the embers in the coffin?" Joe queried.

"I sure do," said Frank. "Maybe the intruder believes the story of the curse and was trying to break it."

As Joe poured a glass of milk, he suddenly recalled that Aunt Gertrude's lecture on their sleuthing had been interrupted by Wortman's visit. "As you were saying," he joked, "we should give up chasing danger."

"Why," Miss Hardy snapped, ignoring the remark, "you boys can't even eat your breakfast in peace. You go running off with total strangers in the middle of a meal."

"We do that just to work up an appetite," Joe said, reaching for another bun. "There's nothing like a little road work between courses."

At that moment, Frank, who had been lost in thought, interrupted his aunt and brother to suggest that there was another lead to follow.

"We might inquire from Mr Cosgrove at the New York bank that's acting as executor of Roberto Prito's will, if he's come across these medallions."

"Good idea, Frank, but Tony ought to be the one to do it," Joe said.

A few minutes after they had been in touch with Tony, their friend called back. He said the bank had reported that there was no record of the two medallions.

Where could they be? What had Roberto Prito done with these items? Had he sold them?

The boys' discussion was halted when their mother called that Mr Hardy was on the telephone. "Hurry! He's phoning from New York."

"Wait till he hears about our latest mystery!" Joe exclaimed.

Mr Hardy told his sons news of general interest about his work, then said, "I had a case that sounded baffling, but I had to turn it down because I'm too busy. Upon the recommendation of a detective agency here, an Alberto Torres called on me at my hotel.

"He claimed to be the head of a Guatemalan

patriotic society," Mr Hardy explained. "He says that his group is trying to uncover a treasure, the location of which they suspect is known by some unscrupulous persons who are trying to steal it. Naturally, the treasure belongs to the government."

"Maybe Frank and I could work on the case until you'd be ready to take over," Joe said enthusiastically. "Did Torres give you any clues?"

"He said that their only clue is a couple of medallions which have disappeared," Mr Hardy answered.

"Medallions!" Joe exclaimed, and quickly related what had happened in the famous detective's absence. Mr Hardy listened intently and told Joe that he would try at once to contact Torres.

"Hang up," he said, "and I'll call you back as soon as I've talked with him."

Minutes passed. Finally the phone rang.

"Bad luck," the boys' father reported. "Torres checked out of his hotel and left no forwarding address."

"Can't we do something about finding him?" Frank asked. "Maybe he's going to contact Willie Wortman in New York City."

His father agreed that this was a possibility but said that he had to leave for Washington on another case. He suggested that the boys fly to New York and check again with the bank's records regarding the curios. There might be a tie-in between the two men interested in the medallions. Perhaps they could pick up a clue on Torres and Wortman.

"What does Torres look like?" Frank asked.

"Short, slender, dark. He has a prominent chin and a black moustache."

"That description fits the blowgun man!" Frank exclaimed.

Mr Hardy said that it couldn't be the same man because Torres had been talking to him in New York at the time the missile had been fired at Joe.

An hour later Frank, Joe, and Tony were winging towards New York on a double mission.

"Where should we start work?" Joe asked.

"First thing to do," Frank suggested, "is to call on Mr Cosgrove and get his permission to check through the list ourselves. There's a good chance that he may have overlooked something."

At the bank the boys were received cordially by Mr Cosgrove and another man who was assisting him in the execution of the Prito estate. The trio was given permission to investigate the shopkeeper's private records. In the cool vault of the bank building the boys began their examination with the help of Mr Cosgrove. Page after page was eagerly scanned in a search for the two items that might have escaped the bankers' eyes.

Finding nothing, the boys turned to a diary and quickly looked over the notations. "Here's something of interest!" Joe exclaimed. He pointed to an entry written in a fine hand. "I'll read it to you.

"It says, first of all, that Roberto Prito did buy the medallions from Willie Wortman."

"That confirms part of Willie's story," Frank said.

"And according to this diary," Joe continued, "they were actually in the possession of Tony's uncle when he died. But now listen. In a separate notation it says, 'These medallions seem old and valuable. The strange design may indicate they are a clue to something. I will study them later.'"

"Mr Cosgrove," Frank said abruptly, "may we look over Mr Prito's store?"

"Of course. I'll get the key for you from the safe-deposit box."

"Torres can wait," Joe said excitedly as the banker went off. "Let's try to find the medallions or the reason why they've disappeared!"

Twenty minutes later they were inserting the key into the padlock of the late Roberto Prito's shop in a Greenwich Village street. Pending settlement of the estate, it had not been re-rented.

"I'll lead the way," Tony said. "I know where the office is."

Bolting the door on the inside, the trio started for the rear of the empty shop, now dimly lighted by the late afternoon sun. Joe followed close behind Tony towards a small office.

Frank, a few strides behind, noticed an unusual looking showcase standing at an odd angle. His detecting instincts aroused, he moved the case and dropped to his knees. At first glance the floor boards under it looked the same as the others. But after a few moments of intent study Frank thought he could see the outline of what might be a trap door.

"Maybe there's a secret cellar under here!" he thought excitedly.

He tried to pull up the boards with his fingers. Failing, Frank pressed each board separately.

A moment later the whole section suddenly caved in. Frank lost his balance and crashed downwards into inky blackness!

·6· *Mr Bones*

PITCHING headlong into the dark cellar below the shop of Tony's deceased uncle, Frank struck his head sharply against a packing case. He fell on to the concrete floor, unconscious!

In the store above, Tony had led Joe into the small office at the rear of the long room. A high partition darkened this section of the shop. Tony switched on a light.

"Where's Frank?" he asked.

"He was right behind me—" Joe began, looking out of the office door. "What could have happened?"

"Frank!" Tony called. "Frank, where are you?" His voice echoed emptily.

Retracing their steps, the two boys peered into the street. Frank was not in sight.

"It's just as if he were swallowed up in the—" Joe suddenly had an idea and began to look for an opening in the floor. He spotted the black rectangle behind the showcase.

"Look!" he cried. "A trap door! Frank must have fallen through." He called his brother's name but there was no response.

From his coat pocket Joe took the small flashlight he always carried and beamed it below.

"There he is!" Joe gasped. "I've got to get down and help him! Must be a ladder here somewhere."

He beamed his light under the flooring and found a

short ladder hinged flat under the floor. Unhooking it, he let the ladder down. Both boys scampered below.

Using precaution in case of broken bones, Joe checked Frank's condition. "Wind's knocked out of him," he told Tony a moment later, "and he has a nasty bruise on his head, but I guess that's all."

As Joe spoke, Frank moved for the first time. He shook his head and made an attempt to sit up.

"Take it easy, fellow," Joe warned him.

With the boys' assistance Frank climbed to his feet. "What hit me?" he asked dazedly.

Tony raised the beam of his flashlight to the trap door and explained what had happened. Revived, but still somewhat groggy, Frank started for the ladder. "Guess I touched a secret spring," he said.

"Just a second," Tony said. "Let's take a look in these packing cases. We may find something interesting."

Near him on the floor lay a claw hammer. Tony prised open a single board on each of the cases. "Here's something I didn't see on the lists." He held up a small antique statuette of a Chinese horseman.

"Mr Cosgrove evidently doesn't know about these boxes," Joe remarked.

Tony was excited. "This may be the answer to the missing medallions," he said. "Let's look through them."

But Joe, seeing that Frank was not steady on his feet, suggested that they postpone searching the crates and look for a hotel where his brother could rest and recover from the accident.

"We'll return tomorrow and investigate this cellar with Mr Cosgrove," Tony said.

Before they left, Joe examined the trap door, and

discovering how the hidden spring worked, closed it. Then the boys locked up and departed.

After getting settled in their hotel room, Tony phoned Mr Cosgrove and it was arranged that he and his associate would accompany the boys to the shop the next morning. The bank knew nothing about the cellar room, he said, and the curios stored there had not been listed.

Meanwhile, Frank had undressed. Joe said to him, "I think Tony and I will do a little looking around town for Torres while you relax."

Joe asked at the information desk in the foyer for a list of hotels in New York where Central Americans might go to be with other Spanish-speaking people, then he and Tony set out. It was several hours later when they returned.

Frank said he was feeling fine and asked what they had learned.

"Nothing," Joe reported. "Torres has probably left town."

After a hearty breakfast the next morning, the boys returned to the Prito shop. Mr Cosgrove and his assistant, named Jones, arrived a short time later and the examination of the secret cellar began. They opened crate after crate.

"It appears that Mr Prito stored his queerest objects here," Mr Cosgrove remarked, after several cases had been unpacked and revealed an array of skulls, animal teeth, an Egyptian toy ferry and all kinds of odd theatrical costumes.

"That's why I think there's a good chance of our finding the medallions here," said Tony. "The notation my uncle made proves that he didn't consider the medallions just routine curios."

Working methodically, the group had almost completed the inventory by noon. But there was no sign of the mysterious medallions.

"I'm afraid that you're going to be disappointed about them," said Mr Cosgrove as he wrote down the final item on his long list. "For you, Tony, this has been a very profitable morning, but unless your uncle had another hiding place that we haven't discovered, it would seem as if the medallions are gone."

Mr Cosgrove picked up his lists and started for the ladder. The others followed one by one to the main floor. Frank, the last to leave, reluctantly set his foot on the bottom rung. Could there be another hiding place? he mused. Stopping, he played his flashlight slowly back and forth along the solid walls of the cramped storage space.

Suddenly he saw, about eight feet from the floor, a faint series of slits that formed a rectangle in the wall. Quickly he stepped down, clambered over some cases, and ran his hand along the wooden slits. Tapping with his knuckles, he heard the hollow sound of space behind the rectangle.

"Looks like the transom of a door," Frank thought. "The door has been sealed off."

With his thumbnail he tried to prise open the thin section. "I'll need a chisel," he decided.

His heart pounding, Frank scrambled up the ladder and cried out his discovery to the others.

"It looks as if it might be a secret passage!" he exclaimed as he looked for a chisel. Finding one in a rusted tool chest in a drawer of the office desk, Frank led the others back into the cellar.

"This beats me!" Mr Cosgrove exclaimed as Frank's flashlight outlined the rectangle in the wall. "How could we have missed this?" The executor chuckled. "I can see how you Hardys have earned such a fine reputation as detectives."

Frank climbed on to a packing case and started testing the section with the sharp edge of the chisel while Joe held the flashlight. The first attempts failed. Then, as he moved the tool to a spot along the right vertical line, he felt the whole section tremble.

"It's coming!" he cried out. Again he forced the cutting tool into the slit, got a stronger bite, and wrenched the partition open. Dropping the chisel, he gripped the wood with his strong fingers and tugged the whole partition free from its position.

"Jumpin' Jehoshaphat!" Frank cried. He almost fell off the packing case as he reared back from the sight that met his eyes.

"What is it?" Joe asked.

Frank thrust one arm into the opening. Slowly he dragged out a human skeleton! Its white ghostliness at first shocked the group into silence.

Then, as Joe realized it was a medical specimen, his humour came to the rescue. "A room-mate for you, Tony." He grinned.

Frank lowered the skeleton to Tony, who gingerly placed it on a packing case. "I just remembered something," he said. "My uncle was very superstitious about skeletons. I guess he didn't plan on our finding this fellow. Anybody who wants this bag of bones can have him!"

"How about giving him to a medical school?" Mr Cosgrove suggested.

After making several calls from the office, he said that a small private institution would be glad to accept the specimen. He gave the boys directions to the medical school, adding, "Tony, will you leave the key to the shop at the bank when you're through with it? And I hope you find those medallions." The executors bade the boys good-bye.

"Who wants to carry Mr Bones to his next place of residence?" Tony asked. "I'll give up the pleasure. He's not my type!"

Joe looked at his brother. "He can sit on our lap while we ride there. After all, you found him."

Grinning, Frank said, "Guess I'm really stuck." He clutched the skeleton and started climbing the ladder. The others followed him up and Joe stepped out on to the sidewalk to hail a taxi.

Placing Mr Bones on the outside of the seat next to Frank, the group headed for the medical school. They had gone only a block when a police siren sounded behind them!

·7· A Street Chase

"THE motorcycle cop is after *us*!" Frank exclaimed. "He must have seen the skeleton!"

The sound of the siren grew louder and the taxi was ordered to pull over to the kerb. The policeman, a big, red-faced man, climbed off his motorcycle and walked slowly back to the taxi. He stared at Mr Bones.

"Where'd that come from?" he roared.

"We—we found him in a cellar," Tony explained, feeling a little foolish.

"Breakin' an' enterin'," the cop accused. "Driver, where did you pick up these fellows?"

The driver said that they had hailed him at Prito's Curio Shop.

"So!" the policeman exclaimed, looking stern. "That shop's locked up. I knew old Prito well. You fellows have got some explainin' to do."

Tony suddenly recalled that in his pocket was a letter from Mr Cosgrove. "Just a minute, officer. I can explain everything to you." He pulled out the letter and handed it over. The burly policeman read the paper, eyed Tony, then handed it back.

"So you're a Prito!" he exclaimed. "Now that I look at you, I can see you're like Roberto. Same snappy black eyes."

The boys breathed more easily. The cop began to laugh. "Just to show that my heart's in the right place, I'll give Billy Bones here an escort as far as the end of my beat." He gunned his motorcycle out ahead of the taxi and headed for the East River Drive. There, the policeman slowed down.

"Good-bye!" he called as he made a U-turn and left them.

The taxi droned on its way. Twenty blocks north the driver pulled into a side street and drew up to a white cement building.

As the taxi disappeared into the city traffic, the boys walked through the hospital doorway. A young intern who passed them grinned. "Who's your air-conditioned pal?" he cracked.

The boys chuckled and walked to a desk where a nurse was on duty. The pleasant woman, about fifty years old, smiled as the group approached her, four abreast.

The nurse directed the boys to the school, across a wide centre court. There, a genial white-haired physician welcomed Mr Bones and thanked the boys.

As the trio walked down the hospital steps, Tony said, "Are we going back to Bayport now? We have a plane reservation, you know."

"That's right," said Frank. "Well, I guess there's not much chance of finding Torres, so we may as well leave."

"We must return the shop key to Mr Cosgrove," Tony reminded them.

At the bank the boys were told that the newly found curios were being appraised at the shop and Tony could take any of them he wished. After lunch the boys brought their bags from the hotel and stuffed several of the smaller objects into them.

"We'd better hurry," Tony observed. "Our plane leaves in less than an hour."

He called a taxi and the boys headed for the airport. As it stopped at a busy intersection near the East River, Frank suddenly gripped his brother's arm. "Look!" he cried. "Over there on the sidewalk. Willie Wortman!"

The recent visitor to the Hardy home appeared to be walking with another man. Wortman's broad shoulders partially blocked his companion from view. But as the taxi passed them, Joe caught a glimpse of the other man's face. He was dark-haired and black-moustached.

"Say, he could be the blowgun man or Torres!" Frank exclaimed. "Come on. We're getting off right here!"

"We'll miss our plane," Tony protested.

"We'll catch the next one," Joe replied.

The light turned green and the taxi started up.

"Hold it, driver!" Frank called, and the man pulled to the kerb. "We're getting out."

Frank paid him and the boys got out. "Tony, you stay here with the suitcases," Frank instructed. "Joe and I will talk to Willie."

"Okay," Tony agreed. He pushed the three bags into a pile and watched his pals dash through the crowd after the two men who had crossed the street.

The moustached stranger had now dropped slightly behind Wortman. As the boys hurried after them, the pair turned up a side street.

The brothers dodged through the crowd. The red-haired sailor seemed to be walking with unconcern, but the other man glanced from side to side uneasily. He acted almost as if he feared someone were trailing him.

Willie Wortman suddenly looked back. Catching sight of the boys, he called out, "Frank and Joe Hardy!" The moustached man also glanced back, then he broke into a run.

Frank stayed to speak to the sailor while Joe continued the chase after the stranger. But the man, having a head start, ran through an alley leading to another street. Joe lost the trail completely. Disappointed, he walked back to where his brother was talking to Wortman.

"What are you fellows doin' here in the city?" the seaman was saying. He did not seem at all curious as to where Joe had been.

"Just came up for a short visit," Frank replied non-committally. "We were on our way to the airport when we saw you. Have you any news about the medallions? We haven't found anything."

Wortman shook his head. "No luck so far."

The brothers said nothing about the other man.

Neither of them was absolutely certain that he had been with Wortman, nor that he was the blowgun suspect.

Before the Hardys had a chance to learn if Willie had been alone, the sailor said, "I'll be glad when I ship out on another voyage. It's sure lonely in New York when you don't know anyone." Turning to Frank, he said, "Don't forget about the medallions. That curse business is getting under my skin. You know what? I think it might have been the cause of old Mr Prito's death!"

"That's ridiculous," Frank told him. "And stop worrying about the curse."

"I'll try," Wortman promised.

The boys assured him that they would keep on searching for the medallions, then Joe said, "Sorry to have kept you from your friend."

"Friend?" Willie asked, a puzzled look on his face.

The Hardys exchanged glances. If the suspected man had been with him, didn't Willie want to admit it? Or, perhaps, had the moustached man been following the seaman unknown to him? At this moment it seemed as if the latter possibility were true, so they did not pursue the subject. The boys said good-bye and returned to Tony.

"Didn't learn a thing," Frank said. He hailed another cab and once they were inside, told Tony about their brief conversation with Wortman.

When they arrived at the airport, the boys were informed that they had just missed the flight to Bayport. There would be a two-hour wait for the next plane.

"Hold on!" Frank exclaimed, as they stood trying to decide what to do. "Looks like George Simons over there near that new four-seater job."

"It's George and nobody else!" Joe agreed. "I wonder if he's heading for Bayport."

George Simons was a close friend of Mr Hardy. He owned a helicopter and several small planes. Frank got permission from a gatekeeper to run out and talk to Simons.

"Frank Hardy!" the flier exclaimed. "Are you snoopin' for clues in the big city?"

"Yes." Frank smiled. "And we've just missed the flight back home."

"You didn't miss this one." George grinned. "I'm about to take off. Are you alone?"

Frank explained that Joe and Tony Prito were with him.

"Perfect!" George said heartily. "Three and one is four. Get your gang together and let's go."

It was late afternoon when the plane circled the Bayport field and landed. The boys drove back to town in the Hardy's convertible with Frank at the wheel.

As Tony got out, Joe removed the curios from the Hardys' bags and helped his friend carry his luggage and the other articles to the front door.

At seven-thirty the morning of the second day after their return from New York, the boys were shaken out of a sound sleep by a frantic hammering at the front door.

"Who's there?" Joe called through the screened bedroom window.

A figure ran on to the lawn. It was Chet Morton. "Hurry out!" he cried.

Frank and Joe raced down the stairs and flung open the door.

"Look!" Chet said breathlessly, pointing.

On the floor of the porch a foot from the railing stood a six-inch-high, cone-shaped pile of ashes!

· 8 · *A Suspicious Barber*

THE mysterious enemy's latest warning struck fear into Chet's heart. "This must be the work of that fire guy in the museum!" the chubby boy exclaimed. "And now he's—he's threatening you both personally."

"We've already been threatened personally," Frank replied. He told of the warning Tony had been given by Valez over the phone. "And this makes me think Valez was the person in the museum."

"Maybe he's putting a curse on you," Chet quavered. "The—the medallion curse!"

"Could be," Frank agreed, smiling. "But he may find it'll backfire."

As Joe and Chet watched, Frank got a small box and swept the ashes into it. "I'll get dressed and then take these to our lab and analyze them. You fellows may as well start breakfast. I smell blueberry muffins baking."

Chet was eating his sixth muffin by the time Frank returned. Dashing into the room he announced that the photomicrographs showed the burned material to be bones!

"Human bones!" Chet almost choked on the muffin. "Ugh, maybe this is a warning that we'll all be roasted alive by some lunatic!"

"Take it easy, Chet." Frank grinned. "The bones were from a chicken."

As Chet took another muffin, Joe slyly remarked that it was strange how the magic of food worked on

49

their friend. "You don't seem to be afraid of anything now."

"That's not quite true," Chet replied, grinning. "I'm afraid we'll run out of muffins!"

After the meal Chet went on his way to buy the tractor part. Joe phoned Tony to tell him about the latest warning and to find out if he had had any further word from Valez.

"Not a peep," Tony answered. "Do you think he's the one who left the ashes on your porch?"

"If he was," Frank replied, "it means he's still in Bayport. Want to come on a search for Valez?"

"You bet. Why don't you pick me up?"

The three boys spent the entire day sleuthing. After consulting the police records and learning nothing, they went to hotels, motels, boarding-houses and real-estate agencies. No one could give them a lead.

"There's one place in Bayport we haven't investigated," Frank remarked. "The new development on the edge of town. People are moving there every day and hardly know one another yet. If there's any place where a stranger could live unnoticed, that would be it!"

"Of course!" Joe agreed instantly. "Let's go!"

The boys cruised in their convertible through the recently paved streets of the development, looking for any Spanish-type person.

"I don't recognize anyone," Joe remarked, as they drove past adults and children working or playing on their front lawns. "And I haven't seen a glimpse of the Latin type of person we're looking for."

As the car pulled out of the development around five-thirty and turned on to the highway, Tony suddenly cried out:

"Stop! There's the name Valez!"

On the front window of a barber shop, occupying the corner of a new block of stores, the name S. VALEZ was stamped in large gold letters! Parking the car, the boys headed for the shop. The screen door was locked.

In the rear of the establishment they saw a dark-haired man sitting hunched over a small desk. He appeared to be writing. Frank knocked on the door. The man swung round abruptly.

"Too late!" he called in a nervous voice. "Come back tomorrow. Shop is closed."

"Are you Mr Valez?" Frank asked.

"Yes," the barber replied. "What do you want?"

"Not a haircut," Frank replied and said they had come to get some information from him.

This statement seemed to upset the man. "What kind?" he sputtered. "I am a good man. I come from Spain. Everything legal. You boys hoodlums? Since I came here I've heard a lot about holdups. Please, I have no money."

Hastily Frank assured Mr Valez that they were not going to rob him. To himself Frank said, "He's from Spain. This can't be our man."

The barber relaxed and smiled. He walked forward and began to talk freely, though he did not unlock the door. Mr Valez asked what he could do to help the boys. His straightforward answers quickly convinced them that he was above suspicion.

The barber explained that he had been in this country only a short time and had not met anyone else of the same name. Then he excused himself, saying he was writing a letter to his mother in Spain and wanted to catch the outgoing evening airmail. The boys thanked him and left.

"Only one Valez in town and he's not our man," moaned Tony, as they let him off at his house.

The Hardys drove to Elm Street, turned into their driveway, and put the car away. When they entered the kitchen, Joe found a pinned-up note near the refrigerator telling them that Mrs Hardy and her sister-in-law had gone out for dinner and the evening. The boys' dinner was on the stove, ready for warming. Also, their father had phoned to say he was still in Washington but might be home later that evening.

"Let's turn on the TV news before we eat," Frank said, and the brothers headed for the living-room. As Joe led the way through the dining-room, he stopped in his tracks. Then he pointed to the floor, crying, "Look at those sideboard drawers!"

The four large drawers had been pulled out and their contents dumped out. Silverware and linen lay scattered on the floor.

"A burglary!" Joe exclaimed.

The brothers dashed into the living-room and the hall. These, too, were a shambles!

·9· *An Amazing Discovery*

FRANK and Joe ran through the house. From top to bottom every drawer in the place had been pulled out and rifled with one exception. The locked files in Mr Hardy's study had not been broken into, probably because they had a secret combination.

"Joe," said Frank presently, "do you realize that nothing seems to be missing? Not silver, jewellery, or anything valuable. What *was* the housebreaker after?"

"Something he didn't find, that's sure."

Frank had just about concluded that the mysterious person was connected with one of their father's cases rather than their own when an idea suddenly occurred to him. He hurried back to the brothers' bedroom.

"I know what that fellow was after and he got it!" Frank called as he opened his cupboard door.

Joe dashed in. The cigarette-type box from Tony's collection of curios was missing from the closet shelf. "But why would anyone break in here just to carry off that worthless box!" he exclaimed.

"Perhaps it wasn't so worthless after all," Frank reflected. He was about to add something else when his speculating was interrupted by the arrival of Mrs Hardy and Aunt Gertrude in a friend's car. As the boys ran downstairs to tell what had happened, Joe remarked, "Guess they decided to come home right after dinner."

The two women were alarmed when Frank told them what had happened, but a quick investigation by the women showed that no articles were missing.

"Except for our curio box," said Joe.

Aunt Gertrude blushed with embarrassment. "Oh, that box!" she said. "Maybe it wasn't stolen after all!" Her announcement surprised the boys as much as their earlier discovery of the ransacking.

"What do you mean?" Frank asked her, mystified.

"If the burglar didn't take it," she replied sheepishly, "the box is inside my sewing machine. I borrowed it this afternoon to use for a button box. I didn't think you'd mind."

"Of course not, Aunty," Frank replied. "But it's possible that we've been underrating that object. Will you see if it's still there?"

The box was found, exactly where the chagrined woman had placed it—not in a drawer but down inside the covered sewing-machine. Frank and Joe teased their aunt, telling her how glad they were that it had been she, and not the housebreaker, who had taken the curio.

"I think we'd better look this over," said Frank. "It might be the object of the man's search."

"What makes you think so?" Mrs Hardy asked.

Frank laughed. "Aunt Gertrude's button box may be more valuable than we thought. Don't forget, it's the only souvenir we own from Tony's collection. The intruder at the museum might have seen Mr Scath hand me the box, and knowing its worth, came searching for it."

"That sounds reasonable," his mother agreed.

Frank eyed the curio for a moment, then asked, "Do you folks realize what this is made of? It looks like Central American mahogany! The same as the charred bits we analyzed."

"What!" Aunt Gertrude exclaimed.

Frank was examining the box carefully and now using pressure on each side of it to see if the curio had a secret compartment. "It has a fake bottom!" he exclaimed triumphantly a moment later, sliding it off.

Then, with his thumbnail, Frank prised out a thin piece of wood built in above the bottom of the box. In it was wedged a large, engraved golden coin! Eagerly he took out the piece and held it up.

"One of the medallions!" Joe exclaimed. "And it

looks like real gold. Boy, am I glad that burglar didn't find it!"

"And see!" Frank cried. "It has the large opal set in it that Wortman told us about!" The stone was set on one of the lines that crossed the medallion. It was a beautiful opal, not a cheap one as Wortman had stated.

"Tony's uncle thought it had a special meaning," Frank said. "I have an idea that these engraved lines may form a map of some kind."

"What was it Wortman said was on the other medallion?" Joe asked.

"It was a word," his brother replied. "Sounded like Texichapi."

As Mrs Hardy and Aunt Gertrude examined the gold coin, Joe said, "Maybe these engraved lines show the exact spot where some treasure is buried in Texichapi! Remember what Torres told Dad."

"Let's look up Texichapi," Frank suggested, and went for the atlas. The boys studied the entire area from Mexico to the tip of South America. Their search yielded nothing. Nor was there any place in the world with that name.

"Apparently," Frank concluded, "Texichapi means something else. What about it being a secret password?"

"Maybe," spoke up Mrs Hardy, a dreamy expression in her eyes. "But it could be the name of a person. Some ancient king buried with a ransom in jewels."

Aunt Gertrude snorted. "Huh! Sounds more to me like one of those peppery fire-spitting South American recipes!" she exclaimed.

Everyone laughed and Frank said, "Probably the answer to the riddle depends on having both medallions. In the meanwhile, I think we ought to memorize the exact position of these lines and where the opal is placed."

"Good idea," Joe said.

"While you're doing that," said Mrs Hardy, "I'll warm up your supper."

The boys concentrated on the lines for several minutes, then tried drawing them from memory on paper. It was necessary for both Frank and Joe to do this again and again until they had memorized the lines perfectly.

While the brothers ate a late supper, Mrs Hardy remarked that she thought they ought to notify the police of the attempted burglary.

"I know that as detectives you would like to solve this yourself, but as proper-acting citizens of Bayport we're bound to report it," she insisted. "What kind of law and order would we have if people didn't notify the police when their homes were broken into?"

"You're right," her sons agreed. As Frank arose from the table and was about to call headquarters, the telephone rang.

"I'll take it," Aunt Gertrude called from the hall. A moment later she said, "It's Fenton! He's on his way home. Says he wants someone to meet him at the airport at nine o'clock."

"I'll go," the brothers chorused, then Frank said, "You pick him up, Joe. Drop me at the police station and I'll talk to Captain Collig personally."

"How about this medallion?" Joe asked. "Don't you think we ought to give it to Tony? After all, it belongs to him."

"You're right. Take it along and show Dad, then leave it at Tony's."

Putting the medallion into his pocket, Joe started for

the garage. Frank followed directly and the brothers set off on their double errand.

"Whatever you do," Frank warned as he hopped out at the police station, "watch yourself."

Joe headed the car towards the airport. Halfway there he remembered that the main road was cut off because of road repairs. That meant he would have to take the lonely one that led past the museum.

The night was warm and the air still. "Like the one when we brought Tony's stuff out to the museum," Joe thought as the convertible purred along. He came to the building and slowed up. "Most of Tony's inheritance is in there now. But the most valuable piece may be the medallion I have," he mused, fingering the outline of the object in his sports shirt pocket.

As he drove along, there were fewer trees and the countryside became flatter. "About one more mile and I'll be at the field. It'll be great to see Dad and tell him first-hand all the new developments," Joe said to himself.

The road took a long bend to the right and then straightened out. As the car approached the highway, its headlights picked up a frightening sight. Several yards ahead a man lay at the edge of the road. Joe wondered if he was the victim of a hit-and-run driver.

The brakes screeched as he slowed his car. Near the prostrate figure, another person staggered forward, shielding his face from the glare of the headlights and signalled Joe to stop.

"What happened?" the Hardy boy asked, as he jumped out to help.

"Don't know," the man who had signalled mumbled in reply. Now Joe could dimly see his face—enough to learn that he had a moustache.

Suddenly the roadside victim leaped to his feet. He too shielded his face so completely that Joe could see nothing of it but his eyes.

Too late Joe realized that this was a trap. He tried to jump back into the car, but the man nearest him let go a powerful blow that sent Joe reeling against the wing.

Recovering his balance, Joe lashed out at his assailant, but the next instant the other man struck a blow from behind. Quick as lightning, Joe whirled and connected with a smash that sent his adversary sprawling on the pavement.

If only a car would come by, there might be some hope for him. But none did.

"If I could get back behind the wheel, I'd have a chance to drive away!" Joe thought desperately.

He got one foot inside the car, but his assailants closed in again. They yanked him out and twisted his arms.

"Let go, you goons!" he cried out in pain.

He managed to tear away from their grip for a second, but one of the thugs shot a smashing blow to his chin. Joe blacked out!

When he came to seconds later his mouth was gagged and a handkerchief was tied over his eyes. He was bound hand and foot, and lay in a thicket.

Joe realized that not once during the struggle had either of the men spoken a word. Even now, when a hand started to frisk his pockets, not a sound came from his enemies.

To Joe's dismay, he felt the hand go into the pocket that held the medallion!

·10· *The Peculiar Ping*

LYING bound and gagged in the underbrush off the highway, Joe struggled to loosen the cords that cut into his wrists. Somewhere nearby in the darkness, his assailants were talking. They seemed to be very excited. Joe strained to hear what they were saying.

"They're speaking Spanish!" he thought, catching a phrase or two of their chatter that he could understand. He heard one of them say, "Now we can find the place." A moment later the other broke out fiercely, "I want that fortune!"

The talk was suddenly drowned out by the sound of a car engine roaring to life. The men were leaving! Joe had not seen a car when he stopped to help the "victim." But now he realized the sound of the motor was different from that of the Hardy's convertible. The men probably had concealed their car in the thicket along the road.

Joe wondered how they knew he would be passing this very spot. He concluded that they must have been eavesdropping below the windows at the Hardy house when plans for going to the airport were being made.

He heard his own car being driven off the road into the brush and then came the sound of running feet às the driver returned to the getaway car. Next minute the car sped off.

"I didn't get a single clue, except that one of the

men had a moustache," Joe moaned. Suddenly, however, he recalled something. The sound of the getaway car's engine. It had a very strange *ping*!

Meanwhile, at the airport, the plane from Washington had landed, and Mr Hardy, a tall, handsome man in his forties, strode down the passenger gangway to the field. Looking hurriedly about for some member of his family and failing to see one, he started for the waiting room. "Perhaps they missed the announcement," he thought. But there was no sign of any of the Hardy family in the waiting room. Mr Hardy decided to wait a few minutes before phoning home.

Ten minutes later the detective inquired at the main desk if any call had come in for him before his arrival. Upon being told that none had, he hurried to the telephone and called home.

"Oh, Fenton," Mrs Hardy sighed, "I'm so glad to hear your voice and know that you're back!" She went on to tell of the attempted burglary. Suddenly she stopped, "But you've already heard this from Joe."

"Joe's not here," Mr Hardy replied gravely. "That's the reason I'm calling."

"But he left in plenty of time to meet you," Mrs Hardy said, worried. "Oh, dear, something terrible has happened. I just know it has."

Mr Hardy tried to console his upset wife, by saying that Joe might have had trouble with the car. Then he asked, "Is Frank there?"

Frank had just returned from his talk with Chief Collig. He came to the phone. "Hello, Dad."

"Frank, do you know what route Joe was taking out here?"

Frank told of the detour, adding that Joe would have had to use the lonely road past the Howard Museum.

"Dad, we found one of those medallions and Joe had it with him. Maybe he's been waylaid!"

Mr Hardy snorted. "I don't like the sound of this. Frank, take my car and start a search. I'll grab a taxi here and investigate from this end."

"Okay, Dad, I'll start right away."

Mr Hardy collected his luggage and hurried from the building. Hailing a taxi, he briefly told the driver, who knew him, what had happened, then directed the man to the spot where he and Frank were to meet.

"I've heard lots about the work you and your boys do, but I never thought I'd have a chance to get in on the detectin'. I would hate to have anything bad happen to one of you."

They set off along the highway over which there was now a heavy mist. Inch by inch they searched the roadsides with the taxi's spotlight, but there was no sign of Joe or the boys' convertible. Only one car came along from the opposite direction and the driver was not Frank. Discouraged, Mr Hardy finally drew near the spot where the attack had occured.

"Frank should be meeting me at any moment," Mr Hardy said to the driver, "unless he's found something."

At this moment the headlights of a car appeared from the direction of Bayport.

"This may be Frank. Blink your lights at him."

The taximan flicked his headlights several times and the approaching car answered the signal.

"Is that you, Dad?" Frank called as he pulled alongside.

"Yes. Any luck?"

"None. But I haven't examined the last hundred feet of roadside."

"Then we'll do that together," Mr Hardy called out. "Turn and move on slowly. We'll come directly behind you. Keep your spotlight on the left side of the highway. I'll watch the right."

Crawling at a snail's pace, the cars headed out along the highway. Over fifty feet had been covered with spotlights when suddenly Mr Hardy saw the glint of a shiny surface in some high bushes.

"Stop!" he told the driver. As the taxi backed slowly, the spotlight picked up the glint again. Revealed in the glare was the windshield of the boys' convertible.

"Blow your horn!" Mr Hardy directed. The cab's powerful horn blasted several times. Hearing the signal, Frank roared in reverse back to the taxi.

"I've got the spot on your car!" Mr Hardy cried.

Frank backed the saloon behind the taxi, leaped out, and, with his father, crashed through the brush. Quickly examining the convertible and the ground round it, they stood perplexed. There was no trace of Joe. But several sets of footprints were evident in the moist earth.

"Joe must have been ambushed," Mr Hardy said angrily. "And they've either kidnapped him or thrown him somewhere into this brush. We'll scour the whole area."

With flashlights, the two went on foot along both sides of the road, penetrating the clumps of underbrush. A few seconds later Frank discovered the trussed-up figure of his brother. Joe was still trying to fight free from his bonds and the gag in his mouth, but his efforts were feeble.

"Joe!" Frank cried out joyfully.

Yelling to his father, Frank knelt, removed the gag, and with his pocketknife severed the cords from

Joe's wrists and ankles. Exhausted from his ordeal and his mouth dry as paper, Joe could scarcely speak. But he whispered how glad he was to see his father and brother.

When they reached the taxi, the driver grinned. "I'm sure relieved that you're all right, boy. Whatever happened?" Realizing Joe could not talk easily, he reached under the seat and brought out a thermos bottle of water.

The water revived Joe considerably and he gave a sketchy account of the holdup but did not mention the stolen coin. Mr Hardy paid the taximan, included a generous extra amount for his time and trouble, and the man drove off.

"Now, Joe," Mr Hardy said. "I'm sure that there's more to your story. Are you up to telling us?"

Joe nodded, saying he felt much stronger. He told in detail about the ambush. "And now they have the medallion!" he moaned. "We've got to get it back for Tony! One of the men had a moustache. He might have been the blowgun man. There's just one other clue," and he explained about the *ping* in the enemies' engine.

"We'll notify the police at once," Mr Hardy declared. "We'll need as many men as possible to listen for that sound. If we act fast, there's an outside chance we can pick up those thugs."

Frank and Joe hurried to the convertible and their father to his saloon. Driving directly to police headquarters, Mr Hardy reported the incident. Chief Collig flashed this information over the teletype throughout the state. Then he assigned a patrolman to accompany the Hardys as they continued their search. The group, in Mr Hardy's saloon, stationed itself at various main streets and incoming roads to listen for the engine with the strange sound. For an hour they patrolled the town without success.

Then, at an intersection near the waterfront, Joe heard the peculiar *ping*! "That's the car!" he cried out. "After him, Dad!"

Mr Hardy turned round and sped after the car, which was now heading west.

"He's goin' at a pretty good clip!" the officer observed from the back seat. "You'd better open up and stop him!"

As the Hardy car closed the distance between the two cars, the driver of the other vehicle sensed that he was being pursued and instantly gunned his motor. But Mr Hardy manœuvred skilfully and soon caught up to the speeding car.

"Pull over!" the patrolman shouted as they passed the other vehicle.

The driver, realizing that he had no chance of getting away, slowed down and stopped at the side of the road. He was from out of town and confessed that he had stolen the car. Joe whispered that he was younger than either of the men who had held him up and did not speak with a Spanish accent. As the police officer left the Hardys to escort his prisoner to headquarters, Mr Hardy observed that they had helped the law, but so far as their case was concerned, they would have to continue their search.

"But that *ping*," Joe reiterated. "I'm certain it was the identical sound."

Frank felt that his brother's hunch should not be ignored. "I think we ought to follow the car down to the station and find out who owns it," Frank declared.

Mr Hardy agreed and drove back to headquarters.

The young prisoner was being booked when the Hardys arrived. Chief Collig waved to the Hardys as they entered.

"Thanks for helping us out," he said with his usual warm grin. "This seems to be a mighty popular auto. According to our list of stolen cars, this one was taken twice tonight!"

·11· A Shattered Window

"There goes our clue!" Joe exclaimed woefully when the Hardys learned that the car thief had "borrowed" the automobile from the two men who had originally stolen it.

The detective and his sons were assured by Chief Collig that he and the force would maintain a sharp lookout for Joe's Spanish-speaking assailants. Then the Hardys went home, where they continued discussing the mystery.

"Since the medallion was stolen and the only two people we know who are interested in it are Wortman and Torres," Mr Hardy said, "I think we'd better get on the trail of Torres."

"How about his patriotic society?" Frank asked. "Don't you think that's a phoney?"

"Probably," his father agreed. "We may solve this mystery if I play along with Torres, letting him believe that I think he's on the level."

"But," Joe put in, "if they've already discovered that you're our father, they won't retain your services."

"You forget," Mr Hardy replied, "that we're still

not certain who our arch-enemy really is. Is he Valez? Torres? Wortman? Or someone else?"

"They may be working together," Joe ventured.

"I wonder," Frank commented, "if Torres is the man who met Willie Wortman in the seaport and learned about his having the medallions?"

"That could be," Mr Hardy agreed. "And Torres might have made up the whole fantastic story about the curse just to frighten Wortman into giving him the medallions."

"Have you any idea where Torres might be?" Joe asked, and told him of the unsuccessful sleuthing the boys had done in New York.

"You've been reading my mind." Mr Hardy laughed. "Before I turn in I'm going to phone a detective friend of mine in New York and ask him to try tracking down Torres. But since you ask, Joe, I'll tell you something."

"What is it?"

"I have a very strong suspicion," his father replied slowly, "that our friend Torres may be right here in Bayport!"

"Wow! What makes you think so?"

"Because I'm convinced Torres and Valez are working together. If Torres is the boss, he probably came here to see how his agent is doing."

Next morning, at breakfast, a special delivery letter arrived from Chicago for Frank. "It's from your friend Mr Hopewell, who analyzed the missile for us, Dad," he told Mr Hardy. Frank scanned the typewritten sheet of information the expert had sent concerning the arrowhead and the blowgun.

"He writes," Frank began, "that the South American Indians who make this unusual type of arrowhead are known to be dead shots. Also, that this is the first of its kind he's seen in the United States."

"No wonder Mr Scath couldn't identify it," Joe remarked.

"The blowgun used to shoot such a missile," the letter explained, "is a variety considerably shorter than the usual seven-foot one."

Joe grimaced. "That's why I got only a glimpse of it," he remarked. "It must have been small enough so that that fellow could hide it under his shirt when he started running into the woods. Read on, Frank."

"These blowguns," the letter continued, "are made by the South American Indians of either a hollow reed or a length of ironwood bored through with a red-hot iron. Blowguns have crude sights, which are sometimes made of animal teeth. And the blowers often succeed in sending missiles with great accuracy up to distances from fifty to sixty yards."

"The man who fired at me certainly was a crack shot," Joe commented.

"That's one fact," Mr Hardy observed, "which makes the Guatemalan connection a mystery. It's doubtful that a Central American could have used the blowgun with an accurate aim like that fellow had!"

Could it be possible, they wondered, that the enemies of the boys were not Guatemalans at all, but South American Indians or half-breeds of Spanish and Indian background?

Aunt Gertrude, who had been silent up to this point, now burst out, telling her nephews once again that she thought they should drop the case as quickly as possible.

"Why, Aunt Gertrude," Joe said, "we're just starting to get hot on this mystery."

"Don't worry," Frank assured her, "we have Dad around to keep us out of trouble."

Fenton Hardy smiled at this remark, then said, "I'm afraid that it's too late now, Gertrude. Even if the boys give up the case, which is unlikely"—and he chuckled—"their enemies would still keep after them."

The brothers agreed and Frank added, "We're going over to Tony's now."

At the Prito home Tony was taking in the morning mail from the box.

"Any news?" Joe asked him. "Any threats or missiles in your cereal this morning?"

Tony smiled, shaking his head. "Come on in," he said. "It's great that you've come over. I get pretty jittery over here wondering what's going to happen next."

"I'm afraid that our news is going to make you more jittery," Joe told him, as they all went into the living-room. He gave Tony the details of the burglary, the ambush, and the loss of the medallion. "Terribly sorry I muffed everything, Tony."

"Oh, that's okay. I guess what's on the medallion is the important part. And you say you memorized it. No wonder Valez wanted me to—"

Tony stopped speaking abruptly. The sudden crash of a windowpane had cut him short!

"Look!" Joe cried, staring at an arrowhead that had struck the wall and now lay on the rug. "It's exactly like the one that was fired at me!"

"And there's a note attached to this one, too!" Frank exclaimed as he picked up the object.

"What does it say?" Tony asked apprehensively. "Is it addressed to you or to me?"

"I'd guess it's meant for Joe and me," Frank replied. "The printing says 'Stop your detective work!'"

Joe, who had dashed out of the front door a moment after the missile struck, was standing on the porch when the other boys came running out to search for the person with the blowgun.

"We're too late," Joe said. "He's gone!"

"Wait a moment," Frank said. "Judging from the angle at which the shot came in here, the man must have aimed from the trees diagonally across the street."

Near the wooded area, a telephone linesman was at work on his truck. The boys hurried over to him and asked if he had seen a man with a blowgun.

"Blowgun?" The husky linesman laughed. "Are you fellows trying to kid me?"

"Well, did you see anyone near this area in the past few minutes?" Frank queried.

"Yes, come to think of it, I did," the phone man replied. "I saw a man cutting through the trees."

"What did he look like?" Frank asked eagerly.

"Short. A skinny guy with a black moustache."

Frank looked at Joe and Tony and the boys nodded to one another. This might be the same man who had fired the first missile! And possibly he was one of the men who had waylaid Joe on the road to the airport. But again the question of whether the man was Torres or Valez arose in the boys' minds.

"Thanks," Frank said to the linesman, and the trio returned to Tony's.

"Do you suppose Dad's hunch about Torres being in Bayport is right and he's a blowgun man too?" Joe observed, as they prepared to repair the broken window.

"Could be," said Tony, frowning with worry as he left for a nearby hardware store to buy a new pane of glass.

Tony, with the help of the Hardys, soon had the new pane in place. Then they sat down to plan further strategy in tracking down the owner of the blowgun.

"Maybe we ought to wear missile-proof suits if we're to continue looking!" joked Frank.

"Remember, we're to meet every half hour on the through street at the west end of the block we're searching," Frank reminded the others as they started off on their separate ways.

Three times the boys met as they had planned, without any report of success. Then, heading north, towards the poorer, more crowded sections near the electric company's power plant, Frank was startled to see a possible suspect approaching on the same side of the street. He was short, slender, and black-moustached. When Frank got a better look at the man, he was fairly sure that he was the one who had shot the arrowhead at Joe.

"If he's our man, I hope that he doesn't see me," Frank thought as he dodged into a shop entrance. "If he doesn't, I'll be able to find out where he's staying."

But in the same instant the man had evidently recognized Frank. Without a moment's hesitation, he whirled about and disappeared down a dingy apartment-house cellarway!

Frank dashed up the street after him. But just before reaching the apartment house he stopped. Had the man fled through the building? Or at this moment was he aiming one of the deadly missiles, ready to let it fly if Frank appeared?

·12· *The Matter of a Moustache*

REALIZING that he was exposed to the deadly aim of the blowgun marksman should he peer from the cellarway, Frank darted out of range behind a parked car. Ducking low to lessen the chance of being hit by the concealed enemy, he dashed across the street to take refuge in a doorway.

"Hey, Frank!" a familiar voice rang out as the young sleuth crouched, waiting for the moustached man's next move. "What are you doing—playing hide and seek?"

"Chet Morton!" Frank cried as his stout friend ambled across the street towards him. "Come over here. Hurry!"

As Chet joined Frank in the shadows of the doorway, he told him that he was on his way to buy some horse feed. Frank quickly related what had happened to him and asked Chet to run to police headquarters two blocks distant. "Tell them to rush a patrol car to 48 Weller Street!"

Without even a backward glance, Chet hurried away. Frank kept his eyes glued to the building entrance but saw no sign of the fugitive. Minutes passed. Grimly Frank thought, "Did Chet get to the police safely, or was he too ambushed?"

Then the welcome wail of the patrol siren sounded as the radio car streaked round the corner into view. As it pulled alongside, Frank dashed from his hiding place.

"The man's in there!" he cried to Sergeant Murphy, who was in charge of four policemen. They leaped from the car. As everyone ran towards the house, Frank described the suspect. "And be careful," he warned the officers. "He's got a deadly aim!"

"Cover the back entrance!" Murphy tersely commanded two of the officers. Instructing a third policeman to stay with Frank out front, he himself and the fourth man dashed into the building.

Several minutes later, as a small crowd was gathering to watch the action, Sergeant Murphy and the patrolman appeared on the sidewalk.

"Sorry, Frank," he said, "but we've found no trace of a black-moustached man. We checked every apartment. The superintendent tells me that no one in the building matches your description of the guy."

Murphy called back the other patrolmen. Frank, smarting with disappointment at their failure to capture the suspect, thanked the police for their effort. The officers pulled away.

"I'm still not satisfied that that blowgun guy is not in there," Frank told Chet. As they started towards the crosstown avenue, he stopped short and said excitedly, "I have an idea!"

"Tell me!" Chet said.

"We'll circle back round the block," Frank explained, "and approach the building from the other direction for a look."

Puffing, Chet kept up with Frank and the two quickly covered the distance round the block. They took up a position in a café from which they had a clear view of the apartment house.

"Do you really believe he's still in there?" Chet asked, munching on the third jam doughnut he had been unable to resist. "We've been here half an hour."

Without taking his eyes off the entrance, Frank replied, "If we wait long enough we may see him."

Ten more minutes passed. Frank began to think about his brother and Tony. They would be waiting at the crosstown avenue.

"Chet!" he suddenly gasped. "There he is now—what a break!" He pointed to a short, slender man leaving the front door of the building.

"But you said he had a moustache!" Chet exclaimed. "This man doesn't!"

"He must have shaved it off," Frank replied. "And he's also wearing a different suit. But there's no question in my mind that he's our boy!" Quickly Frank opened the café door and motioned for his friend to follow.

"What are we going to do?" Chet asked nervously.

"Trail him!" Frank replied in a low voice. "See, he thinks he's given us the slip. Hasn't even looked over his shoulder."

Keeping a safe distance behind, the boys followed the man as he strode jauntily down the block. They stopped when he entered a hardware store.

"Listen, Chet," Frank whispered. "He wouldn't recognize you. Drift over to the store and see what's going on."

Frank ducked behind a large tree as his pal followed instructions and appeared to be looking at the display in the store window. Soon Chet retraced his steps and hurried back excitedly.

"He's buying a window blind and some brackets!" he whispered, as a milk truck pulled up in front of the tree where the boys stood. "And I heard the clerk call him Mr Valez."

"Watch it!" warned Frank, equally excited, as he saw the man step outside the store. He glanced in both directions, not seeing the boys now concealed by the milk truck, then started back towards the apartment house.

Frank asked Chet to return to the store and see what he could learn about Valez from the clerk. "I'm going to follow him!" he said, still keeping his eyes glued on the man.

"Where shall I meet you?" Chet asked.

"On the corner of the crosstown avenue," his friend replied. "Explain to Joe and Tony if you arrive before I do."

They parted and Frank hurried after the stranger. As the man turned into the apartment entrance, he paused to open a mailbox, calmly inspected some letters, and disappeared into the foyer.

"He certainly seems to live here," thought Frank, wondering where the man had been when Sergeant Murphy had inspected the place. Then, having convinced himself that this was the base of operations for the enemy, Frank headed towards the avenue to join his friends.

"What happened to you?" Joe asked as Frank approached the corner.

"We've been waiting half an hour and nothing to report," said Tony. "How about you?"

Both boys listened wide-eyed to Frank's tale of discovering the suspect at the apartment house. His account was interrupted by the arrival of Chet.

"I'm afraid what I learned is of no help," he panted. "The clerk told me that the man's full name is Eduardo Valez. He's the superintendent of the building and has been for years. Another thing, he's never had a moustache and the clerk said Valez is well thought of in the neighbourhood."

"Guess I jumped to conclusions," said Frank. "But maybe there's a connection between the superintendent and the blowgun guy!"

"Could be!" Joe said thoughtfully. "Perhaps Eduardo wears a fake moustache as a disguise, or"—and his eyes brightened—"he may have a moustached twin who's the real villain!"

"That's a good solution!" exclaimed Tony. "The twin might have hidden in his brother's apartment while the police were searching the building."

Frank proposed that the quartet go to his home and talk over the mysterious twist of events with Mr Hardy. "Maybe Radley ought to cover the apartment house. I think we'd be recognized if our deductions are correct," he added.

"Sorry, fellows, but I promised to get back to the farm and pick apples," Chet said. "It's hard work, but it's safer than this detective business."

"Might not be if you eat too many apples," Joe quipped.

Tony declared that he would like nothing better than to continue work on the case, but he was due to drive a truck for the Prito Construction Company the rest of the afternoon. He accompanied Chet to the car park where he had left his jalopy.

The brothers went directly home and told Mr Hardy of their attempt to capture the assailant. Immediately their father called his assistant, Sam Radley, and asked him to watch the building.

"And now, to save time," the detective told the boys, "I'm going to check with the Immigration Service and learn what people named Valez have come into this country and where they are. Meanwhile, I want you both to go and question the building superintendent."

Eduardo Valez proved to be friendly. Through the speaking tube at the entrance he told the brothers to come to his basement apartment. It was very attractively furnished in mahogany and on a mantel stood several carved figures.

"Are these wooden pieces from your country?" Joe asked with interest. "They're beautiful!"

Without a moment's pause Mr Valez replied, "Yes, from Guatemala—my native land. They are made of the best grade of mahogany," he added proudly.

The Hardys were startled by the fact that this man was from Guatemala—some of the telltale ashes were of Central American mahogany! Frank decided to pursue the subject of a twin brother indirectly.

"You have relatives down there?" he asked casually.

"Ah, yes. Many." The man beamed. "But I'm— how you say—hundred per cent American these past five years," he replied in his soft Spanish accent.

"And relatives in this country?" Joe interrupted with a disarming smile. Valez did not reply at once and the youth realized that he was not being understood. "I mean, do you have, for instance, a brother in the United States?"

The man's pleasant manner was ruffled for a moment. He dropped his eyes and his jaw tightened. Recovering his composure, he smiled and said, "No, I have no brother in this country."

Both boys felt embarrassed, as if they had somehow hurt the man's feelings. The Hardys thanked Eduardo Valez for answering their questions and left.

"Another lead that led nowhere," Frank sighed, as

they headed back home. "You know, Joe, I sort of liked that guy. He seemed on the up-and-up."

Joe nodded and replied, "Well, Dad should have the data by now on other people named Valez."

When the boys entered their home, Mr Hardy called them into the living-room. "All the visas have been checked," he told them. "Each entry has been accounted for and in no way could be called a suspect. We can only conclude that your suspect is either a citizen or that he has entered this country illegally."

"I'll bet that he's here illegally," Joe remarked, and his father agreed.

"I think your man either jumped ship or was smuggled into this country across the border," Mr Hardy continued.

Just then, Mrs Hardy appeared and announced dinner. She had no trouble in getting the three male members of the family to the table.

"Smell the food!" Joe chirped. "That's one clue which isn't false."

After a delicious dinner of charcoal-broiled steak, corn on the cob, and ice-cream cake, the boys went into a huddle with their father on where to tackle their sleuthing next.

"I believe we ought to wait for a report from Sam Radley," Mr Hardy said. "Give yourselves a few hours' rest."

His sons took the advice and went to bed at nine o'clock. As they were dressing the next morning, Mrs Hardy called to say that they were wanted on the phone.

"It sounds like Chet Morton," she added.

Frank hurried to his mother's bedroom to answer on

the extension phone. "Hello," he said. "This is Frank Hardy."

"F-Frank," a quaking voice began. It was Chet's. "I've j-just got a letter with a warning in it. Even has some ashes. The message says, 'You, too, are now c-cursed!' "

·13· A Near Capture

"FRANK," Chet groaned over the phone, "when I offered to help you fellows, I d-didn't bargain for this!"

Calming his friend, Frank said he was sorry and advised Chet to stay close to the Morton farm. "Don't risk any trips to Bayport by yourself," Frank continued. "If you have to go to town, make sure you don't try it alone."

Chet promised. "You couldn't get me away, even if I was offered a whole roast turkey to eat."

Just as Frank hung up, the morning post arrived. A suspicious-looking envelope addressed to "Mr F. Hardy and Sons" lay in the box when Joe opened it. Quickly Joe slit the envelope which was postmarked Bayport. It contained a quantity of ashes!

"Dad, come here quick!" he called. "You too, Frank!"

When they reached the hallway, Joe began to read the printed note. " 'We have sent warnings to your friends Tony Prito and Chet Morton. This is the last time we are warning you to stop your sleuthing in this case or harm will come to you.' "

"No need to microtome these ashes!" Frank exclaimed. "Central American mahogany again!" He looked closely at one unburned bit of the familiar wood which he had picked out of the envelope.

Meanwhile, at the Morton farm, Chet's pretty, dark-haired sister Iola was worried about him. She had never seen him more nervous. And she too was upset over the note. Hoping to take her brother's mind off the threat, she proposed a steak roast that evening at the Elkin Amusement Park.

"We'll go early and have some fun."

Iola, who was usually Joe's date, soon extracted promises from Callie Shaw, the attractive blonde who often dated Frank, and two other girls, Maria Santos and Judy Rankin, to come along. Then she invited Tony and the Hardys.

"Swell idea!" agreed Joe, who answered the phone. "We haven't seen you girls for a long time. Seems like a hundred years."

"To us also," said Iola. "We've reserved fireplace Number Twelve for our picnic," she explained. "An attendant will watch our food and lay the fire for us."

"Sounds like a pretty soft assignment." Joe laughed. "We'll have nothing to do but eat the food."

"Oh, you'll have to do the barbecuing," Iola replied. "And of course we'll go on the rides in the amusement area and visit the Room of Horrors!"

"Just step in and look at Frank's and my room any time," Joe replied, "and you won't need to go to the one at the park."

"Well, you should feel right at home," Iola rejoined, chuckling.

She told him that Chet and Tony were coming. "But seriously, will you both be able to go with us too?"

"You bet. We'll pick up the other girls shortly after five," Joe replied.

"Meet us at the farm," Iola said. "We've fixed up something special. 'Bye now!"

About three o'clock Frank phoned Callie to tell her the plan. After a little conversation she said, "Frank, a funny thing happened here a short while ago. I didn't think anything about it at the time, but now it worries me."

"What is it?"

Callie said she felt that stupidly, but unwittingly, she had told a complete stranger about the picnic plans. A man had come to the Shaw's back door selling novel kitchen gadgets he carried in a small suitcase.

"I bought a couple of them," Callie went on. "Then suddenly the man said, 'You're a friend of Frank Hardy's, aren't you? Nice guy.'"

"I hope you agreed," Frank said teasingly.

Callie did not laugh. "I'm worried, Frank, because I told him about the picnic plans. He seemed so nice, but now I realize he asked me a lot of questions. Frank, he may be a spy—one of those men from the patriotic society Iola was telling me about."

Frank asked if the man spoke with a Spanish accent and had a moustache.

"No," Callie said.

"Then stop worrying," said Frank. "Just concentrate on having a good time."

Callie promised to do so, then Frank put down the phone. Despite his light-hearted attitude about the incident, he was alarmed. There was no question in his mind that the kitchen-gadget salesman was a phoney.

As Frank sat mulling it over, Aunt Gertrude and his

mother came through the hall. "A penny for your thoughts," Mrs Hardy said, smiling.

When Frank told them, Aunt Gertrude was alarmed. "You'd better decide on another picnic spot," she said firmly.

"What do you think, Mother?" Frank asked.

Mrs Hardy thought a moment, then said that if there were any change of plan the girls would have to know why. Then Iola would worry because of Chet's warning, and Callie would be embarrassed because she would feel she was to blame.

"It might be better if you boys just keep alert when you're at the park," she concluded.

Aunt Gertrude started to protest but changed her mind and left for the kitchen.

"After all," Mrs Hardy told Frank, "that salesman may have been an innocent person. But if he has any evil intentions, you boys will be safer at the amusement park—with so many people around—than at any other place." So no change in plans was made.

After picking up the three girls and Tony Prito in their father's car, the brothers set off for the Morton farm at five o'clock. When they arrived, the group learned that Chet had piled hay into his father's truck, so that they could all go together on an old-fashioned hayride to the amusement park.

"This is swell!" Joe exclaimed.

"We're all ready to go!" Chet announced. "Don't forget the food, Iola!"

Callie laughed. "As if you'd let us leave without it!" she teased.

"Len is going to drive us," Iola announced.

A big cheer went up from the boys who had been ready to flip a coin to see who would have to pass up sitting with the crowd to do the driving. Len Wharton, a good-natured former cowboy, had recently come to work on the Morton place.

Len grinned. "Shucks, I figured that if I was seventeen I sure wouldn't want to be stuck with the drivin'."

"Well, what are we waiting for?" Tony asked, and everyone climbed in.

All along the way the group sang. "We'll be hoarse before we get there," Callie said, laughing.

Zigzagging through the back lanes, Len stretched the short run to Elkin Park into an hour-long ride. As the picnickers got out, he said, "You jest call me at the farm when you want to git on back."

The baskets of food were carried to the reserved fireplace, where the attendant stored them away.

"How about taking in the amusements before we eat?" Joe suggested. "I guess you can wait, eh, Chet?"

"Sure." Chet laughed. "Let's go!"

For an hour the four couples whirled about on the thrill rides, took a boat down the chute-the-chutes, and laughed their way through the Fun House, where crazy mirrors made everyone take on all kinds of shapes.

"Look!" Chet roared. "In this mirror I'm skinny!"

"Better stand there until after supper," Tony retorted.

"And now—the best for last," Iola announced. "Before we go back to the fireplace, let's take a ride on the roller coaster."

Climbing into the first four seats of the bright red cars, the young people strapped themselves in. The motor rumbled into action and the caterpillarlike train of cars snaked along the track to start the steep climb to the first turn. As the cars rose higher and higher, the lights of the town flickered into view.

"Feel the wind!" Iola cried. "We're going to blow right out!"

The cars reached the summit and rolled smoothly round the bend. Suddenly they snapped into the steep dive! Maria and Judy screamed as the cars streaked past the white uprights. Hitting the bottom of the run, they plunged into the blackness of a short tunnel, and emerged on a level centre track that passed the entrance booth. As the coaster began another climb, Frank uttered a gasp.

"Joe!" he exclaimed to his brother in the seat behind. "He's there! Near the ticket booth!"

"Who?" Callie asked.

Not wanting to worry her, Frank merely said it was a man for whom he and Joe were looking. Through the rest of the breathtaking swoops and turns, the brothers could think of little else. The chances of spotting the blowgun suspect again in the crowd milling round the park were small. Nevertheless, they would try.

The instant the ride was over, Frank and Joe excused themselves and darted in and out of the crowd, but did not find the man.

"I'm sure that he has left the park," said Frank. "But this means he's still in Bayport. So our case isn't so hopeless after all."

When the boys reached fireplace Number Twelve, they found the picnic baskets placed on a redwood table. The attendant had laid the fire of kindling and charcoal. It was ready to light.

Stars twinkled in the night sky. "How about another song?" Tony suggested to the group.

A merry tune was started and the girls began to spread out the food. Chet knelt at the fireplace, struck a match, and set the fire. The flames, fanned by the stiff breeze, licked rapidly through the kindling. In a short time a fine blaze was roaring.

"When it dies down, we'll put on the steaks," Chef Chet announced.

Suddenly there came a terrific explosion from the fireplace! Chet fell backwards several feet from the flames as glowing embers rained down on the entire group.

•14 • *The Black Sheep*

"HELP!" cried Iola frantically. "My hair's on fire!" Desperately she beat her palms against her head, screaming in terror.

Ripping off his jacket, Frank flung it about her head, snuffing out the flame that endangered the frightened girl. Leading her away from the roaring fireplace, he said reassuringly, "You're okay now. Some of your hair's singed a bit, but it gives you that carefree look!" he added lightly to calm her.

Iola, though still shaky, managed a laugh. "It's one way of getting a new hair style," she replied gamely. "And thanks for the rescue."

Chet declared he was all right—aside from having the breath knocked out of him by his fall. The scare over, they all tried to figure out what had caused the blast. Had some explosive substance been sprayed on the kindling? Or had someone planted a crude bomb in the fireplace?

"If the latter is true," Frank thought, "then the salesman at Callie's *was* a spy!"

The girl ran to his side. "I told you! I'm the cause of this!" She quickly repeated her story of the salesman to the others.

"Did you mention fireplace Number Twelve to the man?" Frank asked.

"Yes, I did. Oh, dear!"

Frank put a hand on her shoulder. "Callie, no real harm has been done, so forget it," he said soothingly.

A crowd quickly gathered and began to ask questions. Several wondered if it would be safe for them to use another fireplace.

"Where's the attendant?" Joe called out.

The worried, grey-haired man who had been laying another fire hurried over. Joe questioned him. "I didn't put anything but wood and paper in the fireplace," he said nervously.

"Was anyone near this spot while we were away?" Joe asked him quietly.

The attendant scratched his head, then said a man with a moustache had offered to help him lay the fire in Number Twelve. "I told him I'd do it myself," the man continued. "He did hang around, though."

The Hardys did not voice aloud the suspicion that the salesman had told Torres or Valez the picnic plans. They merely assured the attendant that he was not to blame. The girls found another fireplace, and Chet and Tony carried the baskets over to it.

"Joe," said Frank, "we'd better search the embers in Number Twelve. We might find a clue."

"Right."

Sprinkling a can of water over the still-burning wood, they raked through the damp remains for evidence.

"Here's something," Joe whispered. He handed Frank one of the mysterious arrowhead missiles! "This explains a lot. The arrowhead was intended for one of us!"

"We were sure lucky," Frank said grimly.

"Something went wrong with the way that fellow had the charge rigged up," Joe suggested. "Let's see if we can find out what." Carefully the boys continued examining the embers.

"Guess this is it," Frank said, pulling out a small metal container. "This homemade bomb had the charge and the missile in it."

"The bottom of the container melted and the arrowhead fell out before the charge went off," Joe continued, "which kept the missile from shooting out."

"Hey, what's this?" Frank said excitedly as he reached into the ashes and pulled out a window-blind bracket. "This must have been part of what triggered the bomb. Say, didn't Chet tell us that Valez, the superintendent, bought some brackets at the hardware store?"

"Exactly," Joe replied. "There's no doubt about it in my mind now. That man's mixed up in the case."

"It's strange, too," Frank added, "because he seemed to be a very nice person, not the kind who'd plant deadly explosives."

The boys decided that they would say nothing about their find, but the next morning would investigate Eduardo Valez again. Together, the brothers joined the other young people. Try as they might, the group found little pleasure in the meal, though the food was delicious. The shock of the explosion and the narrow escape of Chet and Iola had caused them all to lose their appetites.

"Even I don't feel hungry," Chet lamented. "We should have eaten on the way out here."

Iola asked Frank to phone Len to come and get them. "At least," Frank said, smiling, "we had fun here before the explosion."

Early the following day, Mr Hardy and his sons drove across town to the apartment house for the purpose of questioning Valez.

"Good morning," the superintendent said affably as the boys introduced their father. "Come right in."

"We have no time for anything but the truth," Mr Hardy said firmly as he entered the apartment.

"Wh-why what do you mean?" the man replied. "I have not held back anything from your sons."

The detective told in detail the happenings at the amusement park. As he unfolded the account of the explosion and the narrow escape of the young people, Valez's face suddenly whitened. The superintendent raised his hand to stop Mr Hardy's recital. A look of distress came over the man's face and his mouth twitched as he prepared to speak.

"I—I am not the man you are searching for," he began slowly. Looking at Joe and Frank, he said, "I am sorry I did not tell you the truth at first. Now I will explain."

"Thank you," Mr Hardy said. "Go ahead."

"The man with the black moustache," Mr Valez continued with a pained expression, "he is my brother. He is the—what you call—black sheep of our family. Six of us children and he is the only one to break the law."

"What is his name?" Mr Hardy asked.

"Luis."

"Where is he now?" Frank asked.

"I do not know, but he was staying with me for a short time."

"Which explains the moustache mystery," Joe remarked to Frank.

"Luis sneaked into this country," Valez went on. "He promised me the day before yesterday he would return to Guatemala at once, so I did not turn him over to the authorities when they came here asking about a moustached man. Luis left here while I was on an errand at the hardware store."

"Buying brackets," Joe said, half under his breath.

"Did you say something about brackets?" Valez asked quickly.

"We found a bracket in the remains of the fire," Joe replied.

"That is why I went to the hardware store," Mr Valez added. "There was a bracket missing from one of my apartments. So I went to buy another. And I purchased a new blind while I was there."

The superintendent went on to tell Mr Hardy and the boys that he was astonished to learn that his brother had become a suspect in a case of violence. "I thought Luis had come to the United States to get away from some little trouble at home. He said it blew over, so he was going back. Always I have defended my baby brother," said Eduardo, clenching his fists, "but now I see I can no longer do this."

"Is there anything else you think we should know?" Mr Hardy asked.

"Maybe this is not important," Valez replied, "but a couple of small mahogany objects disappeared, too. Luis might have them with him."

The Hardys quizzed the superintendent about the possibility of a connection between mahogany and any

Guatemalan superstitions. Valez explained that among certain people in Central America there was one such superstition, adding, "It's said if a person sends the ashes of a piece of native mahogany to his enemy, that man will be rendered powerless to harm the sender!"

Frank frowned. "That's a very strange idea."

Valez could give the Hardys no further help, so the detective and his sons thanked the superintendent and left. On the sidewalk, Frank and Joe speculated on the mysterious piles of warning embers and ashes.

"Luis must have burned some of his brother's mahogany pieces," Frank stated.

"But why the chicken bones?" asked Joe. "Unless," he added thoughtfully, "he didn't have any of Eduardo's wood handy at the time. He probably figured we wouldn't know the difference."

On the corner, where Mr Hardy had parked his car, the trio met Sam Radley. The assistant reported that the moustached man had not been back to the apartment while either he or his relief man was on duty.

When the Hardys returned home, Aunt Gertrude told the boys that Tony Prito had called. He had said Mr Scath had asked him to take away the part of the inheritance which the museum was unable to use.

"And he wants you to go over there with him this evening," Aunt Gertrude concluded.

Shortly after supper, Frank and Joe drove off in the convertible to Tony's. There, they transferred to Mr Prito's small pickup truck.

"Let's drive out and get Chet," Joe said. "I'll bet he's just sitting around still worrying about the threat he received. Maybe he'd enjoy helping us."

The others grinned and Tony said, "You know how he loves work—not at all!"

Chet was reading a magazine when the trio arrived. At the boys' suggestion that he go along, he puckered his lips. "I don't know about taking a chance on tangling with a bombmaker," he said, "especially in that weird museum."

"Aw, come on—be a sport!" Frank urged.

Chet was finally persuaded to join the group and they drove off. The museum had closed for the evening by the time the boys arrived. While Mr Scath showed Tony what he wanted removed, mostly small articles, the Hardys and Chet wandered about the various rooms, now only dimly lit.

At the South American display Frank and Joe noticed that Mr Scath had arranged the shrunken heads on a ledge. The temptation to have some fun with Chet, who was still in the adjoining gallery, was too much for Joe to resist. Gingerly fastening one of the grotesque heads to a window pole, he hid behind a column near the door and called Chet.

"Coming!" his unsuspecting friend replied.

As his footsteps grew louder, Joe stuck the pole farther and farther out and began to swing it gently from side to side. The head, dangling by its glossy black hair, looked ghastly in the dimmed lights.

"*Ee-eee!*" Chet croaked and stopped dead. "Frank! Joe! Where are you?" The startled boy turned and fled back to the other gallery.

Joe quickly restored the head to its place in the exhibit and called Chet again, asking what was wrong. By then, Chet had realized that a prank was being played on him and sheepishly he returned to the room.

The appearance of Tony took Chet's mind off the joke. Mr Scath had finished showing him what he was to take away and given Tony a key. He suggested that the four boys go to the storage shed at the rear of the museum grounds for some crates and pack the articles in them.

"We'll carry the things back to my place," Tony explained, "and put them in the cellar."

As the boys went out of the rear door he handed the key to Chet, who was the last one out. The four youths crossed the dark yard, and entered the shed. A stack of various-sized crates was piled near the door.

Suddenly Joe put his finger to his lips. "Sh-h!" he warned.

The boys stopped short. A faint cry had sounded from the museum.

"Help!" It sounded like Mr Scath's voice.

"H-help!" The cry died out.

·15· *Hunting an Assailant*

DROPPING the crates, the boys ran to answer Mr Scath's call for help. After the two outcries, they had heard nothing more.

"I don't see how anyone could have broken in," Frank said.

"I'm afraid it's my fault," Chet admitted as they reached the rear entrance. "I didn't lock this door— thought we'd be right back."

Frank turned the knob and they hurried inside. Chet locked the door.

"Be careful of a sniper!" Frank warned the others. "And keep together!"

The curator was not in sight and when Frank called

he did not answer. The boys rushed to Mr Scath's office, but he was not in it.

"Mr Scath must be on the side of the building nearest the shed," Joe suggested. "His voice wouldn't have carried from the other sections."

He led the way into the Egyptian Room and switched on the lights. Mr Scath was sprawled on the floor, unconscious! The boys rushed over.

"There's blood on his face!" Tony exclaimed. "He's been slugged."

"And look at his pockets!" Frank cried. "They've been pulled inside out."

"Oh, if I had only locked the door!" Chet wailed, feeling he was responsible.

"Don't worry about that now," Frank replied. "Joe, you and Tony search the building for the slugger, while Chet and I attend to Mr Scath."

Joe and Tony headed for the opposite end of the museum, and Frank and Chet knelt beside the injured man and inspected the head wound. Fortunately, it was not deep and the curator's colour was returning to normal. A moment later Mr Scath gave a low moan and his eyes flickered open.

"Help me up," he said feebly, trying to rise.

"Lie still," Frank urged. "Don't try to move."

He recalled having seen a first-aid kit on an open shelf in the curator's office and asked Chet to get it.

Anxious to make amends for his carelessness, the stout youth hurried off. A whiff of spirits of ammonia revived Mr Scath. Frank gently swabbed away the blood. Luckily the man had been struck only a glancing blow.

"Feeling better?" he asked.

"My head feels clearer," Mr Scath replied. He sat up with Chet's assistance.

"Here, let me put a patch over that cut," Frank said.

When this was done, the boys helped the curator to his feet and back to his office.

"What happened?" Frank asked, after Mr Scath had seated himself in a comfortable chair.

"I was in here alone, waiting for you fellows, when I heard a noise in the Egyptian Room. I went to investigate."

"Did you see someone?" Chet asked.

"Yes. There was a masked man standing alongside the first big column. He demanded that I hand over the Texichapi medallion from Tony's collection."

"Yes?" Frank said eagerly as the man paused.

"I told him that I had no idea what he was talking about," Mr Scath continued. "Then he pulled out a blackjack and threatened me. I got a bit flustered—tried to fight him off—and I shouted a couple of times, hoping you'd hear me. Then he struck me and I blacked out!"

"What was his build?" Frank asked.

"Short, thin. Had black hair."

Frank whistled. "The blowgun man or Torres," he told Mr Scath.

"If it was Luis Valez," Chet exclaimed, "then he didn't go back to Guatemala after all!"

Frank nodded. He asked permission to use Mr Scath's phone, then called Chief Collig and told him about the attack.

"Hold the fort!" the chief responded. "We'll be right there!"

Meanwhile, Joe and Tony had searched the entire north section of the museum without finding the curator's attacker. The boys went back to join the others in the Egyptian Room.

Not finding them there, they decided that their friends must have led Mr Scath back to his office. As they were about to check there, Joe suddenly noticed something on the floor. He hurried over to pick it up. "Tony!" he exclaimed. "This is a Guatemalan coin!"

Joe and Tony hurried to the office and showed the coin to the others. Mr Scath said that it was not a coin from the museum's collection. It was highly probable that his assailant had lost it.

"Let's check Tony's curios," Joe suggested. "If the intruder was Valez, that's what he was after."

They hurried to the gallery containing the old musical instruments and the jewellery. As the ceiling light was turned on, everyone gasped. The glass had been neatly removed from one of the cases. Every ring, bracelet, and necklace was gone!

"Oh, oh!" Mr Scath cried. He wobbled unsteadily and Frank helped him to a marble bench.

At this moment a siren sounded at the front entrance and the night bell rang insistently.

"It's the police," Chet announced.

"Take my key," Mr Scath said to Frank. "Let them in."

Chief Collig strode in with two other officers. Quickly they were told about the attack and theft, and started a thorough search of the building. But it was soon ascertained that the attacker had escaped. Chief Collig said, "From now on we'll keep a guard here on a twenty four-hour basis. Sampson, you stay here right now. I'll send out a teletype on the missing jewels and a description of the intruder."

Mr Scath handed a spare key to Sampson, then said

to the boys, "Come back another time and pick up the curios." Everyone but the officer on duty left.

The next morning Frank and Joe decided to question Eduardo Valez again, hoping he might have heard from his brother. They set out very early for the apartment house.

"My brother?" the man replied to Frank's query. "No, I have not seen or heard of him since you called with your father."

"Did Luis ever tell you the exact nature of the trouble he had in his country?" Frank asked.

"Not really," the superintendent replied. "He did say something about an argument over a buried treasure, but Luis is such a braggart I paid little attention."

"Buried treasure!" Frank exclaimed. "Did he ever say anything about medallions?"

"Medallions?" Eduardo Valez mused. "No, he never did. Oh, I am so sad about the whole affair."

The boys left, feeling sorry for him.

"I think that we ought to spend the rest of this day making an intensive search of Tony's curios for that Texichapi medallion," Joe proposed. "I believe that's what Luis was hunting for when Mr Scath discovered him. So maybe we've overlooked some hiding place where Tony's uncle put it."

"We'll get Tony and Chet," Frank answered. "And, after all, we haven't taken those curios from the museum which the curator didn't want."

At two o'clock they all met at the museum. Mr Scath, still wearing a bandage on his forehead, smiled as the boys started off to the shed for the crates. "I hope we have better luck today!" he said.

The boys brought the crates to the basement and went to work. As each curio was examined closely, those to be taken by Tony were placed in a crate. The others were returned to the shelves. An hour passed. One crate had already been filled but they had not found the medallion.

Chet Morton, still upset over leaving the museum door unlocked the night before, had worked hard, trying to make amends.

At the moment he was fingering a solid mahogany, highly polished ball.

Picking it up, he removed a foil wrapping that covered part of the surface. His sharp eyes detected a thin, almost invisible line that went completely round the circumference of the ball. In his excitement to get a closer view of it, the ball slipped out of his grasp. It hit the cement and rolled across the floor, past the packed crates.

"Playing games?" Joe teased.

"I'm sorry," Chet groaned, going after the ball. "I wasn't playing. I—"

He interrupted himself as he stooped to pick up the ball. It had started to come apart at the seam. A strip of rich blue velvet showed in the opening. Inside he saw the brilliant glint of metal!

Prising apart the two sections, he cried out, "Fellows, come here quick!"

· 16 · *News of Buried Treasure*

"THE second medallion!" Chet exclaimed gleefully. "Fellows, I've found the second medallion!"

Gleaming in the light, on its velvet bed inside the

mahogany ball, lay the medallion. Carefully Frank lifted it from the hollow into which it had been wedged and held it for the others to see.

"There's the clue that Wortman gave us!" he said. "See the word *Texichapi*!"

"And there are strange engraved lines similar to the ones on the stolen medallion," Joe added.

Frank slipped the medallion back into the ball. "I'd like to show this to Dad and examine it very carefully," he said.

"It's okay with me," Tony answered. "But after what happened to Joe with the first medallion, watch your step."

The crates of less valuable objects were taken to the Prito home, then the Hardys sought out their father. To insure complete privacy from eavesdroppers, the trio went to the garage laboratory. There they examined the ball and the medallion. The Hardys concluded that the ball had been designed originally as a secret place to hold small pieces of valuable jewellery.

The boys wrote down from memory the pattern of lines on the stolen coin, then traced the new ones. By comparing markings, the three detectives concluded that the lines from the two coins, when superimposed, did seem to indicate a detailed map.

"It must show the area near the treasure that Luis Valez is looking for," Frank remarked.

"And the opal probably marks the spot where the treasure is hidden," Joe added. "I'm sure it isn't placed on the medallion just for decoration. Boy, I'd like to find that spot myself!"

"But it's in Texichapi—the land of nowhere," Frank reminded him.

"Let's hope we can learn what country Texichapi is

in," said Mr Hardy. "Meanwhile, you boys had better memorize these lines on the medallion and then we'll place it in my safe."

Frank and Joe drew the markings which were on the medallion again and again until they could do them perfectly from memory. Then the papers were burned so that nothing was left for anyone to steal.

"I wonder," mused Mr Hardy, "whether your friend Willie knew the value of both medallions. This one feels like solid gold to me and it certainly has the same lustre as a gold piece. Maybe Willie was just acting dumb because he feared Tony might refuse to sell him the coins once they were located." His sons said that they wished they knew.

The medallion was locked in Mr Hardy's file-safe. Then the boys and their father sat down in his study and continued to discuss the mystery.

"I know that you've consulted all kinds of maps to locate a place called Texichapi," Mr Hardy said, "but I'm going to make another try to find out where it is." He reached for the phone.

Being personally acquainted with various Central and South American consulates, the detective called them one by one and inquired about the place name. None of the men had ever heard of it.

Later in the evening, Mrs Hardy, who had come in with some crocheting, put it down and said, "Fenton, why don't you phone my friend Mrs Putnam? Her husband Roy has just come back from an expedition."

"The Central American explorer?" Mr Hardy asked. "Why, that's a great idea. But it's much too late to call anyone now."

"Not Roy Putnam," Mrs Hardy answered. "He

stays up half the night reading. I'll get him on the line for you."

Mr Putnam answered promptly and Mrs Hardy turned the phone over to her husband. The explorer became so interested in a brief account of the mystery that he offered to drive over at once.

"Be there about midnight," he promised.

The family went down to the living-room to await him. A thunderstorm came up shortly, necessitating the closing of all windows in the house except one near where they were seated. The wind whipped up sharply, banging a shutter on the east side of the house. Frank went to fasten it.

At five minutes before midnight the doorbell rang. Frank opened the door. The explorer, about fifty years old, and a man of commanding figure, removed his raincoat and shook hands with everyone.

"It's about time we got together." He smiled. "I've often heard my wife speak about this fine family."

"But you're so rarely at home," Mrs Hardy replied.

"That's right." The explorer smiled. "I've just returned from Guatemala, as a matter of fact."

"I'm sure then," Mr Hardy said, as his sons' eyes opened wide, "that you can give us a lot of help. Did you ever hear of Texichapi?"

A bolt of lightning flashed, startling them all. Then Mr Putnam said, "When you mentioned Texichapi a moment ago, I was astounded. I never dreamed that anyone way up here would have any knowledge of that place."

"Where is it?" Frank questioned eagerly.

"Well, first of all," Mr Putnam began, "have you ever visited Guatemala?"

The Hardys said they had not.

"As you know," Mr Putnam began, "the country stretches from the Pacific to the Atlantic, just below Mexico. It's a rugged land—full of canyons, towering mountain ranges, and volcanoes.

"It's mostly Indian in population, and has some wonderful ruins. You come upon marvellous stone temples with walls completely carved in rare designs. Even out in the deepest jungle, in the most unsuspected places, one hears about buried temples and palaces."

A crash of thunder made it difficult to hear the explorer for a moment. Through the open window the sound of the driving downpour made an effective background for Mr Putnam's story.

"Guatemala has beautiful cities," he continued. "Beautiful colour splashed everywhere—cobbled streets in the old city sections, bright red roofs, light-blue and white walled houses, tropical flowers—parks full of them."

"Now how about Texichapi?" Mr Hardy asked mildly.

"Oh, yes." Mr Putnam smiled a bit sheepishly.

The boys moved closer to Mr Putnam and listened intently.

"Texichapi," the explorer began, "is a name given by a small tribe of Indians, the Kulkuls, to a mysterious and perhaps even mythical area many miles from Guatemala City."

"Do you mean it's possible that Texichapi really does exist?" Joe asked.

"Oh, there's a place that the Kulkuls call Texichapi," Mr Putnam replied. "I've heard various rumours about the region. The main one, I'd say, concerns a great treasure buried there," the explorer went on, and the boys jumped in amazement. "Though I have many times tried to find out more about Texichapi, the Indians are very close-mouthed. Despite the legends surrounding the whole thing, I feel there may really be such a treasure."

"What makes you think so?" Mr Hardy asked.

Mr Putnam smiled. "Nothing definite," he replied. "Let's call it my explorer's hunch. It's not inconceivable that the Kulkul tribe guards the secret to Texichapi."

Joe's eyes glistened. "Boy, would I like to look for that treasure!"

Aunt Gertrude spoke up for the first time and snapped. "Why, those Indians might kill you if they found you looking for their treasure!"

Mr Putnam smiled tolerantly. "The Indians in Guatemala would not do that. The boys wouldn't have any trouble with them, but I also doubt that they would receive any clues about the treasure. No, you're more likely to have trouble with an occasional band of hostile, renegade Ladinos who have fled to the mountain regions.

"Ladinos," the explorer explained, "are Spanish-speaking, mixed-breed people. They are very proud and do no manual work like labouring in the fields or carrying loads. Mainly, they own stores and cantinas in the towns and villages and hold political offices."

Mr Hardy nodded thoughtfully, then said, "Mr Putnam, do you know whether any Guatemalans have a secret society that was organized to uncover this treasure or any other in the interests of their government?"

"Yes," Mr Putnam replied. "The only trouble is I don't know just which society you mean. They come and go—pop up all of a sudden, make a big noise, and disappear as quickly as they were formed."

The explorer went on to say that he had heard of no such group lately but he could find out. "If you'll allow me to use your phone," he said, "I'll call a friend of mine in Guatemala City whose business it is to investigate such groups. He'll know if there's any such organization operating now."

"Please do so," Mr Hardy said, showing the visitor to the hall phone.

"They won't mind my calling at this time of night." Mr Putnam grinned good-naturedly. "It's three hours earlier there."

The Hardys returned to the living-room while Mr Putnam put through his call. Several minutes passed before the man came back.

"My friend Soldo, who works for a government agency, tells me that there are rumours of another so-called patriotic society forming right now," Mr Putnam reported as he sat down. "His agency would welcome any information about it. If anything subversive is going on, he says, there'd be a good chance of nipping the plans in the bud."

The Hardys noticed that Mr Putnam had suddenly slumped in his chair, giving a tremendous yawn. Almost at the same moment, Frank and Joe themselves began to experience a queer lethargy. The boys sensed dimly that this was not a natural sleepiness!

Their father, too, felt himself growing drowsy. With a great effort, he tried to speak to the boys, but at this moment both his sons and Mr Putnam slipped from their chairs to the floor, unconscious. Fighting to remain awake, the detective got to his feet and moved across the room to assist his already sleeping wife and sister. But before he could reach them, he stumbled and blacked out!

· 17 · *A Ruse Works*

As the storm raged, the Hardy family and their guest remained in a deep stupor on the living-room floor. For twenty minutes none of the silent forms moved. Then the wind shifted, and the rain started pelting through the open window into the room.

Frank, lying nearest the window, was within range of the cold rain that was blowing in. Its continual spray across his upturned face gradually aroused him. Fighting desperately against the drowsiness that still engulfed him, the boy struggled to sit up. He looked dazedly around.

"They're all asleep!" he thought. "At least I hope it's just sleep."

Fearful, he spent the next few moments stumbling from one to another, feeling for pulses. All were alive! He wondered what had happened to cause this weird scene. Suddenly an answer came to Frank.

"Sleeping gas," he decided. "Where did it come from, though?"

Reviving a little more, Frank went to close the window against the storm. As he did so, he noticed the screening had been cut from its frame and lay on the floor. There was a slit in the centre of the wire mesh. Near it were several punctured, greenish pellets the size of a golf ball.

As he picked one up and examined it, Frank mused,

"These are gas pellets and must have been tossed in here."

He decided that the noise of the storm and the family's rapt interest in Mr Putnam's story would have prevented their noticing any sound at the window.

His legs steady now, Frank went to his mother's side, patted her face gently, and chafed her wrists. A few moments later Mrs Hardy's eyelids started to flutter open. Frank heard Mr Putnam talking indistinctly, but saw that he had not returned to consciousness.

"That's what happens to some people under the influence of gas," the boy thought.

The rest of the family began stirring. Frank, sensing that the danger of any lasting effect had passed, turned his thoughts in another direction. Who had hurled the pellets? Suddenly he remembered the screening on the floor. Had the person who threw the pellets in through the slit in the screen, then removed it while they were all unconscious and climbed into the house?

As if in answer to his unspoken query, Frank saw a masked man coming down the stairs! The intruder, apparently startled by Frank's unexpectedly quick recovery, jumped over the remaining steps and dashed for the front door.

Frank made a flying leap into the hall, realizing that here was an enemy who would spare no one to get what he wanted. Before the intruder could turn the doorknob, Frank crashed into him, sending the man sprawling on the hall floor.

Catlike, the masked man leaped to his feet and flailed out at Frank with both fists. One blow caught the boy on the cheekbone and split the skin. Enraged by this, Frank hurled himself in a fierce flying tackle at the man and knocked him against the steps!

While the fight was going on, Joe had regained consciousness. He stood up unsteadily and now glanced around. Out of the corner of his eye he saw the struggle and staggered to the hall. He was just in time to see Frank leap back as the man rolled off the stairs.

Frank, momentarily dazed by the impact of his tackle, raised both fists as his adversary scrambled to his feet pulling a blackjack from his pocket.

"No, you don't!" Joe roared. He leaped forward and swung a left uppercut to the man's chin that sent him to the floor.

Both boys jumped the intruder, stripped him of his blackjack, and pulled off his mask. The blowgun suspect!

"You're Luis Valez!" Frank accused him.

"No, that is not my name."

"Then what is it?" Joe demanded.

"I—I am not Valez," the suspect replied. "You have made a big mistake. I insist you let me go."

"You're in no position to insist on anything!" Frank replied harshly. "Breaking in here after having attempted to injure our whole family, you expect us to let me go! What do you take us for?"

"I have done nothing bad," the stranger insisted. "I have come into the wrong house."

Joe exploded. "You sure have! Now get up on your feet!"

Holding the man in a tight grip, the boys searched him quickly. Frank located a gas pellet in one of their prisoner's jacket pockets. In another, Joe felt something smooth and hard. He pulled it out. The Texichapi medallion!

"You still claim you entered the wrong house!"

Frank said in a steely voice. "How did you get into the file-safe?"

The man admitted hacking it with a hatchet which he had left upstairs. Then he refused to answer any more questions, though his eyes remained glued on the medallion Joe still held.

Frank, recalling that the gas pellets sometimes make a victim talk, decided to use a ruse to make Valez confess! Pretending to tear open the end of the one he had found, he said in a firm voice:

"This'll make you talk!"

The ruse worked. "Don't do that!" the man cried, terrified. "I will tell everything!"

By now, the others in the living-room had recovered from their enforced sleep. They expressed amazement that Frank had caught the burglar. Frank smiled, then said to the man, "Now tell your story."

"You are right," the stranger began slowly. "I am Luis Valez from Guatemala. But please, do not arrest my brother Eduardo. He knows nothing of what I do."

"And what *are* you doing?" Mr Hardy asked.

"I cannot tell you. All I want is to be shipped back to Guatemala."

"How can you go back without this medallion?" Joe asked, holding it up. "You wouldn't be very popular if you came back empty-handed."

The man hung his head and Frank demanded to know who had sent him to steal the coin. The dejected Guatemalan admitted that it was Torres, head of a patriotic society of which he was a member.

"We are searching for the treasure of Texichapi," he said quietly. "That is why we wanted this medallion."

"And why you stole the matching medallion," Joe said.

Valez denied this.

"How do we know you're not just part of a gang that's planning to keep this treasure for itself and not give it to your country?" Mr Hardy asked. "You've got a great deal of explaining to do. The police will want to hear it."

Frank went to the phone and called headquarters. "We didn't have to go chasing the blowgun man this time," he told the lieutenant on duty. "Caught him right in our home. He's the one who fired at Joe."

As Frank hung up, Valez protested vigorously that he had never seen Joe before tonight. In spite of the Hardy's accusations, the man stuck to his story. He admitted trying to buy Tony's curios, but denied having sent any threats or knowing anything about the stolen scimitar, the ashes, the museum theft, or the explosion in the picnic fireplace. He became sullen and seated himself on the steps, staring at the floor.

Mr Putnam, who until this moment had been looking on, got up and approached Frank and Joe. "Good work, boys!" the explorer praised them. "By the way, my friend in Guatemala will be glad to help you at any time. And now I think I'd better get home."

The Hardy family thanked him for coming and for the information he had given them.

"Just call me any time," Mr Putnam said as he started for the door. Then he smiled. "But next time ask your other guests to leave their sleeping gas at home!"

When Mr Hardy returned from escorting Mr Putnam to his car, he said, "It's too bad Willie Wortman isn't here too. He probably could give us some valuable information about Valez." The detective winked at his sons.

At the sound of the sailor's name, the prisoner leaped up from his chair. "Willie Wortman!" he exclaimed. "What do you know about him?"

"Plenty," Joe said noncommittally.

"How you know him?"

"Willie paid us a visit," Frank replied, "and told us about the medallions."

The Guatemalan's face went white with fear. He clenched his fists and made a break for the door but was promptly stopped by the boys.

"Valez, what do *you* know about Wortman?" Mr Hardy asked.

Assuming that the red-haired seaman had revealed more than he actually had, the prisoner admitted having met Wortman in a Guatemalan seaport.

"That sailor!" Valez snorted in disgust. "I fix him! He talk too much!"

When Valez had cooled down a little, Frank asked him where Wortman was at the moment.

"I don't know," Valez replied. "I have not seen him for a long time."

"It'll go easier with you if you tell the truth," Mr Hardy told him.

Valez shook his head determinedly. "I know nothing of things like that. I just want to go home to Guatemala."

The Hardys decided that there was little use in trying to question the man further. After sitting in a jail for a while, he might change his mind.

"Here come the police!" Joe said as a car pulled to a stop in the Hardy driveway.

Before leading Valez away, Chief Collig informed the Hardys that the stolen museum jewellery, including the scimitar, had been located in various pawnshops round the state. All of the proprietors described the seller as a dark-haired and moustached man who spoke with a Spanish accent. He had given his name as Romano.

Still protesting that he was innocent, Valez was handcuffed and led through the downpour by two officers to the waiting car.

·18· *A Helpful Confession*

THE next morning a surprise awaited Frank and Joe when they met their father at the breakfast table.

"Boys," he said, "I'll stake you to a trip to Guatemala —that is, if you want to go."

"Wow! Do we want to go!" Joe exclaimed, and Frank beamed.

The detective said he felt that they had come to an impasse in the solving of the mystery from the Bayport end. Furthermore, if an unscrupulous group was after the ancient treasure, the Guatemalan government would no doubt appreciate having it located by honest people.

"So we have two assignments," Frank said. "To keep the treasure from being stolen, and to locate it ourselves."

Mr Hardy nodded. "I'd like nothing better than to go with you, but since I'm on an important government case, I can't leave the country. I would like you to have company, though. How about Tony and Chet?"

"Bet you couldn't keep Tony home," said Joe. "About Chet, I don't know. He may be needed on the farm."

"Let's find out," Frank urged, and went to the phone.

Both Tony and Chet were flabbergasted to hear about all that had transpired at the Hardy home in the space of a few hours. And the idea of a trip intrigued them, though Chet began worrying about what kind of food he would have to eat in Central America. Mr Prito and Mr Morton gave permission for their sons to go.

Returning to Joe and his father, Frank reported the good news and said, "I'll call the airline office now for reservations." He did this, giving all the necessary data.

The following afternoon the four boys met and drove to the airfield, expecting to pick up their tickets for a flight early the next morning.

On the way Tony gave them some news of his inheritance. "Mr Scath called me a while ago," he said. "He has made an estimate of the total value of the curios I took home. If I can sell them for what he thinks they're worth, I'll have a nice sum of money."

"That's great," said Frank, and the other boys added their congratulations.

"Boy, I never dreamed that getting a shipment of curios would send us to Central America on a treasure hunt!" Tony exclaimed gleefully.

"I'm keen about going," Chet added, "but the idea of riding in those mountains and canyons on a mule sort of worries me."

"Maybe you can rent a water buffalo," Joe teased. When the boys walked up to the clerk with whom

Frank had talked and gave their names, the man's face took on a disturbed look.

"Frank and Joe Hardy and Tony Prito have been cleared," he said, "but Chet Morton is not allowed to leave the country. I'm sorry, but he has been refused a permit."

"W-what?" Chet burst out, stunned by the news.

Joe demanded to know why their friend had been turned down.

"I don't know," the clerk replied, "but it must be a serious charge."

"Charge?" Chet gulped. "I haven't done anything!"

"This is the craziest thing I ever heard!" Joe stormed. "Someone has made a mistake."

The clerk explained that the manager of the office had told him about the Hardys being detectives. "Why don't you fellows do some investigating?" he suggested. "Unless your friend is cleared, he just won't be allowed to make the trip with you."

Frank asked for the card with the information on Chet Morton. The clerk passed it to him. It read simply: *Chester Morton, Bayport—request denied. Under restriction.*

"I wish you luck," the clerk said. "Your friend certainly doesn't look like the kind of a fellow who'd be in trouble with the authorities."

"I'm not!" Chet shouted. "Fellows, do something!" he begged.

"We'll try," Frank offered. "You and Tony stay here. Come on, Joe. We'll go over to police headquarters and find out what's wrong."

Chet slumped into a seat. He was dazed by the strange turn of events. "You don't think it's Torres's way of getting even, do you?" he asked Tony.

"Search me," his friend answered, "but it might well be."

Ten minutes passed, and Chet was now pacing up and down the airline office, sighing and muttering to himself. Finally the Hardys returned.

"Make that *four* reservations!" Joe called out cheerfully to the clerk. "Chet, everything's okay. You've been cleared!"

"You mean it? Honest? No foolin'?" Chet could hardly believe his good luck.

"That's right, unless you're a jailbird out on parole."

"What! You know I—"

Frank waved his hand for silence and explained that another Chester Morton, who had just moved to Bayport and was living on a farm at the northern end of the city limits, was out from the state prison on parole!

"You had better get yourself a city address," Joe said. "Otherwise, you might be getting invitations from the prison to drop in once in a while."

Chet, with a wide grin on his pleasant, pudgy face, stepped up and got his ticket and tourist card along with the other boys. They were now advised that their flight was at ten o'clock the following morning. It would land them at one New York airport from which they would go to another field for the journey to Guatemala.

"We'll have to work fast," Frank said, as the boys started for the car. "We'll need both light and heavy clothes."

As the Hardys each packed a suitcase and a duffle bag, their father recommended that they again test their memories on the markings on the two Texichapi medallions. Both had them letter-perfect.

"I think Tony and Chet should also learn them," Frank said, and phoned the boys to come over.

Neither of their friends, however, could seem to memorize the strange markings on the medallions.

"Let me give you a tip," Mr Hardy said. "You begin, Chet. Take a good look at our drawings and then, with your eyes closed, sketch them in your mind. Mark Twain did this to memorize the Mississippi River when he was a young river pilot."

The memory trick worked and soon both boys had memorized the strange lines which the Hardys believed were directions to the treasure.

At eight o'clock Mr Hardy was ready to go out of town on his case. He wished the boys luck on their exciting trip, reminding them to get in touch with Mr Putman's friend at the consulate if they needed help.

"Sam Radley will drive you to the airport and keep his eyes open for suspicious persons interested in your trip."

When Sam Radley appeared the next morning to drive the boys to the airport, he reported that Luis Valez had still admitted nothing and was being held for the federal authorities.

"He may break yet," Frank prophesied.

As he and Joe kissed Mrs Hardy and Aunt Gertrude good-bye, both women came close to shedding tears. "Please take good care of yourselves," their mother pleaded, and their aunt said, "Watch out in those mountains, you could catch your death of cold!"

Sam Radley, in high spirits, cheered up the women with his jokes, then he and the brothers drove off to pick up Tony and Chet. At the airfield Sam showed the boys his new magnifying spectacles.

"Here," he said to Tony with a wink, "put them on

and you'll see a little strand of a girl's hair on Chet's jacket."

The stout boy blushed. "That's not a girl's hair. That's only Iola's." The others roared with laughter.

"I guess you don't miss much with these spectacles," said Tony, after putting them on for a moment. "Sam, you haven't shaved since last night."

The detective laughed. "You're right, of course."

While the boys were waiting for their bags to be weighed, a familiar voice said, "Hello, boys!"

Willie Wortman! The big redhead seemed as jovial as ever. "I missed you by a couple of minutes at your house," he said. "I was up this way and dropped by to see how you were making out about those medallions. I'd sure like to get 'em."

The four boys looked inquiringly at one another. Did he or did he not know anything about what had happened? Tony at once decided to let the Hardys do all the talking. Chet was introduced but said nothing more than "Hi!"

Feeling that secrecy was the best policy, Frank said, "About the medallions, Willie—we've had bad luck."

"That's a shame," Wortman said. "Don't forget about the curse that's on 'em. I expect bad luck to overtake me any time."

The Hardys felt sure that Willie's trip to Bayport had something to do with the man who was now in jail. Watching the seaman closely, Frank said, "Your friend Luis Valez was arrested last night."

"Valez arrested!" Wortman cried out. "What for?" Then the sailor suddenly realized what he had said. His eyes opening wide, he asked, "How did you find out I know Valez? Did he tell you?"

"No." Joe grinned. "We just guessed it."

Wortman took no offence at this. "You *are* good detectives," he said.

Joe went on, "Valez is the fellow who told you about the medallions' curse, isn't he?"

Paling slightly, Wortman nodded. Joe now questioned him about the man with him on the New York street. The seaman denied having been with anyone.

Frank looked straight at Wortman. "Do you know a friend of Valez's who sells kitchen gadgets?"

"No."

Just then the loud-speaker announced that it was time for passengers to board the New York flight.

"Come on," Tony urged.

Frank hung back a moment. "Willie," he said, "that salesman was responsible for us boys and some girls nearly being seriously injured. That's one of the reasons Luis Valez is now in jail. You'd better watch your step about the company you keep!"

The boys moved off, leaving Wortman with his jaw sagging and his eyes popping.

When they reached the gate, Sam Radley was waiting for them. In a loud voice he called, "Have a swell trip, fellows!"

The detective took hold of Frank's arm and pulled him aside. In a quick whisper he said, "Frank. I think there's a Ladino man on the plane masquerading as a woman. I've got a hunch that it has to do with your case. Watch out!"

•19• *The Masquerader*

AMAZED by Sam Radley's warning words about the masquerader on the plane, Frank hurried after the other boys.

"What did Radley tell you?" asked Joe, as the quartet started up the aircraft steps to the cabin. "You look upset."

"Let you know later," Frank whispered.

As the craft flew out over the bay, Frank, pretending to be trying for a better view of the harbour, leaned close to his brother. "Sam Radley thinks there's a Ladino man dressed as a woman on the plane," he whispered tensely. "I guess Sam got a good look at her through his magnifying spectacles and figures she has a shaven face and wears a wig. He thinks this 'woman' may be mixed up in our case."

"Oh, help!" Joe exclaimed under his breath. "But say, what gave Sam the clue to this Ladino stuff?"

"Don't know. That's what I mean to find out."

Sitting back in his seat, Frank joked with Tony. He got up, leaned over his friend's shoulder, and in between laughs told him the news.

"Pass it on to Chet," he whispered. Then Frank started to look through a magazine.

After a moment, Frank arose, saying he was going to talk to the stewardess and incidentally try to spot the suspected person. The three boys watched eagerly as Frank started up the narrow passageway to where the blonde flight hostess was preparing coffee for the passengers.

Halfway there he spotted someone he was sure was the Ladino. The woman was seated alone. Frank wondered if she had purchased both chairs on purpose to keep a seatmate from becoming suspicious. The boy was tempted to sit down alongside her but decided not to.

The suspect had very dark skin and black eyes. She wore a dark-blue dress with a small white collar. Her hair was black with a Spanish-type comb in it. A narrow shawl was pulled round her shoulders. She was reading a book.

"That's a man wearing a wig, all right," Frank thought as he reached the stewardess and asked to see the passenger list.

The Spanish-looking woman was listed as Mrs John Macky, New York City. The adjoining seat was for Mr Macky. A fake reservation, just as Frank had thought!

As Frank was returning to his seat he saw that the so-called Mrs Macky was turning the pages of her book. With a sense of shock, but one that made him almost certain that she was disguised, he noticed that her hands were large and masculine in appearance.

A moment later he said to Joe, "Radley was right. And I have a hunch the fellow in disguise may be Torres minus his moustache. He has a prominent chin, as Dad said."

Joe was thunderstruck. "Do you think Willie was here to see him off?"

"Who knows?" Frank replied. "Anyway, Radley will keep an eye on Willie."

The problem of what strategy to pursue raced

through the Hardys' minds. Was this woman following the boys, or was the masquerade for some completely different reason? Was the suspect really Torres, and did he know that the boys were headed for Texichapi? If so, they should try to elude him and in turn follow him.

At Frank's suggestion he and Tony exchanged places and the Hardys' friends were told of the plans. But Tony did not want to wait to unmask the imposter. "I'm going back there and pull off her wig!" he declared.

"Suppose we're wrong," Joe countered. "We'd better do what Frank suggests."

"What's that?"

"Wait till we arrive in New York before we take any action. Then we'll use an FBI tactic. Let the enemy follow us till he tips his hand. But, in the meantime, we'll give him a false impression of our plans."

When the plane approached the airport, the boys fastened their seat belts, but decided to be the first ones to alight. The wheels touched down gently and the massive craft rolled swiftly towards the passenger terminal.

"Keep together now!" Frank passed the word.

The boys succeeded in being the first to descend the high steps to the runway. Mrs Macky, they took note, was not far behind.

"I'm sure looking forward to a stay at the Kampton Hotel here," Joe said in a loud voice.

Tony carried on the ruse by stating that there were a lot of sights he wanted to see in the city. Actually, the boys planned to climb into a waiting taxicab and be driven to the other airport as originally planned.

Suddenly the boys stopped dead in their tracks.

"Tony Prito!" a loud voice was calling. "Telegram for Tony Prito!"

Seeing the youth hold up his hand, a messenger hurried over, handed him the envelope, and left.

Opening the envelope, Tony pulled out the message. It was not a telegram at all, but a hand-printed warning: *Stay out of Guatemala or your life will be in danger!*

"And the thing's full of ashes!" Chet whispered nervously.

"This settles it," said Frank grimly. "We get out of here as fast as we can."

By this time their luggage had come through and the boys quickly claimed it. Frank whispered directions and they followed him to a coach that would take passengers into the heart of the city. In the line of those waiting stood Mrs Macky!

"We're in luck!" Joe thought elatedly.

The Bayport group waited until the suspect was seated in the coach and other people piling in. Then they made a dash for a waiting taxi and rode off.

Frank directed the driver to the other airport and the taxi was soon speeding towards the plane that was to carry them to Guatemala. As they reached the mammoth, busy airport, Tony began looking round frantically.

"What's up?" Joe asked.

"The number of bags," Tony replied. "We had nine. And now I can count only eight!"

Tony was right. One bag was missing!

"And it's mine!" Tony moaned. "It had all my clothes in it."

"Couldn't we return to the other field?" Chet asked, but Frank pointed out that they could never get back in time to catch the Central American flight.

Tony was grim. "What'll I do?" he asked woefully.

"You'll just have to dress like an Injun!" Joe laughed and folded his arms across his chest Indian style. "You heap big chief of our tribe."

·20· *Volcano!*

THE remark about Tony having to wear Indian garb gave Frank an idea. "That might be a smart thing to do," he said. "In Indian dress, with his black hair and dark skin, Tony might pass for a native guide."

"Sure," Tony agreed. "I might be able to learn things the rest of you couldn't that would help us in our search. Only trouble is," he sighed, "I can't speak any Spanish or Indian dialect."

Frank grinned and Joe said, "Oh, you can act like an anti-social Indian and say nothing."

The boys boarded the plane. Presently the hostess came round with magazines and Tony asked whether she had any literature on Guatemala. The pleasant young woman brought him a book, in which he was soon absorbed.

As the plane took off and the other boys stared out the windows at the ground below, Tony discovered an item of interest in the Guatemalan book. It concerned an eccentric type of Indian, who rarely spoke and roamed the countryside looking for the sacred quetzal bird. "This would make a perfect disguise for me," thought Tony. In another chapter, he studied and memorized some simple, useful words common to all Indians.

Then, excited by the prospect of playing the role of Indian, he showed the book to his friends. After they, too, had read of the bird-searching Indians, Tony flipped back to a page where a picture of the quetzal bird was shown. About the size of a turtle dove, it was emerald green in colour, with a shining crown containing ruby-red and blue tints.

"To keep from disarranging its beautiful, yard-long tail," the caption underneath the picture explained, "the bird builds both an entrance and an exit to its nest."

"Sure is pretty," observed Joe, reading on. "Say, fellows!" he exclaimed. "Listen to this! The bird cannot live in captivity, and is loved by the people for its free, wild, independent spirit. Because of this, the rare quetzal bird has become the national symbol of Guatemala. In ancient times only the chiefs were allowed to wear this bird's exquisite plumage."

Chet sighed. "I'll take a good domestic broiled chicken any day," he remarked, as the others laughed.

The transport plane winged its way down the coast and the four boys finally dozed in their deep, comfortable seats.

At sunrise the plane was over the Caribbean, nearing the eastern coast of Guatemala.

"There's the shore line!" Joe cried, as he noticed that the vivid blue sea water was changing to a lighter hue. A glimpse at the white strip of beach and the mountains beyond excited all the boys.

"I can hardly wait to land!" Frank exclaimed.

At the Guatemala City airfield, the boys were cleared through customs. Then, gathering their bags, they went outside to look for a taxi. A driver approached and introduced himself as Jorge Almeida.

Smiling broadly as he picked up two bags, Almeida said, "This way, *amigos*. I have a fine taxi waiting for you!"

Grinning, they followed his slender but wiry figure to an old open car parked by the kerb. The driver strapped the bags on the running board and the boys got inside.

The affable driver turned round from his seat in the front and said, "Now where shall my little taxi take you?"

"Texichapi," Joe replied with a grin.

Then Chet said, "Better take us to a hotel first—some place where they have good food," he added hopefully.

"Hokay!" Jorge Almeida replied, and like a stock-car racer coming out of the pits, the taxi joined the highway and started speeding towards the city.

As he drove, the man chatted like an over-talkative parrot. He told the boys he knew of no place near Guatemala City named Texichapi. "But," he admitted modestly, "it is possible for it to be somewhere else. I have not been everywhere."

They reached a crossroad and another taxi approached from the highway to the right. Instead of slowing down, Jorge started blowing his horn wildly. Then he stepped on the accelerator and whizzed across the path of the other cab, missing it by inches.

"Brakes no good," Jorge explained, flashing an engaging grin at his dumbfounded passengers. "Don't use much, anyway. Horn much better!"

The boys crossed their fingers for luck, hoping that they would reach the hotel without a car crash. Meanwhile, Jorge pointed out the sights of the plaza, at times leaning far out the side of the cab to indicate a certain place.

"Say, this is better than a Hollywood movie setting," Joe said, chuckling, as Jorge finally slowed down and drove them round the big square and past the arcades where natives sold food from small booths.

In the centre of the plaza, men were arranging chairs on a bandstand in preparation for the evening's concert, Jorge informed his passengers. Gaily dressed pedestrians were strolling along the promenades, admiring the beds of gorgeous, brightly coloured flowers.

"Look at those men!" Joe exclaimed.

A group of small-statured Indians in red serapes, shawl-like blankets thrown over their shoulders, sat crouched in the shade of the arcades. "Tony, that's what you'll look like in your new clothes!"

Tony grunted. "*Sí*, me searchum quetzal bird!"

The others grinned at his odd combination of Spanish and American-Indian dialect.

"Everybody like that bird." Jorge laughed as he circled the square twice and finally stopped at the entrance of a clean, whitewashed hotel near the end of the plaza. "This place hokay!" he announced, unloading the baggage as they got out of the vehicle.

Frank added a generous tip to the taxi fare and Jorge said, "You fine boys! More fun to drive than fat lady tourists!" He laughed. "I drive you cheap from now on—maybe almost free!"

The boys thanked Jorge for this offer, and obtaining his address, promised to get in touch with him when they were ready for another ride.

After checking into the hotel and stowing their gear in two airy bedrooms, the boys set out to learn what they could about the road to Texichapi.

"Look!" Chet exclaimed, pointing out a booth near the square where native dishes were displayed.

"I'm going to get a few *tortillas* and all the fixin's."

The boys then continued walking round the promenade. At the side opposite the hotel, Joe spotted a shop that sold Indian goods. "Let's go in and find a travelling outfit for Tony," he suggested.

While Tony was buying wool trousers and a warm jacket, the other boys had a great deal of fun. Each tried on serapes, moccasins, and embroidered shirts. Finally Tony's costume, including a shoulder-length wig, was wrapped and the group returned to the hotel.

Half an hour later, the quartet appeared on the plaza. Tony made an odd-looking companion in his Indian clothes and wig.

"Now I'm ready for the quetzal bird!" he said, laughing.

A Spanish-looking Ladino, standing nearby, stared darkly at Tony and spat on the ground. Then he savagely spoke a Spanish phrase that Frank understood to mean:

"*A curse on you!*"

As the boys hurried away, Chet said fearfully, "Hadn't we better give up this scheme? You might get all of us in trouble, Tony, pretending to be hunting for their sacred bird."

"I won't mention it again," Tony promised.

After eating lunch in a nearby restaurant Jorge had recommended, the boys hunted up Mr Putnam's friend. To their disappointment, he had gone to Brazil.

"We'll just have to inquire where Texichapi is," said Frank.

But when they did, the various men shook their heads. No one had ever heard of it. A few knew where the Kulkuls lived—in a northwesterly direction from the city, but were vague as to any details about them.

"I guess that we'll have to map out a route to the Kulkul area and take a chance that the Indians will tell us where Texichapi is," Frank concluded.

He bought a road map and the boys pored over it until late that night. A route was finally decided upon.

"We can go one hundred miles to this point in a car," Joe pointed out. "After that, we'll have to try to hire mules to use from there on."

"We'd better let Dad know how we're making out," suggested Frank, and sent an airmail letter to Mr Hardy bringing him up to date on their plans.

The next morning, the hotel clerk was very accommodating and directed them to a food supply store. Here they purchased a quantity of canned goods and bread. In the course of their conversation with the shopkeeper, he remarked that he had a relative at the one-hundred-mile point who rented out mules, saddles, and blankets to tourists who wanted to explore the mountainous country.

"Shall we take a chance on Jorge and his daredevil driving to get us there?" Tony asked, grinning.

"I'm game," Joe replied, "as long as he fixes those brakes."

They got in touch with the native driver. His face became one expansive smile when he was given the assignment. As the boys walked back to the hotel, Joe remarked, "Doesn't it seem queer to you that we haven't been followed or bothered even once by our enemies?"

"How about the one who cursed Tony?" Chet asked.

"I don't think he was part of any gang," Joe replied. "He probably was one of those people who are superstitious about the quetzal bird and thought Tony was making fun of it."

"Don't forget," said Frank, "that we don't know who all our enemies are. We may meet more of them yet. I suggest that we leave here early tomorrow morning before anyone's up."

By phone they completed arrangements with Jorge Almeida and soon after sunrise he was at the hotel entrance. The clothing the boys were not taking was checked at the hotel, and they set off in rough, warm mountain apparel. Tony, in his Indian costume, stowed the two duffle bags inside the taxi.

"You turn Indian?" Jorge grinned. "Almost fool me," he added.

"Good," said Tony. "But I don't know how to manage this blanket!" He grabbed his serape as it started to slip off his shoulders. Jorge explained how Tony could secure it. Then the boys climbed into the car and started their exciting journey to look for the Texichapi treasure.

In high spirits, Jorge sang a witty native tune as the road started to climb into the mountainous country. "Now we make with the speed!" he announced, driving like a daredevil round a sharp turn.

The boys' hair was standing on end as the car screeched round another narrow bend, where the valley dropped away a thousand feet below. "Good-bye, Bayport!" cried Chet, shuddering.

"What the matter?" Jorge asked, between puffs of an aromatic cigarette he was smoking furiously.

"Please take it easy!" Chet moaned.

Just then a great roaring sound rumbled through the mountains. "What's that?" Tony cried.

"Volcano, I think," Jorge replied, concern on his face. "We see."

As the car completed the next sharp turn, the boys gasped in wonder. The mountain-top above them was exploding in a giant fountain of liquid fire! The boiling 2000-degree lava was already pouring down the slope. In a few minutes it would reach the road!

"We're trapped!" cried Chet.

"No, no, we have ten minutes," said Jorge. "We beat it!"

He raced the car along the road, but had gone only a hundred yards when there was another ominous rumble. Then, almost directly in front of the boys, a second eruption gushed up.

"We're lost!" cried Tony, as the lava spray came within a few feet of the car.

"I manage!" Jorge cried. "Beat other fire river before it run across road."

The driver put the gear in reverse, and steered the taxi back along the treacherous roadway.

"We'll never make it!" Chet groaned. "The volcano will get us!"

Sweat poured out on Jorge's swarthy face as he steered the swaying taxi. Could he get beyond the lava flow before it was too late?

· 21 · A Kidnapped Companion

JORGE ALMEIDA worked desperately to bring his car past the danger area. It swayed and skidded. Once he scraped against the stony mountain wall. With a ripping noise a bumper sheared off.

But Jorge did not slow down. Pressing the accelerator to the floor board, he backed round the serpent-like turn.

"Faster! Faster!" urged Chet, eyeing the hundred-foot-wide, red-hot lava flow above them.

It was so close the boys could feel the intense heat from it.

In a moment it would reach the road. Unless they could get beyond the liquid fire—!

With another burst of speed the taxi shot round the turn. Too late the boys saw that the road was blocked by several massive rocks that had rolled down the mountainside.

"We'll crack up!" Tony yelled.

Jorge braked the speeding car and succeeded in slowing it. But not enough. The taxi smashed into the boulders, throwing the boys violently forward in their seats.

All were dazed by the shock, but managed to climb out of the car. Jorge, who was partly stunned, was pulled out by Joe and Frank. The trio scrambled over the boulders, following Tony and Chet in their desperate flight to get as far away as possible from the taxi which was directly in the path of the fiery lava oozing down the cliff. Seconds later, the destructive stream gushed over Jorge's wrecked car, carrying the taxi with it to the valley below.

"Whew!" sighed Joe, when they stopped running and looked back at the fiery spectacle. "Boy, that was a close call!"

"Y-yes," stammered Chet, dropping exhausted to the roadway.

"Thank goodness we're all safe!" said Frank.

"All but my little taxi," moaned Jorge. Then suddenly his face brightened. "It's hokay! We got insurance. I will get new taxi from the company," he said, "with louder horn."

"But what'll *we* do?" asked Chet. "We've lost our supplies and equipment. All that food," he moaned.

"We get more!" Jorge said cheerfully.

Both Frank and Joe looked doubtful, for they did not share his lightheartedness. They were miles from any city or town and now had no means of transportation.

"My cousin, Alvero Montero, owns *fianca*," he said. "It is long distance back but we can walk it easily. He has mules we can borrow."

The boys gladly accepted the offer and followed Jorge down the mountainside. For the remainder of the day, they trekked through the thick undergrowth of the valley. Chet was the first to start complaining of hunger.

"It's six hours since our last meal," he moaned, "and all that food buried in the lava. If I don't find something soon, I'll have to turn cannibal and eat one of you."

"Huh," said Joe, "your teeth aren't that good. Haven't you found out how tough we are?"

Shortly before dusk, the group arrived at the charming, typically Spanish Montero plantation. Work had ended for the day, and as the boys approached, the aroma of cooking meat, onion and spices reached them.

A tall, pleasant-looking man, dressed in work clothes, appeared at the front of the main house.

"My cousin," said Jorge, and hooted a signal to his relative.

Montero waved and hurried to meet his unexpected

guests. "Welcome, Jorge!" he cried in Spanish. "You bring friends? Good. You are all just in time to take dinner with us."

Then, as the group came closer, he noticed their dishevelled condition. "You have been in a battle with rebels?" he continued. "And what are you doing on foot? Where is your taxi, Jorge?"

Almeida introduced the boys and told his cousin of the near tragedy. After expressing his sympathy, the planter looked in amusement at Tony's disguise. "You had me fooled." Montero laughed. "And I see Indians every day. They work here."

The planter invited the group inside and presented the boys to his beautiful Spanish wife and their two small sons. He provided the visitors with swimming trunks, and the men and boys swam in the cold, clear mountain water of a dammed-up stream near the house. Later, they sat down to eat a lavish steak dinner.

Chet could hardly listen to the conversation as he eyed the platters of juicy meat. The hungry boys had never tasted a better meal, especially the dessert— bowls piled high with papayas and pineapples.

After the meal, Mr Montero, smoking a slender black cigar, told the boys that he had never heard of Texichapi. But he would be glad to lend them four mules to take them to the point where they planned to rent animals and equipment for the rest of their trip.

"If anyone in Guatemala knows about Texichapi," Montero continued, "it will be a remarkable old Indian who lives in a village across the next mountain. You'll go through it."

"Will he talk to us?" Frank asked.

"Yes," Montero replied. "His name is Tecum-Uman. Tell him I sent you—he knows me well."

Jorge arranged with his cousin to let the travellers stay overnight and they all slept soundly. Early in the morning he excused himself, saying he would go back to Guatemala City on one of Alvero's mules and report the loss of his car to the taxi company. A few minutes later he was riding away on a cocoa-brown burro, waving in his cheerful, carefree way.

"Good luck, *amigos*!" he called, just before he disappeared round a turn.

The Hardys and their friends prepared to start for the village where Tecum-Uman lived. Mr Montero gave them a supply of food and handed each boy a machete. "With this, you can chop your way through the thickets."

Thanking the planter for all the favours he had shown them and saying good-bye to his family, the boys mounted their animals. Mr Montero said that the mules could be left at the place where the boys would pick up the others. Two of his plantation workers would bring them back later.

With Tony still wearing the Indian outfit, the quartet began their arduous ride. Because the road was cut off, they were forced to take a path through the dense forest of the valley.

"I wish we had a guide with us," Chet remarked.

"What do we need a guide for," Joe asked, "when we have Big Chief Tony? He will lead us to Tecum-Uman."

"*Sí*, we no get lost, *amigos*," Tony said with a stony face. "Only trouble is, wig itches!" He scratched his head and laughed.

The talk shifted to the treasure.

"What do you think it is?" Chet asked.

Frank said, "I've read that when Cortez's captain,

Alvarado, conquered this country over four hundred years ago, he reported that the Indians had great quantities of gold and precious jewels. Some of this treasure was buried by earthquakes, floods, and volcanic eruptions, and people have been searching for it ever since."

"Don't let your hopes soar too high," said Joe. "You may end up with some worthless three-eyed stone monsters."

Several times along the way, the quartet overtook small groups of homeless refugees whose houses and land had been devastated by the same volcano which nearly cost the boys their lives.

Each time the boys met these groups, Tony tried out his dialect, asking the people about the location of Texichapi. To his delight, they understood him and seemed to accept him as a member of some other tribe, but the boys were disappointed not to learn anything about Texichapi from the natives.

Travelling at a brisker pace than the heavily laden people, the boys quickly moved out ahead of the refugees. In mid-afternoon, as they approached the Indian village where they thought Tecum-Uman might live, the four riders came upon another group of natives on the narrow trail. Tony prepared to try out his disguise once again.

As the group rode up, the mounted Indians suddenly spotted Tony and cried out frantically, *"Shaman! Shaman!"*

They made a quick, flanking movement and encircled the stunned boys. Before Tony could even open his mouth, the attackers had grabbed him, pulled him on to a horse ridden by the fiercest-looking of the lot, and galloped off.

"They've kidnapped him!" Chet cried out.

·22· *The Weird Ceremony*

As Chet made a mad dash after Tony's kidnappers, Frank called him back.

"What's the big idea?" the boy cried, returning to the brothers. To his amazement, they wore broad grins.

"How can you stand there laughing when Tony's in trouble? Why don't we *do* something instead of just looking?"

"Calm down, Chet," Joe said. "Didn't you hear what those Indians were yelling when they captured Tony?"

"It sounded like *shaman*," Chet replied.

"Exactly," Frank said. "And that means sooth-sayer." Shading his eyes from the sun the Hardy boy peered ahead. "Looks as if they're taking Tony to the village. They probably think he's some sort of travelling magic man."

"Oh," Chet sighed in relief.

Joe, however, was worried. "I sure hope Tony can get away with it," he reflected. "If they find out he's not a shaman—"

"Suppose we all wander into the village," Frank proposed. "By the time we get there they'll probably have elected Tony chief of the tribe!"

With Joe leading Tony's mule, the little procession started along the trail.

"What's so wonderful about a shaman?" Chet questioned.

"He's a mixture of priest and poet," Frank replied. "Whatever the shaman says goes. He is supposed to be able to see into the future. One ritual he performs is called 'telling the mixes.' "

"What's that?" Chet asked eagerly.

"When a person plans to do something on a certain day," Frank explained, "and he wants to be sure it's the right time, he calls on a shaman. This man arranges some red beans from a pita tree—"

"Did you say Prito?" Chet interrupted.

"No." Frank laughed. "I said pita. Then he burns some stuff called copal, says his mumbo-jumbo and announces to the man whether it's the lucky day or not."

"We could use a shaman for our Bayport football schedule," Joe remarked with a laugh.

Suddenly the trail turned sharply into the cobbled main street of the village. Adobe shacks with thatched roofs lined both sides. Just as in Guatemala City, the Indians here, too, huddled against the poles that supported the shop roofs.

"You know, in those red bandannas and felt hats," Joe remarked, "those fellows look just like Tony in disguise."

There was no sign of their friend or of the group that had borne him off. But Frank felt certain that the Indians would release Tony as soon as they discovered their mistake.

"While we're waiting, let's ask one of these men about Tecum-Uman," he suggested.

Frank went along the line asking the same question of each of the stolid, poker-faced natives. He got only a cold stare in return.

"Well, that idea went over like a lead balloon," he said a bit angrily. "Let's look for Tony."

At the end of the street stood a low, whitewashed building with a long porch. It looked like a shop. Half a dozen natives were moving about in front of the place, which appeared to be the only spot in the village with any activity.

"That must be where they took Tony," Joe said.

"Unless they have some kind of a temple," Frank added.

"Let's try this place, anyway," Chet urged.

The trio rode to the end of the street and dismounted near the building. At first the natives paid little attention to the boys. But when Joe walked up to a man near the door and asked him in Spanish if he might go in and look round, the native scowled. He shook his head as if he did not understand Spanish and made a threatening gesture.

"Don't get tough," Joe said in English. "I'll just walk in."

"Careful, Joe!" Frank called.

But his brother reached for the knob. At once two Indians stepped up, one on each side of the boy and struck him across the cheeks with the butt of their hard, bony hands. The force of the unexpected blows caused Joe to lose his balance and fall backwards. Furious, he picked himself up and rushed at the bigger Indian, punching him soundly on the jaw.

"That was a beauty!" Frank cried.

The man's eyes glazed and his knees sagged, then he dropped with a half-turn to the porch.

"We'll take this one!" Frank yelled as he swept past Joe to meet the charge of the second Indian. Dodging a vicious blow, Frank swiftly crouched, grabbed the man round the knees, and hurled him to the floor. As Frank leaped to his feet and turned to his brother, the doors of the building were flung wide open. Through the entrance swarmed the whole group of kidnappers. Seeing their guards lying stunned on the floor, the angered Indians attacked the boys. The three friends fought violently but, being greatly outnumbered, were overwhelmed and quickly bound.

The kidnappers, who had not spoken a word, led them through the doorway. Here other natives were carrying armfuls of mahogany wood to the centre of the large main room. Other men sat silently in a circle. This was not a shop after all, but some kind of ceremonial hall. Tony was not in sight. The captured boys were taken to the centre of the circle.

"Look, they're starting a fire!" Chet's face turned white when he saw an old man step forward from the circle and ignite the chips. The stout boy gulped. "They're going to use us as human sacrifices!" he cried, panic-stricken.

Standing inside the ring of about forty Indians who sat glowering at them, the Hardys whispered words of encouragement to each other and to Chet.

"But look!" he gasped. "They're coming after us! They'll toss us into the fire!"

The men walked past the boys, however, and went for more wood which they laid across the blaze.

Some of the smoke was escaping through an opening in the roof, but the place was already hazy. The three boys began to cough.

"Maybe this is part of the curse that Willie Wortman warned us about!" Chet moaned. "We'll never get out of here alive!"

Frank, trying to keep up his courage, said he was

afraid that the Indians had overheard the boys talking
about the treasure. If this were the case and he could
convince them that they did not intend to steal any of
it, the boys might go free. But before Frank had a
chance to try to find out, Joe suddenly exclaimed, "I
think Chet was right! Look what's happening now!"

The men in the circle began to chant on a single low
note. Without getting any louder, they continued to
chant for many minutes. Then two drummers entered
the circle and started in accompaniment to the singing.

"If only someone would say something!" Joe burst
out.

The sound of the beating drums grew louder. The
men seated in the ring made rhythmic motions with
their hands. The chanting increased in fervour—
louder and louder, until the boys could no longer hear
each other speak.

The singing became an angry, wild outcry that
sounded like war-dance music. Snake-like, the circle
came to life as the men, one by one, slowly rose to their
feet and started stamping, sending clouds of dust swirling off the dirt floor into the smoky blue atmosphere.

At the entrance to the building, there now appeared
four weirdly painted dancers wearing feathered head-
dresses. With a savage throbbing of the drums, these
half-naked Indians, brandishing long spears, leaped
through space into the moving circle of stamping
fanatics. As they whirled past the boys, the prisoners
could see the milk-white and scarlet streaks of paint on
the dancers' faces and the eerie blue lines daubed along
their sweating shoulders.

"*Kai-ee tamooka! Kai-ee tamooka!*" the entire circle
bellowed as the big dance got under way.

The solo dancers moved to the right as the circle stamped clockwise. Dust and smoke almost blinded the boys. The drummers started a faster beat that sounded as if it would tear the skin off their instruments. The chanting became a half-scream.

Then, as if by some invisible signal, the wild frenzy came to a sudden end. The performers stood as if frozen. Not a muscle of a single man moved. Then a slow thump—thump—thumping of a lone drum began. Slowly the men in the circle reformed their ring and crouched in silence on the dirt floor. A moment later the circle moved in on the boys and the dying fire.

Now the oldest man rose and approached the low-burning fire. With his arms extended, palms up, he stood for several moments without uttering a sound. Then, as several of the elder members of the circle began to murmur some gibberish, the leader pulled a long stick from a sheath. With it he poked about in the embers. Scraping carefully, he heaped up a cone-shaped pile like those the boys had seen before!

The chanting ceased. The circle closed even smaller. The leader extended his arms a second time and the murmuring began again, a little louder than before. Now, with his stick, the man scraped some of the warm ashes into a wooden bowl.

"*Kai-ee! Kai-ee!*" The chant picked up volume and the leader turned from the fire to face the Hardys and Chet. Holding the bowl out stiffly, chest high, he stopped directly in front of the boys. Inwardly quaking, the captives tried to appear unperturbed.

Murmuring the chant himself, the old Indian sprinkled the hot ashes on the foreheads of the trio. The boys winced as the fragments struck their bare skin but did not cry out.

There was a sudden commotion at the entrance. Then came a booming, commanding voice over the heads of the people, The leader, lowering the bowl, cried out:

"*Tecum-Uman!*"

The man for whom the boys had been searching! What would happen to them now?

· 23 · *Into Dangerous Country*

A HANDSOME, elderly Indian, taller than the other tribesmen, walked with stately steps towards the Hardys and Chet. He motioned to a native that they be unbound at once.

After this was done, the tall Indian addressed Frank in Spanish. "Do you speak this language?"

"A little," Frank replied, then hastened to ask, "Where is our friend? Is he all right?"

For the first time a faint smile played round the Indian's mouth. "He is quite safe. He is changing his clothes and will be brought here shortly. Your mules, also, are unharmed."

Frank told the other boys this news, then said, "I don't understand what has happened, Tecum-Uman. We were advised to ask your aid by Señor Montero."

"Yes," the elderly man nodded. "The Señor is an old friend of mine. I am sorry you have been poorly treated here."

Mystified, Frank asked him to explain the reasons for the odd happenings they had just experienced. For answer, Tecum-Uman motioned for the boys to follow him outside. Reaching a secluded spot, the man turned again to Frank and began to speak.

"I am chief of the three Kulkul Indian villages," he said. "This village is one of them but not where I live. I came here because certain men have been causing much trouble. They are the ones who captured young Prito and took you into the ceremonial hall."

Tecum-Uman explained that he was sure a certain dishonest Ladino in the area was responsible for the recent unrest in the village. "I believe he was the man who told my tribesmen that your friend was disguised as a shaman. This thing is regarded as a great evil by my people," he concluded. "The fire dance you witnessed is an old custom performed to break such a curse."

Frank said he regretted the misunderstanding. "Our reason for coming here," he told the chief, "is to find Texichapi. Do you know where it is?"

If the Kulkul chief was surprised by the question, he did not show it.

"Texichapi—as it is called by the Kulkuls—is reputed to be a day's walk west of the place where Prito said you were to get fresh mules and supplies." Tecum-Uman gave no further information. "You will be free to go with your friend when he arrives here. My loyal tribesmen wish you no harm."

As the old man concluded his statement, Tony Prito was led towards them. Dressed in a blue cotton shirt and a pair of nondescript but clean brown trousers, he rushed up to the boys.

"Am I glad to see you!" he cried. "I thought all of us were goners."

"S-so did we!" Chet stammered.

There was no sign of the unfriendly natives as

Tecum-Uman accompanied the boys to their mules. As a gesture of good will, he handed the boys a sack of food and repeated the directions to Texichapi.

"You will arrive at the village where you change mules and equipment within one hour," Tecum-Uman said. "If you do not leave this trail, you cannot miss it."

The four travellers expressed hearty thanks for his help, and the elderly man waved good-bye to them. As they rode away, the boys told Tony about their ordeal in the whitewashed building and about Tecum-Uman's explanation of it.

"He sure arrived at that clambake in the nick of time," Joe said. "Now tell us what happened to you."

Tony sobered. "This shaman business was a fake," he said. "They knew right away I wasn't an Indian. What they wanted was to find out why we're here. They sure made it hard for me—tried several torture tricks. I guess I can thank Tecum-Uman that things weren't any worse. He arrived in the midst of it. But the guys that were holding me warned that if I told the chief anything, it would go badly with me later."

The Hardys were afraid that the group might be followed and urged their mules forward at a faster pace to outdistance any enemy native runners. Several times Frank dismounted and put his ear to the ground to detect any sounds of horsemen trailing them, but he heard nothing.

"I guess we're safe," he concluded.

Exactly as the old man had predicted, the boys arrived at the next village in one hour. They sought out the shopkeeper's relative who rented mules. He made arrangements for the group to remain overnight, and promised to have their mounts ready for an early-morning start.

After buying fresh supplies for the trip, the boys were shown to the cabin where they were to sleep. The four agreed that they would ask no questions about Texichapi while they stayed in the village.

"We can't tell friend from foe in these mountains," Frank said, "so we'd better just be mum about the treasure."

Before the sun went down, the boys took a short walk round the trading post, inspecting the various supplies that were bought by traders, explorers, and settling farmers. Chet picked up a short-handled miner's shovel.

"Say, here's a tool we might need in Texichapi!" he exclaimed, unwittingly breaking the pledge to silence concerning their destination that the boys had made.

An Indian standing nearby flashed a strange look at Chet. The boys expected him to vanish in the next instant and bring back reinforcements to harm them. But instead the man walked closer and spoke to them in broken Spanish.

"Texichapi?" he asked. "You going there?"

Since Chet had already given away their destination, the boys admitted that they were.

"Bad place," the Indian told them. "Stay away from Texichapi. It is valley of evil."

The man said that Texichapi was hard on a man physically because of its sudden and extreme changes in temperature.

"And besides," he went on, "there are many mahogany trees in Texichapi which are protected by spirits. When someone not wanted tries to enter that section, a curse is put on him!"

The boys looked at one another, dismayed. But the part about the curse did not seem to ring true.

"Where did you learn about the curse?" Frank asked the Indian. The man failed to understand his stilted high school Spanish.

For the next ten minutes, the Hardys and their friends tried to get the native to tell them whether this tale of the curse and the place being called the valley of evil was an old legend of the Indians or whether it was just a recent man-made story. It might be another stratagem of the boys' enemies, the patriotic society, to frighten away the quartet.

"No, sorry," the Indian replied time after time.

"The more I think about going into the Kulkuls' valley," Chet said waveringly, "or about being left behind here, I go cold all over."

The Indian drifted away and the boys returned to their cabin. All were uneasy about going to sleep, not knowing what might happen. But nothing disturbed them except the howling of wild animals in the nearby forest.

At the crack of dawn, the group headed west as Tecum-Uman had instructed them. There was no indication that they were being followed. The boys pushed on and did not take a break in their difficult journey until the sun was directly overhead. Then they lunched briefly on their new provisions and set off again.

Much of the way seemed to be along dry river beds and across streams which appeared to have changed course and left their former beds to flow in adjacent ravines.

"There sure are a lot of crisscrossing trails," observed Frank, who was leading the cavalcade. "The trail to

Texichapi would be mighty tough to follow if Tecum-Uman had not insisted that we keep heading straight west all the time."

Suddenly he stopped, and as the others waited, dismounted and picked up a stick. With it Frank scratched several marks in the dirt. Finishing the last line, he asked the others to look at what he had drawn. "Do these seem familiar?" he asked.

The boys studied the lines for only a few moments, then Joe exclaimed, "Of course. They're the ones on the medallions!"

Frank explained that he had traced the curves of the several streams that they had just passed. "They exactly match the lines that we memorized! We must be in the middle of the Texichapi country!"

Joe looked around excitedly. "I wonder what the opal really meant—should we look for a certain tree, a cave, or maybe a particular hill?"

No one knew the answer. Taking their bearings on the curve of the last stream, the boys changed course slightly. For half a mile they beat their way through swampy ground until they saw, sparkling like a jewel, a small lake at the base of a distant cliff.

"Do you think this lake corresponds to the location of the opal on the medallion?" asked Tony.

"I doubt that the treasure would be buried underwater," replied Frank. "Besides, we have to travel a little farther if my memory is correct."

The riders broke into a jog as the wooded countryside became more open. Within a few minutes they arrived at the lake.

"Look up there!" Joe cried suddenly.

Two figures stood at the top of a sheer wall of rock that dropped seventy or eight feet straight down to the

water. The sight of people in this apparently unin-
habited area startled the boys.

As the figures moved close to the rim of the cliff, the
watchers could see that they were an Indian man and a
small boy.

Frank was about to shout to the Indian when they
saw the little boy break away from the man and run
along the cliff's edge. They could hear the man give a
warning shout. Abruptly, the little boy turned to face
the man, but lost his balance and hurtled towards the
water.

The four boys gasped in horror as the small form
struck the lake surface and disappeared. They realized
that, even if the youngster knew how to swim, a fall
from such a height would knock the wind out of him
and he would drown. The same would be true of the
child's companion if he should dive in and attempt a
rescue.

"I'm going after that boy!" Joe cried. Slipping off
his moccasins and jacket, he dived into the lake!

·24· *Followed!*

As Joe dived into the lake, his friends watched with
concern from the water's edge. Would he be able to
reach the drowning child in time? There was still no
sign of the boy who had fallen from the cliff.

"Perhaps it's already too late," Joe thought fearfully as he swam underwater with strong, sure strokes.

Suddenly Joe saw the boy. His limp body was entangled in the branches of a sunken tree trunk. Re-

lieved, but with the air in his lungs almost gone, Joe swam over and frantically tried to release the unconscious boy. Just as Joe felt his lungs might burst, the branches gave way, and grasping the child firmly, he quickly rose to the surface.

As Joe emerged into the brilliant sunlight and inhaled great gulps of air, Frank cried out, "Great! Over here, Joe!"

His brother, still clutching the helpless child, headed for shore. As he drew near, Frank jumped into the water and said, "I'll take him!"

He reached for the little boy and carried him ashore. Then he laid the child on the ground and he and Tony began artificial respiration to force the water from his lungs. A few minutes later Chet took a turn.

Presently the Indian who had been on the cliff appeared, tears streaming from his eyes. Jabbering in a language unintelligible to the boys and gesticulating, he indicated that the youngster was his son.

As the water was forced from the little boy's mouth, his limbs began to twitch, and his breathing became more regular. Soon the child's eyes opened. Through gestures, Frank indicated to the Indian that his son was definitely out of danger, but should be put to bed for the rest of the day.

When the child was ready to travel, his father gently picked him up. The man, his face beaming with gratitude, nodded to each boy, then started homeward.

"That was a great rescue you made, Joe," Chet praised his pal, "You've made a real friend of that Indian."

Joe blushed and started removing his wet clothes. The warm breeze quickly dried them. After putting them back on, he said, "All set? Let's head for the treasure spot of Texichapi."

The four riders started towards the place, which, according to the stranger at the trading centre, had the power to cast an evil spell. After making two wrong turns, they finally rode into an area which matched the one on the medallions.

"Why, it's beautiful here!" Tony exclaimed.

"Not windy and cold like that Indian said. And it certainly is cheerful," Chet added, watching the brilliantly coloured birds which flitted among the trees.

Small clumps of spruce filled the valley, and as the mules moved silently over the pine-needled ground, the boys breathed in the crisp air.

"There's a big stand of mahogany trees ahead!" Frank said excitedly. "And that's the spot indicated on the map by the opal."

Eagerly the boys urged their mounts towards it. Reaching the grove of giant trees, they held a conference about where to begin their digging. Frank took a pad from his pocket and once more sketched all the lines from the medallions. Then he sketched in the exact location of the opal.

"At the centre of this gem is where we start digging," he announced and marked the exact area. Then he tore the paper into small bits and scattered them in the breeze.

During the next five hours the boys dug without interruption. Nothing came to light. Finally, tired from the heavy work, they were about to quit for the day when Tony's pick struck a hard surface. It made a slightly different sound from that of the rocks he had come against before.

"Fellows," he said excitedly, "start shovelling here!" Working furiously the group gradually made out the shape of first one, then another heavy stone step leading into the earth.

"This is the beginning!" Joe cried. "Let's really dig!"

Into the dusk, then after a brief night's rest, all through the next morning, the quartet continued their excavation work. After uncovering a dozen steps with a carved balustrade, they came to a stone of a different type.

"I don't think this is a step," said Frank. "It's a slab laid across something."

They decided to prise the slab loose. This proved to be a backbreaking job, but at last they managed to up-end the slab. Below it were more steps, almost free of earth.

Their hearts pounding, the boys beamed their lights ahead and descended. "I feel as if I were walking back through the centuries," Frank commented in a whisper.

In a few moments he and his companions found themselves standing in the anteroom of a huge building. "This must have been a palace!" Joe cried excitedly, as his light picked up carved columns, benches, and walls.

As they made their way through richly carved reception rooms, altar rooms, and finally reached the vast throne room, Chet broke the stillness to exclaim, "Wowee! What a treasure!" The frescoed walls and throne were of solid gold!

"Look at those chairs!" Tony gasped.

The carved seats were inlaid with varicoloured woods. Opals and costly jade crowned the backs of each. Emeralds and rubies glistened from their settings in the golden throne. Eight-foot vases with mosaic figures of Aztec royalty filled the corners of the room.

"These treasures are certainly government property!" Frank said. "No one must be allowed to steal them. We must notify the Guatemalan government at once."

Retracing their steps towards the exit, the boys saw one entire room filled with golden figures. Some were of Aztec men, others of animals and birds.

"Why, this one room alone is worth a fortune!" Joe exclaimed. "No wonder Torres and Valez were ready to kill us to obtain the medallions. If they get hold of this treasure, they'll be the richest men on this side of the world!"

Passing through the reception room hung with tapestries of golden thread woven through the brilliant plumage of tropical birds, the boys approached the steps.

"It seems darker here than when we came down," Tony remarked.

It was true, and the reason soon became obvious to the boys. Several shadowy forms were standing guard at the entrance! Some of them were the boys' tormentors from the Kulkul village, others were white men.

"They've followed us here," Frank whispered. "Even the masquerading 'woman' from the plane!" he groaned. "I recognize his face."

These words were no sooner spoken than the man stepped forward. He announced himself as Alberto Torres, leader of the "patriots". Torres was now dressed in a red-and-white wool shirt and khaki trousers. Smirking, he said:

"I am glad to see the detectives from the States. Of

course it will be impossible for you to escape," he added in a sneering tone. "Permit me to thank you for leading us to the treasure we have sought for so long."

Torres went on, "And now that the fabled treasure has been located, we have no time to lose. You boys will be sealed inside this palace to die while we go for more equipment."

As if the power he held over the boys suddenly inflated him, Torres began to strut before them, talking fast as he walked. "I fooled you all, you and your father," he boasted. "That Valez—he is as stupid as you to let himself be caught. Maybe all detectives in the States are dumb. And that Willie Wortman is dumb too. He sells the medallions—the key to this treasure."

"Where did the medallions come from?" Frank spoke up.

"I can at least amuse you before you die by answering some of your stupid questions," the pompous leader replied. "To begin with, those medallions were cleverly and secretly made by an old Kulkul Indian who had wandered away from his tribe. Most likely he had discovered the treasure and made the medallions as a future guide for Tecum-Uman. He died suddenly in the forest and Wortman's buddy found them on the body of the old Indian. He showed them to me. When I realized later that they must be of great value, I tried to get them from Wortman's friend. But he had disappeared with the medallions.

"I sent Luis Valez," he continued, "to find the fellow who had them. He learned that Willie Wortman had received them in the meantime and sold them to Roberto Prito in New York. Valez went there, then on to Bayport. Willie Wortman, meanwhile, had begun to suspect something, and he too began to search for the medallions."

"Were you the man who got away from me in New York?" Joe interrupted.

"I was," Torres replied in a grand manner. "When Valez seemed to be failing in his mission," he continued, "I hunted up Willie Wortman in New York. I was following him that day when you saw us. I didn't find out anything from him, so I went to Bayport to check on Valez. He was in jail and I learned you were coming to Guatemala, so I took the same plane to New York. You got away at the airport, but I took the next plane down here."

Torres's statement that he had arrived in Bayport after his henchman's arrest cleared up one of the questions in the minds of the Hardys. He was not the man who had helped Valez when he had waylaid Joe and stolen the opal medallion.

"How did you find out we were coming to Guatemala?" Frank asked.

"I learned about it from a friend of mine at the consulate in New York. The patriotic society kept track of you. They traced you through a Guatemala City taxicab company and found that you were already headed out here to the hills."

"Did you arrange what happened to us at the fire ceremony?" Frank queried.

"Yes. And one of my spies tried to keep you from this place by telling you that it is a valley of evil."

After a pause, Torres added, "Tecum-Uman himself hates me, but I have many friends in one of his villages. I sent word to them to bring you in and torture you. The old man of course knew nothing of this. But when he showed up he was told a story of his people having to break a curse you had brought them because of a false shaman."

"You didn't plan on our leaving that village," Joe said.

"No. I was going to get the truth out of you about the treasure right there. But it does not matter. You found it for us, anyway."

"It's too bad," Frank said, "that Tecum-Uman doesn't have a loyal following in all his villages. He'd drive a thief like you right out of the country."

"I warn you," Torres responded angrily, "no more talk like that or I won't even bother to seal you in! I'll kill you right now!" He started pacing again.

Frank, stalling for time and hoping that the boys could think of some way to outwit Torres and escape, questioned the vain man again. "How about the first medallion that Valez stole?" he asked.

The leader of the so-called patriotic society stopped pacing, whirled round, and asked Frank to repeat the question. Frank did as Torres commanded.

"You say he stole it!"

"Yes."

"That dirty double-crosser!" Torres roared. "He was playing his own game and must still have the medallion. Valez never told me he got it. The skunk!"

In spite of Frank's attempt to stall for time, Torres, ruffled by the news of Valez's betrayal, suddenly yelled, "Enough of this delay! Strip these four of their tools and seal them in!"

The leader headed for the steps, and without looking back, climbed the steps to ground level. The six guards closed in!

·25· *The Secret Revealed*

"OUR only chance is to slug it out with them," whispered Frank. The other boys grimly agreed, though Tony pointed out that they were weaponless and outnumbered.

Quickly the boys retreated to the middle of the room and braced themselves for attack. Two of the enemy headed for Joe, who ducked, grabbed one native's arm, and swiftly slung him jujitsu fashion over his shoulder. The man crashed against a heavy stone idol and lay dazed. Joe's second opponent caught the boy square on the chest and the two fell, rolling over and over.

Chet, knocked to the floor by a husky Indian, decided to use strategy. As the native above him closed in, the boy pretended to let himself be taken. The man relaxed and motioned for Chet to stand up. As he rose, Chet brought the back of his head up flush under the jaw of the unsuspecting enemy, who at once collapsed.

"Two down—four to go!" cried Chet, running towards Tony, who was being backed into a corner. Remembering a recent movie he had seen with Tony, Chet cried out, "Smash!"

At once Tony reached out with both hands and caught the coarse black hair of the man nearest him. Chet did the same to another Indian. With a quick, jerking motion the boys banged the skulls of the natives together with such a crack that the two dropped in a heap, unconscious.

Tony and Chet now looked to see what was happening to the Hardys. Joe was still struggling with his man and Frank was being beaten by the biggest of the attacking group.

"Come on, Chet!" yelled Tony, racing across the room. With only two natives left to subdue, the boys had a chance for escape!

But just then six more Indians swarmed down the steps. There was nothing for the boys to do but surrender. They were lashed tightly together, then laid at the foot of the steps.

The bandits were jubilant! Shouting words of self-praise, they started up the steps. Suddenly, in the bright light of the opening, an Indian with drawn bow appeared on the steps. He let fly with the arrow. One of the bandits screamed in pain as the flint arrowhead seared into his raised right arm.

Several Indians came running down the steps after their leader. Herding the boys' captors into a corner, they ordered one of them to release Frank and Tony from their bonds and then helped Joe and Chet to their feet.

"We're mighty glad to see you!" Frank said. "But where did you come from?"

"Kulkul village," was the reply.

"But how did you know—" Frank began.

Joe interrupted Frank's question by pointing to the steps. The boys turned to look. At the top of the stairs, with broad smiles on their faces, stood the little boy the Hardys had rescued and his father.

"There's our answer!" Joe cried.

The quartet rushed up the steps to thank the man. Again the grateful native tried to explain, using sign language, but failing in this, he asked one of his friends who could speak a little broken English to act as interpreter.

"He say after you save boy he see you go on path to Texichapi. He start to worry," the man began.

"But how did he know we were coming here after the treasure?" Joe asked.

"He not know that. He know we have some bad people in one Kulkul village. When he see them after you, he run to loyal Kulkuls and tell us come quick with him. Our village not far away."

"We want to thank you and all the loyal Kulkuls for saving our lives," Frank said, shaking the spokesman's hand.

"Tomas, the boy's father, he say we even—equal," the man replied. "You save boy. We save you."

A moment later they saw Tecum-Uman approaching the buried palace. He told the boys that Torres and his gang were under guard, awaiting the arrival of the federal police. He added that he had already sent a messenger to inform the officials.

"You boys have done a noble act for the Guatemalan government," the old man said to Frank as he excitedly started on a tour through the palace with the discoverers.

"Yes," the interpreter added, "place belong to ancestor. Thank you for find. Nobody steal. Sacred for government fathers."

The boys led the way through the wealth and beauty of the rooms they had already seen. The Indians were overcome with joy as they saw the splendour of their earlier civilization. Tears of happiness filled Tecum-Uman's eyes.

"With Torres arrested and in jail," the old man said, "the Kulkul tribe will become united again. And this wonderful palace can be restored. The tribal gods have looked on us with favour."

As they moved along, playing their flashlights from one priceless object to another, Chet, who had been leaning against a jewel-panelled wall, suddenly cried, "Hey, what's this?" as the panel swung open. "A whole new passageway!"

Eagerly the boys beamed their lights into this area. On their previous trip through they had thought this decorated rectangle was part of a solid wall.

Tecum-Uman and the others accompanied them into the newly found section. The old man's eyes glistened as he explained to the boys that this must have been a sacred ceremonial room. It was fashioned of pale-pink granite, which probably had been transported from South America, Tecum-Uman explained. Here, too, were costly idols made of beautifully carved woods, silver, or gold set with precious jewels.

The inspection ended, the party retraced their way through the palace and climbed the steps to the sunlight. Across a small clearing the notorious Torres, guarded by several Indians, stood staring glumly at the ground. At the sight of the boys, the leader of the criminals flew into a rage again.

"I will get my revenge!" he yelled. In spite of the Kulkuls' efforts to silence him, he continued screaming at the boys.

"Say, Torres," Chet called, "next time you impersonate a woman, remember to wear gloves—your hands gave you away!"

Torres, incensed by Chet's remark, clenched his large fists and increased his shouting. But a moment later, when reinforcements of loyal Kulkuls ran into the clearing, the man became silent. Tecum-Uman told the boys that they had nothing to worry about concerning further trouble with Torres and his gang.

Posting a guard at the entrance to the palace, the tribal chief asked the boys to get their mules and walk with him at the head of a procession back to the nearby Kulkul village.

"You are heroes," he said, "and my people will want to thank you. But tell me how you learned of this treasure."

The Hardys explained about the medallions and Torres. When they finished the story, Tecum-Uman nodded his head. He said that an elderly member of his tribe had been taken ill while on a hunting trip and died before he could get back to his village. The old man probably was the Indian from whom Willie Wortman's sailor friend had got the medallions.

The exciting news of the Hardy's discovery of the long-buried palace and the arrest of the law-breaker Torres turned the sleepy village into a buzzing bee-hive. Everywhere the usually silent natives talked excitedly about the details that trickled in ahead of the heroes.

"Tecum-Uman, he say big celebration to honour four boys," a panting messenger had told the villagers, running from house to house.

Immediately, all of the Indians' brightly-coloured finery was brought out. Women adorned themselves in gay festival dresses and prepared great dishes of food for the banquet.

Meanwhile, the menfolk had built fires in the barbecue pits and started roasting chunks of tender beef and pork on the turning spits. The children linked fresh flowers into streamers and strung them above the entrance to the village. Each cottage flew the Guatemalan flag. Musicians tuned up their primitive instruments and waited the arrival of the heroes. By the time the Hardys arrived with Chet and Tony, everything was ready.

"Smell that!" Chet said, as the delicious aroma of the roasting meat reached him. "It must be true that we're going to have a feast. Boy, I can't wait!"

The native band started playing as the boys looked round, smiling. To the cheers of the Indians, the visitors were escorted to a low, decorated table in the public square.

Young Indian girls passed huge dishes of fruits, maize, beans, and meat.

During the meal Tecum-Uman told the boys that he had already sent word to the Guatemalan president requesting that each boy be given a gold souvenir from the buried palace as a token of the country's gratefulness to them.

"We don't expect a reward," said Joe. "We've had a grand time visiting your beautiful country. I wish that everyone in the States could come down here to see it." The old chief looked pleased.

The boys remained in the village for the next two days. Finally federal officers arrived to take the prisoners away. And with them, bearing a large white envelope with an elaborate seal, was a grinning Jorge Almeida.

Jorge hopped off the mule he was riding, with the same adeptness that he had driven his taxi round the mountain curves. "You heroes, *amigos*!" he cried. "Why you not tell me you look for this treasure? Never would I go back to the city!"

After explaining why secrecy had been important,

Tony asked how Jorge had learned about the treasure.

"Why all the papers tell about the great thing you have did," the man said enthusiastically.

Then Jorge told how he had personally called on the president and related his part in the adventure. When he had requested permission that he might be able to come out and see the treasure, the president had said that he could accompany the police and deliver the letter he now carried.

"It is for all of you," he said importantly, handing the envelope to Joe. The letter, signed with the president's name, thanked the boys for the discovery and requested that they each take home a small souvenir from the palace.

Later that afternoon, the four boys and Jorge journeyed out to the ancient site with Tecum-Uman. While the chief led Jorge, highly excited, through the palace rooms, the boys decided on what souvenirs they would choose.

Chet picked up a large, jewelled bowl. "This must be what the king used for his special dinners," he said. "It's just the thing for me!"

A delicately carved bracelet of gold was Frank's choice. He knew Mrs Hardy would like it. And Joe could not resist a small golden idol as a gift for Aunt Gertrude. "It may even try to talk back to her!" He laughed.

As Tony selected an ancient, gold-encrusted bow and arrow, he said, "We mustn't forget Willie Wortman. Those medallions have served their purpose, so I'll give him the one I have. The curse is broken!"

For a short time the Hardys were to be free of a mystery. Then another, called *What Happened at Midnight* was to come their way and involve the brothers in

a series of harrowing experiences. But at the moment
this was far from their thoughts.

Just then, their cheerful friend Jorge walked in with
Tecum-Uman. "This palace hokay!" he exclaimed.
His eyes sparkling, he added, "But you must see my
new taxi! The horn she is like music. And," he concluded, "brakes very good. I park her back at trading
village. We pick her up and you ride to city with me?"

"Sure. But how about that volcano?" Joe asked.

Jorge grinned. "I find new way."

What Happened at Midnight

What Happened at Midnight was first published in a single volume in the
U.S. in 1968 by Grosset & Dunlap, Inc.
First published in the U.K. in 1972 by
William Collins Sons & Co. Ltd.

Copyright © 1968 by Grosset & Dunlap, Inc.

·1·

Burglars

"WHAT an assignment! And from our own Dad!"

Joe Hardy grinned at his brother Frank as the two boys slipped into ripple soled shoes and put on dark jackets.

"First time we've ever been asked to play burglar," Frank answered with a chuckle.

A few days before, their father, an ace detective, and Malcolm Wright, an inventor, had left for California to hunt for Wright's valuable stolen antique plane. Because they would be delayed in returning, the inventor had requested the brothers to "break into" his home and retrieve a top-secret invention before thieves took it.

"A little nefarious work around midnight," Joe mused, "and all because Mr Wright left his keys inside the house and locked everything but one bedroom window with a broken lock."

"The invention must be something super or Dad and Mr Wright wouldn't have asked us to guard it with our lives," Frank remarked. "I wonder what it is."

"Dad gave us permission to find out. Say, suppose we can't locate that secret compartment we think is in Mr Wright's desk before those thieves arrive?" Joe asked. "I wish Dad could have given us all the details before the call was cut off and we couldn't get it back."

Joe, who had blond hair, was a year younger than his dark-haired, eighteen-year-old brother Frank. Both had solved many mysteries, some of them for their father.

Fenton Hardy had told the boys on the telephone that just before Mr Wright had left Bayport, where they all lived, he had been threatened by a mysterious gang. They had learned about the invention from a worker in a factory that had made some of the parts. He had breached the confidence placed in him.

The caller had told Mr Wright that if he did not voluntarily turn over his invention before a certain time, "visitors" would come for it. The date they had set was the following day!

"Mr Wright didn't have time to put the invention in a safe-deposit box, so he hid it in his study," Fenton Hardy had said. "He's afraid the thieves may break into his house, so he has alerted the police to be there tomorrow morning. But he's worried and he wants you boys to get the small box containing the invention before then. Don't leave it at our house when you're not there. Keep it with you at all times but well hidden."

Frank and Joe relayed the conversation to their pretty, understanding mother, and to Aunt Gertrude, their father's maiden sister who lived with them. She was inclined to be critical of her nephews' involvement in detective work.

Instantly she said, "Be burglars! The idea! Why, suppose you fall off that house—!"

"Gertrude, *please!*" Mrs Hardy broke in. "Don't even mention such a possibility. I know the boys will be careful."

"Of course," said Joe. "Let's go, Frank!"

The brothers hurried to the garage where their shiny convertible gleamed in the light of a street lamp on the corner of High and Elm streets. Frank took the wheel and drove to within a block of Mr Wright's rambling, old-fashioned house. The boys walked to it and were glad to see that the building stood in deep shadows.

They reconnoitred the grounds in silence. No one was about. Finally Frank whispered, "I guess our best bet to the upper story is that trellis. It looks sturdy. We'll go across the roof over the kitchen door and edge round to the unlocked window."

"I'll stay close by and hold on to your legs until you make it," Joe answered.

They followed each other up the trellis and crossed the narrow roof. Fortunately there was not much pitch to it. Joe crouched and grasped his brother's right leg.

"All set," he announced in a whisper.

Frank stretched over to the window ledge but could not reach the top of the sash to raise it.

"Give me a push up," he murmured to Joe, who hoisted his brother until his fingers reached the top of the sash.

The window lifted easily. Frank pulled himself sideways through it. "Your turn, Joe." He reached out and grasped his brother's outstretched hands.

Joe, a little shorter than Frank, found he could not reach the window without swinging precariously in space. If Frank couldn't hold his brother's weight, he would be dragged outside. Both boys would plunge to the ground!

"No use being silly about this," Frank said. "I'll open the rear door for you."

Joe was about to climb down the trellis when a strong light suddenly lit the area.

"A car!" Frank exclaimed as the driver beamed a searchlight on their side of the street. "Maybe the thieves are in it! Duck!"

Frank quickly closed the window, while Joe flattened himself face down on the roof. He did not stand up until the area was in darkness again. Then he hurried down the trellis and through the rear door.

"Close call!" said Frank.

Joe nodded. "I thought maybe it was a police car, but I guess not. It had no revolving top light."

His brother agreed. "I'm sure Mr Wright's enemies are casing this place!"

"Yes. And they'll probably be back soon! We'd better get moving."

Holding their flashlights low to the floor, the boys sped up the stairs and found Mr Wright's study. A large walnut desk stood in the centre of the room. Frank and Joe walked to the front of it, where there were drawers to left and right of the wide kneehole.

"The secret compartment may be in one of them," Joe suggested.

"They're not locked," Frank whispered in amazement.

The boys searched diligently, lifting aside letters and other papers. They found nothing.

"Now what?" Joe asked.

"A car!" Frank exclaimed. "Maybe the thieves are in it!"

Frank had an idea. "I'll look in the kneehole while you hunt for movable panels on the outside of the desk."

Again there was silence as the two boys began to finger the woodwork. Minutes went by, then Joe said, "I've found something that moves."

Frank crawled out and watched as his brother slid open a panel, revealing a long, narrow space.

"Anything in it?" Frank asked.

Joe beamed his flashlight inside. A look of disappointment came over his face.

"Nothing," he announced. "There might have been at some time, though."

"You mean the invention?"

"Maybe. How are you making out?"

"Something in the kneehole looks suspicious," Frank answered.

Just then the boys heard the crash of glass and immediately clicked off their flashlights. Someone had broken a windowpane, and at this moment was no doubt reaching inside for the lock. Any minute one or more men might mount the stairs and enter the study!

The boys looked for a hiding place. There were no draperies, sofa, or large chairs, and no cupboard.

"Let's hide in the kneehole," Frank whispered, "then use our hand signals."

Some time before this, the Hardys had devised a series of hand-squeeze signals. One hard squeeze meant, "Let's attack!" Two indicated caution. Long, short, long meant, "We'd better scram." An ordinary handshake was, "Agreed".

"If there are not more than two men, let's attack," Joe said in a barely audible tone.

"Okay.".

Quickly the two crawled into the kneehole and pulled the desk chair into place. The boys were well hidden when they heard footsteps on the stairs, then voices.

"No failing this time or Shorty'll take us on our last ride," said a man with a nasal voice.

Frank and Joe wondered if the men had tried to break in earlier but failed.

The man's companion spoke in lower tones of disgust. "Oh, you'd believe Shorty invented fire if he told you he did. He ain't so great. Takes orders from the boss, don't he?" The other did not reply.

The two men entered the room and beamed flashlights around. "Where did Wright say he kept the invention?" the deep-toned man asked.

"I got in late on the conversation when I tapped that telephone call to the Hardy house," the other answered. "But I did hear the words 'secret compartment'. Where would that be? The desk?"

Frank and Joe froze. Were they about to be discovered?

"No, not the desk," the other man said. "The safe."

For the first time the boys noticed a small safe standing against the wall opposite them. Frank and Joe were fearful the men would detect their hiding place, but the attention of the burglars was focused on the safe. In a moment they squatted and the boys got a good glimpse of their faces. Both were swarthy and hard-looking.

At that moment the tower clock of the town hall began to strike. It was midnight!

The men waited until the echo of the twelfth stroke had died away, then the one with the nasal twang put his ear to the dial of the safe and began to turn the knob.

After a few moments his companion asked impatiently, "What's the matter? That safecrackin' ear of yours turned to tin?"

"Tumblers are noiseless," the other said. "Guess we'll have to blow it." He began to take some wire from his pocket.

Frank and Joe were trapped. If the door of the safe were blown off, it might head right in their direction!

Quickly Joe felt for Frank's hand and gave it a hard squeeze, meaning, "Let's attack!"

Instantly Frank answered with the "Agreed!" handshake.

In a flash Joe flung the desk chair at the two men, then the boys jumped them!

·2·

Amazing Invention

TAKEN by surprise the burglars were at a disadvantage. Frank and Joe knocked them to the floor and sat on their backs.

"Ugh! What's going—?" one mumbled.

The men were strong and with great heaves they tried to shake off the boys. Frank and Joe pressed down hard.

"Who are you?" Frank demanded.

No answer. Then suddenly the man Joe was holding rolled over and tried to sit up. Joe kept him down and the two, locked in a vice-like grip, twisted to and fro across the floor.

Frank, meanwhile, had found his deep-voiced opponent a kicker, who viciously jabbed his heels into the boy's back. Angry, Frank sent two swift blows which grazed the man's chin.

The other two fighters bumped into them. In the mix-up the burglars were able to throw off their attackers and scramble to their feet. The four began to exchange punches.

"Finish off these guys!" the nasal-voiced man rasped.

For several seconds it looked as if they would. Their blows were swift and well-aimed. Then both men,

172

breathing heavily, relaxed their guard. In a flash Frank and Joe delivered stinging uppercuts to their opponents' jaws. The burglars fell to the floor with thuds that shook the house. They lay quiet.

The boys grinned at each other and Joe said, "Knockouts!"

Frank nodded. "We must notify the police to get out here before these men come to."

"We can wait," Joe answered. "They'll sleep for at least half an hour. Let's find that invention first!"

"Good idea."

Though bruised and weary the boys eagerly searched the side of the kneehole where Frank thought he had found a clue. There was a slight bulge in the wood. After pressing it in several directions, a panel began to slide counter-clockwise. There was a click.

Just then one of the burglars groaned. The Hardys tensed. Was the man coming to? Joe leaned forward and beamed his flashlight on the two figures. Both were still unconscious.

Meanwhile, Frank had lifted out the panel. The space behind it contained a small metal box. Written on the box was: *Property of Malcolm Wright. Valuable. Reward for return.*

"I've found it!" Frank exclaimed.

"Then let's go!" Joe urged.

"Okay," Frank agreed. "You'll find a phone in the lower hall. Call the police while I slip this panel back. Take the box."

In a minute Joe was dialling headquarters. Without giving his name, he said, "Come to Malcolm Wright's house at once. There are burglars in it." He hung up.

Frank joined him and the boys dashed out of the rear door. They took a circuitous route to their convertible to avoid being questioned by the police. At an intersection they saw a police car apparently speeding to the inventor's house.

"Where do you suppose the burglars' car is?" Joe asked. "You'd think they'd have a lookout."

"Maybe it's cruising," Frank suggested.

The boys hopped into their convertible. As an extra precaution against a holdup and possible loss of Mr Wright's invention, they locked themselves in.

"Boy, a lot can happen in an hour," Joe said, looking at the car clock. He reached over and turned on their two-way radio to police headquarters. "I wonder if there's any news yet from the Wright house."

The boys were just in time to pick up a broadcast. An officer was saying, "Send the ambulance to Wright's house."

"Ambulance?" Frank echoed. "Joe, we didn't hit 'em that hard—or did we?"

The policeman went on, "These guys aren't too bad, but they sure got knocked out. Looks like a gang feud. The men who hit them may have done the stealing."

Frank and Joe chuckled. "Some day we'll tell Chief Collig," Frank said, "but right now—"

He stopped speaking as a loud crack of static burst from the radio and a vivid flash of lightning made the night turn to day momentarily. A long roll of thunder followed.

"Looks as if we're in for a bad storm," Joe commented, and Frank put on speed.

A few minutes later the car was parked in the Hardys'

garage. They were mounting the steps of the back porch when the storm broke. Quickly Frank inserted his key in the kitchen door and turned the knob. At once the burglar alarm rang loudly and all the ground floor lights went on.

Joe chuckled. "That'll bring Mother and Aunt Gertrude down in a hurry." He flicked off the alarm.

"And bring the police, too," Frank added. He picked up the kitchen phone and dialled headquarters. "This is Frank Hardy. Our alarm went off by accident. Forget it."

"Okay. You sure everything's all right?" the desk sergeant asked.

"Yes. Thank you. Good night."

By this time the two women had appeared and Mrs Hardy said, "I didn't know the alarm was turned on."

"Well, I did," Aunt Gertrude spoke up. "I wanted to be sure to wake up and see how you boys made out. You must be starved. I'll fix some cocoa and cut slices of cake while you tell—Frank, look at your clothes! Your jacket's torn. And you, Joe, where did you get that lump on your forehead? And your faces—the two of you look as if you've been rolling in the dirt."

"We have." Joe grinned. "Had a big fight. But we saved this!" He pulled the box from his pocket.

As the boys related their adventure, crashing thunder lent a booming orchestration to the story.

"This is the worst storm we've had in years," Mrs Hardy remarked. "I'm glad you boys didn't have to be out in it." When Frank and Joe finished eating, she added, "And now you must get a good night's sleep."

"But first I'd like to open Mr Wright's box and see

just what we have to guard so carefully," Frank said.

Everyone watched excitedly as Joe unwrapped the package. Inside was a small transistor radio.

"Is that all it is?" Aunt Gertrude burst out. "You risked your lives to get *that*?"

The boys were puzzled. Surely their father would not have made such a request if this invention were not unusually valuable.

"Let's turn it on," Frank suggested.

Joe clicked the switch. A man was speaking in Spanish from Madrid, Spain, and announcing the start of a newscast. His voice was very clear.

Frank grabbed his brother's arm. "Do you hear that?" he cried. "The receiver is not picking up one bit of static!"

"You're right!" Joe agreed. "It must be designed to work in the high-frequency bands."

"But how can we be receiving a broadcast direct from Madrid? That Spanish station must be transmitting by short-wave. Yet, we're hearing it loud and clear. This is amazing!"

Joe gazed at the miniature radio with great interest. "I'll bet there's a lot more to Mr Wright's invention than just being able to hear overseas stations without static," he observed. "After all, why is he so anxious to keep it a secret?"

Just then there was a loud knock on the back door and a voice from outside said, "Let me in! I'm a ham! I have a message for you!"

·3·

Warning Message

FOR a few seconds none of the Hardys spoke. They were trying to decide if the caller at the kitchen door really was a radio ham with a message. Or a member of the burglary gang?

Finally Mrs Hardy said, "We can't let the man stand out there in the rain."

Frank called, "Where's the message from?"

"Mr Hardy in San Francisco."

"Open the door," Mrs Hardy said quietly.

Joe hid the box containing the invention, then he and Frank stood on either side of the door, poised for any attack. Aunt Gertrude had armed herself with a broom. Joe turned the knob and a water-drenched figure in raincoat and hat stepped into the kitchen.

"Thanks," the man said, removing his hat. "What a night! My wife told me I was crazy to come out."

The speaker was an honest-faced man of about thirty-five. He noticed Aunt Gertrude's broom and smiled. "You can put that away," he said. "I'm harmless."

Miss Hardy looked embarrassed. "Take off your coat," she said. "I'll get you some coffee."

The man nodded. "I could use it. I got cold walking over here. My car wouldn't start."

"Did you come far?" Joe asked.

"About five blocks. I'm Larry Burton, 69 Meadow-brook Road. I've always wanted to meet the Hardy boys. This all came about in a funny way. I have a short-wave set. Tonight I picked up your father. He said he couldn't get through to you or the police on the phone—lines tied up—and you didn't answer his signal on your short-wave set."

"We weren't expecting a call," Frank answered. He did not say that he and Joe had not been at home and that their mother and Aunt Gertrude rarely paid attention to the set unless specifically asked to do so.

"By the time I phoned you, the lightning was fierce," Burton went on. "My wife's scared to death of lightning. She wouldn't let me use the phone, so I walked over."

Aunt Gertrude served the visitor coffee and cake as they all sat around the big kitchen table.

"What was the message, Mr Burton?" Joe asked.

"That you boys are in great danger. A gang is after you and will stop at nothing to get what they want."

"How dreadful!" Mrs Hardy exclaimed. "Did my husband name this—this gang?"

"No. That's all there was to the message," Burton replied. "I'm sorry to bring you bad news, but I guess that's to be expected in a detective's family. Well, I must get along." He stood up.

Frank shook the man's hand. "We sure appreciate this. Maybe some time we can return the favour."

"Forget it," Burton said. "I only hope that gang doesn't harm you fellows."

Joe helped him on with his coat and he went out. The storm had passed over.

For a few minutes the Hardys discussed the visitor and confirmed his address in the telephone directory. Joe was a bit sceptical, however. "Either he made up the whole story, or else Dad is really concerned for our safety."

Frank was inclined to think Burton had told the truth. Had he and Joe already encountered two members of the gang at the Wright home?

Aunt Gertrude spoke up. "How in the world did my brother Fenton hear this in California?"

"News travels," said Mrs Hardy. "Especially among detectives and police."

"Hmmm!" Aunt Gertrude murmured, then announced she was going to bed.

Ten minutes later Frank and Joe were asleep and did not waken until ten o'clock. At once Frank got up and opened a wooden chest of sports equipment under which he had hidden the box containing Mr Wright's invention. It was still there.

"Where do you think we should keep this?" he asked Joe as they were dressing. "Dad said not to leave the box at home."

"A tough problem, Frank. With that gang after us, we can't take the chance of carrying it round with us," Joe answered.

"Right. And they may not be after us, but after the invention," Frank answered.

While they were having breakfast, Frank came up with the idea of a unique hiding place for the invention. "Let's put it in the well under the spare tyre in the boot of our car," he said.

Joe laughed. "Now you're using that old brain of

yours. Best place you could have picked. The car's
vibrations can't hurt the radio and no one would think
of looking there."

Mrs Hardy asked her sons what their plans were for
the day.

"Dad told us to drop into the antique aeroplane
show and see if we could spot anybody who seemed
overly interested," Frank replied. "He thought the
person who stole Mr Wright's old plane might be
planning another theft."

"Tonight," Joe continued, "we're going to Chet's
party and staying until tomorrow. Okay?"

"Of course," his mother answered.

Chet Morton, an overweight, good-natured school-
mate, lived on a farm at the edge of Bayport. A group
of boys and girls had been invited there to a barn dance
and late supper. Frank and Joe would pick up Callie
Shaw, a special friend of Frank's. His brother's date
was usually Chet's sister Iola.

Mrs Hardy remarked that since the boys would be
away, she would spend the night with a friend. "Your
aunt plans to visit Cousin Helen in Gresham, anyhow."

During the conversation Aunt Gertrude had left the
table. She returned holding the local morning newspaper. "Well, you boys are in for real trouble!" she
exclaimed. "Listen to this!"

Miss Hardy read an account of the captured burglars
at the Wright home and the mysterious summons to the
police. The item stressed the fact that the men's
assailants, when caught, should be dealt with severely.

"When caught, eh?" Joe burst into laughter. "We're
going to be mighty hard to find, aren't we, Frank?"

His brother grinned, but Mrs Hardy looked worried. "Maybe you boys should explain everything to Chief Collig."

"Not without Dad's and Mr Wright's permission," Frank answered. "For the time being—"

"I haven't finished," Aunt Gertrude interrupted. "It says here that the police think this incident might be part of a gang feud." She removed her reading glasses and gazed at her nephews. "You two are now considered to be part of a gang and the rival gang is about to harm you."

"Wow!" said Joe, pulling his hair over his eyes and striking the pose of a belligerent "bad guy". "We'd better look the part!"

Since the antique aeroplane show did not open until two o'clock, the boys did various chores during the morning. They also hid Mr Wright's invention in the tyre well and bolted the spare wheel back into place.

After lunch Frank and Joe drove Aunt Gertrude to the train. From there they went directly to the Bayport Air Terminal where the antique aeroplane exhibit was housed in the spacious lobby. The first person they saw was Chet Morton.

"Hi, fellows!" he greeted them. "Say, take a look at those old planes. Aren't they beauties?"

"Sure are," Frank agreed. "I notice that most of them are biplanes. It must have been fun flying in the days of the open cockpits."

"You can say that again!" Chet declared. As he stepped back for a better view, his foot slammed down on the toe of a man standing directly behind him.

"Ow!" the stranger yelped.

The boys turned to see the man hopping about on one foot. "You stupid, overgrown kid!" he screamed.

"I'm awfully sorry," Chet said apologetically.

The tall, muscular man, who had blond hair and hard features, looked at the youth menacingly. "You idiot!" he snarled.

Frank and Joe stepped in front of Chet as he stammered, "Who—who are you calling an idiot?"

"Now just a minute!" Joe interrupted. "It was an accident. No sense getting upset about this!"

"Can I be of any help?" the boys heard someone say. They looked round to see a lanky young man walking towards them. He had rust-coloured hair and leathery skin that was deeply tanned.

"What are you butting in for?" snapped the stranger.

"This boy didn't step on you intentionally," the young man insisted. "I saw the whole thing. You were trying to listen to their conversation and got too close."

The tall stranger was about to say something, but hesitated. For a moment he glared at Chet and his companions, then stamped out of the lobby, swinging his briefcase.

Frank and Joe looked at each other. Why had the man been listening to their conversation? Did he belong to the gang they had been warned about?

Meanwhile, Chet was saying, "Thanks for your help, Mr—"

"My name is Cole Weber," the young man introduced himself. "I'm president of the Central Antique Aeroplane Club. We own the exhibit and are taking it to several airports. We're trying to encourage public interest in vintage aircraft."

"Sounds like a great club," Joe remarked.

"We think so," Weber said. "The majority of the models you see here are replicas of real aeroplanes owned and operated by our members."

"You mean that some of those old crates still fly?" Chet asked.

Weber grinned. "Well . . . we don't think of them as crates. When properly rebuilt, most antique planes are as safe and reliable as the day they were originally made. I own one myself. It's outside on the ramp. Would you like to see it?"

"Would we?" Joe exclaimed.

Mr Weber led the boys to the airport ramp. A short distance ahead stood an orange-and-white biplane. The boys peered into the two open cockpits.

"This is cool!" Joe declared.

The pilot smiled. "Compared to modern planes, mine doesn't have many instruments. But since we fly the antiques only for fun, we don't need elaborate equipment, such as that required for all-weather operations."

The boys looked closely at the diagonal pattern of wires stretching between the wings. Then they examined the plane's radial engine and the long, slender wooden propeller.

"How many passengers can you carry?" Frank asked.

"Two in the front cockpit," Weber answered. "Say! Would two of you like to go for a ride?"

The boys' eyes widened with excitement. Then Frank and Joe remembered the sleuthing they had promised to do for their father.

"Thanks just the same," Frank said, "but I'm afraid Joe and I can't go this time."

"But I'd like to," Chet spoke up. "Say, fellows, could you drive me to the farm afterwards?"

"Farm?" Weber interrupted. "Are there any level stretches of ground in the area?"

"Plenty of them. Why?"

"I'll fly you home if you'd like."

Chet tingled with excitement. "Great! Thanks."

The flier opened the baggage compartment and took out a parachute, helmet, and goggles. "Put these on and climb into the front cockpit."

"Mr Weber, do you know Mr Malcolm Wright?" Frank asked.

"Yes, indeed. He's a member of our club."

"Did you hear that his antique plane was stolen?" Joe put in.

Weber nodded. "Too bad. I understand he has some secret invention he was trying out in the plane. I hope that wasn't stolen too."

The boys caught their breath in astonishment but said nothing. They had not heard this. Weber did not seem to notice. He donned his own parachute and summoned a mechanic to twirl the propeller and start the engine. Then he climbed into the rear cockpit.

"Brakes on! Switch off!" the mechanic called.

"Brakes on! Switch off!" Weber echoed.

The mechanic pulled the propeller through several times. Then he stepped back and yelled:

"Contact!"

"Contact!" the pilot responded.

The engine caught on the first try. A staccato

popping developed into a steady roar. Chet's goggled face turned towards the Hardys. He waved wildly as Weber taxied out for take-off.

"See you at the party!" Chet shouted over the roar of the engine.

Minutes later the plane, looking like a box kite, was climbing above the Bayport field. As the Hardys turned to leave, Frank caught his brother's arm.

"There's that man Chet stepped on! He's watching us from the doorway! This time I mean to find out why." Frank started to run. "Come on, Joe!"

·4·

The Cold Trail

As soon as the man saw Frank and Joe, he turned to hurry off. In doing so, he bumped into the frame of the door and dropped his briefcase, which burst open. At a distance the boys could not read any of the printing on the letters that fell out, but one had red and blue stripes at the top.

The tall, blond man snatched up the papers and stuffed them into the briefcase. He quickly zipped it shut and began to run.

"He sure isn't on the level," Joe remarked, "or he wouldn't race off like that. We can't let him get away!"

The stranger's long legs and agility helped him cover a wide stretch in a short time. Before the Hardys could catch up to him, he reached the exit and jumped into a waiting car which zoomed off.

Frank and Joe stopped short, puzzled. Was the man afraid of them? And if so, why?

"Maybe that briefcase had something to do with his running off," Frank said.

The boys went inside the terminal building. They continued to look at the planes while keeping their eyes open for any other suspicious characters. They saw none and finally returned home.

"You must be hungry," said Mrs Hardy. "I have hot apple pie, but it's getting cold."

Joe patted her shoulder. "Shall we eat dessert first?" he teased.

Later the boys went upstairs to change for Chet's barn dance. Both put on jeans, plaid shirts, and big straw hats. They packed overnight bags, then joined their mother who was waiting to be driven to her friend's home.

Just before leaving the house, Frank heard a signal from their private short-wave set. "Dad must be calling," he said, and raced upstairs to Mr Hardy's study.

"FH home," he said into the mike. "Over."

"Frank," said his father, "how's everything?"

"Okay, Dad. How about you?"

"Fair," the detective said. "But I have a new lead to follow. You won't be able to get in touch with me for a couple of days. Did you get my message from the ham operator?"

"Yes, Dad." Frank told him all that had happened in the past twenty-four hours, including the wire-tapping.

Mr Hardy whistled. "Then the gang knew where you were going."

"Shall Joe and I tell Chief Collig we were the first burglars?" Frank asked.

"I guess you'd better," the detective agreed. "But warn him the information is confidential and don't tell him what the invention is you were after."

He now explained that he had been tipped off by Chicago police that a gang suspected of robbery there had suddenly vanished. A "squealer" had reported

they were out to "get" the Hardy detectives. The boys'
father did not know why, but surmised it might concern
Mr Wright's invention.

"And now let me speak to your mother," Mr Hardy
said.

Half an hour later Frank and Joe stopped at Chief
Collig's home and made their report. The chief burst
into laughter. "So you're the ones who knocked out
those men. I guess they had a real scare. They haven't
talked since."

By the time the boys reached the Mortons' farm with
Callie Shaw, the dance was under way. A Bayport
High School group was playing.

"Hi, masterminds!" Chet shouted as the Hardys
strolled in. "I thought you'd never get here. Boy! Wait
till I tell you about my flight!" He began to describe
the adventure, supplementing his words with swooping
motions of both hands.

His sister Iola joined Callie and the boys. She was a
slim, dark-haired girl and very pretty. "Hi, Joe, Frank,
Callie!" Then hearing her brother, she said laughingly,
"Oh no! Is Chet talking about his flight again? He
hasn't stopped since he landed."

"You just don't know anything about real flying,"
her brother said, "until you've been in one of those old
biplanes."

"Our turn's next," Joe reminded him.

The following hours passed quickly When it was
time for supper, Joe and Iola decided to eat outside.
They filled their paper plates with sandwiches,
chocolate cake and cups of lemonade, and went to sit
on the steps of the Mortons' front veranda.

As they ate, Iola glanced towards the driveway in which many of the guests had parked their cars. The Hardys' convertible was near the end of the long queue.

Suddenly Iola touched Joe's arm. "What's the matter?" he asked.

"I saw someone lurking behind your car," Iola replied. "Yes, There he is."

Joe peered into the darkness. He saw a man, his hat pulled low, pop up from behind the car, then duck down again. At once the young detective sprang to his feet and ran towards the mysterious figure. The fellow might be after the secret radio!

"Who are you?" he shouted, seeing the boot lid rise and the light go on. "What are you doing?"

The intruder ran from behind the car and disappeared into the darkness. Joe dashed after him.

"Keep your distance or you'll get hurt!" the man shouted. But Joe went on.

Iola screamed for help. Frank, Chet, and their classmates, Biff Hooper and Jerry Gilroy, raced from the barn.

"What's wrong?" Frank asked.

"We saw a man lurking behind your car," Iola answered in a trembling voice. "Joe ran after him through the woods but was warned away."

At once Frank and his companions rushed in that direction. The boys had not gone far when they heard a muffled cry for help, followed by the roar of a car speeding off.

Coming to a halt, Frank signalled to his friends for silence. The sounds of the car faded away. Everything was still, except the big grandfather clock in the hall of the Morton home. It began to strike. Midnight! Frank thought of what had happened just twenty-four hours earlier.

"Joe!" he shouted. "Joe! Where are you?"

His call went unanswered. The young detective stood frozen in his tracks. Had his brother become the victim of the gang?

By this time everyone at the party had raced outside to learn what had happened. They joined in a frantic search but without success.

"I'm afraid he was kidnapped," Frank said grimly.

"In the car we heard roar off?" Biff Hooper asked.

"Yes."

Jerry Gilroy chimed in, "But by whom? And for what reason?"

"I don't know," Frank said. He turned and rushed back to the convertible. Seeing the boot open, he immediately looked in the tyre well. The secret radio was still there.

"Joe must have blocked an attempted theft and been taken away so that he couldn't identify the man," Frank thought.

He slammed the boot shut, asked his friends to guard the car, and ran to the house. He scooped up the telephone and dialled the home number of Chief Collig.

"What!" the officer exclaimed when Frank told him about Joe's probable kidnapping. "I'll call the FBI and also get some of my own men out there right away! And I'll come myself."

He and three officers arrived shortly and were given a briefing. The place was carefully examined, but the searchlights picked up little.

There was such a profusion of tyre tracks on the main road that those of the mystery car could not be detected. Iola, the only one except Joe who had seen the suspect, could give little information other than that he was tall, heavy set, and wore gloves.

"Then we won't find any fingerprints on your car," the chief said to Frank.

Frank nodded. "He could be the man who ran from Joe and me at the airport." Frank told the police about him and gave a fuller description.

"We'll be on the lookout for him, as well as for Joe," Collig said. "There's nothing more we can do here, but I'll leave two of my men."

Solemnly the group left the barn dance and each guest expressed a hope for Joe's speedy return. The Mortons tried to comfort Frank and discussed whether or not they should call Mrs Hardy and tell her the disturbing news.

"I don't see that anything can be gained by that," Chet's mother said. "Let's wait."

She insisted Frank try to get some sleep, but he lay wide awake, hoping the phone would ring with good news from Collig. But none came. Chet, in the same room, was restless.

Finally at five o'clock he said, "Where do we go from here?"

"I'm not sure." Frank sighed. "We've absolutely no clue. In fact, we don't even have a description of the car we heard drive off last night."

"Joe could be miles from here by now," his chum remarked.

Frank thought for a moment. "Let's drive down the

road and make some inquiries at the farmhouses along the way. There's a slim chance someone may have spotted the kidnap car."

The boys left the house quietly and jumped into the Hardys' convertible. They waved to the patrolling police guards. Frank drove along the narrow, tree-lined road. As they feared, all their inquiries were fruitless. Most of the farmers they questioned had retired long before midnight, and had neither seen nor heard anything.

"Guess we may as well go home," Chet suggested.

But Frank was not ready to give up. "Let's drive on a little farther," he said.

About six-thirty, the boys spotted a farmer cutting weeds by the roadside and stopped to question him. He rubbed his chin dubiously while listening to their story.

"Quite a few cars go past my place every night," he said. "But now you come to mention it, there was an automobile came whizzin' along and stopped here right after midnight. It woke me up, what with two men in it shoutin' at each other."

"Did you see the car?" Frank asked.

"No. I didn't get up. Course my home is right beside the road, and I couldn't help but hear some o' what the men were sayin'. The car come along at a mighty lively clip, but when it got in front of the house, the driver slammed on the brakes and stopped.

"There was an argument. I heard him tellin' somebody they must have gone past the crossroads in the dark. The other man started jawin' at him and they had quite a row. Finally they turned the car round and went back."

"To the crossroads?" said Chet.

"Yes. That's about two miles back."

"I remember. One road goes to Gresham, the other heads up through the market gardens."

Frank and Chet returned to the crossroads. But which way should they go? Right to the market gardens, left to Gresham?

"The kidnappers might have hidden Joe on one of the market gardens," Chet suggested.

"Yes, except that all those farms are close together and everybody knows everybody else's business," said Frank. "I'd rather tackle the road to Gresham. If we don't find Joe, we can come back and try the other road." He took the turn to the left.

As they sped along, the boys spotted the wreckage of a black car in a roadside ditch. Afraid that this was the kidnap car, Frank pulled up.

"Some accident!" Chet observed.

The licence plates had already been removed from the badly smashed-up car.

"If anybody was hurt," Frank said, "they'll know it in Gresham. We'll ask the police there."

Suddenly a black saloon swung out of a lane some distance ahead and roared off towards the town. Frank stared fixedly at the back seat.

"Look!" he exclaimed, gripping Chet's arm. "Do you see what I see?"

"What?"

"A hand. Isn't that someone signalling?"

Chet gazed ahead and saw a hand wave frantically for a moment at the rear window, then suddenly withdraw.

"You're right!" Chet snapped. "Joe!"

Frank started the convertible and sped off in pursuit.

The other car had a good lead and was increasing speed. It was almost obscured by a cloud of dust, but Frank memorized the out-of-state licence number.

"We're gaining on them!" Chet declared.

Frank nodded. Inch by inch the intervening distance lessened. Trees, farms, and hedges flashed by. At times the boys could hardly see the saloon through the swirling clouds of dust.

Suddenly the steady hum of the convertible's engine changed its rhythm. The motor spluttered.

Chet groaned. "Now what?" he muttered as the car slowed down.

The boys' hearts sank when the engine stopped completely. They looked dismally at the other car as it disappeared round a distant bend in the road.

· 5 ·

The Hunt

FRANTICALLY Frank flung open the hood and examined the engine. In a few minutes he discovered the trouble.

"Fuel pump," he announced.

"Oh—oh!" Chet sighed. "And we're miles from a service garage."

"We're not stranded," Frank assured him. "I suspected the pump was going so I put a spare in the boot. But it's going to take fifteen or twenty minutes to change the pump, and—"

"And by that time the kidnap car will be far away," Chet finished.

"I'd better notify Bayport Police Headquarters." Frank turned on the car's two-way radio to the proper frequency and gave the licence number of the suspect's car.

"We'll get busy on it right away," came the answer. "Incidentally, FBI men have been here and out to the Morton farm. I'll contact them. There's no news so far."

Frank replaced the mike. He and Chet worked feverishly to install the new fuel pump and soon had the engine running.

"No chance of our catching up with the saloon now,"

Chet remarked as the boys once again got under way. "It has nearly half an hour's head start."

"I'll bet that the kidnappers won't stop at Gresham, now that they've learned we're after them."

Ten minutes later Frank stopped the car. He backed into a side road, pulled out again, then turned to retrace his route. "I want to go up that lane the kidnap car came out of and see what we can find."

Reaching it, Frank turned in. The ground was stony and full of holes. Progress was slow.

Half a mile farther on, an old inn, apparently closed, came into view. It was a long, low, white building with a wide veranda. The boys got out of the car and Frank knocked several times, hoping someone might be inside. There was no response.

"Nobody's home," Chet mumbled.

Just then the sound of heavy footsteps could be heard. The door sprang open and a surly-faced man confronted them.

"What is it?" he growled.

"Sorry to bother you, sir," Frank said, "but have you seen a black four-door saloon within the past hour?"

"You've got a nerve waking me up to ask such a stupid question!" the man snapped. "I don't know anything about a saloon!"

"Have you had any visitors recently?" Frank persisted. "There's a wrecked car lying in a ditch close to the spot where your lane leads in from the road. Did anyone come here for help?"

The man looked at the boys suspiciously. "Get out of here before I kick you off the porch!"

"Have it your way!" Frank retorted. "I'm certain

"Get out of here before I kick you off the porch!"
the man growled.

there were kidnappers in that saloon I asked you about. If you know anything, you'd better tell me, or be held as an accessory!"

"Kidnappers?" the man cried out. "Okay! So there were some guys walked in here late last night."

"How many were there?" Frank demanded.

"Three. One said they'd had an accident, and asked if they could stay at my place for a while. They paid me real good, so I let 'em come in."

"Please describe these men."

"One was tall, one short," the proprietor replied nervously. "The big guy said they're brothers named Wagner. They were carrying the third guy—he was wrapped in a blanket 'cause he got knocked out. I couldn't see his face. The big guy made a telephone call to Gresham. A car picked 'em up about an hour and a half ago. I can't tell you any more!"

He stepped back inside the house and slammed the door in the boys' faces.

"Sociable guy," Chet commented as the boys drove off. "He did give us one lead," Frank said. "The wreck was theirs and the pickup car came from the direction of Gresham. Chet, I'm afraid Joe was hurt. We're going to Gresham. I'll call Collig and tell him what we've just heard." He tuned in Bayport headquarters and left the message.

On reaching Gresham, Frank cruised up and down the side streets flanking the main boulevard, hoping to spot the saloon but had no luck. He then headed for the local police headquarters. "Dad introduced me to Police Chief Stanton when we were passing through this town several months ago," he said.

The boys entered the neat, red-brick building and Frank introduced himself and Chet to the desk sergeant on duty. They were ushered into the office of the chief.

"Frank Hardy, how are you?" Stanton said, extending his hand in greeting. "Sit down."

"Has Chief Collig in Bayport been in touch with you?" Frank asked.

"Yes. So far we have no word on the saloon or the men travelling in it, one of them injured. You're sure your brother was kidnapped?"

"Without a doubt!"

"Hmm!" Stanton muttered. "The saloon's probably miles away by now with a different licence plate. But our men will keep on the lookout."

Realizing they could do no more here, Frank and Chet decided to return to Bayport.

"What's our next move?" Chet asked.

"Whoever kidnapped Joe might ask for ransom, Chet. I'd better stick close to the phone at home in case someone tries to establish contact."

Then Frank's heart sank as he thought of having to tell his mother and father and aunt that Joe was missing! When he pulled into the Hardy garage some time later, Frank shut off the ignition and sat quiet for several seconds. Then he took a deep breath and climbed out of the car.

He had no sooner entered the house when Mrs Hardy rushed to meet him. "What happened to Joe?" she cried.

Frank was startled by her question. Before answering, he hugged his mother and led her into the living room.

"I'd just got home, and decided to telephone the

Morton farm. I spoke to Iola," Mrs Hardy explained. "She seemed terribly upset and started to tell me something about Joe, then stopped. She said you were on your way here and would explain."

Frank related the whole story of Joe's disappearance. Mrs Hardy was stunned by the news and tears filled her eyes.

"I would have told you sooner," Frank said, "but I was hoping to find Joe before this."

Although Mrs Hardy worried about the dangers involved in her family's sleuthing activities, she rarely displayed her concern openly. But now she could not hide her anxiety. She began to tremble.

"We must do something!" she pleaded. "Have you notified the police?"

"Yes," Frank answered. "And the FBI."

"Your father! He should be told about this at once!"

"But we can't reach him," Frank reminded her.

The hours dragged on into early evening. Mrs Hardy continually walked the floor, saying over and over, "This is dreadful, dreadful!"

Frank paced around nervously, mulling over in his mind the events that had taken place during the past two days. The telephone rang. Was it the kidnapper calling? Frank rushed to answer the call.

"Frank, this is Chief Collig!"

"Yes, Chief! Any news?"

"Not much. The police managed to detect the scratched-off serial number on the engine block of the car lying in the ditch. It was traced through the State Bureau of Motor Vehicles. The car was stolen yesterday evening from a man in Lewiston. No one saw the thief."

"Well, we're right back where we started," Frank said.

After a light late supper, Frank settled himself into a wing chair within reach of the telephone. The hours ticked by with no word from Joe or his abductors. Finally, through sheer exhaustion, Frank dozed off.

When he awoke, the sun was already sending bright, warm rays into the room. Frank got up and began to pace back and forth. He and his mother ate a sketchy breakfast. They grew more uneasy when the morning passed without any news of Joe.

Shortly after noon a taxi stopped in front of the Hardy home. A tall, angular woman, carrying a small suitcase, got out of the cab and hurried towards the house.

"It's Aunt Gertrude," Frank announced to his mother.

"I'm glad to be home!" Miss Hardy exclaimed as she entered the house like a rush of wind.

She glanced at Mrs Hardy and immediately sensed that something was troubling her. "Laura! You look exhausted. Haven't you been getting enough sleep? What's wrong?"

"We have something to tell you," Frank declared. "You'd better sit down."

He broke the news about Joe's disappearance as gently as he could. His story, however, sent Aunt Gertrude springing from her chair.

"That's terrible! Poor Joe! Call the police!" she cried. "Call the FBI! Do something!"

"Try to be calm," Frank pleaded. "The police and the FBI have already been notified."

"I felt it in my bones!" Aunt Gertrude exclaimed. "Something like this was bound to happen."

"Now, Gertrude, please," Mrs Hardy interrupted.

Aunt Gertrude continued to rattle on. "You can't be too careful these days. The world is full of rude and nasty people. Now you take this morning, for example, when I was walking on the platform at Gresham. Suddenly this big, fair-haired man stepped right in front of me, carrying a bulging briefcase. Part of its zipper was torn and some of the papers inside were sticking through.

"Well, this clumsy ox gave me a hard bang on my arm with that dirty, beat-up briefcase. I was about to give him a piece of my mind, when he deliberately pushed me aside!"

Her words had seized Frank's attention. The man sounded like the one that Chet had stepped on in the airport terminal and Frank and Joe had chased later. He might be one of the kidnappers! The suspects' car had gone towards Gresham!

"Then came the crowning insult," she went on. "He called me—he called me—an old whaler! Can you imagine? I never fished for a whale in my life! Next, this big, fair-haired lummox walked over to two other men and handed them the briefcase," Aunt Gertrude continued. "I was so furious, I decided to demand an apology. I went up to the big man and tapped him on the shoulder. He must know me because just then he said 'Hardy'. Well, he turned and glared at me, then hurried off with his friends. The nerve, indeed!"

Frank had already jumped to his feet. He was obviously excited. "Did you see what was written on the papers in the briefcase?"

"I wasn't close enough to read them. But one had red and blue stripes on it."

"He's one of the men we suspect!" Frank cried out. "Aunty, did you hear any more of the men's conversation? Anything at all?"

"No, not really," she answered, somewhat puzzled by her nephew's questioning. "I only caught a word or two. The fair-haired man said something about caves. Yes, that's it—caves! I remember because it struck me at the time that with his bad manners, he should be living in one."

Frank darted to the telephone and called Chet. "I'm sure I've latched on to an important lead," he told his chum. "I'll need your help."

"I'm ready to go any time you say."

"Okay! I'll be right over!"

·6·

Fogged In

FRANK leaped into the convertible and headed for the Morton farm. He began piecing together the details of Aunt Gertrude's story about the fair-haired man at Gresham. He had said, "Hardy!"

"I'm sure he didn't mean Aunt Gertrude. He could have meant Dad or Joe!"

Then the man had made a reference to caves! There were many to be found in the cliffs which formed the north shore of Barmet Bay. Was Joe being held in one of them? Frank smiled, recalling his aunt's indignation at being called an "old whaler" by the big fair-haired man.

"He might not have been referring to whales at all," Frank thought. "There's a small, flat-hulled motorboat known as a motor whaler. Maybe that's what he had in mind."

Frank told himself that using such a term would be unusual for any person unless he was familiar with boats. The young sleuth was certain that he had a real lead at last!

As Frank drew up before the Morton house, Chet came down the steps at a run. "What's up?" he asked eagerly.

Frank repeated Aunt Gertrude's story of the man mentioning the name Hardy and making the mysterious reference to whaler and caves.

Chet whistled, then suddenly his eyes widened. "You mean Joe might be a prisoner in a shore cave?"

"Exactly!" Frank answered. "And I'll search every one of them if I have to!"

"I'm with you! How about the other fellows? Let's get Biff and Jerry to come along. They'd be mad as hornets if they weren't in on the search."

"Okay!" Frank replied. "We'll use the *Sleuth.*" This was the Hardys' sleek motorboat.

"Let's go!" Chet said briskly. Then the ever-present problem of food occurred to him. "If you'll wait a few minutes I'll ask Mom to fix up a lunch for us. We may get hungry. At least you *may*, but I'm sure I will."

Both boys dashed into the house. While Mrs Morton was making up a package of sandwiches and cake, Frank reached Jerry and Biff by telephone and gave them an inkling of what was afoot. They were eager to help and promised to be at the Hardy boathouse within twenty minutes.

In a short time Chet was ready and scrambled into the convertible beside Frank. At the boathouse Jerry and Biff were waiting for them. Biff was a tall, lanky blond whose perpetual good humour was indicated by the slight tilt to the outer corners of his lips. Jerry, medium height and dark, was wiry and more serious. Both boys were agog with curiosity.

"What's the clue?" Jerry asked, and Frank gave the details as he unlocked the door of the boathouse.

The boys quickly unmoored the *Sleuth* and jumped

aboard. The engine spluttered spasmodically a few times, then burst into a roar. Frank opened the throttle and the craft shot into the bay, gradually increasing speed.

"If we don't find Joe, then what?" Jerry asked.

Frank answered promptly, "Go down the coast tomorrow. There are a few caves along the beach. You fellows game?"

"You bet," they chorused.

There were clouds in the sky and far off towards the open water at the distant end of the bay was a hint of fog. Frank eyed the mist doubtfully. It would take some time to make a close search of the caves on the north shore, and if fog came up, a hunt would be difficult. Chet, thinking the same thing, mentioned it aloud.

"We'll just have to hope for the best," Biff spoke up.

As they zipped along, the boys talked over Miss Hardy's encounter with the fair-haired man.

"He may be tall," said Biff, "but he sure sounds short on brains!"

"He'll need all the brains he has if we get on his trail," Chet affirmed.

"But why would he be mixed up in Joe's disappearance?" said Biff. "Surely he wouldn't kidnap Joe just because Chet stepped on him."

"There's something deeper behind it," Frank said, thinking of the secret radio, "but I'm not at liberty to tell you fellows. Sorry."

The *Sleuth* sped on towards the north shore and gradually drew closer to the high cliffs that rose sheer from the waters of the bay. The fog was coming up the bay now in a high, menacing grey wall.

Chet grimaced. "We're not going to make it. That fog will be on us before we get within a quarter of a mile of the caves."

"I'm afraid so," Frank said. "But I hate to give up now that we've come this far."

"I've had a few experiences in fog out on this bay," Biff Hooper remarked, "and I don't want to repeat 'em if it can be helped. You never know when some other boat is going to come along and run you down. You can't see it until the boat's right on top of you. Let one of those big ships wallop you and you're done for!"

"A horn isn't much good," said Jerry, "because the fog seems to make the sound come from a different direction than the true one."

The fog swirled down on the boys, hiding the shore from view. It enveloped them so completely that they could scarcely see more than a few yards ahead. Frank had already turned on his yellow fog light and suddenly they saw a small tug a short distance up the bay. The craft was heading towards the city, but now it vanished. Frank reduced speed and pressed the horn. No sound!

"This," said Jerry, "is bad. If it weren't for Joe, I'd say go home. I wonder how long the pea soup will last."

No one ventured a guess. Frank said tensely, "Watch for that tug, fellows. My horn won't blow."

As the *Sleuth* groped blindly through the clammy mist, Frank thought he heard the faint throb of the tug's engines. His light did not pick up the craft and it was impossible to estimate its distance or direction.

Then came the blast of the tug's whistle, low and mournful through the heavy fog. It seemed to be far to

the right, and Frank hoped to avoid it by going straight
ahead.

When the whistle sounded again, it was louder and
seemed to come from a point just to their left. It was
drawing closer!

"That old tug must have travelled about two miles
clean across the bay in half a minute," Chet remarked.
"Frank, I—look out!"

As he spoke, the whistle sounded again. This time Biff
straightened up in alarm. The tug seemed to be
directly ahead.

"How do you figure its position, Frank?"

"I think the tug is mighty close. It's hard to tell
where the sound's coming from. We'll just have to go
easy and hope we see it first."

Biff could hardly make out the stern of the *Sleuth*.
"This is worse than a blackout," he commented.

Once more the whistle blew, this time so terrifyingly
loud that the tug seemed to be only a few yards away.
The boys could hear its engines. Still their light revealed
nothing.

"Up in front, Chet!" snapped Frank. "If you see it,
sing out!"

Chet scrambled on to the bow and peered into the
grey gloom ahead. Suddenly, he gave a yell of terror.

"It's bearing right down on us!"

Even as he shouted, a heavy dark shadow loomed out
of the fog. The *Sleuth* was about to be rammed!

The tug was sweeping down on the boys. It was only
a few yards away! The boys could see a man on deck,
waving his arms wildly. The whistle shrieked.

No time to lose! The engine of the *Sleuth* broke into a

sudden clamour as Frank opened the throttle wide. At the same instant he swung the wheel hard to port. The motorboat swerved and shot directly across the bow of the larger boat.

For a breathless second it seemed that nothing could save the boys. They waited for the jarring impact that seemed only seconds away!

But the *Sleuth* had speed, and Frank handled his craft masterfully. His boat shot clear!

The tug went roaring astern. It had missed the *Sleuth* with less than a yard to spare! The Hardys' boat was caught in the heavy swell and pitched to and fro, but rode it out.

Chet Morton broke the silence. "Wow, that was a close call!"

Jerry Gilroy, who had been thrown off balance when the *Sleuth* altered its course so suddenly, scrambled to his feet, blinking. "I'll say! Were we hit?"

"We're still here." Biff grinned. Nevertheless, he had been badly frightened. "That's the last time I'll ever come out on the bay when there's a fog brewing," he announced solemnly. "That was too narrow a squeak!"

Chet, now that the peril had passed, leaned down from the bow. He shook hands with the other three boys, then gravely clasped his own.

"What's that for?" Jerry asked.

"Congratulating you—and myself on still being alive." The others smiled weakly.

Frank steered the *Sleuth* back to its previous course. Again the boat crept towards the north shore, invisible beyond the wall of mist. Frank did not dare venture closer for fear of piling his craft on to the rocks at the foot of the cliffs. He cruised aimlessly back and forth, but within half an hour the fog began to lift. It thinned out, writhing and twisting like plumes of smoke.

"The cliffs!" Chet cried in relief as the boys caught sight of the land rising sharply just ahead. They were less than two hundred yards off shore and already far down the bay, abreast of the caves.

"We can make our search after all," Frank said.

He brought the *Sleuth* as near the base of the cliffs as he dared, skilfully avoiding the menacing black rocks that thrust above the water.

Jerry, who had scrambled out on the bow, gestured towards an outcropping of rocks about a hundred yards away.

"Here's our first cave," he announced.

"I remember it," said Frank. "Joe and I went into that one when we were on a car-theft case. It looks like a cave, but is only a few feet deep. No use looking here."

The searchers passed several shallow openings, but at last Chet gave a jubilant shout. "Here're the deeper ones!"

They had rounded a little promontory and the boys saw a ragged row of gaping holes in the face of the rock. Most were just a few feet above the waterline.

Chet said, "I know them. Some are small but others are big enough for an elephant to walk through side-ways."

Frank brought the *Sleuth* in still closer to the base of the two-hundred-foot-high cliffs.

"Great place to hide someone," Biff commented. "I bet there are hundreds of those caverns."

"We have our work cut out for us," Frank agreed.

Some distance on, he spotted the first of the larger holes in the rock. The cave was six feet wide and high above the water. Frank ran the boat in close enough so that by scrambling over its bow one could land on the tumbled heaps of rocks and boulders just beneath the opening.

"Let's take a look," he said eagerly. "Jerry, will you hold the boat here?"

"Sure. Go ahead."

Within a few minutes the others were climbing up the boulders towards the cave mouth. Presently they vanished into the dark interior.

·7·

The Escape

JERRY held the nose of the *Sleuth* inshore and manœuvred so that the propeller remained in deep water. He waited impatiently for news of Joe.

It did not take the others long to find that the big cave they had entered was unoccupied. They reappeared a few minutes later.

"Did you find him?" Jerry called.

"No luck," Biff reported.

Chet was discouraged and said so. "We're working on the slimmest of clues," he said. "The fair-haired man and his friends might not have meant the Shore Road caves. Don't forget, there are hundreds of subterranean caverns between Gresham and Bayport."

"But the caves here are the best known," Frank remarked. "Let's look some more. I'll cruise along the shore and pick out the more likely caves to hide a prisoner."

The motorboat edged its way along the face of the cliff. Whenever the boys noticed one of the larger openings that could be reached easily from the shore, Frank ran the boat in among the rocks. Then, while one boy stayed in the *Sleuth*, the others would scramble up to investigate the cave.

The hours dragged by. Finally, they navigated to a place where the cliff sloped and began to give way to sandy hills and wooded inclines.

Biff gave a sigh. "Guess we'll have to give up. There's only one small opening left to investigate."

"But why would kidnappers go up to that cave when there are so many that are easier to reach?" Chet protested. "They'd have to climb fifty feet up to the mouth."

"It isn't as steep as it looks," Frank remarked thoughtfully. "And I can see a winding trail up the slope."

"I'm game," Jerry said.

"Me too," Biff added.

Frank brought the *Sleuth* in towards the rocks. The boys craned their necks to look up at the tiny opening in the face of the cliff above.

"I guess you're right, Chet," Jerry admitted. "Joe's kidnappers wouldn't climb all the way up there, with so many better caves to pick from."

Chet gave a loud groan. "I've lost about three pounds already, climbing these cliffs."

Despite the worry over Joe, Biff could not refrain from saying, "Then, Chet, you'd better tackle about fifty more caves."

Frank, meanwhile, had seen something that had gone unnoticed by his friends. A piece of newspaper was lodged among the stones under the cave's mouth. The scrap of paper might be significant! The fact that it was within a few feet of the cave was suspicious and warranted investigation.

This time Chet volunteered to stand watch and

manœuvred the boat round so that the others could reach the shore from the bow. Frank went first. Biff and Jerry followed.

They climbed the slope, following the trail Frank had spotted. But the incline was so steep and winding that they could make only slow progress in a diagonal direction. The path ended abruptly at a ledge some fifteen feet below the cave. From there they had to climb directly upwards over the rocks.

When Frank reached the piece of newspaper, he picked it up. The sheet was wet and soggy from the fog, but he recognized it as a copy of the *Gresham Times*, dated the previous day.

His hopes rose with this discovery. Gresham! For the third time since Joe's disappearance the name of that town had come into the mystery! Excited, Frank thrust the paper into his pocket and scrambled up towards the entrance of the cave.

"What did you find?" Jerry demanded, panting.

"Newspaper. It looks like a clue."

Frank reached the cave mouth and stepped inside. The interior was larger than he had thought. Though the entrance was small, the cave widened and seemed to be very deep.

The young detective took a flashlight from his pocket and clicked it. He played the beam on the rugged, rocky walls, the fairly level floor, and finally focused on a wooden box like those used for shipping food.

"Someone's been here!" he shouted eagerly as the others entered the cave. "Look at that box! Fresh bread crusts around it!"

"Don't see anyone now," Jerry observed. "Listen!"

The boys heard a peculiar sound, which seemed to come from the back of the cave. The sound was repeated. They listened, staring at one another in surprise.

"Someone's groaning!" Frank exclaimed.

Biff pointed a trembling finger toward a large section of rock about twenty feet away. "From there."

Again they heard groaning.

"Somebody's behind there!" Frank declared.

He ran towards the mass of rocks and directed the light into the shadows beyond. Frank gasped as its beam fell upon a figure lying bound and gagged on a crude pallet of sacking.

"Joe!" Frank shouted. He sprang forward and removed the gag.

His brother answered feebly, "Frank!"

Biff and Jerry gave a joint yell of delight. They scrambled in behind the wall of rocks and bent over their friend.

Joe looked white and ill. He could scarcely talk to them. His feet were bound together with rope and his hands were tied behind his back.

"To think that we weren't going to search this cave at all!" Biff exclaimed. "And wait until Chet learns we've found you. He's down there guarding the *Sleuth*."

Frank had already opened his pocketknife and was hacking at the ropes that bound his brother's ankles. Jerry was working at the other knots.

"I'm hungry," said Joe, when all the ropes had been loosened and he was able to sit up. "I haven't had anything to eat since yesterday noon."

The boys helped him to his feet. "They drugged me," Joe went on shakily, "and I can still feel the effects. But tell me, how did you find me?"

"Aunt Gertrude gets the credit." Frank quickly told of her encounter with the fair-haired man at Gresham, and his reference to "Hardy" and "caves".

"But Frank put two and two together," Biff spoke up, and mentioned the newspaper clue.

"It was lucky for me you saw the paper," Joe declared. "One of the kidnappers had some food wrapped in a newspaper yesterday. He must have dropped one of the sheets."

"Was the big, fair-haired man really mixed up in it?" Frank asked.

Joe nodded. "He was in it, all right. But there were others. They were after that secret in our car. It's a long story. Let me tell you about it later."

The boys refrained from asking more questions.

"Do you feel strong enough to come with us now?" Frank asked.

Joe, with a flash of spirit, started to walk. He wavered for a moment and would have fallen if Frank had not caught him.

"If you can't make it, we'll carry you," Jerry offered.

Joe shook his head and sat down weakly. "My legs are so numb from being tied up, I don't seem to have any strength in them. I'd better wait a few minutes."

At that moment they heard a loud noise. It was a clattering, rolling sound, as if a rock had been dislodged and gone tumbling down the steep incline.

"What was that?" Biff whispered.

Joe got to his feet. "My captors are coming back! Quick! We'll have to clear out!"

"Can they get in here through the rear of the cave?" Frank wanted to know.

"Yes, a passage leads down from the top of the cliff."

Frank and Jerry each slipped an arm round Joe's shoulders and helped him towards the mouth of the cave. Biff ran on ahead.

When Chet saw Joe, he gave a war whoop of joy. The others motioned frantically for silence, but their jubilant chum did not understand their urgent signals. He proceeded to put on a noisy celebration. He yelled, waved his arms, and then, to their horror, began whistling shrilly.

The men coming down the passage into the cave would certainly hear the commotion and hurry to investigate. The boys must flee quickly!

Frank and Jerry scrambled down the slope with Joe. They reached the first ledge in safety, with Biff slipping and sliding along the path ahead of them. As they commenced the second half of the descent the boys heard a yell behind them.

Frank looked back. A man was standing at the mouth of the cave. He glared at the boys a moment, then turned and shouted to someone behind him. Two other men quickly joined him.

"Go on!" Joe cried. "I'm holding you up! If they catch us, we'll all be in trouble."

"Leave you, my eye!" Jerry growled.

By this time Biff had nearly reached the boat. He called out to Chet, who apparently had not seen the men in the mouth of the cave. At Biff's warning, Chet stopped his noise. Frank and Jerry clung to Joe on the narrow path, with loose rocks sliding treacherously beneath their feet.

Frank glanced back again. One of the men had drawn a revolver from his pocket and was pointing it at them. Another had stooped and was snatching up stones.

The revolver barked. A bullet whistled overhead. Frank and Jerry ducked and almost lost hold of Joe. A heavy stone hurtled past them and splashed into the water beside the boat.

A hail of stones followed. The man with the revolver fired again and again and several bullets came dangerously close to their mark.

Chet had revved up the engine, ready to take off as soon as his passengers climbed aboard.

"Hurry!" Biff yelled. "Only a few yards more!"

Frank and Jerry scrambled to the bottom of the incline with Joe. One of the three men was stumbling down the path in pursuit.

Jerry leaped on to the bow. With Frank on the shore and Jerry helping from the boat, Joe was hauled aboard. Frank was about to jump on to the bow when he felt a heavy, sharp blow on his left leg. He lost his balance and fell partly into the water. When he tried to rise, his leg doubled beneath him. One of the rocks hurled by the men had found its mark!

Shots sounded again. A splinter flew from the bow of the boat.

"Hurry, Frank!" Chet urged.

"Give me a hand," Frank said grimly.

Biff scrambled over the side, seized Frank, and laid

him on deck. Frank's leg throbbed and he could scarcely keep from crying out.

The man on the path was only a few yards away now! He showered the air with rocks!

8

An Astounding Report

SMACK! A large rock hit the water with a resounding crash only inches from the *Sleuth*. A deluge of spray drenched the boys.

Chet, at the helm, could hardly see. Wiping the water from his eyes, he revved the motor and took off. The *Sleuth* made sternway from shore.

"Gadzooks!" cried Jerry, mopping his face and looking towards the kidnappers. "They've gone!"

"They sure disappeared in a hurry," said Jerry. "I wish we could have captured them. Frank, how's your leg?"

"Oh, it'll be all right, but it hurts." He gave a wan smile. "Never mind that, though. The main thing is that we found Joe."

"Yes, thank goodness," his brother said weakly.

Chet had taken the *Sleuth* into deep water and was now speeding towards Bayport. Jerry and Biff were busy trying to make Frank and Joe comfortable on one of the long seats.

"To think I missed finding Joe!" Chet said in disgust. "I climbed those cliffs every other time and searched. When Joe was found, where was I? Sitting in the boat!"

"Good thing you were," Jerry retorted. "It's lucky

for us someone was here to have the *Sleuth* ready for a fast getaway."

"Why did it have to be me?" Chet complained. "Some fellows have all the luck. Joe, tell me about your capture. Who were those men who shot at you and heaved all those rocks? When did they take you to the cave?"

"Better let Joe rest awhile," Frank advised.

"I think we ought to go back and clean up on that gang!" Jerry put in.

"I'd like to learn more about them myself," Frank said, "but I think we'd better leave it to the police. Those kidnappers are a tough outfit, and we have Joe to look after. He's in bad shape. We should get him home."

"He looks hungry," Chet observed sympathetically, as Frank tuned in their radio and called police headquarters to report the rescue.

Joe opened his eyes. "You bet I'm hungry."

Chet grabbed the package of sandwiches he had brought with him and handed them to his chum. "I knew these would come in handy," he said. "Dig in."

"Hold it!" Frank warned. "No solid food until the doctor says it's all right."

"Then how about the milk in this Thermos?"

"Okay."

Joe drank the milk slowly and gratefully while Jerry satisfied Chet's curiosity about their experience in the cave rescue.

Chet whistled. "That was a close squeak."

When the Hardys reached home, their mother was overwhelmed with relief at seeing Joe safe.

Aunt Gertrude hugged her nephew and said, "Well, this time you deserve sympathy. At least you didn't do something harum-scarum and propel yourself right into a mess of trouble."

Dr Bates, the family physician, was summoned to examine the young detectives. "No internal damage," he declared. "Just exhaustion. Joe'll be fit in just a day or two. Frank has a deep bruise which will be sore for a while."

Joe was given a steaming bowl of hot soup, then put to bed. He immediately fell asleep.

Frank related the story of the rescue and gave Aunt Gertrude credit for the clue. She smiled and blushed but said nothing.

It was not until late that evening, after he had been refreshed by a long, sound sleep, that Joe was able to tell the others what had happened to him. He still looked pale, but good food and rest were beginning to do their work and a trace of colour had returned to his cheeks.

"As you know," he said, "at Chet's party I chased into the woods after that man who was looking in our car boot. As I got near, someone reached out and grabbed me. I couldn't see his face."

Joe said a gag had been jammed into his mouth and a hand clapped over it. Then he was dragged to a car.

"Mercy!" exclaimed Aunt Gertrude.

"But why did he kidnap you if he was only after the secret radio?" Frank asked.

"There's another reason," Joe replied. "I'll come to that. When we got to his car I tried to fight him, but he's as strong as an ox and managed to tie me up and put me in the back seat.

"Then he drove away. We went down the road for some distance and stopped. Two men came out of the bushes and walked over to us. One said, 'Is that you, Gross?' and my captor growled at them, 'No names.' When they saw me in the car, the men wanted to know who I was. It seems they didn't know Gross was going to kidnap me."

Joe said there had been a row about it. The other two men had wanted Gross to bring him back, but he was stubborn. "This kid knows too much," Gross had said. "He saw the rocks. Besides, his father is a detective."

"The other men called him a fool and said he should have left me alone and let the other thing go.

"One of them told Gross they didn't want the authorities after them for kidnapping. Then they realized it was too late to let me go, because there would be trouble when I got back to Bayport and told my story."

Joe said that the two men got into the car and they all rode for about two miles. Then one of the men climbed out and headed across a field towards the bay.

"We went on, but we hadn't gone far when Gross lost control of the wheel and we crashed into a ditch. The car was wrecked but no one was hurt. Gross and the other man seemed worried because they were afraid somebody would come along and find them. They took off the licence plates.

"Gross knew there was an old inn nearby. They agreed to go to it and telephone a friend of theirs to bring a saloon. They took a blanket out of the car. We walked up the road and into a lane where the inn was. Without any warning one of them slugged me from behind."

Frank said, "And put you in the blanket."

Joe said that later, as he started to come to in the inn, a drug was forced into his mouth and he was made to drink some water. He passed out, and did not wake up until morning, when they were carrying him in the blanket to their friend's saloon.

"Just as we drove out of the lane and on to the Gresham road," Joe continued, "I heard a car coming and managed to raise up. It looked like ours, so I tried to signal. Then Gross shoved me down."

Joe had been driven to Shore Road and taken to the cave through an abandoned shaft.

"You were there nearly two whole days!" Frank said.

"Most of the time I was alone. They fixed up a few sacks for me to lie on, but they didn't pay much attention to me. Once in a while they would bring in sandwiches and water and feed them to me."

"Did you find out what they're up to?" Frank asked.

"At night, when they thought I was asleep, I overheard enough to learn one of the gang's secrets. They're smugglers!"

Aunt Gertrude opened her mouth wide. "Smugglers!" she gasped. "What kind?"

"Diamonds and electronic equipment. That's probably why they wanted to get Mr Wright's special radio."

Joe paused and Mrs Hardy asked if he were too tired to go on. "No, I'm okay, Mother. I also learned that one of the top men is named Chris. From what was said, I'd guess he's that big fair-haired man who's been watching us."

Frank was excited by this news. Now they had something definite to go on! If Joe were right, they could concentrate on finding Chris and turning him over to the police.

Joe spoke up. "There are four or five in the gang working with Chris, and others offshore. Chris delivers smuggled diamonds. His pals in the cave—one tall and dark, one red-haired, and one short—mentioned that he had diamonds in his briefcase. Chris thought we had seen them when the case burst open. Gross saw a chance to kidnap one of us to keep us from talking."

"A stupid move," Frank commented. "Even if we had seen the diamonds, we wouldn't have known they'd been smuggled. What about Mr Wright's secret radio? Did they talk about that?"

"I'm not sure," Joe answered. "Gross mentioned a secret gadget, but since they smuggle electronic equipment, it could be anything. Do we still have the transistor?" he asked.

"Yes. But it's my guess someone connected with the smugglers figured out that we have the radio and thought it might be in our boot. Do you know the names of any of the others in the gang?"

Joe shook his head. "I'm sure there's a big boss, but they never mentioned him. One man who came to the cave had a nasal voice. He sounded like one of those burglars at Mr Wright's house."

"And he's afraid of someone named Shorty," Frank added. "This is a real clue." After a moment he said thoughtfully, "So we're up against a gang of smugglers."

"I think," Aunt Gertrude said firmly, "that you boys should leave well enough alone. Joe is back safe and sound, and we ought to be satisfied. If you try tracking down those smugglers, you'll only end up in trouble. Leave it to the police."

The conversation was interrupted by the ringing of the telephone. Frank answered the call.

"Are you one of the Hardy boys?" a strange voice asked.

"Yes. Who is this?"

"The inventor of the secret radio."

"What's your name?" Frank asked.

"You know I don't want to mention it on the phone. All I want to find out is whether you still have it," the man replied.

Frank was suspicious at once. He beckoned his mother and wrote on the telephone pad, *Go next door and try to have this call traced. Then call the police and give them Joe's clues to the kidnappers.*

Aloud Frank was saying, "Why are you so interested, sir?"

"'Cause I'm the inventor and I want the radio back." The stranger spoke sharply.

A long parley followed. Finally, when Frank was sure his mother had had time to call the police, he said, "Sorry not to help you, sir, but you'll have to get your information from my father. He isn't here right this minute."

"Your father!" the man shrieked. "Why, you impudent young pup! I'll be right over and you'll give me that radio or I'll—I'll—"

The caller hung up.

·9·

Smuggler's Trail

THE evening passed with no further word from the mysterious caller who had phoned from a public booth but had disappeared before the police could track him down. Frank and Joe discussed the situation.

"Maybe he was scared off," Joe suggested. "And what about the secret radio? Somebody may look in the boot again."

"Right," Frank agreed. "I'll bring it in here. But each time we leave the house let's take the invention along."

Before the family went to bed, Mrs Hardy turned on the burglar alarm, which was connected to every door and window in the house and garage. There was no disturbance during the night.

"We're safe so far," Frank remarked at breakfast. "Maybe the police have caught Chris and the others. I'll phone Chief Collig."

"Sorry, Frank," came the report from headquarters. "None of my men has picked up a clue."

Almost a week passed. Still there was no news. The kidnapper-smugglers had covered their tracks well.

Joe had recovered from his experience and Frank's

injured leg had healed. The brothers were ready to continue their sleuthing. They asked Chet, Jerry, and Biff to help them.

"Gross and the others may sneak back to Bayport," Frank prophesied. "They'll get nervy soon and we may have a chance to trip them up."

"Where do we go from here?" Biff asked.

"A tour of the docks," Frank answered, "to hunt for a whaler."

A long but wary search of Bayport's busy waterfront yielded nothing. Finally all the boys went home.

Frank and Joe found that Aunt Gertrude had been shopping. "Who is that new young man working in Bickford's jewellery shop?" she asked abruptly.

"I never saw a *young* man working in there," Frank replied. "The only assistant I know of is elderly and he's in the hospital right now."

"A young man, I said," Aunt Gertrude repeated in a tone that did not invite contradiction. "A very suspicious-looking young man. He wasn't there the last time I went in."

"He's new to me," Joe remarked. "What happened?"

"You see this diamond pin I'm wearing?" Aunt Gertrude pointed to a small one on the shoulder of her dress. "Well, he kept eying it while I was looking at some inexpensive watches."

"He was probably just admiring it, Aunty," Frank suggested.

"Admiring it, yes. With the thought of stealing it!" Aunt Gertrude was warming to her subject. "You can't fool me about young men. Besides, I've seen that assistant somewhere before."

"Where?" Joe asked.

"I'm not sure, but I know I have seen him."

"Is that all you have against the poor fellow?" Frank asked jokingly.

"It's enough. Mark my words, that young jewellery assistant is bad. Next thing we hear of him he'll be in prison for robbing his employer!"

This dire prediction left the Hardy boys wondering. Aunt Gertrude's intuition was amazing. They would drop into Bickford's tomorrow and talk to the assistant.

The following morning the boys decided to walk downtown. They made sure their mother and aunt would be at home to guard Mr Wright's invention.

On the way Frank said, "I wonder why those smugglers operate in Bayport. Wouldn't you think they'd pick one of the larger cities?"

"Perhaps they are known in those places," Joe suggested. "I wish I could have heard more when I listened to them in the cave—like where the diamonds and electronic stuff came from and where they make their headquarters."

Suddenly Joe gripped his brother's arm. "Look!" he said tensely.

He gestured towards a man walking on the other side of the relatively deserted street and Frank almost shouted with excitement. The man was tall and muscular, with a shock of fair hair protruding from beneath his hat. He was the person who had been at the airport—the one they now suspected might be part of the kidnap-smuggler gang.

"I'll bet his name is Chris!" Frank whispered.

"Let's trail him and see where he's going."

"We'd better cross the street. He may catch sight of us."

Excitedly the Hardys hurried to the opposite side and fell in behind the fair-haired man. "Chris," apparently unaware that he was being followed, strode along at a rapid pace.

"Perhaps he's going to meet some of his pals," Joe said.

"We won't let him out of our sight," Frank said, "and if we meet a policeman I'll ask him to notify headquarters."

They were careful to remain far enough behind so that there were always several people between them and their quarry. The fair-haired man did not look back. He seemed to be in a hurry.

"You'd think Bayport has no cops," Joe complained when the boys had gone several blocks without meeting one.

The Hardys trailed the big man for several blocks. Abruptly he struck off down a side street. The boys had to run in order to keep him in sight.

"Perhaps," Joe said, "he saw you and me and is trying to shake us off."

"I don't think so. I believe he's going to the railway station."

"Good grief! If he takes a train out of town, we'll lose him."

"I don't intend to lose him," Frank declared. "How much money do you have with you?"

Joe groped in his pockets. "About seven dollars."

"Luck's with us. I have thirty. We can take the train if he does, but I hope he won't go far."

It was soon evident that Chris was indeed bound for the station. When he came in sight of the big brick building, he broke into a run and disappeared through the massive doorway.

The Hardys hastened in pursuit, still looking for a policeman. Just before reaching the station, they saw one of their father's friends. Quickly Frank told him the story and added, "Call headquarters and my mother." He dashed after Joe.

When the boys entered the station they saw Chris just leaving one of the ticket windows. He ran across to an exit, raced through it, and darted towards a waiting train.

Frank stepped up to the window which the fair-haired man had just left.

"Where to?" the agent asked.

"We wanted to meet a man here," Frank explained. "He's a big fellow with blond hair. Have you seen him?"

"Just bought a ticket to New York City a minute ago."

Frank was taken aback. He had not anticipated that Chris would be going as far as New York. However, having once picked up the trail, the young detective decided to follow it.

"Two one-way tickets," he said.

"You'll have to hurry," the agent said. "The express is due to leave right away."

Frank grabbed the tickets. He heard a whistle and saw that the train was beginning to move.

The boys dashed to the platform. Joe, in the lead, scrambled up the rear steps of the last coach. Frank followed.

When the boys had recovered their breath, they went through to the coach Chris occupied. They halted in the rear doorway and made a quick survey of the occupants.

Alone in a front seat they saw a familiar thatch of yellow hair. Chris was unaware that he had been followed.

The boys took seats at the rear of the coach, and settled down for the journey.

·10·

Elevator Chase

"I HOPE the Bayport police communicate with the authorities in New York," Frank remarked. "If they meet the train and arrest Chris, our worries will be over."

"And if they don't?" Joe asked.

Frank gave a wan smile. "Our troubles will just be starting. There'll be crowds and it'll be tough to keep track of him."

The train did not make many stops, but each time it did, Frank and Joe were ready to hop off in case Chris should alight. At length the train reached the suburbs, clattering past miles of factories and houses, and finally lurched to a halt in the underground station in New York City.

The boys watched Chris intently as the passengers prepared to leave. The fair-haired man did not look back once. He put on his hat and strolled towards the front of the coach.

"We'll get out at the back and keep an eye on him from there," Frank said.

The Hardys scrambled on to the platform where passengers were just beginning to file up the ramp to the waiting room. Chris had not yet appeared, so the

234

brothers, shielding their faces, made their way quickly to the exit gate.

"I don't see any police," Frank remarked, disappointed.

"No," Joe replied. "I guess we'll have to take over."

The boys emerged into the concourse. There, in the enormous, high-vaulted station, booming with hollow echoes, they waited for Chris to appear.

He stalked through the gate, looking neither to right nor left. The boys quickly fell in behind him. He towered above the throng, and they had little difficulty following him. Despite the crowds that jostled them, the Hardys managed to keep Chris in view and pursued him out into the street.

"What'll we do if he hops into a taxi?" Joe asked.

"Hop into one ourselves and hope we can trail him," Frank said.

"I'd feel better if we had more money with us," Joe mumbled.

The man they were trailing still seemed unaware that he was being followed.

"It's going to be mighty hard for one taxi to follow another in this traffic," Frank remarked.

"Maybe we won't need one," his brother suggested. "Anyhow, these New York taxi drivers are pretty clever. I think if we tell one to follow a car we point out and make it worth his while, he could do it."

"Going to cost a lot of moolah," Frank said.

They were relieved when their quarry continued walking.

"Come on!" Frank called.

The two sleuths had a twofold problem: to follow

Chris and be careful he did not suspect they were after him. Twice he swung round while they hurried along the crowded sidewalk, and it seemed as if he were suspicious.

On these occasions the boys dodged behind passers-by. After two momentary surveys, Chris hastened on again.

"I don't believe he saw us," Frank murmured as they again took up the chase.

"No, evidently not. But we're coming to heavy congestion. Look at the crowd and there are traffic signals. If he gets across the street ahead of us and you and I are held up by a red light, we'll lose him."

The boys were anxious as they approached a busy corner where a policeman was directing the flow of traffic and pedestrians.

"Shall we ask his help?" Joe asked.

"I doubt if he could leave his post," Frank answered.

Just what Joe had feared took place. Chris was among the last to slip across the street before the lights flashed from green to red and the officer blew his whistle sharply. Joe groaned.

"Just our luck!" he cried.

"Look!" Frank exclaimed. "We're in luck!"

Chris was speaking to a man on the other side of the street. Evidently the stranger had asked directions and Chris had halted to explain and point out the location of a certain street. He took such pains with the man that by the time he finished, the traffic light had again flashed green.

"Let's go!" Joe cried.

They trailed Chris along the street for several blocks,

then he turned into a large office building. Inside was a row of elevators opposite the entrance. Frank and Joe hesitated for a few seconds before following Chris.

"Come on!" Joe urged. "If he gets in an elevator, and we aren't there, we won't know what office he's going to."

"You're right!" Frank agreed.

They hurried into the lobby just as Chris stepped into one of the cars. The door closed and he shot upwards. Fortunately he was the only passenger and the boys watched the dial. The lift stopped at the tenth floor.

"I hope he doesn't get away," Joe murmured excitedly.

"We never would have dared get into the same elevator with him," Frank said. "He'd have recognized us."

The boys stepped into the next lift, which soon filled up. The boys left it at the tenth floor. Each wondered if they could locate Chris in the maze of offices.

Again luck was with them. As Frank and Joe looked down a corridor, Chris was just entering an office. Evidently he had been delayed looking for his destination.

The Hardys hurried to the door as it closed behind the suspect. It was a green-painted steel door with an open transom. The sign read:

SOUTH AFRICAN IMPORTING COMPANY
WHOLESALE ONLY

"I wonder what he's doing in there," Joe murmured.

Frank put a finger to his lips. The sound of muffled voices could be heard from the office. Apparently

Chris and the others inside were so far from the door that their conversation was indistinct.

A moment later Chris's voice came loud and clear. He must be walking towards the outer door!

"We'd better scram," Frank advised.

"When he comes out, shall we grab him?" Joe asked.

Frank shook his head. "If those are buddies of his in there, they may grab *us*."

The boys scooted up the corridor and watched Chris over their shoulders. He did not notice Frank and Joe. The suspect was looking intently at some papers in his hand as he went to the elevators and pushed a button for an ascending car. He was going to a higher floor.

"Shall we follow him?" Joe whispered.

"Too risky. Let's go down and wait in the lobby, then take up the trail again."

After Chris had gone up, the boys took a down lift. On the ground floor they watched each descending elevator. After half an hour had passed, their patience was rewarded. Amid a carload of businessmen, they saw the burly form of the big blond man towering above all the others.

"Come on!" Frank whispered to Joe as Chris moved towards the street doors.

Again the chase was resumed in the crowded street. For several blocks Chris maintained a straight course. Then he swung round a corner and stalked down a side street. The sleuths hurried after their quarry and saw him dip beneath a restaurant sign below street level.

"Oh—oh!" Joe muttered. "If we follow him in there, he can't miss us."

"Let's see if there are many customers inside," Frank

suggested. "If so, we just might be able to get away with it. Could be he's meeting someone there."

Frank went down the steps leading to the restaurant and made a quick survey of the place through the door. It was almost full.

"Chris is taking a table in the rear, and he's not facing the door. Come on, Joe! We're not letting him out of our sight."

Boldly Frank and Joe entered the place. It was a cheap restaurant, with a row of booths along one side. The boys slipped quickly into one of the compartments. They could watch Chris but he could not see them.

"This is a break!" Joe whispered.

An untidy-looking waiter came over and they gave their orders. After he had gone to the kitchen, the boys put their money on the table.

"There's enough to pay for a hotel room if we have to stay over, and a few more meals."

"We can't afford to hang around New York long," Joe remarked, eyeing their available cash. "I guess we'd better tell the police about Chris and forget trying to spot his buddies."

Suddenly Frank sat bolt upright. "Chris is getting up from his table."

"Leaping lizards!" Joe exclaimed. "He's heading right for us!"

·11·

Discovered!

JOE pretended to be searching for something he had dropped and quickly ducked his head underneath the table as the fair-haired man approached. Frank snatched up a menu and held it in front of his face.

There was a tense moment as Chris drew nearer. To the boys' relief, he brushed past without noticing them and walked directly to the cashier's counter. The Hardys got ready to pursue him, but he only stopped to glance at a newspaper lying there, then returned to his own table.

"Whew, that was close!" Joe murmured as he raised his head.

"It sure was," Frank agreed. "But we have one thing in our favour. We're the last persons in the world Chris would expect to find trailing him in New York City."

The Hardys watched as a waiter walked up to the big man's table. Apparently Chris was well known in the restaurant, for the two exchanged a few words, laughing all the while. Presently a slim, sharp-featured man emerged from a door to the kitchen and went directly to Chris. He sat down, then began to talk.

"I think," Joe whispered, "it's time for some action. How about my going outside and looking for a policeman?"

"Good idea, Joe. I have a feeling the man with Chris should be investigated, too. He may be one of the smugglers."

Joe slid from the booth and went outside. No officer was in sight, but there was a public-telephone booth nearby. "I'll call headquarters from here," Joe decided and dialled the number.

He was connected with a lieutenant, who said they had been alerted by Chief Collig, but the boys' message to him had been delayed, and the call to New York had come too late for the police to meet the train from Bayport. "I will send two officers to the restaurant. If this man Chris hasn't started to eat yet, he'll be there a while. By the way, we got a message that you are to phone your home at once."

"Thank you," said Joe and hung up.

He immediately dialled the Hardy House. Aunt Gertrude answered. "My, you boys certainly take off fast! You ought to be right here taking care of the secret radio mystery."

"What do you mean, Aunty?"

"I mean that I can't understand your father. He sent a telegram saying, 'Inventor will phone. Do as directed.' Well, the inventor called and said we should leave the radio on the front steps at ten o'clock tonight."

Joe was astounded. After a moment's thought he said, "I think the telegram was a hoax. Dad would never do such a thing. Somebody may be listening in on this call, but I'll take a chance. Put a package on the steps but not the radio. Then ask the police to shadow the house and pick up this fake inventor. I have to say good-bye now. Frank and I have one of the gang almost nabbed. Give my love to Mother. Tell her we're sorry we couldn't call before this."

Joe returned to the restaurant and in whispers repeated his whole conversation. Frank nodded, then pointed to Chris's table.

"I heard that thin guy call him Chris, so we know for sure we're on the right track."

The smuggler and his companion were busily engaged with pencil and paper. Chris seemed to be explaining something that did not please the other man, for he shook his head doubtfully and crossed out what Chris had already jotted down.

"I'd give anything to know what those two are talking about," Frank said in a low tone.

"So would I," Joe replied and started to eat.

At that instant the boys' attention was diverted to a stocky man who had just entered the restaurant. He glanced in their direction, then made his way towards them. He planted himself in front of their table and glared at the Hardys.

"What's the idea of sittin' at my table?" he demanded.

"*Your* table?" Frank asked in surprise.

"Yes. This is my table you're sittin' at. You'd better clear out!"

"There are lots of other tables," Frank retorted in a low voice.

"Sure. And you can have any one of 'em you want."

Frank decided that nothing would be gained by

arguing with the stranger. Both boys returned quietly to their meal and did not look up.

"Well," the man roared, "are you gonna move?"

"As soon as we've finished our lunch," Joe snapped.

"You'll move now! This is my table you're sittin' at, and I mean to have it!"

The young sleuths were infuriated by the intrusion. Unknowingly the man was putting them in a difficult position. If they stood up to walk to another table, Chris would surely spot them and might escape before the police arrived! If they remained where they were, they probably would be discovered, since the incident was beginning to attract attention.

Frank signalled a waiter standing nearby.

"What's the trouble, Mr Melvin?" he asked.

"These kids are sittin' at my table," Melvin protested. "Make 'em move!"

The waiter looked uneasy. "I can't ask these young men to move, Mr Melvin. They were here first."

"Ain't I a good customer of this restaurant?"

"Yes, indeed. But there are plenty of other tables, sir. If you don't mind—"

"I *do* mind. These boys can get outta here or I won't come back to this restaurant again!" Melvin shouted.

Frank saw that Chris and his friend had turned and were looking in the Hardys' direction. At once Chris spoke to the sharp-featured man, who nodded. Then both darted towards the kitchen door and disappeared through it.

Joe said to the waiter, "We're not afraid of this fellow, but we'll leave just to save trouble."

The boys got up. Melvin, breathing defiance and

declaring that no person could sit at *his* table and get away with it, promptly sat down in the seat Frank had just vacated.

Joe dashed to the back of the restaurant and whirled into the kitchen. Chris and his friend were not in sight, but a back door was open and Joe assumed the men had ducked outside and up a delivery alley to the street. He hurried back into the restaurant.

Frank had hastened to the cashier's desk and paid the boys' bill. Then he ran up the front steps and into the street. The police had not arrived.

Joe joined his brother. "Chris left by the back door," he said. "He should be coming up that alley." When the two men did not put in an appearance, he added, "You stay here, Frank. I'll run down."

Joe returned in a short time. "Come on!" he cried, and explained that the alley joined another one that led to the busy street beyond. They followed it to the sidewalk, which was teeming with pedestrians. Chris was not in sight.

"We've really lost him this time," Joe commented in disgust.

"I have an idea," Frank said. "Let's walk along this street in opposite directions for about ten or twelve blocks. I'll head downtown, you uptown. There's a slight chance one of us might spot Chris."

"But he might have gone across town," Joe argued.

"You're right. But what have we to lose?"

"Okay, Frank, I'm game. But there's just one hitch. If I should see Chris, how do I let you know and vice versa?"

Frank looked around and pointed to a public-telephone booth. He walked over and jotted down the number.

Rejoining his brother, he said, "We'll meet back here in half an hour. However, if one of us gets back and the other isn't here, I say stay by the phone and wait for a call." He handed Joe a copy of the number and took one himself.

"Here's hoping!" Joe declared with a grin as the boys went their separate ways.

Frank walked along slowly, dividing his attention between weaving among pedestrians and searching for his quarry. When he had covered nearly fifteen blocks, Frank decided to work his way back on the opposite side of the street.

He stopped for a moment at an amusement arcade to watch the people playing the various coin-operated machines.

As Frank was about to continue walking, his eyes widened in surprise. Towards the rear of the arcade a big fair-haired man was engaged in conversation with three ominous-looking characters. Frank carefully edged his way inside the arcade for a better look. He was certain now.

The man was Chris!

·12·

Tunnel Scare

FRANK mingled with the crowd in the arcade and cautiously worked his way towards the spot where Chris and his companions were standing. He kept glancing towards the street, hoping a policeman would come along. Soon the young sleuth was close enough to overhear the men's conversation.

"Sounds like you got in with a gang that's going places," declared one of Chris's companions. "How about talkin' to your boss and gettin' us in on the action?"

"Sorry, but I can't help you guys," the fair-haired man answered. "The big boss has all the men he needs."

"Keep us in mind if anything comes up," one of the trio chimed in.

Just then a man who had been playing one of the game machines beside Frank shouted, "Whee! I've won ten in a row. I musta broke some kind o' record!"

The outburst caused Chris and his friends to look in the man's direction—and therefore right at Frank. The boy turned quickly and gazed into one of the coin-operated machines. In its highly polished surface he could see Chris's reflection.

"He must have recognized me!" Frank thought, noting a look of surprise on the smuggler's face.

Frank watched as the fair-haired man whispered something to his friends then left for the street.

Determined not to let the big man out of his sight, and to contact the first police officer he met, the young detective started off in pursuit. To his dismay, he was intercepted at the entrance by Chris's three companions.

"Where d'you think you're goin', kid?" one of them growled.

Another said, "We don't like the idea of our pal being shadowed."

"Get out of my way!" Frank demanded.

One man stepped behind the youth. The other two each grabbed an arm and led him out of the arcade.

"We're goin' for a little walk," one of them snarled, "and if you make one sound, it'll be curtains for you!"

Frank was forced to walk about half a block, then he was led into a dark, narrow alley.

"You need to be taught a lesson, kid," the man behind Frank said. "We don't like snoopers."

Frank was in a desperate situation, but he did not panic. With catlike speed he thrust out his leg and tripped the man on his right, then he flung him down so hard that the grasp on his right arm was broken. With his free arm Frank jabbed an elbow into the midriff of the man behind him.

"Ouch!" his opponent grunted loudly.

The third man, who still had a firm grip on Frank's left arm, was unable to dodge the boy's blow. It caught him on the chin and he crumpled to the ground.

Frank had only a second to collect his wits. One of his stunned opponents had recovered quickly, scrambled to his feet, and was now prepared to attack him. Just as Frank dealt the man a staggering blow, he heard a noise behind him. Before Frank could turn, he was struck on the head with a hard object.

Several minutes passed before Frank regained consciousness. He slowly got to his feet and looked around. The three men were gone. Frank grimaced as he felt a large swelling on the back of his head. Then he noticed that his wrist watch and wallet were missing.

"Chris has some rough playmates," he thought. "And they're petty thieves to boot."

Still a bit unsteady on his legs, Frank finally started uptown to rendezvous with his brother. Frank's body ached, but a light rain which was falling seemed cool and refreshing to him.

When Joe saw Frank's condition, he exclaimed, "Leaping hyenas! You look as if you'd fallen into a cement mixer!"

"Not quite," Frank replied. "I ran into some of Chris's pals."

"What! You mean you caught up with the smuggler?"

"Yes, but lost him again. I'll tell you all about it later. But first let's find some shelter from this rain. I'm cold."

They ducked into a doorway. Frank straightened his tie and brushed off his clothes in an effort to look more presentable.

"My wallet was stolen," he said. "How much money do you have left?"

Joe dug into his pockets. "Exactly six dollars and thirty-seven cents."

"I'm starved," Frank announced. "And we'll need most of that to get a good meal. Anyway, it's not enough for our fare back home. Let's find a restaurant and a phone. We can call Mother and let her know what has happened so far. Hope she can wire us some money."

The rain lessened and the boys hurried along the street in search of an eating place. They examined the menus posted in the windows of several restaurants, hoping to find one that would not exceed their budget.

"Here's a possibility," Joe said. "The menu looks good and the prices are reasonable."

The boys entered the restaurant and sat down. Shortly a waiter walked over to them. He eyed Frank's rumpled clothes and the man's manner became abrupt. The Hardys had already selected a dinner listed on the window menu and ordered immediately.

"I have a feeling he's in a hurry to get rid of us." Joe grinned as the waiter walked off.

"Did you see the way he stared at me when he came over?" Frank laughed. "I admit I look a little shabby. He probably thinks we're not going to pay our bill."

After finishing dessert, Frank rose. "Give me some change and I'll place a call home," he told Joe. "Meanwhile, you take care of the bill."

Locating a phone booth at the rear of the restaurant, the young detective deposited the coin and dialled the operator.

"I'm sorry," said a feminine voice when Frank tried to make a collect call to Bayport. "Violent storms up there have temporarily affected the service. I suggest you try again in about an hour."

Disappointed, Frank returned to the table. To his surprise, Joe was involved in an argument with their waiter.

"What's wrong?" Frank asked.

"There seems to be a misunderstanding about our check," Joe declared. "It's almost double the amount listed on the menu we saw in the window."

"I already told you," the waiter growled. "Those prices are good only up to three o'clock. After that, you pay more."

"I'll say you do," Joe retorted. "But how were we supposed to know?"

The waiter picked up a copy of the menu the boys had seen in the window and thrust it at them. "Can't you read?" He pointed to a line of fine print at the bottom of the menu:

> THIS MANAGEMENT RESERVES THE
> PRIVILEGE TO CHANGE LISTED MENU
> PRICES AFTER THREE P.M.

"Wow! You almost need a magnifying glass to read it!" Joe snapped.

"Don't try to squirm out of this," the waiter said harshly. "I had you kids sized up the minute you walked in here. I'm going to get the manager!"

The waiter reappeared shortly with a short, stocky man wearing a dark suit and a bow tie.

"I hear you boys can't pay your bill," he said.

Joe started to explain. "We can pay you half of it now and . . ."

"We don't sell meals on the instalment plan," the manager stated tersely.

"Give us a little time," Frank pleaded. "Just as soon as we can get a call through to our home, we'll have some money wired."

"A lot of good that will do me," the manager answered. Suddenly his expression changed. His face broke into a wide grin. "Tell you what! I'm in need of a couple of dishwashers right now. Each of you work for three hours and I'll call it square. You keep your money."

The Hardys were reluctant, but being short on funds, with no place to go, and unable to get through to Mrs Hardy yet, they agreed.

After working a while Joe said in disgust, "A couple of private detectives end up in New York as kitchen police!"

"I wouldn't complain too much," Frank said, grinning. "What if we had to wash these dishes by hand!"

"Why do we have to do them at all?" Joe complained. "Dad has several friends here in the city. They'd be willing to help us out with some money."

"I know! But I think we should go to them only as a last resort."

Frank waited nearly four hours before getting a call through to Bayport. Finally the lines were repaired, and a long-distance operator connected him with Mrs Hardy.

"Your Aunt Gertrude and I have been worried sick about you and Joe," she said. "There's been a bad storm here. Where *are* you?"

"Still in New York. But guess what? Joe and I are washing dishes to pay for our dinner."

Mrs Hardy laughed and promised to wire them money right away.

"Send it to the telegraph office at Grand Central Terminal," Frank requested. "And don't worry about us. We're fine, and we'll probably be home tomorrow. Now tell me, did that fake inventor show up?"

"No. I guess the storm was too bad. The detectives stationed here were needed elsewhere and had to leave. The box on the steps is soaked. We turned the lights off and have been watching from the window. Maybe we can catch a glimpse of whoever comes."

"Good. 'Bye now. I hope nobody tapped this call."

When Frank and Joe finished their work, they hurried from the restaurant. It was still raining when they stepped on to the street. "It's almost midnight. What now?" Joe asked.

"Let's take the subway to Times Square," Frank said. "Then we can get the cross-town shuttle train to Grand Central. At least we can keep dry there until our money arrives."

There were only a few people waiting for the shuttle train when the boys arrived at Times Square. Several minutes passed, then suddenly Frank clutched his brother's arm.

"What's the matter?" Joe asked.

"That man behind the post!" Frank whispered. "He's one of Chris's friends!"

Just as Joe glanced up, the man brushed against one of the strolling passengers on the platform. The young detectives' keen eyes saw him lift a wallet from his victim's pocket.

"Hey! You!" Frank shouted, rushing towards the pickpocket with Joe close behind him.

Startled at Frank's outcry, the thief quickly removed the money and dropped the wallet. He leaped off the platform on to the tracks and disappeared into the dark tunnel. The boys took off in pursuit.

"Watch that side rail!" Frank warned his brother. "It's charged with high-voltage electricity!"

The young detectives had run a considerable distance into the yawning tunnel when they halted abruptly.

"What's that rumbling noise?" Joe asked.

"It's the shuttle train!" Frank screamed. "And it's coming our way!"

Seconds later the fast-moving train loomed round the bend. Would the Hardys escape in time?

·13·

Exciting Assignment

"RUN for it!" Joe yelled.

The boys whirled and dashed through the tunnel. As the train rapidly gained on them, its headlight illuminated the walls. Stretching along one side was a power line encased in metal piping. Frank spotted it.

"That's a conduit line!" he shouted. "Grab it and flatten yourself against the wall!"

They made a desperate leap, caught hold of the narrow piping, and stiffened themselves hard against the wall. Seconds later the train sped past them. The roar was deafening and the mass of air that was pulled along lashed the Hardys like a gale. The sides of the carriages were barely inches away as the lighted windows passed by in a blur.

Soon the last coach disappeared round a bend. The youths jumped on to the tracks and made their way back to the Times Square station platform. Both were trembling.

"What do you think happened to the man we were chasing?" Joe asked finally.

"Probably he's used this tunnel before as a means of escape," Frank replied, "and knows the layout well. I'm sure he's heading for Grand Central station."

Arriving at the platform, the boys spotted the man Chris's pal had tried to rob. He was talking to a police officer.

"These are the two boys who chased the pickpocket into the tunnel," the man told the policeman as the brothers walked towards them.

The officer turned to Frank and Joe. "This man claims someone stole his wallet."

"That's right," Frank said, "and the thief is probably the same one who lifted mine this afternoon. We chased him but he got away."

"By now he has no doubt reached Grand Central," Joe added.

"I've alerted a couple of the men on duty there," the policeman said. "They'll be on the lookout for him." He stared at the boys curiously. "Say, that was a risky job for you fellows to take on!"

The boys introduced themselves to the officer and showed him their credentials.

"So you're the Hardys," the policeman remarked.

"I'm Reilly. Your father's name is something of a legend round the department."

"Dad is a great detective," Joe said proudly.

At the officer's request, the boys gave him a description of the pickpocket. Reilly then took the name and address of the man who had been robbed.

Shortly the next train arrived and the Hardys stepped aboard. When they got off at Grand Central station, Frank and Joe noticed a commotion at the far end of the platform. A group of spectators had assembled.

"Let's see what's going on," Frank suggested.

As the boys walked forward, Joe's eyes widened. "Hey, look!" he yelled. "There's the pickpocket we chased!"

"He's being questioned by two policemen," Frank observed. "That was quick work. They must've nabbed him coming out of the tunnel."

The boys pressed their way through the spectators.

"I ain't done nothin'," they heard the pickpocket snarl.

"That's not true!" Joe declared. "He tried to steal a man's wallet. My brother and I saw the whole thing!"

"And I suspect he took mine and is a pal of some smugglers," Frank added.

"Who are you?" one of the policemen asked.

The boys identified themselves once more, then related the incident at the Times Square station.

One of the officers nodded. "We were alerted to be on the lookout for this guy."

"We know all about him," the second policeman said. "His name is Torchy Murks. Has two convictions for petty larceny. We had reports of a pickpocket that looks like him working the subways recently."

"You're crazy!" Murks growled. "I'm being framed!"

"We'll see about that."

The officers requested the boys to accompany them. At the police station Murks was marched off to the interrogation room.

A few minutes later a tall, muscular, square-jawed man emerged from the squad room. He walked directly to the Hardys and extended his hand in greeting.

"One of the officers has just told me that you're the sons of Fenton Hardy," he said.

"That's right."

"It's a pleasure to meet you. I'm Detective Lieutenant Danson. I joined the force as a rookie just before your father left the department. A great detective. Come into my office."

The youths were ushered into a small but comfortable office, where Danson offered them chairs and seated himself behind his desk.

"I hear you fellows had a scrap with Torchy Murks," he said. "Slippery character. Well, tell me, what brings the famous Hardys to New York City?"

The boys related their experiences of the past two weeks, ending with an account of how they had trailed the smuggler-kidnapper Chris to New York.

Lieutenant Danson sat thoughtfully for several moments. "That's strange," he mumbled to himself.

"What is?" Joe inquired curiously.

"It might be just a coincidence," Danson muttered. "Then again . . ."

The boys watched with interest as the lieutenant thumbed through his private list of telephone numbers. "An FBI agent I know, named Emery Keith, dropped into my office a couple of days ago and told me about two suspects his office wants for questioning. From his description of the men, one of them sounds like this big blond fellow Chris. Of course our men have been on the lookout, but I'd like Keith to hear your story."

Twenty minutes later two neatly dressed men arrived at the lieutenant's office.

"I'm Agent Keith," the tall, light-haired one said to the Hardys. Then he introduced his shorter, dark-haired companion. "And this is my assistant, George

Mallett. I've heard a lot about your father. Some of our agents have worked with him."

After the formalities, they all sat down to discuss the case. Frank and Joe told their story about the kidnapping and smuggling.

"Hmm!" Keith muttered. "Interesting lead!" The agent eyed the Hardys for a moment before speaking again. "Does the name Taffy Marr ring a bell with you fellows?" he asked.

"I'm afraid not," Frank replied.

"Taffy Marr," Keith said, "is one of the slickest crooks in the country. He's the leader of the smuggling ring and I suspect is the boss of Shorty, Chris, and their pals. Marr is young—the innocent-looking type—but as clever and cold-blooded a crook as you'll ever come up against."

"What else can you tell us about his looks?" Frank asked.

"Not much. Taffy is slender, of average height, and uses a lot of disguises, so we're not exactly sure what he does look like. One of our men did spot a triangular scar on Marr's left forearm. No doubt he's self-conscious about this identification and he usually wears long sleeves.

"Taffy came from the West Coast a few months ago and organized a gang," Keith went on. "The group's been flooding the country with smuggled diamonds. It's so bad that the Jewellers Association is offering a sizeable reward to anyone who can trip up Marr. As for me, I'd give a year's salary to put him in prison."

Joe volunteered the information that the gang also

smuggled electronic equipment, and added, "Have you any leads on Marr's whereabouts?"

"The last report shows he was here in New York," the agent answered. "Before that, it was Florida, then Virginia, Connecticut, New Jersey, and the Carolinas."

"He certainly gets around," Frank commented.

"Apparently he's confining his operations now to the East Coast," Keith said. "But the problem is where. He has dropped out of sight completely."

"How long do you two plan to be in New York?" Keith asked the Hardys.

"Not much longer," Joe said. "We called home for money, and it should be at the Grand Central telegraph office by now. We plan to take the first train back to Bayport."

"Tell you what," Keith said. "Why not let us put you up at a hotel tonight at our expense? Then you can catch the morning train. I'd like to have breakfast with you fellows and discuss the possibility of your working with us. But I'll have to talk with my chief first."

Frank and Joe were excited at this prospect and quickly consented. Lieutenant Danson drove them to Grand Central, where they found their money waiting, then they went to a nearby hotel. Completely exhausted, Frank and Joe were sound asleep within minutes.

Early the next morning they met Keith in the hotel restaurant and enjoyed a breakfast of sausage, wheat cakes, and fruit. Then the agent reviewed the facts on Marr and his gang.

"I realize our information is sketchy," the agent said. "But you've given us some good leads and maybe you can dig up a few more."

"We'll certainly try," Frank said.

"I'd like you fellows to be on the lookout for Marr in the Bayport area. The same goes for Chris. He may turn up there again—perhaps to meet Marr, if they're in the same racket."

"You can count on us!" Joe said eagerly.

Keith reached into his pocket and took out a small business card. On the back he jotted down a series of digits.

"I suggest you memorize this telephone number," he said. "You'll be able to get in touch with me or my assistant Mallet at any time."

"Right!" The Hardys repeated the digits several times until both were sure they would not forget them.

Frank telephoned to check the trains and learned that one would depart for Bayport within half an hour. Keith drove them to the station and shook hands.

"Good luck, and good hunting," he said with a smile. "I can assure you that the entire Bureau will be grateful for whatever help you can give it."

When the boys arrived home, Joe jokingly stuck out his chest and said to Mrs Hardy and Aunt Gertrude, "Meet a couple of Federal men!"

"Whatever do you mean?" his mother asked.

Frank told of Keith's request and the women smiled. "It's a big assignment," Mrs Hardy remarked, and Aunt Gertrude added, "You'd better watch your step. This Marr fellow sounds pretty dangerous for you to tackle."

"Now tell us," Joe requested, changing the subject, "about that fake inventor. Did the mysterious caller ever come for the box with the secret radio in it?"

"Yes," their mother replied.

"Was he caught?" Frank asked eagerly.

·14·

Identification Diamond

AUNT Gertrude answered Frank's question. "Of course that crook was caught. The police came back and nabbed him. Inventor, nothing."

"Hurrah!" Joe shouted. "Who is he?"

"He won't talk and he had no identification on him. But I'll bet he belongs to Chris's gang," Miss Hardy said.

"You're probably right," Frank agreed. "And they may all belong to Marr's racket." After a few moments' thought, he added, "I think I know a way to find out."

"How?" Joe asked.

Frank grinned. "I'll pretend I'm a fellow gang member and go and talk to him."

The young detective telephoned Chief Collig, who gave his consent to the plan.

"What can you tell me about this man?" Frank asked.

Hearing that the prisoner was very short and strong, Frank instantly thought of the man the burglars at the Wright home had mentioned.

"Sounds like Shorty," he said. After hanging up, he asked Mrs Hardy, "Have you an unmounted diamond?"

"Yes. One that fell out of a ring. Why?"

261

"I'd like to borrow one as a sort of identification with the gang."

"Swell idea," said Joe. "I'll help you get fixed up." The boys went upstairs and rummaged through their father's supply of disguises.

When Frank emerged from the house, his best friends would not have recognized him. He wore a long cut wig and beard, tight-fitting slacks, and a turtleneck sweater. He roared off on his motorcycle, and on purpose went past the cell block.

As prearranged, Chief Collig met him at the entrance to headquarters and escorted Frank to the prisoner, who looked idly through the bars.

"Friend of yours to see you," said the chief. "Maybe he can persuade you to unbutton your lips."

Frank gazed through the bars. "Like nuttin' I will," he whispered to the prisoner in a tough voice as soon as Collig had moved off. "Hi, Shorty! I'm sorry the cops got yuh. But yuh didn't tell 'em nuttin', did yuh?"

"Naw."

Frank was jubilant. He had scored one point. The man's nickname *was* Shorty.

"Did yuh hear my new motorcycle?" he asked.

"Yeah, I heard it," Shorty answered. "Whaddaya pay for it with?"

Frank pulled the diamond from his pocket. "With some o' dese."

Shorty seemed impressed. "Say, what's yer name?"

Frank assumed an air of annoyance. "Ain't Taffy told yuh 'bout me yet?"

"Naw."

The young sleuth's heart was thumping with excitement as he said, "Name's Youngster. I got a bonus on the last haul. Just joined up with Marr—when *smacko!* —I run into *the* toughest setup."

Shorty, apparently convinced by Frank's story, said, "I was lookin' fer some chips, too. But Marr'll probably have me rubbed out for gettin' in here."

"Did the cops take the Hardys' package from yuh?" Frank asked.

"Yeah. Before I could open it."

"How'd yuh like me to lift it? I could do it easy," Frank boasted.

"From the cops?" Shorty asked, astonished.

"Naw. The Hardys. The chief'll give it back to 'em."

Shorty's thin lips broke into a smile. "Then Taffy'll think I didn't bungle after all?" His face clouded again, however. "Lessen yuh double-cross me," he added.

"I won't squeal," Frank said. "I'll tell Marr yuh give it to me to deliver. Say, where's he holin' up now? I seen him in New York an' he told me to come here an' wait till I heard from him."

"Guess he's still at Bickford's," Shorty answered, and added with a smirk, "Best place to hide out with a wad o' rocks."

At that moment a voice called, "Time's up for visitors." A guard came in Frank's direction.

"Okay, but don't rush me," the elated boy said in a tough voice.

He swaggered out of the police station and walked towards his motorcycle. What should he do now? Divulge the information to Collig at once and have the police pick up Taffy Marr?

"I'll call him, anyway," Frank decided, "and he can notify Keith."

Collig said he would stake plain clothesmen at the shop. "I'll let you know what happens."

When Frank reached home, Aunt Gertrude met him at the door. "I'm glad you've come," she said excitedly. "We must do something at once about that young clerk at Bickford's."

"We are going to," her nephew assured her. "That is, the police are."

"Well, I can tell them something," Aunt Gertrude said. "I was going to tell you what I remembered about him."

"You know something about him?" Frank asked.

"I'll say I do. You recall the tall, fair-haired man who bumped into me at the Gresham railroad station and called me an old whaler? Well, it suddenly came to me that one of the men he was talking to was the very same young man who's working at Bickford's!"

"What!" Frank exclaimed. "You're sure?"

"Now listen here," his aunt said sharply. "When I'm sure, I'm sure."

"Aunty, this is great news!" Frank exclaimed.

Her announcement changed the whole scheme of attack. "Does Joe know about this and where is he?" Frank asked.

"He hasn't heard my story because I just remembered. Joe went— Here he comes now."

As Joe came in, he asked, "Frank, how did you make out?"

"Great! Listen! Taffy Marr is working at Bickford's!"

"No kidding?"

"It's straight. I got the tip from Shorty, the prisoner," Frank answered. "And listen to this. Aunt Gertrude saw Marr with Chris in Gresham! While I remove my disguise, will you call Chief Collig and tell him this?"

"Okay, and let's go down and watch the fun when Marr is arrested," Joe urged.

It took Frank only five minutes to take off his costume and make-up. Since Mrs Hardy and Aunt Gertrude planned to leave the house, Joe put Mr Wright's invention in the tyre well of the boys' car. Then he and Frank rode downtown in the convertible. When they reached Bickford's, there was a good-sized crowd in front of the jewellery store.

"What's going on?" Joe asked a bystander.

"Don't know. An attempted holdup, I guess. Police arrived and circled the building. We've been waiting for them to bring somebody out."

A siren began to wail and seconds later an ambulance raced up the street. It stopped in front of the jewellery store. A hush fell over the crowd as they waited for the victim to be brought out. Would it be Taffy Marr, or a policeman who had gone in to arrest him or would it be the shop owner?

A stretcher was carried in and a little later it was brought out bearing a man. His eyes were closed and his face ghostly white.

"It's Mr Bickford!" Joe exclaimed.

Instantly the boys pushed through the crowd and rushed up to an officer just emerging from the store. He knew the Hardys and beckoned to them.

"We were just a little too late arriving to catch

Marr," he said. "Marr must have attacked Mr Bickford and cleaned the place out before he skipped."

"A complete haul, you mean?" Joe asked.

"Took everything."

"How bad is Mr Bickford?" Frank inquired.

The officer shrugged. "He's unconscious and his pulse is weak."

Joe spluttered angrily, "If I get my hands on Marr, I'll—I'll—"

"It's going to be tough tracking him down," Frank predicted. "I'll bet by this time he's wearing a disguise and has already left town."

Joe snapped his fingers. "If he owns a suitcase full of disguises, he probably went back to wherever he's living to pick them up. Officer, have you any idea where he's living?"

"No, but our men are questioning people in the neighbourhood."

As the ambulance pulled away, the boys asked permission to check out the jewellery shop for a clue to Marr's address.

The officer smiled. "Go ahead. You fellows may manage to pick up a lead before the police check. I'm to stay on duty outside so take all the time you want."

Frank told his brother he was sure Mr Bickford would have some kind of record concerning his assistant.

"No doubt they will be under an assumed name, but let's have a look."

The boys found a drawer full of papers. Under them was an account book. They read each name listed in the book and at last came to one with recent, regular notations of payments.

"This might be him," Frank observed. "Ray Stokeley, 49 New Street."

"It's worth following," Joe said.

Frank and Joe briefly told the officer on duty they might have a lead and dashed off to their car. They soon reached New Street, where most of the old-fashioned houses had "Rooms for Rent" signs in windows. Number 49 was a large run-down mansion, set far back from the street.

Frank and Joe climbed the high steps and rang the bell. A neatly dressed, middle-aged woman opened the door.

"Is Mr Stokeley at home?" Frank inquired.

"No, he left—moved out, not ten minutes ago."

The woman started to close the door, but Frank, smiling at her, said, "We think he's the man we're looking for, but we're not sure. Would you mind describing Mr Stokeley for us?"

Her description fitted Marr. Frank nodded. "He's our man. Do you know where he went?"

There was no answer for a few seconds, then the woman said jokingly, "Who are you? Boy detectives?"

"Yes," Joe replied promptly, "and Mr Stokeley is wanted by the FBI and police. You'd be doing them a great favour if you tell us all you know."

"Oh!" she gasped. "I know very little about Mr Stokeley. But I did hear part of a phone call he made early this morning. He said, 'Then to the airport.' Does that help you?"

"Yes indeed. Thanks," Frank answered as he and Joe raced down the steps.

They arrived at the airport in record time. As they

rushed through the terminal lobby, the boys caught sight of Cole Weber, the pilot, looking at the antique aircraft and waved.

"If Marr's wearing a disguise, how can we spot him?" Frank said.

Joe was staring at a man with grey hair, moustache, and a beard. He stood near a counter, talking to a red-haired fellow.

"Frank, look! That guy the grey-haired man's talking to looks like one of the kidnappers!"

"Sure?"

"Positive! And I'll bet Grey Beard is Taffy Marr!"

The men turned and went out to the field. Frank and Joe followed. The suspects started running towards a small white single-engine plane that was ready for take-off. They climbed aboard quickly.

"Now what'll we do?" Frank asked.

"Only one thing we can do," Joe replied. "Follow them!"

·15·

Pursuit

"BUT how can we follow Marr?" Frank asked. "If only Dad's plane were here, we could do it easily."

He was referring to the sleek, six-seater aircraft owned by their father. However, Mr Hardy and his pilot Jack Wayne had flown it to California with Mr Wright.

"Keep an eye on that white bird," Joe ordered. "I'll run into the administration building and telephone Agent Keith. Then I'll go to Manson's Charter Service and see if we can rent a plane."

"You'd better make it quick!" Frank warned.

Joe rushed to a phone booth inside the administration building and dialled Keith's code number. It took only seconds to make the connection.

"Agent Mallett speaking!" crackled a deep, firm voice.

"This is Joe Hardy. Is Agent Keith there?"

"No, but he should be back in a few minutes."

"Can't wait!" Joe declared. "Tell him my brother and I are trailing a man we're sure is Taffy Marr. We're at Bayport field. The suspect and another man are about to take off in a white single-engine job. We'll try to follow them. I'll keep you posted!"

"Good work!" Mallett said. "Try to get the registration number of their plane so that we can trace its owner."

"Right!"

Joe hung up quickly and went directly to one of the terminal's counters. Behind it stood a plumpish, pleasant-faced man. On the wall hung a sign which read:

MANSON'S CHARTER SERVICE

"Well, if it isn't Joe Hardy!" the man declared.

"Hello, Mr Manson."

"Where have you been keeping yourself? Haven't seen you around the airport lately."

"We've been sleuthing," Joe answered with a wink. "I'd like to charter one of your planes right away!"

"Gosh, Joe, I'm sorry, but all my aircraft are out on flights," Manson said apologetically. "Haven't had such a busy day in months."

Suddenly Joe had an idea. How about Cole Weber? He rushed off and in a few moments found the lanky owner of an antique plane.

"Nice to see you again," the pilot greeted him. "What's the rush?"

"I'm looking for a ride."

"You've come to the right man. I'll be glad to fly you wherever you want to go," Weber told him.

Joe drew the pilot aside and in a low voice briefly explained the situation to him. "Could your aircraft keep up with a fast plane?"

Frank rushed into the lobby. "Marr and his friend are getting ready to take off!" he exclaimed.

Followed by his brother and Weber, Joe ran to a window overlooking the field. They spotted the small, single-engine plane taxiing to the active runway for take-off. Frank jotted down the registration number.

"Is this the one you want to follow?" Weber commented. "That type isn't too fast. I'm sure I could keep up with it."

"Great!" said Frank.

"We'll have to make it snappy!" Joe urged.

"Maybe not," Weber answered. "There's a long line of planes waiting for take-off clearance. It'll be at least ten minutes before those men can clear ground. That'll give me time to telephone the control tower. Since my plane is not equipped with radio, they'll have to okay me for take-off by flashing a green light."

Frank said, "How about warning the control tower not to let Marr take off?"

Weber looked surprised. "Are you completely sure that one of those passengers is Marr?" he asked.

"Well, no, we're not," Joe confessed.

"Then I think we'd better not make such a request," the pilot advised. "All of us might get into trouble."

The boys nodded and Joe said, "We'll just make a chase of it."

Weber went off but soon returned. "Everything's set," he said. "And we're in luck! The control-tower boys are going to let us take off from the grass shoulder of Runway Six. It means we won't have to wait in line for clearance. Chances are we'll be off the ground ahead of your friends."

The Hardys followed the pilot to his orange-and-white biplane. He drew three parachutes from the baggage compartment and instructed Frank and Joe to put them on while he fastened his own.

"Climb aboard!" he said.

The boys seated themselves side by side in the front cockpit. Weber signalled a mechanic to help start the engine, then jumped into the rear cockpit.

"Brakes on! Contact!" the mechanic shouted.

"Brakes on! Contact!" Weber replied.

With a single whirl of the propeller, the engine roared to life. The boys were so thrilled by the chance to fly in an old biplane that for a moment they had almost dismissed Taffy Marr from their minds.

Weber began to glide his wood-and-fabric craft down the runway. Nearing Runway Six, he veered on to the grass shoulder which paralleled it.

"All set?" the boys heard him shout over the sound of the engine.

"All set!" Frank and Joe answered.

Their pilot pivoted the craft round and pointed its nose into the wind. Shortly a bright disc of green light beamed from the control tower. The engine emitted a loud, steady roar as Weber advanced the throttle. The plane bounced across the grass surface, then cleared it. Frank looked down and spotted Marr's craft just taxiing into position for take-off.

After reaching a couple of thousand feet, Weber circled the airport. He and the Hardys watched intently as the other plane sped down the runway and became airborne far below them.

Weber manœuvred his craft at a safe distance behind Marr's plane, which was now heading on a north-easterly course.

"So far so good!" Frank exclaimed, noting that their quarry was not outdistancing them. The boys waved happily to Weber, who responded with a wide grin.

Nearly half an hour had passed when they noticed a build-up of haze ahead. It seemed to thicken as they drew closer. Soon the antique craft was skirting an ocean of milky-white mist which obscured the country-side below.

"What a cloud!" Joe shouted.

"And we'll head right into it on our present course!" Frank observed.

Weber signalled that he would try flying above it. By now Marr's plane was also climbing. To the Hardys' dismay, their quarry vanished behind a screen of whiteness.

Weber signalled that he was going to turn back. But as he banked the biplane, it suddenly plunged into a misty void!

·16·

Bail Out!

WEBER struggled to keep the aircraft under control in the fog. He shifted his attention to the *turn-and-bank* indicator mounted on the instrument panel. What the dial showed would help prevent the pilot from rolling into an uncontrollable spiral.

Then, suddenly, the plane broke out into a cavity of clear air. The boys spotted the other aircraft and saw that it had altered its course. It was now heading south. Weber immediately banked and took the same direction, hoping to close the gap and come in on the tail of the other plane.

It was then that the Hardys realized the extent of the fog bank. Already obscuring a great area of the coast, it stretched far out to sea. Ahead they saw their quarry flying directly towards a looming wall of thick mist.

Weber altered course again and headed north-west in an effort to skirt the edge of the fog bank. But the mist built up rapidly in swirling clouds.

"I guess if we hope to keep the other plane in sight, we can't go too far to the west," Frank observed.

Weber began to climb, hoping to get above the fog. But as he turned north to meet the advancing cloud, his craft was enveloped in mist before he could gain altitude. Marr's plane had vanished.

"The other ship is equipped to fly on instruments!" Weber shouted. "We're not!"

Their pilot held to a straight course and increased his speed, hoping to run through the fog and pick up the other plane when visibility improved. The great bank of mist evidently extended over a greater area than he had first supposed.

Minutes ticked by and still the opaque greyness persisted. Frank and Joe turned to watch the pilot. Weber was peering at the instrument panel.

"At least we're flying straight and level," he announced.

Frank and Joe tried to remain calm but inwardly they were worried. Their craft might ram another plane at any moment!

Weber continued on into the limitless white wall. Not a glimpse of blue sky. Not a patch of earth to be seen.

"I guess we've lost Marr for sure," Joe remarked.

"Yes," Frank agreed. His voice showed his disappointment.

Suddenly the roar of the engine stopped. The only sound was the hum of the rigging. The nose of the plane dropped sharply and the craft went into a dive.

"The engine's stopped!" Joe yelled.

The pilot waved at them in an encouraging gesture. He had thrust the stick far forward and the plane was plunging through the fog at terrific speed.

On and on it went. The boys were alarmed. They knew engine trouble had developed and a forced landing in the fog would be perilous. But there must still be some hope: otherwise their pilot would have signalled to abandon ship.

The rush of air took their breath away. Then, as abruptly as it had ceased, the roar of the engine broke out again.

"Boy, what a welcome sound!" Joe exclaimed.

Weber eased the stick back slowly and the plane gradually recovered from the dive. It flattened out and began to climb again. Frank took a deep breath. Joe grinned.

But their relief was short-lived. Again the engine began to act up. It spluttered, balked, misfired, and picked up again. No longer was it throbbing with its previous regularity.

The boys looked back at the pilot's anxious face. They all knew a blind landing could be disastrous! For a moment the Hardys stiffened as the engine died, then coughed once more.

"Carburettor ice, I'll bet," Frank said to himself.

The plane they had been pursuing was forgotten. Their whole concern now was safety—to escape the grey blanket. If only they could sight ground to attempt a forced landing!

Frank felt for the harness of his parachute. "We may have to jump," he thought, not relishing the prospect. To leap from a crippled plane, with fog blanketing the earth below, was an experience he could do without.

Joe was alarmed too. "If only the fog would lift!"

The pilot was desperately trying to revive the engine's old steady clamour. But it was useless.

The engine stopped again. The nose of the machine

dropped and the plane repeated a long, swift dive. It straightened out, banked, then dived again at screaming speed.

Coming out of the second dive, the nose rose abruptly. They all waited for the reassuring catch of the engine but it remained mute.

The speed gained in the dive steadily decreased as the craft soared upwards in a steep climb. Then it fell off on one wing and went into a descending spiral.

"I have a feeling we're going in circles!" Joe shouted to his brother. "I think Weber is becoming disoriented."

"We're sunk!" Weber yelled at the boys. "You'll have to take to the chutes!"

"Jump?" Joe shouted.

The man nodded. "The engine is done for. Choked up. I don't dare try a landing in this fog. We'll crack up for sure. Hurry! I'll keep her under control as long as I can. Crawl out on the wing, watch for my signal, then jump clear! Count ten, then yank the rip cord!"

The boys scrambled out on the swaying wing in dead silence as the plane coasted through the grey mist.

"Jump clear!" Frank reminded his brother.

"It's not the jumping that worries me," said Joe. "It's the landing."

The boys knew that they had no control over their direction and had no idea of what lay beneath. They might be plunging directly towards a lake or into a city street!

Out on the wing Frank and Joe clung for a moment, their eyes on the pilot. Weber raised his hand, then brought it down sharply.

"Jump!"

Since the parachutes could easily become entangled if the boys jumped together, Frank went first. He leaped away from the swaying plane and plummeted through the fog. Then Joe followed suit.

Twisting and turning through the air, the boys plunged towards the earth. Desperately Frank groped for the rip-cord. It eluded his grasp. Sudden panic gripped him.

He was falling towards the earth at terrific speed and could not find the parachute's Dee ring!

Every second was precious. He knew that even if he found the ring, it would be a few moments before the parachute opened. By then he might already have reached an altitude too low to permit the chute to billow out in time!

His groping hand found the ring and he tugged. Nothing happened. He was still tumbling through the clouds of mist!

About to give up hope, Frank heard a crackling sound above him. There was a sudden jerk as though a gigantic hand had grabbed him and he found himself floating gently through space.

Through the wreaths of mist he glimpsed another object. It was a parachute similar to his own, dropping slowly through the fog. Joe, at least, was safe.

But what of the pilot and the crippled plane? Where were they?

· 17 ·

The Trapped Pilot

FEAR gripping them, the Hardys drifted down silently through the fog. The only sound was an occasional flapping of the canopies looming above their heads.

"The ground can't be too far below!" Frank thought. "What kind of terrain? Sharp rocks? Trees? Open water?"

He and Joe heard a muffled explosion some distance away.

"Weber's biplane must have crashed!" Joe concluded. "Hope he bailed out in time."

Suddenly the milky void vanished. The Hardys blinked in relief. They were less than a hundred feet above a farmland area.

They settled down in a ploughed field a short distance from each other. Frank tumbled across the soft ground a couple of times, then hauled in a section of shroud lines to spill the air from the canopy of his chute.

"You all right?" he shouted to Joe, throwing off his harness and running towards him.

"I'm okay! That was wild! But I wouldn't want to do it again under the same conditions!"

Frank pointed to a plume of smoke rising behind a hill about half a mile away.

"That must be the explosion!" he yelled. "Let's see if it's Weber's plane."

They raced towards the spot. In a few minutes they came to a charred, twisted mass of wreckage. A pool of oil still burned.

"At least Weber wasn't in the wreck," said Joe. "But where is he?"

At that instant the pilot called out to them. "Hey, fellows!" he shouted. "Give me a hand!"

The voice seemed to come from a small clump of trees located about five hundred feet away. When the boys reached it, they saw Weber dangling in his harness high among some branches.

"Are you hurt?" Joe asked with concern.

"No—only my pride," the pilot answered. "I'm supposed to be an expert at handling a parachute. And where do I land and get trapped? In the only grove of trees within a mile!"

"You're too far above the ground to try dropping free," Frank warned. "We'd better get help."

People from the surrounding farms who had seen the smoke began to arrive at the scene. When the boys asked for some rope, one of the farmers rushed off. He returned in a few minutes with a coil of one-inch hemp.

Joe took it and began shinning up the tree in which Weber's chute was entangled. Everyone watched the rescue as he edged out along a branch directly above the pilot and tied one end of the rope to it. Seconds later they both were sliding to the ground.

The farmer on whose property they had landed stepped up. "My name is Hank Olsen," he said. "Was anybody injured?"

*People from the surrounding farms began to arrive
at the scene*

"No," Frank replied. "Sorry about the plane coming down on your land."

"That's all right. I haven't done any planting in that section yet," the farmer explained.

Weber spoke up. "I'd like to telephone a report of the crash."

"You can use the phone at my house," Olsen offered. "I'll drive you there. My pickup truck is just on the other side of the hill."

When they arrived at the farmhouse, the pilot called the control tower at Bayport field to report the accident. Frank phoned Mrs Hardy to let her know where he and Joe were, and then got in touch with Chet Morton for a ride home.

"What!" Chet exclaimed in disbelief when he heard about the Hardys' adventure. "Say that again."

"I said we had to bail out of Weber's biplane," Frank declared.

"Aw, come on," his chum muttered, unbelieving.

"It's true," Frank replied. "We need a ride home. Do you think your jalopy would hang together long enough for you to pick us up?"

"Hang together?" Chet retorted. "That's no way to talk about one of the finest pieces of machinery going. Where are you?"

Frank asked the farmer for their exact location. Olsen unfolded a road map and pointed to a spot about ninety miles north-east of Bayport. Frank traced the route with his finger and relayed instructions to his friend.

"Okay! I'm on my way!" Chet answered.

Nearly three hours passed before the Hardys

spotted their chum's yellow jalopy bouncing along the narrow road leading to Olsen's house. Weber and the boys thanked the farmer and his wife for their hospitality, then started for Bayport.

As they rode along, the Hardys and Weber discussed their pursuit of Marr's plane. "I wonder if he ran into any trouble," Joe mused.

"When I called control tower, I asked if they knew about the stretch of fog north of them," Weber explained. "They did, and said it was only two or three miles across, with clear air on the other side."

"And since Marr's plane was equipped with radio," Frank interrupted, "the pilot would have received the latest weather reports. He knew he could fly through the fog bank and be in the clear again within a few minutes."

"Do you think Marr knew he was being followed?" Joe asked.

"My guess is that he didn't," Weber said. "At least his pilot wasn't attempting any evasive action."

"Sorry about your plane," Joe said sympathetically.

"It was a great ship," Weber declared sadly. "But I have enough parts to rebuild another one. That's some consolation."

Chet dropped off Weber and the Hardys at Bayport field, where the pilot made arrangements to fly home. After expressing their thanks to him for his help and saying good-bye, the boys walked towards their car.

"We'd better call Agent Keith before we go home," Joe suggested, and they went inside to telephone.

"Too bad Marr got away," the agent said when

Frank told him about their recent adventure. "But I'm glad you and your brother are safe."

Frank drew a notebook from his pocket and opened it. "I have the registration number of the getaway plane."

"Good!" Keith said. "Let's have it. I'll check it out with the Federal Aviation Agency."

Frank gave it and hung up. The boys went to the parking lot. In a moment Frank frowned. "I thought I left our car here."

"You did," Joe said with a sinking feeling. "It—it's been stolen!"

The Hardys were momentarily paralyzed. Not only their fine convertible, but also Mr Wright's highly secret invention was gone!

Frank spoke first. "Come on, Joe! We must call the police."

The boys ran to the administration building and telephoned. They were told by the sergeant on duty that state troopers had picked up a car fitting the convertible's description. "Will you Hardys go out to the end of Pleasantdale Road and look at it?" the officer requested.

Frank hailed a taxi which took them to the spot, then back to Bayport. The convertible was a sorry sight. Every bit of the upholstery had been slashed and the contents dumped out. Articles had been removed from the front compartment and the boot. The spare tyre had been ripped open.

"Too bad, fellows," a trooper said.

"Yes," Frank answered, testing the rack.

It was still bolted in place, but he winked at Joe, a

signal that he wanted to be alone for a further search. On a pretext Joe got the trooper round to the front of the car. Quickly Frank looked under the tyre well. The box and invention were still there.

Frank slammed the lid shut. He called out, "Joe, if this baby still runs, let's go home."

The engine started promptly and the steering mechanism was undamaged. Frank signed a paper for the police, saying he was the owner of the car, then the boys rode off. As soon as they reached home, Joe carried the invention to the boys' room and hid it.

"I'm afraid that next time the gang's going to find this," he told his brother.

"I agree," Frank answered. "What do you say we ask Mother to put it in her safe-deposit box? I'm sure Dad would agree."

Mrs Hardy and Aunt Gertrude approved this idea and as soon as the bank was open the next morning, took the invention downtown. A little later the phone rang. Mrs Hardy was calling to assure her sons of its safety.

A few moments later Agent Keith telephoned. "We've lost Marr again," he said. "The FAA looked up the registration number of his plane. It belongs to a fixed base operator at a small airport in Connecticut. Marr's pilot rented the plane for the day."

"Did the owner see the pilot's flying licence?" Frank inquired.

"Yes," Keith replied. "The name listed was Harold Clark. It's a forgery! Such a licence was never issued!"

"What about the plane?"

"It was returned some time last night. The owner found it tied down on his ramp when he went to the airport early this morning."

The Hardys were downcast by the situation. Marr had vanished and they did not have the slightest lead on him. Furthermore, their car was a wreck. They reported the damage to the insurance company and waited for an investigator to come.

"We'll have to rent a car while ours is being repaired," Frank said.

He made the arrangements by phone and within half an hour a car stood in the driveway.

The boys had just sat down to lunch in the dining room when the telephone rang. Aunt Gertrude went to the kitchen to take the call.

"Yes, they're at home," the others heard her say. Presently she darted into the room. "It's about Mr Bickford!" she said quietly.

·18·

Outsmarting the Enemy

MRS HARDY and her sons lowered their eyes. They were sure Aunt Gertrude was about to announce that the kindly jeweller had died because of Marr's beating.

"Mr Bickford is—is—?" Frank asked.

"He wants to see you at the hospital," his aunt replied.

"Then he's alive!" Joe exclaimed.

"Of course he's alive," Aunt Gertrude said. "Very weak naturally, so I don't think you boys should stay long."

"When are we to go?" Frank asked.

"Mr Bickford got permission for you to come any time. He has something urgent to tell you."

Curious as to why they were being summoned, Frank and Joe left immediately to see the elderly man. Mr Bickford was partially propped up in bed. He looked ill, but he gave his visitors a warm smile.

"I'm so glad you came," he said in a voice barely above a whisper. "The doctor said a ten-minute visit so I'll get right down to business. Sit down, please. I feel it my duty to warn you boys."

"Warn us?" Frank asked. "About what?"

"That assistant who slugged me and his pals are determined to get you," Bickford answered. "Stokeley thought he was in the shop alone, but I came in the back door quietly. He was talking on the phone and seemed to be giving orders."

Mr Bickford stopped speaking and closed his eyes. He began to gasp a little. Frank jumped up and pressed a cup of ice water to the man's lips. Mr Bickford sipped it gratefully.

"Perhaps we should go," Frank suggested.

"No, no, not yet. This won't take long," Mr Bickford insisted, opening his eyes again. "I must tell you. Stokely was saying, 'Don't tell me you couldn't help your stupid mistakes. Just don't make any more! I want the Hardys on the whaler.'

"Just then Stokeley caught sight of me and hung up the phone. He turned livid, and before I could defend myself, he punched me, kicked, hit me with a stool, and acted like a crazy man. I blacked out and wakened up here." He closed his eyes and shuddered a little.

Frank and Joe stood up, sensing that Mr Bickford was exhausted and had told all he knew.

"Thanks a lot," Frank said. "Joe and I are certainly sorry we were the cause of the attack on you."

"And we'll profit from your warning, you can bet," Joe added. "Now take care of yourself."

When Frank and Joe reached home, they at once told their mother and aunt about Mr Bickford's report. "So you see, Aunt Gertrude," said Joe, "that man Chris wasn't calling you an old whaler. He was talking about trying to get us boys on their motor whaler."

"Hmm!" said Aunt Gertrude. "Well, just the same he has very bad manners. Doesn't know how to treat a lady."

Mrs Hardy was extremely concerned and said so. "I believe if Joe hadn't been rescued from that cave, those dreadful men would have put him aboard the whaler and taken him far away. Frank would have been next."

"Exactly," said Aunt Gertrude, "and I'm sure your father never intended you boys to become so deeply involved in this horrible case. I believe my brother would thank you, Laura, to forbid these boys from any further detective work against such men as Taffy Marr."

Frank and Joe were fearful their mother might take Aunt Gertrude's advice. After several moments of silence, Mrs Hardy answered. "Fenton expects his sons to follow through and see justice done. He doesn't want me to pamper them into being cowards. However," she added, "I expect them to be cautious and alert. Frank and Joe don't deliberately run into trouble."

The boys were relieved. Each kissed their mother and thanked her for her confidence. Now that the tension was over, Joe grinned and said, "Mother, we should have been born with extra eyes in the back of our heads, so that we could see in all directions."

"You could wear those special spectacles that reflect what's at the back of you," Aunt Gertrude suggested.

"But they don't work at night," Joe replied, "and that's when most of the sluggings take place."

The conversation was interrupted by the doorbell. Frank answered and was handed a special-delivery letter.

"It's for you, Mother. From Dad," he called.

Mrs Hardy opened the envelope quickly. Presently she said, "Good! Your father's coming home. That will solve a lot of problems."

She read further. "But not right away. He and Mr Wright have to testify against two men suspected of stealing the antique plane."

"Dad found it?" Joe burst out.

"Yes. Listen to this: 'I have good reason to believe the hijackers are part of the gang I've warned the boys about. I'm sure these men have pals who are watching me, tapping my phone, and intercepting radio messages, so I decided to use the mail. In an emergency you can contact me care of Elmer Hunt, president of the Oceanic Electronic Company, San Francisco.' " The rest of the note was for her personally.

Frank and Joe went upstairs and discussed their next move. Both agreed they should do everything possible to learn where the whaler was moored.

"I guess it wouldn't be too smart to use our *Sleuth* to hunt down the whaler," Frank remarked. "We'd be spotted in a moment. And anyway we haven't fixed the horn yet."

"I don't think it'd be good to take Tony's boat, either," Joe said. He was referring to their school friend Tony Prito.

"How about arranging with somebody who has a cabin cruiser to help us make a search?" Frank suggested.

Joe's eyes twinkled. "Pretty expensive. How about the tug that nearly rammed you in the fog. Was there a name on it?"

"I'm not sure, Joe. I was pretty busy getting out of the

way! But I think I saw the word *Annie* on the side."

The boys decided to go to the docks on their motor-cycles. These were easier to manœuvre and hide than their rented car.

Soon after they left, Frank and Joe noticed that a car with three men in it was following them. None of the passengers looked familiar.

"We'd better do something fast and shake off those men!" Frank advised.

"Guess we'll have to play *hare and hounds*," Joe observed. "What do you suggest?"

"Head for Biff Hooper's and pretend to be staying there," Frank answered. "We can sneak out of their back door before those men have a chance to go round to the garden."

Joe nodded. "And take a back street to the docks. Score one for us!"

They explained their plan to Mrs Hooper, who let them out of the kitchen door. Frank and Joe hurriedly crossed the back lawn, which was out of sight of the street. They jumped the hedge. Twenty minutes later the Hardys were in Harbour Master Crogan's office inquiring about a tugboat named *Annie*.

The man flipped open a large ledger and ran down a list. "I guess you mean the *Annie K*. She comes in here once in a while."

"Is she docked now?" Joe asked.

"I'll see." Crogan consulted a chart on the wall. "Yes, she is. Waiting for some kind of shipment that's been delayed."

Frank and Joe glanced at each other. There might be a chance of chartering the tug!

"Does the captain own the *Annie K*?" Frank inquired.

"Yes, and a real nice man he is too. Name's Captain Volper."

The Hardys got directions on where to find the tugboat, thanked Crogan, and left. Captain Volper was seated cross-legged on the deck of the *Annie K*, reading the morning paper. He was a ruddy-complexioned, slightly plump, good-natured man.

"Howdy, boys!" he greeted the brothers. "And what can I do for you?"

Frank made their request.

"So you want to take a cruise round the bay, up and down the coast, eh? Well, I guess I could do it." He laughed. "You fellows got some money with you?"

"Sure thing," Frank replied. "Can we cast off now?"

"Soon's I can get my crew out o' the coffee shop across the street."

He ambled off down the gangplank and was gone nearly fifteen minutes while the boys walked up and down impatiently. Then Volper returned with two sailors, whom he introduced as Hank and Marcy.

A few minutes later the old tugboat pulled away from the dock. The boys decided to stay in the cabin so as not to be seen by anyone going past in other boats.

"Captain Volper, did you ever notice a motor whaler around here?" Frank asked.

"Yes, about two weeks ago. Then I got caught in the fog and plumb near run somebody down." Frank and Joe glanced at each other.

"Does the whaler have a name on it?" Joe asked.

The captain tilted back his cap and scratched his

head. "Seems to me it did. That's harbour regulations, you know. Let me see now." Unable to recall the name he summoned Hank and Marcy and asked them.

"Sure I remember it," Marcy replied. "Man alive, I wish I could own one o' them plastic boats. They got speed. The name o' this one I seen anchored up near the caves was *Water Devil*."

"I'll bet it is, too," Joe commented, but did not explain the double meaning in his remark.

The tug went directly to the spot and the boys gazed at the sleek whaler, which was anchored in shallow water. No one seemed to be around.

"Ship ahoy!" Volper shouted. There was no answer.

"I'm going aboard," Frank announced. When the captain reminded him that the law dealt harshly with snoopers, the young detective said, "Did you know smugglers are operating in this territory?"

Volper and his crew were amazed.

"And you think this is their boat?" the captain asked.

"We suspect so," Frank replied. "We'd like to go aboard and hunt for clues."

The captain sighed. "Boys today are too smart for me. Go ahead."

He pulled up close to the whaler and the Hardys jumped down on to the deck of the *Water Devil*. At first they made a casual surveillance. Seeing nothing suspicious, the boys began opening lockers.

"This is the gang's boat all right," Joe sang out, holding up a piece of paper with red and blue stripes on it. A few figures had been scrawled on it.

"Say, Frank, do you suppose there are any diamonds or electronic equipment hidden aboard?"

"Let's look!"

Nothing came to light until they opened a dashboard compartment. A sack lay inside. Both boys reached for it at once. The next second they were hurled violently across the deck. They blacked out and toppled into the water.

·19·

Anchor Pete

On the deck of the *Annie K*, Captain Volper and his crewmen stood stunned by the sudden accident. But not for long. Instantly Hank and Marcy jumped into the water.

"I'll get this one," Hank called, indicating Joe as the boy's limp form bobbed to the surface.

Marcy set off with fast strokes to rescue Frank. In less than a minute the two Hardys were lying on the deck of the tugboat and being given first aid. They did not respond.

"We'd better get these boys to the hospital as soon as possible," Captain Volper said worriedly.

He set the ship's engines to maximum capacity and sent a radio message for an ambulance to meet him at the dock. By the time Frank and Joe regained consciousness, they were in a Bayport Hospital room and Dr Bates was there, as well as Mrs Hardy and Aunt Gertrude.

Relief spread across the watchers' faces as the boys managed wan smiles. "I guess we gave you all a good scare," Joe remarked. "Say, where are we?"

When the boys were told, Frank said, "Joe and I must have been *out* a long time. I remember we touched a sack in that whaler and then—wham! What happened to us?"

"You fellows got a bad electric shock," Dr Bates explained, "and were thrown into the water. If Captain Volper hadn't been there, you would have drowned. Hank and Marcy rescued you."

"Thank goodness," Mrs Hardy murmured.

"The person who rigged up that device got a shock of his own," Aunt Gertrude said crisply, "and I'm glad he did."

"He was caught?" Joe asked. "Who is he?"

"Your kidnapper—at least this is what the police think from your description of him," Aunt Gertrude said. "When you feel well enough, you're to go down to headquarters and identify this man you call Gross."

"How was he captured?" Joe asked impatiently.

The boys sat open-mouthed in astonishment as they listened. Captain Volper had notified the Coast Guard and the Harbour Police. Both had gone out at once to the spot where the *Water Devil* was moored. Nothing had been disturbed and the men were sure no one would show up until the launches moved away.

"The police decided to leave a couple of their skin divers to watch," Dr Bates told Frank and Joe. "Soon after the others had left, a rowing-boat came from shore. The man in it boarded the whaler. He looked worried at seeing the compartment open, but seemed relieved that the sack was still there. He clicked off a switch, then picked up the sack with no harm to himself. As he reboarded the rowing-boat with it, the man was overpowered by the two skin divers."

"What was in the sack?" Joe queried.

"Exactly what you might expect," Aunt Gertrude said. "Diamonds and valuable electronic equipment."

Mrs Hardy told her sons that both the *Water Devil* and the rowing-boat had been impounded by the authorities and were being examined for further clues since the prisoner would reveal nothing.

Joe wanted to go right down to headquarters and see the man, but Dr Bates forbade this.

"May I call Chief Collig?" Joe asked.

A phone was brought to the room and plugged in. Soon Joe was talking to the chief, who was amazed and delighted that the Hardys had recovered.

"I want to see the prisoner," Joe told him. "Dr Bates says I can't come down. Could you possibly bring him here?"

The others in the room gasped at the request, but Dr Bates nodded his approval after the chief had said, "If the doctor thinks it's okay." The physician left but Mrs Hardy and Aunt Gertrude remained.

Twenty minutes later the prisoner arrived with two officers, one of them with a tape recorder already turned on.

"He's Gross all right!" Joe burst out. "My kidnapper!"

The man was sullen. He murmured defiantly, "You can't prove a thing."

"Proof?" Joe scoffed. "I heard plenty in the cave. And somebody else besides me got a look at you when you were snooping in our car." He did not mention Iola's name.

When Gross made no answer, Aunt Gertrude cried out, "You ought to be horsewhipped! Jail's too good for people like you. Kidnapper, smuggler, and goodness knows what else!"

As she paused to take a deep breath, Frank spoke up. "Gross, you tried to starve my brother and you doped him."

The prisoner finally began to talk. "I—I had to do what I was told or risk being killed myself."

"You mean by Taffy Marr?" Frank shot at him.

Gross winced. "Yes. I shouldn't tell you, but it don't matter now. I got nothing to lose. Marr takes away every diamond and electronic gadget we steal and smuggle in and threatens us besides. I'm better off in jail."

One of the officers remarked, "Things will go a lot better for you if you tell everything. Where is Marr now?"

"I don't know. He was watching me from the shore with binoculars. When I got caught I'm sure he ducked into hiding. That's the way he does. When things get too hot, every man for himself. Then in one month we meet up again."

"What's the next place?" the officer asked.

"Portland, Maine."

"No plans until then?"

Several seconds passed before Gross answered. Finally he said, "Each man was ordered to get the Hardy boys one way or another. Maybe some of 'em will stay around here and try it."

"Oh, I hope not!" Mrs Hardy exclaimed.

Frank asked the prisoner, "Who do you think will get after us first? And where?"

Gross did not answer directly. "I don't want to see

you guys get hurt, but I can't help you. Chris might decide to stick around, or Anchor Pete."

"Anchor Pete?" Joe repeated.

"Yeah—he's a sailor and a smuggler. Used to pitch an anchor like you'd pitch horseshoes and he'd bet he could throw one farther'n anybody else. He could, too. You guys had better watch out."

Gross, who finally said his first name was John, had no record. Marr had saved him from being beaten up by a gang, so Gross had felt indebted to him. "But I was wrong. He made a no-good out o' me. And what do I get? Jail!"

The bitter prisoner was led away. A nurse came in with food for the boys and announced that as soon as they had eaten they were to go to sleep.

Mrs Hardy and Aunt Gertrude kissed Frank and Joe good night and left. As the boys ate, they discussed the latest developments in the case and how they should tackle them when they resumed their detective work.

"I have an idea," Frank said. "How about asking Chet and Biff and Jerry to shadow us while we let ourselves be seen around?"

Joe grinned. "Hoping to be attacked, you mean?"

"Right." Frank thought it doubtful that this would occur in daylight. "We'll reverse our schedule—sleep in the daytime and roam at night."

From his bed Joe shook hands with himself, indicating, "Agreed."

Three days went by before Dr Bates told the boys they were as good as new. "And stay that way!" he advised with a meaningful laugh.

Meanwhile, Frank and Joe had arranged with their friends to carry out the sleuthing programme.

"Okay," said Chet, "but I think your scheme is pretty risky. Taffy Marr may have shadows following his men and they could be behind the other fellows and me."

"We'll just have to take that chance," Biff had said.

The first night was spent along the waterfront where the Hardys were sure Anchor Pete would be stationed. Frank and Joe walked together at times, then would separate. They deliberately went into dark areas and deserted spots. No one bothered them and later their friends reported having seen nothing suspicious.

"Tomorrow night," said Frank as the group separated, "we'll try the high school and athletic grounds and football stadium."

Again the boys were not disturbed and so far as they could judge were not followed.

"What's next?" Biff asked.

Joe felt that perhaps Marr's gang had learned the Hardys' friends were helping them and suggested he and Frank try the sleuthing alone.

"Nothing doing," Chet spoke up.

It was decided that the third night would be spent in the heart of town and would last only until just before midnight. It rained, but once more Frank and Joe led the way through dark streets and up and down deserted alleys. Finally, at ten minutes to twelve, they heard Biff whistle, Jerry give the sound of a hoot owl, and Chet yap like a dog.

"Quitting time," Frank remarked.

"Yes," Joe said. "Three nights of walking and not

one thing happening. By this time Marr and the rest of his gang could be halfway round the world."

Frank sighed from weariness and disappointment. "Let's take a short cut across the square."

They headed for the small park which lay in the centre of Bayport. Various municipal buildings, including the town hall with its large illuminated clock, outlined the four sides.

Frank and Joe reached the square and took a diagonal path through it. The place seemed empty. Part way across, Joe suddenly said, "I just saw someone dodge behind that big tree ahead."

"We'd better wait," Frank answered.

The Hardys jumped at the back of a wide-trunked maple. When no one ventured towards them, the boys peered out, looking in opposite directions for a possible attacker. Seconds later there was a shuffling sound behind them.

"Look out!" a voice yelled.

Frank and Joe turned in time to see a masked sailor swinging a heavy anchor. He was about to crash it on Frank's head!

·20·

Captives' Hideout

THE sailor's diabolical move was accompanied by the midnight striking of the clock, shouts from all directions, and a prolonged war whoop that could come from no one but Chet Morton. As Frank and Joe dodged the anchor, footsteps pounded in their direction.

The boys grabbed the sailor and held him tightly. In a moment Chet, Biff, Jerry, and Mr Hardy rushed up.

"Dad!" his sons cried. "When did you get home?"

"I haven't been home yet," the detective answered. "Came from the airport and dropped off Mr Wright. As I rode past here, Chet hailed me."

Frank stared at the other boys and said, "I thought you'd gone."

"What do you take us for?" Chet asked. "Did you think we'd run out on you? We were planning to follow you to your house."

All this time the sailor was wriggling, trying to break away from his captors.

Joe looked at him hard. "Hold still, Anchor Pete." he ordered. "You'll stay right here until the police come for you."

"And his pal," Biff put in. "I kayoed him back by that tree."

The sailor's jaw dropped. "Ben?" he said unbelievingly. "And you know my name too?"

"Sure," Frank answered. "Your buddy Gross squealed."

Meanwhile, Mr Hardy had pulled his two-way short-wave set from a pocket and began talking to police headquarters. He told what had happened and asked that Keith and Mallett of the FBI be notified. The sergeant agreed and said he would send a squad car and four men to the park immediately.

While waiting, Frank and Joe asked the other boys to hold the captive sailor so that they could take a look at Biff's victim. When Joe beamed his flashlight on the man's face, he exclaimed, "This guy was in the cave with my kidnapper!"

The boys dragged the man back to where Anchor Pete was standing. The sight made the sailor blanch and the Hardys figured that maybe he was so frightened he might talk if quizzed.

"Pete, the game's up!" Frank said. "You can tell us about Taffy Marr now."

The sailor squinted his eyes and looked into space, as if trying to make up his mind what he should do. At last he said, "I'll talk. Marr's gone to make a pickup."

"Diamonds? Electronic parts?" Joe asked.

"Yeah."

"Where?"

"Along the bay. Maybe near the caves."

At that moment the police car arrived and the two prisoners were put inside. Before the driver pulled away, he said to the Hardys, "Sergeant asked me to give you a message. Keith and his assistant Mallet are already in town. They're at your house."

The Hardys said goodnight to Chet, Biff, and Jerry, thanking them for their fine work.

"Any time," the three responded.

On their way home Frank and Joe asked their father how he had learned about the gang. "I got a tip from a detective friend in Chicago, but he wasn't sure just which gang it was."

When the three reached home they found Mrs Hardy and Aunt Gertrude with the two FBI agents. They had already briefed the men on the latest developments in the case.

"Our night's work isn't finished," Frank spoke up. "We have a new lead to Taffy Marr."

"We'll go right after him," Keith said.

"As soon as we put on dry clothes and get raincoats," Mr Hardy said.

Within ten minutes the five were ready to leave the house. Mr Hardy drove his car. The gentle rain had now changed to a severe storm. Thunder boomed and vivid flashes of lightning streaked down from the black sky.

When the Hardys and the two agents reached the area of the caves, the detective parked and the searchers groped their way down the hillside.

"There's a narrow path between the cliffs just ahead," Frank told the others. "It leads directly down to the water."

He led the way to the path and started down it. The teeming rain made the footing treacherous. Occasionally a flash of lightning illuminated the entire hillside, forcing the sleuths to crouch low to avoid detection.

During one of the flashes, Joe pointed to the shore below. "I saw a man standing down there! He could be Marr!"

The searchers continued to stalk their way along the steep path. When they were a little more than halfway to the bottom, Mr Hardy signalled for his companions to stop.

"Keith, how about our sitting here for a while and seeing what that man is up to," Mr Hardy whispered. "This spot is a good vantage point, and there are enough bushes to provide cover."

"Good idea."

As they watched the shore below, the watchers suddenly saw a flashlight beam flicker on and off several times.

"Marr must be signalling to someone," Mallet said.

"What's that?" Keith snapped, pointing off into the distance.

There had been an answering gleam from far out in the bay. The light flashed once, twice, then out completely.

A few minutes later there was a flash of lightning that bathed the entire area in a blue-white glare. In that moment the boys and their companions caught a glimpse of a small rowing-boat making its way inshore across the choppy waters.

"Did you see that?" Frank cried. "Four men in that boat."

"Let's go down for a closer look," Joe suggested.

They descended cautiously, edging their way through

the bushes towards the spot where the man was standing. Through the storm they heard a faint shout. Again the suspect signalled with his flashlight. He was guiding the boat inland.

As it drew closer, the sleuths heard the rattle of oar-locks. They crept a bit nearer and, about forty feet away, they could clearly distinguish the waiting figure near the water's edge.

The gang-leader switched on his flashlight again. The rowing-boat was approaching. It rocked to and fro, its bow high in the water.

"That you, Marr?" someone called.

"Yes, but shut up!"

At last they were going to confront Marr!

"We can't risk letting those men get away," Keith muttered. "When the boat lands, we'll arrest them!"

The agents drew their pistols. With Mr Hardy they poised for action. The detective ordered his sons to step back.

The rowing-boat was now in shallow water. Two of the occupants leaped out and pushed the craft on to the beach.

"This is it!" Keith declared. "Let's go!"

He sprang from the bushes with Mallett and Mr Hardy.

"Put up your hands!" the agent shouted. "And don't make a move!"

There was a yell from the dim figures on the beach. One of the men was about to push the rowing-boat back into deep water when Mallet fired two shots over his head.

As the agents ran towards the suspects, Frank caught

sight of a man running off down the beach and he raced after him. Behind him he could hear shouts, another shot, then the sounds of a struggle.

The fleeing man plunged on into the darkness, but the young detective overtook him quickly. His quarry suddenly turned, crouched low, and as Frank came up he lashed out with his fists.

The boy dodged the blow, then grappled with the man. A clenched fist struck the young sleuth in the face and sent him sprawling.

Frank recovered instantly and scrambled to his feet. His opponent turned and fled. Again Frank overtook him and brought the man down with a flying tackle. In a tight clinch they rolled across the beach and into shallow water. Finally Frank managed to get in a blow that knocked his opponent unconscious. He dragged him out of the water.

Joe, meanwhile, had plunged knee-deep into the water and grabbed a man who was trying to haul the boat away from shore. They lashed out at each other. Joe was knocked down. He struggled to his feet, choking and gasping, and followed his tall, muscular opponent on to the beach. The man aimed a blow, but Joe side-stepped it, then rushed in and drove his fists into the other's body. The gangster grunted and doubled up with pain.

Joe noticed that Mallet was sprawled on the ground apparently unconscious and that Mr Hardy and Keith were still battling two men.

Joe suddenly realized that Taffy Marr had escaped and was now rowing off in a sheet of rain.

"Marr is getting away!" he shouted.

"What!" Keith yelled. "And we don't have a boat to go after him!" He fired a shot in the air, but the suspect did not halt.

Mallet recovered and got to his feet just as Frank arrived, shoving his prisoner ahead of him.

"Marr escaped in the rowing-boat!" Joe told his brother, and picked up the flashlight Marr had dropped. He directed its beam on the prisoners.

"I recognize three of these guys!" he exclaimed as Keith and Mallet handcuffed the men. "They visited Chris in the cave when I was there."

They were searched and bags of diamonds and small electronic equipment were removed from their pockets.

"Where'd you get these?" Mr Hardy asked.

"They're legit," one man said.

"We know you're smugglers," the detective said, "and we can trace these."

"Okay. They were dropped to us off a ship. In this storm I didn't see the name of it."

"Where's Marr going?" Frank asked one prisoner.

"You're not gettin' anything more out of us!"

"That's not being smart," Keith said. "After all, Marr left you behind to face the music. It might help you get off with lighter sentences if you co-operate." Silence.

"Why don't you tell us what you know?" Frank queried.

"I—I want to," the man stammered. "But I'm afraid of—of the boss."

"You mean Marr? Where is he?"

"I guess up on the north shore of Barmet Bay. Place

called Rocky Point. Marr had me rent an old shack there. He uses it as a hideout.''

"Where's Chris?" Joe questioned.

"Probably waiting for Marr."

Mr Hardy radioed Bayport Police Headquarters again and told them that they had captured more of the smugglers. The sergeant promised to notify the Harbour Police to pick them up.

"I hope they come soon," Joe said. "We must go after Marr before he skips."

The launch arrived in an incredibly short time and the prisoners were handed over. Then Frank said to the captain, "We may need you again soon. Up at Rocky Point."

"Let us know," the skipper said and chugged off.

The Hardys and the FBI agents climbed the cliff, then rode along Shore Road to Rocky Point. In this area the bluff was not as steep and the sleuths had no trouble descending it. They were just in time to see a man with a lantern meeting an arriving rowing-boat.

"That's Chris!" Frank whispered.

"And Marr," Joe added. "Let's rush 'em!"

"Not yet," Keith said. "I have a tape recorder in my pocket. We may find their conversation useful."

As Keith had hoped, the two smugglers talked freely.

"I guess we can now clear out of Bayport for good," Marr said. "Chris, when we get to Portland, you set up a whole new gang. Make friends with the crew of a new ship and pick out one like Beef Danion on the *Rizzolo*. Too bad we have to chuck him."

"But, Taffy," said Chris, "you goin' to leave here without getting Wright's secret radio? You said that if you used that, nobody could ever catch us. It would scramble messages among the gang and from ship to shore. And the dicks couldn't interfere, or a bad storm stop your orders from reaching us."

"I know," Marr answered, "but right now our skin's more important. Maybe I shouldn't have hung around after I slugged Bickford. But I needed tonight's haul."

"What about your stealin' Wright's antique plane?" Chris asked.

Marr gave a sardonic laugh. "It served its purpose—kept Mr Wright and Mr Hardy away from here. But those kids, Frank and Joe, are pests. All the Hardys are too clever."

The boys were smiling. Marr did not know that one of the secret radios was hidden in Wright's plane, and now it had been recovered!

By this time Marr and Chris had reached the one-room shack and went inside. Again the boys wanted to rush the place, but their father held them back.

"You watch through that window," he ordered.

Going off a little distance, the detective radioed the Harbour Police.

Then he and the FBI men got ready to burst open the unlocked door. Inside, the smugglers were busily packing suitcases. They had stopped talking.

At a signal Keith opened the door and dashed into the room with Mallett and Mr Hardy. Taken by surprise, Marr and Chris had no chance to put up any resistance and were handcuffed to await the Harbour Police. When Frank and Joe came in, they received looks of furious resentment from the prisoners.

Meanwhile, the smugglers' suitcases were examined.

Many secret pockets and a false bottom were found, each containing a fabulous quantity of jewels and electronic equipment.

Joe broke the silence. "Wowee, these smugglers could have retired rich!" he remarked.

Presently the police arrived and the two men were taken away. Keith and Mallett went with them. As the launch departed, Frank and Joe realized that another mystery had also departed. They were to experience a "lost" feeling until their next case, *The Sinister Signpost*, came along.

On the way home, the boys and their father filled in the gaps of the present mystery. "Mr Wright is very pleased with your work," said Mr Hardy, "but he's ready to sell his antique plane."

"We know who will buy it," Joe spoke up. "Cole Weber."

"What about the special radio, Dad?" Frank asked. "Surely there's more to it than what we know."

Mr Hardy chuckled. He did not answer directly and they guessed the secret was a highly classified one. Instead, he said, "Some day how would you boys like to own pocket radios that can pick up signals from outer space?"

"You mean that's what Mr Wright has done?" Joe cried out.

The detective gave his sons a broad wink.

The Sinister Signpost

The Sinister Signpost was first published in a single volume
in the U.S. in 1968 by Grosset & Dunlap, Inc.
First published in the U.K. in 1972 by
William Collins Sons & Co. Ltd.

Copyright © 1968 by Grosset & Dunlap, Inc.

·1·

Danger on Wheels

"Do you see what I see?" Joe Hardy asked his brother.

"It's a dragster," Frank replied. "They're not supposed to be driven on public roads. At least not in this state."

The Hardys were driving home from Taylorville along Shore Road in their open convertible. It was a sunny, summer afternoon. So far, they had encountered almost no traffic. Now Frank was gaining on the slow-moving, bright-orange racing car. In the driver's seat, situated aft of the car's massive rear wheels, sat a helmeted, black-jacketed figure.

"He's sure travelling at low speed," Joe remarked. "I wonder why."

Frank, dark-haired and eighteen, accelerated and attempted to pass the other vehicle. The driver of the dragster increased his own speed and prevented the convertible from going by.

"What's he trying to do? Cause an accident?" Joe said angrily.

Frank was forced to return to his position behind the dragster. As he did so, the driver again reduced speed to a snail's pace.

Blond-haired Joe, who was a year younger and

more impetuous than Frank, stood up and cupped his hands over his mouth. "Okay!" he shouted at the other driver. "You've had your fun! Now let us by!"

Frank made another attempt to pass. Suddenly the driver of the dragster manœuvred his vehicle in such a way that its left rear wheel slammed up against the right front wheel of the Hardys' car.

"We're out of control!" Joe yelled.

Their car swerved violently as a result of the impact. Frank struggled with the steering wheel and managed to regain control. He quickly came to a stop. The boys watched as the dragster sped down the road out of sight.

"I'd like to get my hands on that clown!" Joe said, fuming.

"So would I," Frank agreed. "But the dragster had no licence plates. We'd have a hard time trying to track down the car."

The boys inspected the damage to their convertible. The right front bumper was crumpled and the rim of the wheel badly bent.

"We'd better replace the wheel with our spare," Frank suggested.

The Hardys jacked up the car. While they worked, a large, open truck approached on the opposite side of the road. As it flashed by, Joe caught a glimpse of a bright-orange dragster in the rear of the vehicle.

"Look!" he exclaimed. "That must be the same racing car that rammed us!"

Frank jumped to his feet and peered in the direction his brother was pointing. By now the speeding truck had vanished round a bend in the road.

"Everything happened so fast," Joe said disappointedly, "I wasn't able to get the licence number of the truck."

"Too bad," Frank commented. "It'll be miles away by the time we finish putting on the spare."

When the job was completed, the boys continued their journey home. Mrs Hardy, a slim, graceful woman, greeted them when they arrived.

"I'm so glad you're back," she announced. "Your father wants to see you right away."

The boys sprinted up the stairs to their father's study on the second floor. Mr Hardy, a distinguished-looking, middle-aged man, was seated behind his desk.

"Hi, Dad!" Joe greeted him. "Mother said you wanted to see us."

"Hello, boys," he replied. "I just accepted a new case that I'd like to discuss with you two."

Frank and Joe glanced at each other excitedly. Then they took seats near Mr Hardy's desk. He sat quietly for a moment, studying a myriad of notes he had spread out in front of him.

Fenton Hardy was an extremely meticulous man. Formerly a member of the New York City Police Department, he now worked as a private detective. His exceptional skill in solving baffling crimes had made him famous. In fact, many of his methods were studied and adopted by law-enforcement agencies throughout the world. Frank and Joe had inherited their father's talent, and often assisted him with his cases.

"Yes," Mr Hardy said finally, as he glanced up from his notes. "I believe we're in for a challenging case."

"We?" Joe exclaimed. "Did you say—we?"

Their father smiled. Although in his mid-forties, he appeared much younger than his years. "That's right," he assured his sons. "I'm going to need your help."

"That's great!" Frank declared. "What kind of case is it?"

Mr Hardy leaned back in his chair. "Have you ever heard of the Alden Automotive Research and Development Company?"

"Yes," Joe answered quickly. "It's a firm just a few miles south of Clayton. I believe they experiment with high-speed cars."

"Correct," the detective replied. "The company makes components for regular stock cars as well. Also—"

"Isn't Keith Alden the president of the company?" Frank interrupted. "I remember reading about him in the newspapers. He was once a famous racing driver."

"That's right," Mr Hardy replied.

He went on to tell his sons Alden had designed an experimental turbine motor for his high-speed racing cars.

"The power plant is so revolutionary that the government has shown an interest in it. However," the detective continued, "despite his efforts to keep the motor a secret, Mr Alden suspects that someone has learned about it and is trying to steal the plans."

"Does he have any idea who the person is?" Joe asked.

"None," his father replied. "And here's something else. Two of his cars, in which the motor was installed, met with accidents of a very mysterious nature."

Mr Hardy stated that Alden wanted to put his motor and car designs to a real test by entering them in road race competitions. "It was during test runs that the vehicles were totally destroyed. The drivers barely escaped with their lives."

"What happened?" Joe asked.

"The windshields of the cars suddenly crazed," he said, "and cut off the drivers' forward vision. As a result, they went out of control and crashed."

"Windshields crazed?" Joe muttered.

"Yes," Mr Hardy answered. "They turned almost a milky white."

"But how could that happen?" Frank asked.

"We don't know," his father admitted. "At first, Alden thought the windshields might have been made of a faulty material. But after a laboratory test, that theory proved to be wrong."

"What's our assignment, Dad?" Joe questioned eagerly.

Mr Hardy rose from his chair and slowly paced the floor. "I'm going to run a check on all of Alden's employees," he said. "That's just a matter of getting hold of the personnel files at the plant. However, such information seldom reveals the whole story about a man. I'd like to place as many of the workers as possible under close observation, especially the men in the research department."

"And you want Joe and me for an undercover job!" Frank exclaimed.

Their father grinned. "You're way ahead of me," he replied. "But you're right. It's exactly what I have in mind."

"That means we'll have to act as employees ourselves," Frank said. "The problem is how can we do it without arousing suspicion?"

"I have an idea," his brother answered. "Bayport High introduced a basic automotive engineering course last term. Suppose we say we want to work at the plant to get some practical experience."

"That's it," Frank said. "And the timing is perfect, since our school vacations have just started."

"Sounds good," Mr Hardy agreed. "You'll have a chance to meet Mr Alden tomorrow. He's permitting an automobile club to use his private race track for a dragster and a stock-car competition. We're invited to be his guests."

"Great!" Joe exclaimed. "Would it be all right to ask Chet to come along?"

"I don't see why not," his father replied.

Chet Morton was a school chum of the Hardys. He was a plump, good-natured boy, who lived with his family on a farm near Bayport.

Just then Mrs Hardy announced that supper was ready. The boys and their father were about to leave the study when an object crashed through one of the windows. It landed in a corner of the room.

"Get down!" Frank yelled.

A split second later there was a muffled explosion!

·2·

Threats

INSTANTLY the room was filled with thick, boiling clouds of smoke.

"What happened?" Joe shouted.

"It must have been a bomb!" Frank cried out.

The Hardys held their breaths and groped their way through the choking smoke. There was no sign of fire. Frank, Joe, and their father soaked handkerchiefs with water, held them over their faces, then began flinging open all the windows on the second floor. Gradually the smoke cleared.

"Eek!" they heard a woman scream. The boys turned to see the tall, angular form of their Aunt Gertrude rushing up the stairs, followed closely by Mrs Hardy.

"Everything's all right!" Frank announced, in an effort to calm the women.

"Smoke!" Aunt Gertrude cried. "Call the fire department! Call the police! Do something!"

"No need to get excited," Mr Hardy said. "There's no fire. Please go back downstairs. We'll explain everything later."

The boys dashed from the house to look for the thrower of the smoke bomb. Not finding him, the young detectives searched in a widening circle. Presently Frank noticed a small, glittering object some distance away. He ran to the spot and picked it up.

"Take a look at this!" he called to his brother.

"Why—it's a rifle cartridge case," Joe said, as he examined Frank's discovery.

"Let's show it to Dad."

The boys returned to their father's study. Mr Hardy was examining fragments of the bomb. He held up a metal tube about a foot long. "This is all that's left of what I'm certain was a rifle grenade."

Frank's eyes widened with astonishment. "A rifle grenade?" he echoed.

"Yes," Mr Hardy replied. "The explosive section is attached to one end of this tube. The other end fits over the muzzle of a rifle. It's then fired from the weapon by means of a blank cartridge shell."

"A shell like this?" Frank said, handing his father the cartridge case he had picked up.

An expression of surprise spread across the older detective's face. "Exactly!" he declared, studying the small object. "Where did you find this?"

"Just a few yards beyond our own grounds," Frank said. "That explains why we saw no footprints on our property."

Mr Hardy handed his sons a fragment of paper. "This was tied to the shaft of the smoke grenade," he told them.

Frank and Joe were amazed to find that it was a handwritten message which read:

You are being watched. Drop the Alden case, or the next smoke will be lethal!

"Leaping lizards!" Joe exclaimed. "We haven't even started on the case yet, and already we're being threatened!"

"This is something we can't ignore," Mr Hardy said. "We'll have to be extra cautious. And as for your mother and aunt, I'm going to ask them to take a little trip. We can't risk leaving them alone in the house."

During supper the two women rebuked the boys' father for suggesting that they go away.

"Would a sea captain be the first to leave his sinking ship?" Aunt Gertrude exclaimed. "Not on your life! I, for one, will not budge from this house!"

Mr Hardy's sister, unmarried, had a peppery temperament. She was always quick to express her opinions openly, and often made dire predictions about the horrible fate awaiting all detectives.

"We know you're concerned for our safety," Mrs Hardy added in her soft-spoken voice. "But we will not leave here."

"Well—all right," her husband conceded reluctantly. "However, I'm going to call Chief Collig at head-quarters and request that a couple of guards be posted near the house day and night."

The next day, Saturday, Mr Hardy and the boys had an early breakfast. Then, after driving to the Morton farm to pick up Chet, they headed for Alden's private race track near Clayton.

"I can't wait to see the stock-car competitions," Chet said, as he peeled a large banana. "In fact, I've been thinking of getting into the sport myself. There's an old car in my father's barn I'm planning to fix up."

"Oh-oh," Joe remarked jokingly. "That's one hobby you had better stay away from."

"Don't worry," Frank added with a laugh. "Chet's car will end up as a diner on wheels, rather than a threat to the racing world."

"Cut the small talk," their friend retorted. "You two master minds are jealous because I'm the daredevil type. We're a species that eat more because we need tons of energy."

The Hardys and Chet arrived at the track in less than an hour. The area was a beehive of activity. Bright-coloured stock cars and dragsters gleamed in the sun as drivers prepared their vehicles for the day's competitions.

"You fellows enjoy yourselves looking at some of these cars," Mr Hardy said. "I'll locate Mr Alden and bring him back here."

"Okay, Dad."

The boys began to stroll around the area. Suddenly Joe grabbed his brother's arm and exclaimed, "There's the dragster that rammed us!"

"It sure looks like it," Frank agreed. "Same colour. But let's not jump to conclusions. We'll ask the driver some questions first."

The Hardys and Chet walked towards the dragster. A slim, sandy-haired young man was working on the engine of the car.

"Are you the owner of this dragster?" Frank queried.

"Yeah," the young man sneered. "What's it to you?"

"Now hold on!" Joe interjected. "No need to get hot about it. He just asked a simple question."

"Were you driving along Shore Road in Bayport yesterday?" Frank continued.

The drag-strip racer hesitated for a moment. "Why don't you guys take a walk?" he shot back finally. "Especially the fat one with you. He looks like he could use some exercise."

"Who do you think you're talking to?" Chet snapped.

"Just a second," Joe said. He ran his hand round the outer surface of the vehicle's left rear wheel. "The wall of this tyre is roughed up. It must have rubbed hard against something."

"Such as our car!" Frank stated.

"Get away from that wheel!" the young man growled.

He gave Joe a shove that sent the boy crashing to the ground. Like a flash Joe was up on his feet. He rushed at his attacker and pinned his opponent's arms behind his back in a jujitsu manœuvre.

"Let me go!" the young man cried.

At that moment Mr Hardy appeared with Keith Alden. He was a tall, slim man with patrician features. His dark hair was slightly grey at the temples.

Mr Alden looked troubled. "What's going on here?" he demanded.

"Are you boys having trouble?" Mr Hardy asked quickly.

The car manufacturer spoke to Joe in a displeased voice. "Why are you holding on to my son like that?"

"Your—your son?" Frank stammered.

Joe released his grip on the young man.

"Yes," Alden continued. "This is my son Roger."

Mr Hardy introduced his client to the boys. Except for Roger, everyone was mutually embarrassed.

"These guys," the young man shouted, "are trying to pin some sort of car accident on me!"

Alden eyed Roger suspiciously. "I don't think the Hardy boys would accuse anyone without good reason. If you were involved in an accident, it wouldn't be the first time."

Frank and Joe glanced at each other. It seemed wise not to force the issue. They told Mr Alden about their encounter with a dragster the previous day, but could not say for certain that the driver of the bright orange car was Roger.

"Then only my son can clear up this matter," Alden said. He put the question to Roger.

The young man became even more arrogant. "I didn't ram into anybody's car, and I never heard of Shore Road!"

His father was in a quandary. Finally he said, "Until this matter can be investigated further, I forbid you to drive your dragster in the competitions today."

"We'll see about that!" Roger muttered defiantly. He glared at the Hardys, then turned and walked off at a furious pace.

"I don't know what to do about my son," Alden said with remorse. "His mother died several years ago, and I haven't been able to spend much time with him. He's been getting more difficult to live with every day."

"I'm sure he'll straighten out," Mr Hardy remarked sympathetically.

"I hope so," Alden replied. Suddenly his mood changed. He turned to Frank and Joe. "Now down to business. Your father tells me you two are going to work with him on the case," he said.

"That's right," Frank replied.

"Excellent! I'm sure you have some questions of your own you'll want to ask me. However, I must fly to Washington immediately after the competitions. How about all of us meeting in my office on Monday morning?"

The Hardys nodded.

Alden looked at his wrist watch. "It is time for me to get to my post. I'm the official timekeeper for the stock-car runs. Perhaps you would like to join me out on the track."

"Would we!" the boys answered excitedly.

As they started to walk off, Frank bent down and picked up a small packet which had fallen from his brother's pocket during the scuffle. It was Joe's detective kit. Each of the Hardys carried one. Among the items that had spilled out was a magnifying glass and a metal signalling mirror. He handed the kit to Joe.

Suddenly a voice crackled from the loudspeaker of the P.A. system.

"The first trial run will be made by car number twenty-two. The driver is Roger Alden!"

"What!" exploded Alden. "How did he get his hands on a car? I must stop him! Roger doesn't have enough experience for closed-circuit racing!"

·3·

Prime Suspect

ALDEN rushed towards the starting line with the Hardys close at his heels.

"Stop that car!" he shouted.

But it was too late. Roger roared off.

"Flag that car down!" Alden ordered one of the track officials.

"I'll try to signal him with my mirror when he comes along the straight," Joe said.

Frank and Joe ran alongside the track opposite to the direction Roger was heading. They watched him as he skidded dangerously on the far turn.

"Did you see that?" Frank yelled.

"Yes. He took that curve too fast."

The boys hurried down the straight. As Roger came round the second far turn, his car spun out of control and crashed through the fence on the sideline. A huge geyser of dust erupted from the spot.

Frank and Joe rushed to the scene of the accident. An ambulance sped by them with its siren screaming. They arrived just as two white-coated men were helping Roger move away from the damaged vehicle.

"Is he hurt?" Joe asked quickly.

"No," one of the men replied. "He's lucky. I think

he just had the wind knocked out of him. But we'll take him to the hospital for an examination, anyway."

Shortly Roger's father and Mr Hardy came running up.

"Are you all right?" Alden asked his son nervously.

"I—I guess so," Roger gasped, still trying to catch his breath. Then he glared at the Hardys and pointed an accusing finger at them. "You guys are the cause of this!" he screamed. "You reflected sunlight into my eyes with that mirror of yours!"

"You're crazy!" Joe retorted.

A rangy young man appeared and gazed at the wrecked car in disbelief. "My car!" he groaned. "It's almost totally demolished!"

"Are you the owner?" Alden queried.

"Yes, I am."

"How is it my son was driving your racer?"

"Roger offered me a hundred bucks if I would let him make the trial run," the young man explained. "Now all I have is a pile of junk."

"Serves you right," Alden snapped, "but I'll pay for the damage."

Roger was helped into the ambulance and taken to the hospital. Although his father was greatly upset over the incident, he did not request that the competitions be discontinued. Instead, Alden told the participants to carry on. At the signal, engines began roaring to life. The Hardys and Chet watched the day's activities and were thrilled by the performance of the skilful drivers.

After dropping Chet off at the Morton farm, the three detectives headed home. When they arrived, Mrs Hardy announced that supper was ready to be served. As they ate, the boys discussed the day's events.

Aunt Gertrude looked at them scornfully. "Racing of any kind is just dreadful! It should be outlawed!"

"When properly organized," Frank put in, "it's a fine sport."

"I call it utter nonsense!" Aunt Gertrude retorted. She hurried out of the room before her nephews could argue the point.

The next day the boys rose late. After eating a hearty breakfast and attending church services, they settled down to read the voluminous Sunday newspapers. Shortly the telephone rang. Frank scooped up the receiver. The caller was Iola Morton, Chet's sister.

"Chet won't be able to see you later," she sobbed. "He's had an accident!"

Frank and Joe leaped into their convertible and drove to the Morton farm. They arrived to find the entire family standing on the front porch of the house. Chet was seated on the steps, exclaiming that he was all right. His face was blackened with soot.

"I don't need a doctor!" the chubby youth insisted.

"What happened?" Frank asked worriedly.

Mr Morton, a good-looking, normally jolly man turned to the Hardys. "Chet was experimenting with a highly volatile fuel on the engine of that old car I keep in the barn. He was pouring some into the carburettor when it suddenly blew up."

"It seems the racing bug has bitten him," said Iola, a slim, pretty girl. She was a witty, light-hearted person and was a school chum of the Hardys. Iola was Joe's favourite date.

"I was afraid something like this would happen,"

Frank remarked. "However, I didn't expect it so soon."

Mrs Morton, an attractive, dark-haired woman, hurried to meet Dr Mills, a Bayport physician, as he drove up to the house. He examined Chet, then left after saying that fortunately the boy had not been injured.

"You'd better call off your experiments," Joe advised his friend.

"I'll make sure he does," Mr Morton said. "I'm getting rid of that old car right away."

"But you can't!" Chet protested. "I'm on the threshold of producing the Morton super-duty racing car!"

Frank and Joe helped to convince him that such experiments should be left to the experts. Chet was crestfallen for a moment, than his face suddenly brightened.

"I'll drop the race-car project in favour of another idea," he said. "A rocket-propelled bicycle!" The Hardys shook their heads in despair and returned home.

Monday morning found Mr Hardy and his sons in Keith Alden's office. The company president was seated comfortably behind his desk, ready to discuss the case with them.

Frank was the first to speak. "Dad says that you suspect someone is trying to steal your experimental motor. Why?"

"My motor," Alden replied, "uses a valve of a very unusual design. In fact, we're not equipped here at the plant to make one. However, I learned of a company on the West Coast that specializes in valve manufacturing. They said they could do the job, so I gave them the green light."

He went on to say that one day Mr Dillon, president of the valve company, had telephoned him excitedly. A stranger, who refused to identify himself, had appeared with the specifications of a valve exactly like the one to be used in Alden's experimental motor.

Keith Alden rubbed the back of his neck. "Beats me how the fellow got hold of my design."

"What's the name of the company, sir?" Joe asked.

"Exeter Valve. It's a small outfit and luckily for me very reputable. Mr Dillon told the guy he'd like to study the specifications further before agreeing to handle the job. The stranger refused and left."

"Did you get a description of him?" Frank asked.

"Yes," Alden replied. "He was tall, wore black-rimmed glasses, and had a beard and moustache that looked phony."

"Obviously a disguise," Mr Hardy commented.

"I'm certain it was by sheer accident that the stranger went to the same company I was dealing with," Alden declared. "And I'm also sure that his valve sketch was a direct copy of my own design."

"Leaping lizards!" Joe interjected. "Maybe the stranger has the plans to your whole motor!"

"We doubt that," Mr Hardy said.

Alden grinned. "Your father is referring to the precautions I have taken to prevent the plans from being stolen."

"What kind of precautions?" Frank asked.

Alden explained that there were only two sets of plans in existence. "One set, the original, is safely hidden. The other set is recorded on film slides."

"The work is divided among the technicians here," the man continued. "No one worker knows what the other is doing. Each receives his assignment in the form of a slide, which is placed in a burglarproof projector. He displays it on a small screen and uses it for his job."

"Sounds foolproof," Joe commented.

"That's what I thought," Alden said. "Yet somehow specifications for my motor must be leaking out of the plant."

"So far," Mr Hardy told his sons, "only half of the slides have ever been seen by anyone other than Mr Alden. That's why we doubt that the entire design has fallen into the wrong hands."

The boys asked Alden if he had the slightest reason to suspect any of his workers.

"No," he replied. "And just to be sure, I had them all double-checked."

"What about ex-employees?" Joe suggested. "Have you had any trouble in the past?"

Alden rubbed his chin dubiously. "Come to think of it, I did. But that was several months ago."

He stated that Vilno Sigor, an engineer and designer, had worked in his research department. The man had created a number of small, but clever inventions which were used by the company.

"Then one day Vilno came to my office and accused me of picking his brain," Alden said. "I told him that was what I was paying him for, and reminded him of the generous bonuses he received for his ideas. Vilno wanted more. He demanded a partnership in my firm.

When I refused, he became furious and left. I haven't seen him since."

"Too bad," Frank muttered. "He might have been our man."

"Now take his twin brother Barto," Alden remarked. "He's still employed in my research department as a sheet-metal worker. An excellent craftsman. His job is to fabricate the bodies of our experimental racing cars."

"A twin brother?" Frank exclaimed. "That's a lead. Barto could be in cahoots with Vilno!"

Alden grinned. "You'd be wasting your time investigating him. He's the direct opposite of Vilno in engineering knowledge and in temperament. Even if he got a look at the plans of my motor, he'd never be able to understand them."

Despite Alden's opinion of Barto, the boys were determined to list the sheet-metal worker as a prime suspect.

The young detectives asked about the two experimental cars that had met with accidents after their windshields had been mysteriously crazed. Alden told them that each of the vehicles was powered by a prototype of his motor.

"But whether the accidents were the result of sabotage, I can't say," he added.

Mr Hardy spoke up. "Right now let's tackle this case one step at a time," he advised his sons. "We have to assume that somewhere in this plant there's a clever crook. He's managing to steal specifications of the experimental motor. Our first job is to find out who he is. And we'll have to find him fast!"

·4·

Fingerprint Hunt

"So you want to work in my plant as undercover agents," Alden said, when told about the boys' plan. "I like the idea."

"Thanks," Frank replied. "When do we start?"

"Tomorrow, if that's all right with you fellows," Alden said. He glanced at his wrist watch. "I see it's nearly lunchtime. Let's have some food."

After a delicious meal in the company's cafeteria, Alden conducted the Hardys on a tour of the plant. The boys watched with interest as various machinists turned out parts for the experimental motor. Each of the men worked from a plan projected on a small screen.

The last item on the tour was a visit to the research department. There Alden introduced the boys and their father to Barto Sigor.

"I am pleased to meet you," Barto said in a quiet voice. He was a short, stocky man with bushy eyebrows and dark, wavy hair. His steel-grey eyes were fixed on the young detectives.

"These two lads will be working here in the plant for a while," Alden told him. "They're taking an automotive engineering course at school and would like to get a little practical experience."

"Ah," Barto responded. "So you want to learn the automobile business. That's good. Do not hesitate to call on me if you have any questions."

"We won't," Joe answered.

Later, while driving home to Bayport, Frank and Joe discussed the case with their father.

Then Joe said, "What's your opinion of Barto, Frank? He seems pleasant enough."

"I agree he's a weak suspect, but—"

"You have something on your mind, son," Mr Hardy guessed. "What is it?"

"Mr Alden said that Barto would not understand the motor specifications even if he got a look at the plans," Frank replied. "However, since Vilno and Barto are twins, it's possible that they could have switched identities."

"There's only one flaw in your theory," Mr Hardy said. "Vilno is not a sheet-metal worker. How could he perform his brother's job at the plant?"

"I didn't think about that," Frank admitted. "Still, I'd like to check it out."

"There's one way of settling the question," the older detective suggested. "Try to get Barto's fingerprints. But do it without his knowledge. We don't want Barto, or anyone else in the plant, to suspect you're working on a case."

The boys retired early that night. The next morning they started for the Alden plant immediately after breakfast. Mr Hardy, who had been supplied with a microfilm report of all the employees' records, remained at home to check the information against his files on criminals.

The boys spent the morning watching the skilled machinists perform their various tasks. Finally they positioned themselves so that they could peer into the research department to observe Barto. The young detectives noticed that he wore a pair of thin rubber gloves constantly. Joe made a casual remark about this to another mechanic.

"Barto always keeps those gloves on," the man said. "He uses certain acids in his work. Also, he says the gloves give him a better grip on his tools."

Eager to discuss the situation, the young detectives retreated to a secluded corner of the plant.

"Those gloves of Barto's make it impossible to get his fingerprints," Joe commented.

"He'll have to take them off some time," Frank pointed out. "Maybe when he has his lunch."

At noon most of the workers went to the cafeteria. Barto, however, did not leave the shop. Instead, he walked to a clothes rack in one corner of the room and pulled a sandwich, wrapped in wax paper, from the pocket of his jacket. He then sat down on a bench, removed his gloves, and unwrapped the sandwich. The boys watched from a distance.

"We might get a good print from that wax paper," Joe whispered.

"Right," his brother agreed. "Let's see what he does with it."

After Barto finished eating, he crumpled up the wax paper, put his gloves back on, and strolled out of the shop through an exit door. The young detectives rushed to a window and peered outside. There they spotted the suspect walking towards a flaming incinerator. The man tossed the wax paper into it and returned to the shop.

"Well, that's that," Joe muttered disappointedly.

"We can't waste too much time trying to get Barto's prints," Frank said. "Let's follow him when he quits work for the day."

A few minutes before five o'clock the boys hurried to the car park to pick up their car. Then they posted themselves outside the main gate. Workers began to spill out of the plant.

"There's Barto!" Joe said.

The boys watched their suspect walk to a street corner and wait. Soon a bus came along and Barto climbed aboard. The boys followed the vehicle. Eventually the trail led them to the centre of Clayton. The bus stopped and Barto got off.

"We'll park the car and follow him on foot," Frank declared.

They shadowed their suspect in the best detective fashion. Barto bought a newspaper. Then he stopped at a refreshment stand and ordered a glass of orange juice. When he had finished and walked off, Joe rushed to the stand to seize the glass. But before he could do so, the stand attendant swept up the tumbler and plunged it into a sink filled with soapy water.

"Out of luck again," Joe grumbled.

Finally Barto led the boys to a small, red-brick apartment house off the main street and entered the building. Frank and Joe waited a few minutes, then dashed into the lobby. They quickly checked the mailboxes and found that Barto lived in apartment 6B.

"Well, there's nothing more we can do today."

Frank sighed. "We may as well go home. Maybe we'll come up with an idea before tomorrow."

After supper the young detectives joined their father in his study.

"Sorry to hear you haven't had any luck with your investigation today," Mr Hardy said. "Neither have I. So far, none of Alden's employees show up in my criminal files."

"Did you check on Barto and his brother?" Frank queried.

"Yes, I have."

Mr Hardy said that according to their records, the twins had been born in a small Midwest community. When they were still very young, their father had moved the family to Switzerland, where he accepted a job as an engineer. It was there that Vilno attended a university, and Barto had learned the sheet-metal trade.

"The twins returned to the United States several years ago and started a business called Inventions, Incorporated," Mr Hardy continued. "They didn't do very well and finally closed the shop. After that, it was a matter of job-hopping until they joined the Alden company."

"Hm! Not much to go on there," Frank muttered. "However, I still want to follow through on the finger-print angle."

"Maybe we could get into Barto's apartment!" Joe suggested.

"We'd need a court order to do that," his brother said. "At present we haven't any reason for justifying such a move."

Frank thought for a moment, then suddenly sat bolt upright in his chair. "Wait a minute! I have an idea!" he exclaimed. "Barto has to grab the doorknob to enter his apartment. I can hide in the hallway and wait until he comes home, then simply lift his prints from the knob."

"Say! That might work!" Joe agreed.

"Go to it, boys. But be careful," Mr Hardy warned.

The hours dragged by slowly during the boys' second day at the plant. At lunch they reviewed their plan. Frank would leave an hour before stopping time and take the bus to Clayton. Joe would drive their car and shadow Barto as they had done the previous day.

A few minutes before four o'clock, Frank hurried from the plant and caught the bus to Clayton. Within half an hour he was climbing the stairs to the sixth floor where Barto's apartment was located. He found 6B, then stepped out through the exit door at the far end of the hallway. The young detective inched the door open so he could watch for his suspect.

"I hope Barto doesn't come home late tonight," he thought.

While Frank waited, an elderly woman in work clothes appeared with a vacuum cleaner and a small trash disposal cart. She unlocked Barto's door and went inside. Shortly she reappeared with a wastebasket and dumped its contents into the cart. Then she went back into the apartment. The whirling sound of a vacuum cleaner could be heard.

"I wonder what was in the wastebasket," Frank mused. "Maybe I'll find a clue."

He dashed to the cart and found several pieces of

crumpled paper. Frank jammed them into his pocket and returned to his hiding place.

Eventually the cleaning woman emerged from the room, locked the door, and disappeared down the hallway with her paraphernalia. Frank ran to the door and wiped it clean so that Barto's prints would be the only ones present.

Half an hour passed. Then, from his hiding place, Frank spotted Barto walking down the hallway. The stocky man unlocked his door, twisted the knob, and went inside. When the door closed behind him, Frank sprang into action.

He dusted the knob with a fine, grey powder. Next, he took a strip of sticky tape from a celluloid container and carefully pressed it on the knob. A split second later he lifted off the tape, placed it back in the container, then rushed down the stairs and out of the building. He saw Joe in their car about a block away.

"Whew!" Frank said, out of breath. "I was afraid Barto was going to open his door any second."

"Mission accomplished?" his brother asked half-jokingly.

Frank held up the celluloid container. "Here are his fingerprints. Let's take them to Chief Collig and have him check them right away."

The boys drove directly to Bayport Police Headquarters. Chief Collig told them that he would send the data to the FBI by teletype and call the Hardys as soon as he received a reply.

Arriving home, the boys had a leisurely supper, then went to their crime lab located above the garage. There they examined the crumpled pieces of paper

Frank had found in the disposal cart. All of them proved to be discarded advertising circulars, except one blank page.

"This looks like the backing sheet for a typewritten letter," Joe observed, as he carefully flattened it out on a table.

"Then there must be word impressions on it," his brother replied. "Let's put it under the ultra-violet light."

The boys treated the blank sheet with a chemical solution and placed it under a special lamp. Gradually, words began to show up clearly. The letter read:

6/2

Dear Eric:

Forgive me for taking so long to write you, but I've been so exhausted from work the last few days that I didn't feel I could write a coherent sentence. How I wish I had the stamina of two hard-working boys who have taken summer jobs at the plant. Any family would be proud to have sons like that.

As I already told you, my brother has left the Alden company. It came as a surprise to me because I did not detect anything in his behaviour to lead me to believe he was dissatisfied with his job. I hope he manages to survive his own idiosyncracies. His reasons for leaving were extremely unreasonable, and I hope he eventually sees the error of his ways.

Because of my brother, I feel a bit embarrassed about continuing to work here. I'm sure they're expecting me to leave also. I must admit I have been investigating other possible jobs, but now I realize it would be foolish of me to quit.

Hoping that luck will not continue to evade us, I am

Your friend,
Barto

The Hardys wondered to whom the letter had been sent, and if it might contain a coded message. After close examination, they concluded that the letter was quite ordinary. They kept it on file, nevertheless.

Later Chief Collig telephoned the boys. "I just got a reply on those prints you wanted checked," he announced. "They belong to a Barto Sigor."

The news was shattering. The Hardys no longer had a prime suspect!

·5·

A Close Call

THE next day and a half at the plant proved disappointing for the boys. Despite their meticulous investigation, they failed to come up with a suspect.

"I'm ready to tackle this case from another angle," Frank said. "We may as well give up our undercover work here at the plant. Nothing more we can do."

"What do you have in mind?" Joe asked.

"Looking into the accidents involving Alden's experimental racing cars."

"Do you think there's some connection between the accidents and the stealing of the motor specifications?"

Frank shrugged. "I don't know. Each of the cars was equipped with a prototype model of the motor. Yet why would anyone risk destroying the cars if that's what they were after?"

"Let's have a talk with Alden," Joe suggested.

In a little while the boys were seated in the president's office.

"So you want to investigate the accidents," Alden said. "That's okay with me."

"We'd like to have a talk with the drivers," Frank replied.

"You'll find them in the garage opposite the research department," Alden told the boys. "They're getting another of my cars ready for a road race competition that's coming up. Their names are Jim Markus and Speed Johnston."

Frank and Joe made their way towards a large, metal-covered building. Inside, a crew of mechanics was busy working on a bright red experimental racing car. Two wiry young men, in their mid-twenties, were watching the proceedings. They turned when the boys called out the names of the drivers.

"I'm Jim Markus," one of them said.

"And my name's Speed Johnston," announced the other, extending his hand in greeting. "What can we do for you?"

Frank and Joe questioned the drivers about their accidents. They told the Hardys that Alden had entered the experimental vehicles in the competitions in order to match their performance against other makes of cars. The explanation of the accidents were the same as Alden had given, except for a couple of interesting facts. First, each of the drivers had experienced a crazing of the windshield immediately after turning a sharp bend in the road. Shortly before it happened, each of them recalled seeing a sign marked DANGER.

"Would you show us on a map where the accidents took place?" Frank asked.

"Sure thing," Johnston replied.

He took out a road map and spread it on the floor. "Mine happened here," he said, jabbing a finger at the spot along a winding red line.

Markus stooped beside his companion. "And my accident took place right here," he added, marking the location with a pencil.

The boys thanked the drivers for their help, then left, taking the map with them.

"The road isn't far from here," Frank commented. "Joe, let's drive there and take a look around."

Half an hour later the Hardys were guiding their convertible along a narrow, winding road. They arrived at the sharply curved segment indicated by Johnston and stopped.

"This is the spot," Frank remarked. "But I don't see a sign marked DANGER."

The boys got out and walked along the shoulder of the road.

"Look!" Joe exclaimed, pointing down at the ground. "There's a little mound of dirt. Someone has filled in a small hole."

"You're right," his brother agreed. "That's where the sign must have been. But why was it taken away?"

Puzzled, the boys returned to their car and drove on to the spot where Markus had said he had his accident. It proved to be another sharply curved segment on the road. The Hardys again examined the shoulder and found a similar mound of dirt.

"Strange," Frank muttered. "I think we're on to something. The only problem is—what?"

It was getting late, so the boys decided to drive home. When they arrived, Mrs Hardy rushed out of the house to meet them.

"Something has happened to your Aunt Gertrude!" she cried out.

"Where is she?" Frank asked.

"In the living room!"

The boys quickly followed their mother inside. There they found Aunt Gertrude slumped in a chair. Mrs Hardy had placed a wet towel on her forehead.

"What's wrong, Aunt Gertrude?" Frank asked.

Miss Hardy suddenly came to life. "The telegram I just received!" she moaned. "What a dreadful inheritance! Read it!"

The boys looked down and saw the telegram on the floor beside her chair. Joe picked it up and they read the message. Both tried hard not to laugh.

"So that's what this is all about," Frank said finally. "You've inherited a stable of race horses."

"A stable of retired race horses, you mean!" she exclaimed. "They're the worst kind. They've already fleeced the public!"

Mrs Hardy smiled. "I think it's wonderful," she commented. "You might get to like horses. They seem to grow on you in time."

"Laura! How can you say such a thing!" Aunt Gertrude rebuked her. She slumped back in her chair. "And to think that this was wished on me by an old friend I forgot even existed. She apparently has no heirs."

"Where is the stable located?" Joe queried.

"In Baltimore," his aunt replied. "Even that is too close for me."

"What do you plan to do with it?" Frank asked.

"Sell the place!" Aunt Gertrude shot back. "And the quicker the better!"

"Now calm down," Mrs Hardy urged. "Tomorrow we'll telephone the attorney handling the estate and see what this is all about."

Aunt Gertrude remained silent all through supper. Finally a teasing cry of "Giddap!" from Joe sent her storming out of the room.

The next morning the boys went straight to Alden's office. They told him about the signs the drivers had mentioned and of their own investigation.

"Sounds mysterious," Alden remarked. "But what harm could a sign do?"

"I can't answer that at the moment," Frank admitted. "But I've a hunch it has something to do with the accidents."

Alden eyed the boys with interest. "How do you plan to follow up your hunch?"

"The last time we talked," Frank recalled, "you said that another of your experimental cars was being got ready for a road race."

"That's right. In fact, the race is scheduled for tomorrow."

"Where is it to take place?" Frank asked.

"On a road not far from the one where the accidents happened. Why?" Alden asked.

"If you'll point out the road for us on a map," Frank explained, "Joe and I will travel the route shortly before the race starts. Maybe we'll spot one of those signs. At least it's worth a try."

Alden pulled a map from his desk drawer and indicated the road to be used for the competition. Then the boys returned home and discussed the plan with their father.

"You might be on to something," Mr Hardy said. "I'll drive the route with you."

"Thanks, Dad," Frank replied. "But we weren't going to use the car."

"You're not planning to walk all the way?" the detective asked with a look of astonishment. "The race will be over a course of several miles."

"We discussed it on the way home, Dad," Joe put in. "We plan to use our old bicycles. They're still stored in the garage."

Mr Hardy leaned back in his chair and grinned. "I get it. Bicycles are noiseless. And if there is anything behind this sign theory of yours, you won't scare off whoever's setting them up."

"Exactly," Frank replied.

Before retiring for the night, the boys went to the garage and inspected their bicycles.

"The tyres have to be inflated, and a few drops of oil are needed here and there," Joe observed. "Otherwise, they're in good shape."

It took only a few minutes to do the job, then they rode their bicycles once around the block for a quick test run.

"Let's load the bikes in our car," Frank suggested, "so we'll be all set to go first thing in the morning."

Frank and Joe got an early start. Mr Hardy accompanied them to the starting line. There were about twenty stock cars lined up for the race. Each was painted in a different colour scheme. Drivers and mechanics were milling around, waiting for the contest to begin. Alden was there and greeted the Hardys.

"How much time do we have before the race gets under way?" Frank asked him.

"About thirty minutes. My car will be the first one off. Johnston is the driver."

"Then we'd better get going right away," Frank declared.

"Be careful," Mr Hardy urged.

The young detectives lifted their bicycles from the boot, then pedalled down the road.

After they had covered most of the route, Joe sighed. "I'd forgotten how slow bicycling can be."

"Keep going," his brother said. "The race will be starting any second now, and it won't take the cars long to travel this far. We should cover as much of the route as we can before they do."

As the boys continued, they noticed that the road was becoming treacherous for racing. It was flanked on one side by a rocky wall, and on the other by a sloping embankment with a drop of nearly a hundred feet.

Eventually Frank and Joe came to a sharp bend in the road. As they rounded it, Frank suddenly locked his brakes. Joe did the same. Just ahead was a large sign marked DANGER!

"Leaping lizards!" Joe declared in a hushed voice.

"That sign is exactly like the ones Johnston and Markus described to us," Frank observed. "Let's take a look at it."

"Maybe we're being watched."

"That's a chance we'll have to take."

The boys laid their bicycles on the embankment and began walking towards the sign. When they reached it, they stopped and gazed at its face.

"What do you make of it?" Joe queried.

"Seems quite ordinary, except for one thing," Frank answered. "It's much thicker than most signs."

At that instant the young detectives heard a faint, whirring noise.

"What's that?" Joe said.

Frank listened. "I'd say it's a generator of some kind," he concluded.

"It's coming from a spot a little farther down the road."

The boys began to inch their way towards the source of the sound. Suddenly the roar of a motor became distinct. Each second it grew louder.

"The first of the racing cars is coming!" Joe gasped.

The Hardys turned just in time to see Alden's entry tearing around the sharp curve in the road. Suddenly it began to swerve out of control. The vehicle bounced into the air and hurtled directly towards the boys!

·6·

Final Warning

THE racing car plunged towards Frank and Joe like some horrible monster eager to crush its prey. In a desperate move the boys leaped down the embankment and went tumbling head over heels to the bottom. They lay stunned. The next thing they knew, Mr Hardy and Alden were leaning over them.

"Are you all right?" their father asked anxiously.

"I'm—I'm okay," Frank assured him.

"Me too," Joe added, rubbing his head gingerly.

"One of the other drivers saw that there had been an accident and reported it," Alden said. "We got here just as fast as we could."

Frank sprang to his feet. "Your driver, Johnston! How is he?"

"Fine, except for a few bruises," Alden replied. He grinned. "I build very strong cars. My drivers are well protected."

The boys told the two men what they had seen.

"And you say there was a signpost marked DANGER?" Mr Hardy asked curiously. "Where?"

Frank pointed towards the top of the embankment. "The one right—" His words trailed off.

"Why—it's gone!" Joe exclaimed.

The boys led the way up the embankment. Then

they slowly walked along the shoulder of the road. In a minute they discovered a small hole that had been hastily filled in.

"Here's the place," Frank said. "This is where we saw the sign."

"I'd call it a sinister signpost," Mr Hardy remarked, rubbing his chin dubiously. "It's here one minute, and gone the next. Obviously someone has carried it off."

Joe casually thrust his hands into the pockets of his jacket. A moment later his face showed surprise and he pulled a piece of paper from one of his pockets. On it was a printed message:

THIS IS A FINAL WARNING!
HANDS OFF THE ALDEN CASE!

"This must have been put in my pocket while we were lying at the bottom of the embankment," Joe said.

"We can be sure of one thing," Frank added. "Whoever's after Mr Alden's experimental motor is also responsible for the accidents."

A car roared up and screeched to a halt. Its driver, one of Alden's racing car mechanics, leaped out.

"Mr Alden!" he shouted excitedly. "We just received a call from one of your watchmen at the plant. The research department is on fire!"

"We'll drive you there," Mr Hardy offered. "There might be a connection with the accident here."

He and his sons hopped into the boys' convertible with Alden. By the time they arrived at the plant, the flames were completely extinguished. Firemen began to rummage through a charred area that once was Alden's research shop.

"This is a terrible blow to my experimental project," he muttered.

The Hardys expressed their regret, then went to talk with the fire chief.

"I can't say what caused the fire," the chief told them. "We'll have to conduct an investigation first."

"Approximately when did it start?" Frank asked.

"We got the alarm about an hour ago."

"I'd appreciate knowing the results of your investigation," Mr Hardy said as he presented his credentials to the fire chief.

The man recognized the name immediately. "It sure is a pleasure to meet you, sir. And these two boys must be your sons, Frank and Joe. My name's Fred Evans." There was an exchange of handshakes. "You can count on me," the fire chief continued. "I'll let you know if we uncover anything."

The Hardys thanked him, then rejoined Alden, who was picking his way through the rubble of his burned shop.

"There's nothing left to salvage," he said dejectedly. "However, I'll set up a temporary research shop in one of the other buildings."

The Hardys expressed their regrets at Alden's loss and returned home. Aunt Gertrude was still greatly upset over her inheritance of a stable filled with retired race horses.

"Fenton!" she exclaimed. "You promised to call the attorney who's handling the estate, and you never did. Please do it right away. I can't rest thinking about that awful place."

Mr Hardy went to telephone, while the boys had a

snack of sandwiches and milk in the kitchen. A few minutes later their father hurried into the room.

"I still have the attorney on the line," Mr Hardy said. "He'd like us to take a look at the stables. However, I have too much work to clean up here, and I'm sure your aunt won't go. So why don't you two boys hop down to Maryland?"

"Sure thing, Dad," Frank replied.

Mr Hardy completed his call, then gave Frank and Joe their instructions.

"You can catch an early train to Baltimore in the morning," the detective explained. "The attorney will meet you at the station there. He'll be waiting in front of the information desk. His name is Steve Benson."

Frank and Joe left Bayport aboard the seven o'clock train. It was nearly noon when they arrived in Baltimore. The boys went directly to the information desk and noticed a tall, even-featured man standing nearby. He appeared to be in his late fifties, and was impeccably dressed.

"Mr Benson?" Frank queried.

"Yes," the man answered. "And you must be the Hardys. I've heard a lot about you and your father." He extended his hand in greeting. "My car is just outside. The stable isn't far from here."

The boys enjoyed the drive through the lush, green countryside. During the journey, the attorney discussed Aunt Gertrude's situation.

"Your father says that she wants to sell the stable as soon as possible," Benson remarked. "We shouldn't have any trouble doing that. In fact, Norman Fowler, the temporary manager out there, would like to buy the place. Unfortunately he doesn't have the money right now."

Nearly an hour passed before Benson guided his car through an arched gateway. Spread across the arch, in gold letters, was the name:

SOUTHERN PINES STABLES

"All told, there are about twenty acres here," the attorney announced. "It's not very big, but it's adequate for the purpose."

Ahead, the boys saw a small house and two other wooden structures. All were painted white and appeared to be in excellent condition. The largest of the buildings contained the stalls for the horses. To the left was a large grassy area surrounded by a wooden fence. About a dozen fine-looking horses were lazily grazing there.

Benson brought the car to a stop near the house and got out. The young detectives followed. Standing on the porch was a bulky, deeply tanned man whom the attorney introduced to the boys as Norman Fowler.

"The Hardys have come to take a look round," Benson told him.

"Glad to be of service," Fowler said cordially. "As you probably know, all the horses here have seen the last of their racing days. The owners want to provide a comfortable retirement for them. That's our job."

The manager invited his guests into the house to lunch, then took them on a tour of the stables. As the day drew to a close, Fowler suggested that the boys remain overnight and return to Bayport in the morning.

"All my stable hands are away for the evening at a

local affair," he said, "and the bunkhouse is empty. You can sleep there."

Benson announced that he had to leave, but promised to return in the morning to drive the Hardys to the railroad station. After a quick supper prepared by Fowler, Frank and Joe went to the bunkhouse. At ten o'clock they retired for the night. Little more than an hour had passed when the boys were awakened by the muffled sound of men talking.

"That's odd," Frank whispered. "I thought all of Fowler's stable hands were away for the evening."

The boys dressed and crept out of the bunkhouse towards the source of the voices.

"We want fifty per cent of the take," they heard one man say.

Joe accidentally stepped on a twig, which snapped with a cracking noise. The boys froze in their tracks and listened. There was only silence.

"Let's move ahead and try to get a glimpse of the men," Frank hissed.

The young detectives cautiously edged their way through the darkness. They saw no one. Then suddenly a voice boomed out from behind them.

"Stay where you are!"

The boys turned to find themselves peering into the muzzle of a rifle.

"Who are you?" Joe demanded.

The armed man directed the beam of a flashlight into the faces of the Hardys.

"Oh, it's you boys," he said. "I thought you were asleep." The man flicked the beam of light on to his own face.

"Mr Fowler!" Frank exclaimed.

"We heard some men talking out here," Joe explained, "and came to investigate."

"Did you see them?" the manager questioned.

"No," Frank replied. "We never got close enough."

"Well, I heard them too," Fowler said. "But I'm sure they were workers from the farm just across the way. They often use our area as a short cut when they walk back from town." He then said good night and went into the house.

Frank and Joe rose early the next morning. They had just finished breakfast when Benson arrived to take them to the railroad station. The boys thanked Fowler for his hospitality, then hurried off to the train. During the drive, the attorney explained some of the legal points involved in their aunt's intended sale, and handed them some documents that she was to examine.

When they arrived in Bayport, the boys wasted no time in telling Aunt Gertrude and their parents what they had seen.

"It's too bad you want to sell the stable," Joe said. "The place is beautiful."

"Say no more!" their aunt retorted. "Just give me the documents the lawyer wants me to read, so that I can get it over with!"

"Once your aunt makes up her mind," Mr Hardy commented, "there's no changing it."

The following morning Alden telephoned Mr Hardy. "Come to the Clayton Police Station right away," he requested. "There's a thief down here who's been stealing information on my experimental motor!"

·7·

The Elusive Stranger

MR HARDY and the boys drove to Clayton immediately. Alden met them at the police station.

"Where is the suspect?" Mr Hardy asked him.

"Detective Lieutenant Swaze is questioning him in the interrogation room," Alden answered. "He said we were to join him the minute you arrived."

Inside, a thin, untidily dressed man was seated in a chair. Lieutenant Swaze, lanky and middle-aged, was pacing the floor in front of him. Alden introduced the detective to the Hardys.

"This man is charged with burglary," Swaze announced. "He was caught rifling Mr Alden's office safe by one of the watchmen at the plant."

"When the police searched him," Alden interrupted, "they found several hollow-core impeller blades for my experimental motor in his pocket. I always keep a supply of them in the safe until an engine is ready for assembly."

Mr Hardy turned to the suspect. "Whom are you working for?" he demanded.

"I ain't workin' for nobody!" the prisoner shouted. "And I don't know nothin' about any experimental motor!"

"Then why did you take the impeller blades?" Frank asked quickly.

"Them things were made out o' shiny metal," the man replied nervously. "I thought it might be silver and I could get some money for 'em."

The interrogation continued for another two hours. The prisoner stuck to his story. Finally the boys and their father left the room with Alden.

"I'm convinced the suspect is telling the truth," Mr Hardy concluded. "He's obviously just a small-time crook who would steal anything."

"Then you don't think he's part of a gang trying to get the plans for my motor?" Alden queried.

"At this point, no," the detective said. "But let's see what the police come up with when they check his record."

Alden glanced at his watch and announced that he would have to return to the plant. The Hardys walked to their car and started back to Bayport, disappointed that nothing had come of their trip.

While driving through the centre of Clayton, Joe suddenly pointed towards two men standing at a street corner. "Look!" he exclaimed. "There's Barto talking to someone!"

"I wonder why he's not at work," Frank remarked.

"Maybe he has the day off," Joe answered.

The boys noticed that Barto's companion had the collar of his jacket turned up high, and his hat pulled low over his eyes.

"That guy he's with sure looks suspicious," Joe commented.

Frank stopped the car at the next corner. "I'll walk

past Barto and try to get a glimpse of the other man's face," he said. "The sidewalk is crowded with pedestrians. Chances are he won't spot me."

Frank made his way towards the two men. When he was within a few feet of them, Barto suddenly gave his companion a hard shove. The man turned and ran down the street. Frank, figuring this was strange, raced off in pursuit.

"Did you see that?" Joe said to his father.

"Yes! Come on! Frank might need our help!"

They leaped out of the car and joined in the chase. Mr Hardy stopped long enough to fire a question at Barto.

"Who was that man you were talking to?"

Barto appeared surprised. "I—I don't know," he stammered. "He was looking for a handout. When I refused, he insulted me and I gave him a shove."

Mr Hardy hurried on and found his sons standing at the entrance of an office building.

"He ran in here," Frank told his father.

"Let's go after him!" Joe urged.

"I'll stay outside," Mr Hardy said. "In case he gives you the slip, I'll go after him."

The boys ran into the building and discovered that the elevator was out of order. They bounded up the stairs. High above them, the two sleuths heard heavy footsteps.

"He must be heading for the roof!" Joe whispered.

Continuing the chase, the boys soon reached the roof. Their quarry was not in sight, but they heard what sounded like a metal door being slammed shut.

"It came from over there!" Joe said, pointing to the roof of an adjacent building.

The boys leaped across the narrow gap separating the two structures, and found a door leading inside. Pulling it open, Frank and Joe rushed down the stairs to the ground floor. Their father met them as they dashed outside.

"Your man came running out of this building," Mr Hardy said. "I was too far away to stop him. By the time I realized what had happened, he disappeared in the crowd."

"Too bad," said Frank.

As the Hardys drove home, the detective told his sons what Barto had said.

"Do you believe him?" Frank asked.

"We have no choice but to take his word for it," Mr Hardy replied. "Yet Barto doesn't strike me as the type that goes shoving people around."

"And why would a man just asking for a handout run off like a fugitive?" Joe interjected.

"There's something fishy about this," Frank added.

The Hardys had just finished supper when the telephone rang. Frank answered.

"This is Mr Alden," the caller said. "I have one more completed racing car fitted with my experimental engine. Luckily it was in the garage when the research shop burned down. I plan to give it a test run tomorrow."

"Another competition?" Frank asked.

"No, this will be a private test. I have permission from the highway department to use a straight stretch of road near the plant. I'd like you boys and your father to be present. I don't expect any trouble, but it pays to be safe."

"Wouldn't it be better to use the drag strip at your track?" Frank suggested. "You'd be less likely to find intruders there."

"The strip is too short for my purpose," Alden explained. "Shall we say ten o'clock tomorrow morning?"

"We'll be there," Frank assured him.

The next day the boys and their father drove to the test site. Alden's experimental racing car was unpainted, and its highly polished metal surface gleamed in the sun. Mechanics were giving the vehicle a final inspection.

"We'll be ready to start in about twenty minutes," Alden told the boys. "I intend to drive the first couple of runs myself. They will be acceleration tests."

He said that the car was a two-seater designed to carry a mechanic in addition to the driver.

"Since I won't be taking a mechanic with me," Alden said, "how would one of you boys like to go along?"

He suggested that the boys draw straws to decide which one would accompany him. They did, and Frank won.

"That's settled," Alden remarked, then added, "Joe, would you mind helping us with the tests?"

"How?"

"Normally, there's not any traffic using this road," Alden replied. "But we can't be sure. So I'd like to post a man with a walkie-talkie at the far end of the stretch to warn me if anything comes along. I have a radio receiver in the car for that purpose."

"I'm your man," Joe assured him.

He could not help but feel a bit envious of his brother as he watched Frank climb into the sleek car with Alden. Mr Hardy drove Joe to his post a couple of miles down the road, which at that point was flanked by heavy woods.

As the detective drove off, Joe heard a voice crackle from the speaker of his walkie-talkie. "All clear ahead?"

"All clear!"

Minutes later, Joe could detect the sound of Alden's car approaching. Then he spotted it far down the road. It was a shining speck of silver that grew larger and larger each second.

As Joe watched, he was startled to see a battered car emerge from the woods.

"Stop!" Joe cried frantically. "Mr Alden, stop!"

·8·

Stolen!

THE dilapidated car turned on to the road, picked up speed, and headed directly for Alden's car. Joe raced after it, calling out into the walkie-talkie.

His pleas went unheeded. Joe was horror-stricken at the small gap between the two vehicles. A head-on collision seemed inevitable.

"Frank! Mr Alden!" Joe screamed. "Watch out!"

Suddenly the mystery car swerved out of control. It went hurtling off the road and tumbled over into a ditch. A split second later the vehicle was a mass of flames.

Alden brought his racer to a screeching halt. He and Frank leaped out and followed Joe towards the disabled vehicle. They managed to get close enough to pull open one of its doors. The three were amazed to find that there was no one inside.

"Get back!" Alden shouted. "The tank may explode any second."

His warning came just in time. As Alden and the boys got clear, there was an explosion. A large ball of orange flame rose above the burning car. It was quickly transformed into a thick cloud of black smoke.

Minutes later a pickup truck arrived on the scene,

carrying a crew of Alden's mechanics. Mr Hardy was with them. The men scrambled out with fire exting-uishers, and directed streams of chemical foam at the burning car. Soon the flames and smoke disappeared.

"You gave us a bad scare," Mr Hardy said, turning to Frank and Alden. "We saw the smoke and came running. We thought you'd had an accident with the car."

"They almost did," Joe said shakily. He told his father what had happened.

When the car cooled sufficiently to be touched, the Hardys examined it. The heat had turned the vehicle into a charred mass of twisted metal.

Frank, looking underneath, made a startling dis-covery. To the underside was attached the remains of an elaborate radio-controlled system. Wires ran from it to the throttle and steering mechanism.

"So that's how the car was operated with no driver!" Joe exclaimed. "But why did it go haywire all of a sudden?"

Frank had an answer. "When Joe used the walkie-talkie to warn us, the signal must have interfered with the radio frequency used to guide the car."

Mr Hardy nodded. "Whoever operated the trans-mitter would have needed a clear view of the road, and at a point not too far away from this spot."

Frank looked towards a high hill, the top of which loomed above the treetops. "There's a perfect spot," he said, pointing to it.

The boys lost no time in climbing to the summit to investigate. The area was covered with thick brush and grass.

"These bushes would provide good cover for anyone watching the road," Frank stated.

"Look! Over here!" Joe cried out. "Some of the grass has been trampled flat. I'd say it was done recently by two or three men."

Frank examined the spot. "This is where the transmitter was set up," he concluded. "From here you get a perfect view of the road."

A further search revealed no other clues. The boys rejoined their father and Alden. Mr Hardy stated that he had given the mystery car a thorough going-over, but found nothing that would permit them to trace its owner.

"The vehicle wasn't carrying licence plates, and the serial numbers on the engine and chassis had been removed," he continued. "Also, the fact that it was burned to a crisp doesn't help either."

Alden decided to carry on with the tests. When he had finished, the Hardys offered to drive him to his office.

As they started off, Alden rested back in the seat. "After all the excitement we've been having lately, I need a little diversion," he said. "I think I'll spend Saturday giving my race horse a workout."

"Race horse?" Joe queried.

"Yes," Alden answered. "I'm interested in racing of all kinds. I bought the horse several months ago. Great animal! I keep him in a rented stable near the plant."

"Our aunt would tell you off quickly if she knew this," Frank remarked laughingly. He then told Alden about Gertrude Hardy's recent inheritance.

"A stable for retired race horses? Sounds like a great

idea," Alden said. "I'll keep it in mind. Perhaps some day I'll send my horse down there."

"Not if Aunt Gertrude has anything to say about it," Joe muttered with a grin. "Anyway, she will have sold her stable by that time."

Alden asked the Hardys if they would like to see his horse. The boys' father had to decline because of a business appointment, but Frank and Joe eagerly accepted the invitation.

"And would you mind if we bring our friend Chet?" Frank asked.

"Please do," Alden replied. "Drop by any time. I'll be at the stable most of the day."

Chet was not able to go until the afternoon because of Saturday chores to do. The Hardys picked him up at the Morton farm.

"A real race horse, eh?" Chet said with a grin. He pulled three apples from his pockets and offered one to each of his friends. "What I wouldn't give to own one!"

When they arrived at the stables, Alden was leading a beautiful, haltered thoroughbred around the paddock. His owner spotted the boys and led the animal towards them.

"How do you like him?" he called out. "His name is Topnotch."

"Nice piece of horseflesh," Chet commented, trying to act like a seasoned equestrian.

The horse was completely chestnut in colour, except for small white areas above its two front hoofs. The boys watched in admiration as Alden removed the halter and permitted Topnotch to trot freely round the paddock.

As Joe glanced towards a row of stalls nearby, he noticed a sandy-haired young man pitching hay into one of them.

"Mr Alden, isn't that your son Roger over there?" Joe asked.

"Yes," Alden replied in a determined voice. "I arranged to get him a job here so that he could help pay for the racing car he damaged. It's about time he developed a sense of responsibility. I'd have given him something to do at the plant, but he can't get along with the other workers."

Chet followed the Hardys to the stall.

"Hello, Roger," Frank said in a friendly voice.

The young man looked surprised. Then his eyes narrowed as he glared at the boys.

"Oh, it's you guys again!" he snapped. "You keep popping up like bad dreams."

"So you're still carrying a chip on your shoulder," Joe retorted.

"You bet I am," Roger shot back angrily. "I've got to work in this lousy place to pay for that stock-race car I had an accident in. You Hardys were the cause of it all!"

Frank kept his temper, but said, "Don't tell us you're sticking to that fairy tale of yours. You know we didn't reflect sunlight into your eyes while you were driving."

"It's my word against yours," Roger snarled. "But what chance do I stand? Because you're the Hardy boys you think you can get away with anything."

Joe's face flushed with anger. However, he managed to exercise self-control. "It's useless trying to talk sense into Roger," he said. "We'd better go."

As they walked away, Chet remarked, "That fellow is about as friendly as an enraged cobra."

Roger, who overheard the comment, gave Chet a black look. He picked up a large mass of hay with his pitchfork and flung it on top of the chubby youth.

Chet scrambled from underneath the pile. He quickly brushed strands of hay from his eyes, ears, and hair. Then, angry, he grabbed a feed bag nearby and pulled it over Roger's head, down to his elbows. The imprisoned boy stumbled around the stall in a frenzy.

"I'll get you for this!" Roger yelled after his tormentor, when he finally pulled the bag free.

The Hardys and their chum strolled back to the paddock. Mr Alden had been too preoccupied with Topnotch to notice what had happened.

"Let's not say anything to him about Roger," Frank suggested.

The boys spent the rest of the afternoon watching Alden exercise his horse, or taking turns riding the mount themselves.

"He's super," Chet remarked. "Sure beats our farm horses."

At sundown the boys thanked the owner and left.

Frank and Joe spent a relaxing Sunday at home and retired early. The family had been asleep only a short time when the telephone rang. Frank got up and rushed to answer it. His father had already picked up the extension by his bed.

"This is Alden," an excited voice was saying. "Sorry to disturb you. But something terrible has happened and I need your help. I'm at the stable. Topnotch has been stolen!"

·9·

Demand for Ransom

FRANK wakened his brother to tell him about Topnotch. The boys and their father dressed quickly, rushed to their car, and headed for the stable.

"This sounds to me like some of Roger's work," Joe suggested.

"Possibly," Frank agreed. "He's pretty mad at his father. Roger could have done it for spite. But stealing a horse is not easy. He'd need help."

"My advice is to wait until we get the facts before coming to any conclusions," Mr Hardy interjected. "I realize Roger would never win a popularity contest. Yet it's hard to believe he'd be mean enough to do a thing like this."

They arrived at the stable to find Alden still greatly distraught over the theft of his horse.

"The police were here to investigate," he told the Hardys. "They left a few minutes ago."

"What did they come up with?" Joe asked.

"Nothing," Alden replied disappointedly. "The thieves were careful not to leave a shred of evidence behind. Even the foot and hoofprints leading from Topnotch's stall were swept away."

"But they must have used some kind of vehicle to carry the horse off," Frank said. "Did the police find any tyre tracks in the area?"

Alden nodded and asked the Hardys to follow him. After walking a short distance, he directed the beam of his flashlight towards the ground and pointed to a set of deep, parallel ruts pressed into the soft earth.

"They must have been made by a truck or a horse van," Joe said.

Mr Hardy stooped down and examined the ruts carefully. "Obviously the thieves covered the wheels with canvas or other heavy material," he concluded. "There aren't any tread marks. Too bad."

"Were there any witnesses to the crime?" Frank queried.

"Only one of the grooms," Alden answered. "But he can't help us. He lives in a room above the stable. When he heard a strange noise in one of the stalls, he came down to investigate and was struck from behind. The police took him to the hospital."

"Has the groom been able to tell when the theft took place?" Mr Hardy questioned.

"Yes. He regained consciousness. The theft was about five hours ago. The groom had been tied and gagged. It took him over four hours to work himself free after he regained consciousness."

Joe let out a whistle. "Five hours!" he exclaimed. "The truck could be hundreds of miles away by now."

The Hardys did not want to upset Alden any further by asking him about Roger's whereabouts that evening. Instead, they discussed the case from another angle.

"We don't know if this was an inside job or not,"

Mr Hardy remarked. "But we can be reasonably sure what the motive is. Ransom!"

"In that case, the thieves will try to contact me," Alden said. "If they do it by telephone, they'll call my office, since I have an unlisted number at home."

"I suggest we go there right away and wait," Frank put in. "The horse thieves may start to call early."

Alden accompanied the Hardys in their car. During the drive, Mr Hardy outlined a basic plan.

"If you should receive a call demanding ransom," he advised the horse's owner, "stall him off. Tell him you want proof that they actually have Topnotch. That'll give us more time to hunt for a lead."

Arriving at the plant, Alden led the way to his office. There he and his companions each selected a comfortable chair and settled down to wait.

"Have you a private line here in addition to your regular company phone?" Mr Hardy asked the executive.

"Yes, I do," Alden replied, pointing to one of two phones on his desk.

"Good," the elder detective said. "I'll use it to have the call traced if the thieves should contact you."

The night dragged on slowly. The boys were restless and found it difficult to sleep. When morning finally came, Alden arranged to have breakfast served in his office.

It was a little after nine when there was a short buzz on the company phone. Alden scooped it up, listened for a moment, then covered the mouthpiece with his hand.

"It's my secretary in the outer office," he informed

the Hardys. "She says a man wants to speak to me. He refuses to identify himself."

"This might be the call we're waiting for!" Joe exclaimed softly.

Mr Hardy rushed to the private phone. "I'll get to work on having the number traced," he announced quickly. Seconds later, he signalled Alden to proceed.

"Okay, put him on," Alden ordered his secretary.

The boys fixed their eyes on the executive and waited anxiously.

Alden suddenly sat bolt upright in his chair. "You want fifty thousand dollars' ransom to return Topnotch?" he shouted into the phone. "You're out of your mind! I'd want absolute proof before I handed out that kind of money!"

A few seconds later the executive put the phone down. "He hung up," Alden announced.

Mr Hardy frowned. "Too bad. There wasn't enough time to trace the call. Obviously we're not dealing with amateurs."

"What did he say when you asked for proof that they had Topnotch?" Frank put in.

"He said he'd think about it and let me know later," Alden replied.

Mr Hardy stretched out his arms and yawned. "You boys must be as exhausted as we are," he said. "Why don't you go home and get some rest? I'll stay here. You'll hear from me immediately if anything comes up."

His sons readily agreed. But it was not rest that interested them. Their father's suggestion offered an

"You want fifty thousand dollars' ransom?" Alden
shouted

excellent opportunity for them to question Roger without Alden's knowledge.

"Let's go back to the stable and see if he's working today," Frank said, as they drove off in their convertible.

When the Hardys arrived, Roger was busy painting a section of the fence that surrounded the paddock.

"We'd like to ask you a few questions," Frank called out.

Roger quickly glanced at his visitors without interrupting his work. "It's you guys again!" he snapped. "Haven't you got a home? Get lost! I don't have time to answer any of your stupid questions."

"Come off it!" Joe shot back angrily. "You must know your father's horse was stolen last night. That's what we want to ask you about."

There was a momentary pause. Roger nervously fingered his paintbrush and kept his face turned away from the Hardys. "Yes, I heard about it," he muttered defiantly. "But you've come to the wrong guy for information. And even if I did know something about it, I wouldn't tell you."

"Where were you last night?" Frank demanded.

"Why don't you try looking into a crystal ball to find out?" the young man retorted.

"Cut the comedy!" Joe exclaimed. "This is serious. A theft has been committed, and there's no reason why you shouldn't be among the suspects."

"Okay! If you have to know, I was working on my dragster all evening," Roger snapped.

"Where?" Frank questioned.

"At home!"

"Can you prove it?" Joe asked. "I mean, was there anyone with you who can back up your statement?"

"No. I was alone," Roger answered.

"What about your father?" Frank put in. "Didn't he see you?"

"He was visiting friends till late. I was already in bed when he got home."

"For your sake," Joe remarked, "I hope you're telling the truth."

Roger suddenly hurled his paintbrush to the ground. His face was flushed with anger. "I've had enough of you two!" he rasped. "What I do is none of your business!"

"We're making it our business," Joe told him.

Frank wanted to avoid a scene. "Simmer down," he said calmly. "We'll have to take your word for what you told us. But if you should run across any information concerning the theft, I advise you not to keep it to yourself."

The Hardys walked back to the convertible and returned to Bayport. Their mother and aunt were disappointed to see that the boys' father had not come with them.

"I suppose he's chasing after some horrible criminal!" Aunt Gertrude remarked. "Your father won't remember where he lives if he keeps up this sort of thing."

"Now calm down, Gertrude," Mrs Hardy pleaded in a soft voice.

Joe playfully sniffed the air. "Smells like roast turkey for supper."

"And coconut-custard pie for dessert," announced Mrs Hardy.

"Let's hope your sons can stay put long enough to eat it," said Aunt Gertrude.

The boys went to bed early that night. They spent the next day puttering around their crime lab and mulling over the case. It was mid afternoon when their father telephoned with an urgent message.

"Mr Alden just received another call from the thieves," said the detective. "He was told that the proof he had asked for would be found in a book entitled *Famous Horses of the World*, at the Clayton Library. Meet us there just as soon as you can."

The boys started out immediately. At the library they found their father and Alden seated at one of the reading tables examining a large book.

Mr Hardy handed his sons a photograph. "This was tucked in between the pages," he whispered.

The boys' eyes widened with surprise. "It's a picture of Topnotch," Frank said.

"Are you absolutely sure?" Joe asked.

"No doubt about it," Alden replied in a low voice.

"And it's a cul-de-sac when it comes to getting a line on who placed the photograph in the book," Mr Hardy said. "I questioned the librarian, but she has been too busy to take note of any strangers."

"May we keep the picture for a while?" Frank queried. "It might provide us with a clue."

"You're welcome to it," Alden replied. He glanced at his watch. "I'd better get back to the plant. The thieves will surely call me again."

Mr Hardy explained that Alden had had one of his drivers bring them to the library. He turned to the executive. "Why don't you send him back to the plant?

You and I can go along with the boys in their car."

"Very well," Alden agreed.

As they drove, Mr Hardy urged his client to stall for more time. "Tell those crooks that you can't get the ransom money until Friday morning," he said.

"I'll try." Alden sighed. "But I don't want to endanger Topnotch any more than I have to."

Soon the plant came into view. As they drove towards the main gate, Alden's experimental racing car suddenly sped out of the driveway.

"I didn't give anyone permission to drive that car!" he shouted.

Frank pressed down on the accelerator and the convertible shot off in pursuit!

·10·

Suspicious Rendezvous

"THAT racer is too fast for us!" Joe yelled. "We'll never catch it."

"Turn on to that side road just ahead!" Alden ordered. "We might be able to head him off!"

Frank followed instructions. It was a wild, bumpy ride and kept the occupants hanging on to their seats. After a couple of miles, the route led them back to the road along which their quarry was travelling.

"There's the experimental car!" Mr Hardy called excitedly, as he peered out of the rear window. "It's about a quarter of a mile behind us and coming fast!"

Frank skilfully manœuvred his convertible to prevent the other driver from passing.

"Hang on!" he cried out. "I'm going to start slowing down!"

As the Hardy car came to a stop, the other driver was forced to do the same.

"Good work!" Alden exclaimed, and leaped out of the convertible. The Hardys followed.

"Roger!" Joe exclaimed, as a sandy-haired young man slowly emerged from the experimental dragster.

Alden was furious. "What do you think you're doing?" he demanded.

"I—I was just taking your car for a little spin," his son stammered.

"Why aren't you working at the stable?" Alden fumed.

"I took the afternoon off," Roger replied.

Alden glared at his son with a look that would have melted ice. "You know my racer is a secret project. How dare you take it for a drive?"

He turned to the Hardys. "I'll meet you back at my office. I'm going to ride to the plant with Roger just to make sure he doesn't get any more wild ideas."

The Hardys reached the office just as Alden finished reprimanding his son.

"Don't send me away to that lumber camp," Roger was pleading.

"I don't see what else I can do with you," his father replied. "I'm fed up with your irresponsibility!"

"But I promise to stick with my job at the stable," Roger replied, "and I won't go near your experimental car again."

Alden rubbed his chin dubiously for a moment. "Well—all right," he finally agreed. "But step out of line once more and off you go."

Roger thanked his father. Then he rushed past the Hardys and out of the office.

At that instant the telephone rang. Alden picked it up. From his expression the Hardys knew it was another call from the thieves.

"Yes, I saw the photograph of Topnotch you placed in the book at the library," Alden informed the stranger. . . . "Will I pay the ransom you demand? I suppose I'll have to. But you must give me until

Friday. It'll take me that long to get such a large sum of money."

When the telephone conversation ended, Alden glanced at the Hardys. "They've agreed to wait till noon on Friday. I'm to receive further instructions then."

Frank jumped up. "That gives us two and a half days to find out who stole your horse."

"We'll get to work on it right away," Mr Hardy said.

"I hope you're successful," Alden commented. "Fifty thousand dollars is a lot of money. But I'll pay it if I have to."

The Hardys hurried home to Bayport. There the elder detective began going through his criminal files. "I'll check to see if I have information on anyone whose speciality is horse-thieving," he said.

Meanwhile, his sons hurried off to their crime lab and studied the photograph of Topnotch.

"What are we looking for?" Joe inquired.

"I thought we might find something in the picture that would help us identify the locality," Frank replied.

"Slim chance. Other than the horse, there's nothing but a few bits of shrubbery."

"Wait a minute! That's it! Perhaps a botanist could tell us if the shrubs are indigenous to a particular region."

"Let's call Mr Scath, curator of the Howard Museum."

Frank rushed to the phone and dialled a number. Soon he had the curator on the line.

"We recently added a botanist to our staff," Scath

said. "His name is Mr Ronald Clause. I'm sure he can be of help to you."

"Would it be possible to see him right away?" Frank asked. "It's urgent."

"Yes," the curator assured him. "We're about to close the museum for the day, but Mr Clause plans to be here for a couple of hours to work on a new exhibit. I'll tell him you're coming."

The boys hurried to their car and drove to the museum, located in the north-western section of Bayport. A lanky, scholarly-looking man admitted them.

"I'm Mr Clause," he announced. "Mr Scath said you wanted to see me."

The boys introduced themselves, then stated their business. They handed the botanist the photograph of Topnotch.

"Hm! The shrubs are a bit out of focus," Clause muttered, "but I'll see what I can do."

"We realize you're very busy," Frank said. "However, we're racing against time. We'd appreciate it if you could give us an answer as soon as possible."

"I'll get to work on it right away," the botanist answered. "Might take me a day or so. If I come up with something, I'll call you."

The Hardys thanked him and left. As they drove back home, Frank's thoughts returned to Alden's son.

"I'm still not convinced that Roger had nothing to do with the theft of Topnotch," he remarked.

"I'm not either," Joe added. "Say, why don't we shadow him tomorrow? If he is in with the crooks, he might try to contact them."

"We've nothing to lose," Frank agreed. "But it

would be safer to have Roger shadowed by someone he doesn't know. That eliminates us and Chet."

"What about Biff Hooper and Tony Prito?" Joe suggested. "They've done a good job of following suspects for us before."

"Good idea. Let's call them when we get home."

Like Chet, Biff Hooper and Tony Prito were classmates of the boys at Bayport High. They always welcomed a chance to work with the Hardys on their cases.

"What's up?" Biff asked eagerly, as he and Tony joined the Hardys in their crime lab. "From your telephone call, I'd say it was important."

"It is," Frank assured him. "And we need your help."

Tony Prito, a dark-haired, lively boy, declared, "Count me in!"

Frank and Joe gave their friends a quick rundown on the case, then furnished them with a description of Roger.

"We'd like you to shadow him and give us a report on everything he does," Joe said.

"You'll find Roger at the stable in the morning," Frank added. "Try to be as inconspicuous as possible. We don't want him to suspect he's being watched."

Biff, a tall, blond, athletic-looking youth, beamed with enthusiasm. "You can depend on us!" he exclaimed.

The next day the Hardy boys stayed close to the telephone. It was almost one o'clock in the afternoon when a call came. Frank answered.

The caller was Biff Hooper. "Tony and I followed

your suspect to a restaurant in Clayton. He's inside talking to a couple of suspicious-looking characters."

"Are you calling from the restaurant?"

"No. I'm in a public phone booth across the street from it, on the corner of Stanton and Winthrop streets."

"Joe and I will come there right away!" Frank declared. "If Roger leaves in the meantime, stick with him. You can let us know where you are by leaving a message with Mother or Aunt Gertrude. We'll check with them every fifteen minutes."

The boys leaped into their car and headed for Clayton. When they arrived, Biff and Tony were still at their posts across the street from the restaurant.

"Your suspect hasn't left yet," Biff said.

Frank pointed to a building behind him. "Let's hide in that doorway, Joe," he advised. "We don't want Roger to spot us when he comes out."

The Hardys and their companions became impatient as the minutes ticked by. Finally Roger emerged from the restaurant with two rough-looking men. Each of them walked off in a different direction.

Frank turned to Biff. "You and Tony follow Roger," he ordered. "Joe and I will split up and trail those two men he was with."

Each boy hurried off on his assignment. Frank trailed his quarry for several blocks. Suddenly the man darted into an alley.

"He must know he's being followed," the young detective thought, and cautiously stalked towards the spot. He peered into the alley. There was nothing in it but a pile of discarded wooden crates at the far end.

"That man must be hiding behind them," Frank decided.

As he edged his way forward, the man leaped from behind the crates and flung a small object towards Frank. It hit the ground a few feet from the boy and exploded!

·11·

A Prize Catch

A THICK, white cloud of smoke erupted from the spot. Frank felt a burning sensation in his eyes and began to cough uncontrollably.

"It's tear gas," he thought. "I must get out of here!"

Frank stumbled backwards away from the smoke. At that instant he saw the blurred figure of a man running past him. The young detective lashed out with his fist and made contact. Then someone grabbed his left arm. Again Frank lashed out with his fist, but his punch was blocked.

"Hold it!" came the voice of his brother. "It's Joe!"

As the effects of the tear gas wore off, Frank saw a man lying unconscious on the ground. Joe pointed at the prone figure. "Looks as if you got your man," he said. "Wish I could say the same."

"You lost the other guy?" Frank asked.

"I had to let him go. He led me round the block and down this street past the alley. Then the smoke attracted my attention and I saw you were in trouble. So I ran to help."

The man regained consciousness. "Who—who are you guys?" he groaned as he struggled to his feet.

"Never mind that," Frank answered. "Suppose you tell us who *you* are?"

"My name's Marty Tempson, if it's any of your business," the man growled.

"Why did you toss that tear-gas bomb at me?"

"I thought you were some guy out to rob me."

"What kind of business did you and your pal have with Roger Alden?" Joe shot at him.

Tempson glared at the boys. "Roger Alden? I don't know no guy by that name," he snarled.

"You're lying," Frank declared. "He's the young man you and your friend were with in the restaurant."

"Never saw him before," Tempson replied. "The restaurant was crowded and he let us share his table."

At that moment a police patrol car arrived on the scene. One of the officers got out and approached the Hardys and Tempson.

"A shop owner across the street reported seeing smoke in this alley," the policeman announced. "What's going on here?"

The boys gave their names and Frank explained what had happened. When Tempson was unable to produce identification, the policeman searched him and discovered a tear-gas bomb in his pocket.

"I'm taking you in!" the officer declared.

Tempson turned pale. "You—you can't arrest me!" he stammered. "I ain't done nothing!"

"That's what you think," the policeman retorted. "There happens to be a law against tossing bombs at people." He glanced at the Hardys. "Will you come to the station and make a statement?"

"Glad to," Frank answered. "We'll pick up our car and meet you there."

Tempson was already being fingerprinted when the

boys arrived at Clayton Police Station. The desk sergeant took down their statement, then said that a complete check would be made on the prisoner.

"You boys must be in court when he's brought up for a preliminary hearing," the sergeant added. "That'll be tomorrow morning."

"We'll be here," Frank assured him.

He and Joe left the building and returned to their car.

"What's our next move?" Joe asked.

"Let's find out if Roger went back to the stable," Frank suggested. "If so, I want to question him."

Arriving at their destination, the boys found Roger seated in front of a stall repairing a harness. He was as belligerent as ever and became enraged when Frank declared that they had seen him in Clayton with two men.

"You lousy snoopers!" Roger yelled. "What right have you to spy on me?"

"Never mind that," Joe put in. "Who were the two men you were with?"

"I don't know," snapped the young man. "I went to the restaurant for lunch. The place was crowded and I let them share my table."

"Very considerate of you," Joe said sarcastically. "What made you so friendly all of a sudden?"

Roger jumped to his feet. "I don't have to take that from you!" he shouted.

In the next instant he swung the harness at Joe. The young detective stepped back, caught the end of the gear, then wrapped it tightly around his opponent's arms.

"Let me go!" Roger demanded.

"Not until you calm down!" Joe shot back.

Frank spoke up. "I don't think you're telling us the truth about not knowing those men."

"I am!" the young man cried out.

"Clayton is about ten miles north of here," Joe said. "Isn't that a long way to go just to have lunch? I've noticed a couple of local restaurants within walking distance."

"I like the food in Clayton," Roger replied mockingly.

"Why did you three walk off in different directions when you left the restaurant?" Frank questioned.

"I went my way, and they went theirs. How am I supposed to know where they were going?"

By now several grooms had collected round the boys. "Hey! Roger's wisecracking must have finally got him in trouble!" one of them yelled to his companion.

"Yeah! And he sure looks funny with that harness wrapped around him," another said, laughing. "I think he should keep it on permanently."

Joe felt a bit embarrassed and released Roger, who glared at the faces around him. Then he stormed off.

The Hardys headed back to Bayport. As they rode along, Joe said, "What do you think about Roger's story?"

"At least it tallies with what Tempson told us," Frank remarked. "But it could have been a pre-arranged alibi between him and the two men."

"If you ask me, there's something fishy about the whole thing."

When the boys got home, they went directly to their father's study.

"Glad to see you're back," Mr Hardy said. "Detective Tanner of the Clayton police telephoned a few minutes ago. He wants to talk to you two."

"What about?" Joe inquired.

"Marty Tempson. Tanner told me all about the tear-gas incident," their father replied. "They checked up on him. Seems his name is not Tempson, but Marty Seegan. He's wanted in Michigan for robbery."

"Then it means that Seegan will be extradited," Frank remarked, "and we won't have a chance to talk to him."

"Afraid so," Mr Hardy commented. "Since the Clayton police are holding Seegan on a lesser charge, the Michigan authorities get first crack at him. I was also asked to tell you," the detective continued, "that the preliminary hearing scheduled in the morning is off."

At that moment the telephone rang. Mr Hardy answered it. "It's for you, Frank."

"This is Mr Clause of the Howard Museum," the caller announced. "I have some information concerning the shrubbery you asked me to identify in the photograph."

·12·

Startling Lead

"WHAT did you find out?" Frank asked him quickly.

"I've identified the shrubs as *Rubus Diparitus*," Clause told him. "They're indigenous to Maryland and parts of Virginia."

Frank thanked the botanist for his help. He then informed his brother and Mr Hardy about Clause's discovery.

"Maryland!" Joe exclaimed. "That's a coincidence. Aunt Gertrude's stable is located there."

"Let's go and see Mr Fowler, the manager, first thing in the morning," Frank suggested. "Maybe he can help us find Topnotch. Is it all right if we have Jack Wayne fly us there, Dad?"

"Sure, boys."

Jack Wayne, a tanned, lean-faced man, was the pilot of Mr Hardy's personal single-engine plane. The boys telephoned him and requested that he be ready for an early departure the next day. Dawn was just breaking as Jack began his take-off roll at the Bayport field.

"Too bad Dad couldn't come with us," Joe remarked, as he watched the ground drop away beneath them.

"Yes," Frank agreed, "but he wants to be within reach of Mr Alden if something should come up."

It took little more than an hour to reach their

destination. Jack landed the plane on a small field about four miles from Aunt Gertrude's stable. The airport operator, a genial man, lent the Hardys a car which he kept for the convenience of visitors.

"We might be gone for several hours," Frank told the pilot.

"Don't worry about me," Jack said. "I'll stick around here and do some hangar flying with the fellows."

As soon as the boys arrived at Southern Pines Stables, they spotted a short, wiry man standing in front of one of the stalls. His hard features and deep-set eyes gave him a forbidding appearance.

"We'd like to see Mr Fowler," Joe informed him.

"Whatcha want to see 'im about?" the man asked in a raspy voice.

"It's confidential," Frank said. "We'd appreciate it if you would tell us where we can find him."

The man stared coldly at the boys for a moment. Then he pointed towards a knoll in the distance. "You'll find 'im on the other side of that hill. He's practice shootin' with his rifle."

The muffled sound of rifle shots could be heard in the distance. Frank thanked the man and the boys started off. As they crossed over the crest of the hill, they spotted Fowler at the bottom of a shallow gully. He was firing at a paper target.

"Well, if it isn't the Hardys!" Fowler called out, when he saw them approaching. "What brings you to this neck of the woods? Business?"

"Not exactly," Frank replied. He then told the manager about the theft of Alden's race horse.

"Why are you telling me all this?" Fowler snapped.
"I've never heard of Topnotch."

"We're pretty sure that the horse is being kept
somewhere here in Maryland or Virginia," Joe explained. "You must come in contact with lots of stable
owners. We thought you might have heard rumours
that . . ."

"Sorry! Can't help you," the manager interrupted.
"Maryland and Virginia cover a lot of territory. That
horse could be anywhere." He squeezed off a couple of
shots, then turned to the Hardys. "I regret I can't spend
more time with you, but I've lots of work to do. I'm
sure you understand."

As the boys followed Fowler out of the gully, Frank
picked up one of the spent cartridge cases from the
manager's rifle. He quickly stuck it into his pocket.

A few minutes later they were back at the stable.
The short, wiry man the boys talked to when they first
arrived was nowhere in sight.

"Sorry to cut your visit so short," Fowler said,
shaking hands with the young detectives. "Come again
when I'm not tied up."

The boys walked back to their car.

"Fowler was certainly in a hurry to get rid of us,"
Joe commented. "He acted mighty suspicious. Why
don't we stick around and see what's going on?"

"No. We're flying back to Bayport right away,"
Frank announced. "If my hunch is right, we'll save a
lot of time in our investigation."

"What hunch?"

Frank dipped into his pocket and pulled out the
cartridge case he had picked up. "This shell is of the

same calibre as the one we found the day the smoke bomb was fired into Dad's study," he said. "But I can't tell whether it was fired from the same rifle until I make a microscopic comparison."

"Leaping lizards!" Joe exclaimed. "If they do check out, it would connect Fowler with the gang that's after Alden's experimental motor!"

"And the same gang might have stolen Topnotch," Frank added.

Soon the boys and their pilot were winging back to Bayport.

Mrs Hardy greeted her sons when they arrived home. "I didn't expect you so soon. Your father left on an errand a few minutes ago. Then he's going directly to Mr Alden's home. He told me he can be reached there in about two hours."

The boys hurried to their crime lab. Frank took the first cartridge case he had found, and placed it with the second in the comparison microscope. He peered into the eyepieces of the apparatus for several minutes.

"What's the verdict?" Joe asked impatiently.

Suddenly Frank leaped to his feet. "My hunch has paid off!" he exclaimed. "Take a look! The markings on the cartridges match exactly!"

"Wait till Dad hears this!"

Frank glanced at his watch. "Let's drive to Alden's home," he suggested. "Dad should be there by the time we arrive."

The boys dashed to their car. An hour went by before they pulled into a driveway leading to a large, white house. It was set back from the road on a spacious, tree-covered lawn.

An elderly servant responded to a single press of the doorbell. "What can I do for you?" he asked.

"We're Mr Hardy's sons," Joe explained. "We must see our father right away."

"Oh, yes," the servant answered, as he pulled the door open all the way. "He arrived with Mr Alden a few minutes ago. Please come in."

The boys were ushered into Alden's study. Mr Hardy was surprised to see them.

"Back from Maryland already?" he said. "Have any luck."

"You bet!" Frank replied excitedly.

Their father and Mr Alden listened with interest as the two boys told them about their startling lead.

The executive sat bolt upright in his chair. "If what you suspect about this man Fowler is true," he said, "then we must do something right away."

"I'm going to call Chief Collig," Mr Hardy declared. He dialled a number and shortly had the officer on the line.

"Those cartridge cases are strong evidence," the chief remarked, when told about Fowler. "I'll contact the Maryland State Police and have him picked up for questioning. You should hear from me within a couple of hours."

Alden arranged to have dinner served while they waited. Nearly three hours passed before the phone rang. Mr Hardy rushed to pick it up.

"This is Chief Collig," the caller said. "Looks like your suspect flew the coop. The Maryland police went to the stable and found no one around."

"In that case, will you issue an APB on him?" Mr

Hardy asked. "Frank and Joe can give you a detailed description of Fowler."

"I'll send it out immediately," Collig assured him.

Frank got on the phone and furnished the police chief with the necessary information. Then he and his companions mulled over the situation.

"No wonder Fowler was eager to get rid of us," Joe muttered. "He was planning a getaway. But we still don't know if he had anything to do with the theft of Topnotch."

Frank was casually gazing at some photographs mounted on the wall of the study. Suddenly his eyes widened in amazement.

"I—I don't believe it!" he shouted.

·13·

No Trespassing!

"WHAT is it?" Joe asked, surprised at Frank's outburst.

Frank pointed to a photograph showing a small group of men. "Take a look at the face of the man standing next to Mr Alden in this picture," he urged.

Joe peered at the photograph in astonishment. "Why—it's Fowler!" he exclaimed.

"The picture you're looking at was taken three years ago during a fishing trip I went on with some friends," Alden interjected as he gazed at the boys curiously. "That man's name is not Fowler. It's Norman Dodson. He's a distant cousin of mine."

"I'm sure we're not mistaken," Frank insisted. "He's the suspect we're after!"

"The idea is utterly ridiculous," the executive countered. "Why would Norman get mixed up with a gang of crooks? He—"

"Think back," Mr Hardy interrupted. "Did you and Dodson ever have a quarrel in the past?"

There was a momentary pause.

"As a matter of fact we did," Alden said finally. "About a year ago."

"What happened?" Frank asked.

"Norman was once a junior partner in my firm," the

executive explained. "However, he became more interested in the raising of race horses than in automobiles. One day he asked to be bought out so that he could purchase a stable. Unfortunately, his venture failed and Norman lost his money."

"The pieces are beginning to fit together," Joe observed.

"Then about a year ago," Alden continued, "he came to my office and demanded more money. He said that I hadn't paid him enough for his share in the firm. I refused, and we had a bitter argument. I haven't seen him since."

"No doubt about it!" Frank declared. "Dodson must have masterminded the theft of Topnotch. And his motive is clear. He's out to get more money from you one way or another."

"I still find it hard to believe," Alden sighed.

The Hardys returned to Bayport. Aunt Gertrude went into a frenzy when she heard about Topnotch and their suspect. "My stable is not only a haven for retired race horses," she cried, "but for stolen ones as well!"

"Let's call Mr Steve Benson, attorney for the estate," Frank suggested to his father. "He should be able to give us more information on Dodson."

Frank dialled the number. It took only seconds to reach the lawyer in Maryland. Benson was shocked to hear about the missing stable manager. He stated that Fowler had worked several months for the previous owner before their aunt inherited the business.

"But I only knew him by the name of Fowler," Benson added. "He was the most competent of all the workers there. When I was placed in charge of the estate I made him temporary manager."

"Is there anything else you can tell us about him?" Frank asked.

"Only that he was interested in buying the stable when he learned it was for sale," the lawyer said. "However, he was unable to raise the cash. Later he asked if I would help him sell a piece of land that he owned."

"A piece of land?" Frank blurted. "Where?"

"In northern Vermont," Benson replied. "He showed me the exact spot on a road map. It consists of about twenty acres and a cabin. But I wasn't really interested in handling the matter."

Frank quickly obtained a map of Vermont. He then asked the attorney to describe where Fowler's land was located. Benson stated that it was just west of Highway 15, twelve miles north of the town of Haversville.

After Frank had hung up, he said, "I'll bet Fowler-Dodson has gone to his cabin!"

"It would be a perfect place to hide out with Top-notch," Joe agreed. "But wouldn't he be taking a big chance? After all, he told Mr Benson where his land was located."

"Dodson might be hoping the attorney forgot about it, or wouldn't think it important enough to mention," Mr Hardy said.

"How about requesting the police up there to check the area?" Frank spoke up. "It's been more than fourteen hours since we last saw Dodson. He could easily be in Vermont by now."

Mr Hardy telephoned Chief Collig again. Two

hours passed before the Bayport officer called back.

"A couple of officers searched the cabin and some of the surrounding land," he informed the detective. "Afraid you're out of luck. They found nothing."

"Thanks, Chief," Mr Hardy replied. "By the way, our suspect would have to transport Topnotch in a horse van. Would you send out an alarm to have all such vehicles—spotted within a six- or seven-hundred-mile radius—stopped and inspected? Although I'm sure it's too late for that now."

"I'll do it, anyway," the chief assured him.

"Guess we've run into another blank wall," Joe muttered.

"Not necessarily," Frank commented. He snapped his fingers. "Let's go to Vermont and take a look ourselves. Dodson's pretty clever. He certainly wouldn't keep Topnotch there at the cabin. It's possible he's hiding somewhere nearby."

"I'm with you," his brother said.

"Go to it," Mr Hardy told them. "I'll have to stay behind and sit it out with Mr Alden. Remember! Noon tomorrow is the deadline for him to pay the ransom."

The boys alerted Jack Wayne for another flight the next morning. After an early breakfast, they drove to the airport and boarded the plane.

"Flight time should be approximately two and a half hours," the pilot announced. "The nearest field is about twenty miles from where you want to go."

Jack's estimated time to reach their destination proved to be correct. After landing, the Hardys arranged to rent a car.

"You stick close to the phone here in operations," Frank instructed Jack. "If you don't hear from us in two hours, notify the police."

"Roger," Jack replied. "Good luck!"

Soon Frank and Joe were driving north on Highway 15. When they were twelve miles north of Haversville, they spotted a crude fence a few yards west of the road. On it was a large sign which read:

PRIVATE PROPERTY
NO TRESPASSING

"This must be Dodson's land," Joe concluded.

Frank turned the car on to a narrow, dirt trail which jutted off the highway. After travelling a short distance, he brought it to a stop.

"We'd better continue on foot," he advised.

The Hardys picked their way through an area of dense woods and brush. Soon they came to a small clearing.

"There's the cabin!" Joe declared, pointing to a dilapidated log structure directly ahead.

"Let's watch it from here for a while," Frank said. "There might be someone inside."

Half an hour went by. There was no sign of life, and the only sound was that of the wind rustling through the trees.

"I think it's safe to go in," Joe remarked impatiently.

"Okay. Let's go!"

They skirted the clearing and approached the cabin from the rear. When they reached it, Frank cautiously peered through a window.

"The place is empty except for a couple of pieces of furniture," he told his brother.

The boys walked round to the front of the cabin and climbed two steps to the porch.

"Careful," Frank warned. "These planks are pretty creaky. Step lightly."

The door of the cabin did not have a lock. The boys pushed it open and went inside. A wooden table stood in the middle of the floor with worn-out chairs set at each end. Suspended from the ceiling above the table was an old paraffin lamp.

Joe walked over to a cupboard mounted against the wall. He pulled open the door. "Look at this!" he exclaimed. "A supply of tinned food!"

Frank inspected his brother's discovery. "These tins look as if they haven't been here long. No dust on them."

Suddenly the boys heard the voices of men in the distance.

"Someone's coming!" Joe said excitedly. "Sounds as if they're approaching from the woods behind the cabin."

"Let's get out of here!" Frank said.

The boys dashed through the door and across the clearing to the edge of the woods. They took cover in a clump of thick brush. A moment later three men appeared from round the corner of the cabin.

"That tall guy is the one I trailed from the restaurant in Clayton," Joe whispered.

"And we met the short one at the Southern Pines Stables when we went to see Dodson," Frank hissed.

Neither of the Hardys recognized the third man, who

remarked, "Dodson would nail us to a wall if he knew we came to the cabin!"

"I'm hungry," another said. "I can't wait till dark to get some of that tinned food!"

The three men hurried into the log structure and slammed the door behind them.

"I'm going back to try to hear what they're saying," Joe announced.

"It's too risky in daylight," his brother warned.

But Joe was already on his way. Frank watched him sprint across the clearing and carefully step up on to the porch of the cabin.

Suddenly there was a loud cracking sound. Frank's pulse quickened. "Some of the planks are giving way underneath Joe!" he thought.

The next instant there was a crash as Joe fell through the porch floor up to his waist. Frank rushed to his aid. As he reached his brother, the three men spilled out of the cabin!

·14·

Daring Escape

THERE was a violent struggle. Frank lashed out at one of the men and sent him hurtling back into the cabin. The remaining two pounced on the dark-haired youth.

"Run for it!" Joe shouted, as he frantically tried to free himself from between the planks.

One of Frank's assailants caught him from behind with a headlock. The young detective flipped him high over his shoulder in judo fashion.

"Hold it!" came an order. Frank suddenly found himself staring into the face of Dodson, who patted a rear pocket significantly.

"Er—hi, Boss," one of the men said nervously. "We came to get some tinned food and caught a couple of snoopers."

"What did I tell you guys about coming here in daylight?" Dodson yelled. He glared at the Hardys. "How did you know where to find me?"

"Trade secret," Joe snapped, as he finally worked himself free of the planks and rejoined his brother.

"These kids probably told somebody they were coming here!" Dodson said to his cohorts. "We'd better move the horse van to another hiding place."

"But what about the ransom money?" said one of the men. "Kurt will be comin' here after he picks it up."

Dodson looked at his watch. "It's early yet. He'll still be in his room at the hotel in Clayton." He turned to the short, wiry man the boys had met at the Southern Pines Stables. "Beaver! Get to a telephone and call Kurt. Tell him to go ahead as planned, then to drive to the bus terminal in Haversville. We'll meet him there tonight."

"Okay, Boss," Beaver replied, as he hurried off.

The boys were ordered to walk ahead of their captors.

"Where are you taking us?" Frank demanded.

"You two went to a lot of trouble to find Topnotch," Dodson snarled. "I'm going to give you a chance to see him."

The Hardys were marched along what appeared to be a very narrow trail through the woods. Actually they saw it was a wide, dirt road, cleverly covered with brush.

Soon the boys were ordered to halt. A huge mound of dried brush loomed in front of them. One of their captors pulled it aside.

"Why—it's a camouflage net," Joe whispered to his brother.

"And it's covering a horse van," Frank answered in a low voice.

"Shut up!" Dodson demanded. "Get inside!"

The boys walked up a ramp which formed the rear door of the van when closed. To the right in the back of the van was a small bedroom for the trainer. Ahead, another door with bars at the top opened into a stall. Inside was Topnotch who began to whinny at the disturbance.

Frank and Joe were roughly pushed into the van. A quick glimpse at the race horse revealed that his distinguishing white marks above the front hoofs had been dyed chestnut to match his coat.

"This animal," Dodson remarked with a laugh, "has been living like a king. After all, he means fifty thousand dollars to me."

"You won't get away with this!" Joe vowed.

"Who's going to stop me?" Dodson retorted. He then barked an order to his pals. "Tie these wise guys up!" His henchman shoved the boys inside the small room and uncoiled lengths of rope.

"No use resisting," Frank told Joe. He winked. "Just relax." Joe nodded in response.

As they were being tied up, the boys took deep breaths and flexed their muscles hard. The men wound the ropes tightly round the boys' bodies, then they left with Dodson. The rear door was slammed shut.

Instantly the Hardys exhaled and relaxed their muscles. The ropes went slack and the boys had little difficulty freeing themselves.

"Thanks for reminding me to relax," Joe said with a grin. "I had almost forgotten that old trick Dad taught us."

"We're lucky Dodson's men don't know much about tying up prisoners," Frank remarked.

A scraping sound outside told the boys that their captors were removing the camouflage net covering the van.

"They're getting ready to move," Frank said. "We must get out of here fast!"

"Let's make a break for it! It's our only chance."

Dodson's henchmen tied the ropes tightly round the Hardy boys

The boys dashed from the small room, but were dismayed to find the door of the van locked.

"There's no other exit!" Joe said frantically.

"I have an idea!" Frank whispered. "We'll ride Topnotch out of here!"

"What! Through a locked door?"

"We'll force Dodson and his men to open it!"

"How?"

"By raising such a racket that they'll let down the door to investigate."

The boys opened the door to the stall, patted the horse, who seemed to recognize them, then bridled him. Quickly they lead Topnotch to within a few feet of the rear door.

"Hey!" came the voice of one of their captors. "Do you hear Topnotch movin' around?"

"Probably just restless," Dodson replied. "He'll calm down."

Frank leaned close to Joe. "All set?" he whispered.

His brother nodded, and the boys began pounding on the door with their fists.

"What's that?" they heard a man shout. "It's comin' from inside the van."

"Maybe the kids got loose!" Dodson declared. "We'd better check. Quick! Open the door!"

The Hardys leaped on to Topnotch and flattened out on his back. As the ramp was pulled down, they nudged the racehorse forward. He sprinted down the ramp, taking the men completely by surprise. Before they could recover, Topnotch had covered a hundred yards.

"They're getting away!" one of the men yelled.

Suddenly Topnotch stumbled and the Hardys were thrown to the ground. They scrambled to their feet just in time to see Dodson take a small object from his pocket and throw it towards them.

"Looks like a tear-gas bomb!" Frank yelled.

Joe darted ahead and caught the object, then tossed it back at their captors. On contact with the ground, the bomb exploded and engulfed Dodson and his henchmen in a thick, white cloud of smoke.

As the choking gas began to drift away, the boys, holding their breaths, pounced on them and wrestled the men into the van. They shut and locked the door.

Joe glanced around. "Where's Topnotch?"

"He ran off!" Frank said. "You stay on guard here. I'll go and look for him."

After a brief search Frank found the horse behind a clump of trees, entangled in heavy brush. He freed him and led the animal back to the van.

At that moment the Hardys were startled to hear their names called. "Frank! Joe! Where are you?"

"Sounds like Jack Wayne," Joe said. "He must be at the cabin."

Frank sprinted down the brush-covered trail. Reaching the clearing, he saw the pilot and two state troopers standing near the cabin.

"Jack!" Frank shouted, as he ran to greet them.

"Am I glad to see you!" Jack said, with a sigh of relief. "I jumped the gun a bit. Didn't quite wait out a full two hours. Thought you'd call me long before that. I began to worry and notified the State Police."

"Glad you did." Frank told Jack and the officers what had happened, then led them to the van.

"You're under arrest!" one of the troopers announced as the boys pulled the door of the vehicle down. Dodson and his henchmen staggered out and were handcuffed.

"There was a fourth man with them," Joe put in. "He went to make a call."

"Where's the nearest telephone?" Frank asked the officers.

"There's a public booth about a mile and a half down the highway," one of them replied.

Frank checked his watch. "Let's drive in that direction," he suggested. "Beaver was on foot. He should be on his way back by now."

"We'll use the patrol car," one of the troopers said, and added, "I'll have to radio headquarters for more help."

Leaving Jack and the other officer behind to guard the prisoners, the Hardys and their companion hurried to the highway. Soon they were cruising in the patrol car.

Minutes later, Joe pointed to a wiry figure trekking back along the highway. "There he is! That's Beaver!"

The officer brought the car to an abrupt halt and leaped out, with the boys close at his heels.

"What—what's this?" Beaver shouted as he was placed under arrest. "How did you kids escape?"

"Save your breath," Joe snapped. "You'll soon have enough talking to do."

It was not long before more troopers arrived on the scene. Two grooms from a nearby stable were summoned to take charge of Topnotch until his owner could claim him.

Dodson and his cohorts were driven to Haversville Police Headquarters. There Frank telephoned Alden's plant.

"Sorry," said the executive's secretary, "but Mr Alden and Mr Hardy left a few minutes ago on urgent business. I don't know when they'll return."

"They're probably on their way to pay the ransom money," Frank remarked as he hung up.

"The guy named Kurt is in for a surprise when he arrives at the bus terminal tonight," Joe commented with a grin. "He'll have quite a reception party waiting for him."

"You can say that again," Frank said. He then turned to their pilot. "Jack, fly back to Bayport and keep trying to contact Dad and Mr Alden. When you do, bring them here."

"Okay."

The Hardys interrogated the prisoners but without success. After an early dinner at a restaurant in town they returned to police headquarters. They were elated to find their father waiting for them.

"Just got here," Mr Hardy said. "Heard you boys cracked the horse-thieving case. Good work."

"Thanks, Dad," Frank answered. "Where's Mr Alden? Didn't he come with you?"

"He intended to. But just as we were leaving his office, he received word that Roger was involved in an automobile accident," the detective explained. "Jack went back to Bayport and will fly Mr Alden here in the morning if Roger isn't seriously hurt."

"What about the ransom?" Joe asked.

"Mr Alden decided to pay it," his father replied.

"He received a call precisely at noon today and was instructed to leave the money in a public locker at the Clayton railroad station. I wanted to stick around and try to nab the pickup man, but Mr Alden wouldn't hear of it. He was afraid of losing Topnotch if anything went wrong."

The boys told him about Kurt.

"This is a great piece of luck!" Mr Hardy exclaimed.

Frank glanced at his watch. "If Kurt picked up the money and departed from Clayton by one o'clock this afternoon, he should reach Haversville about ten or eleven o'clock tonight."

As the hour neared, the three Hardys posted themselves across the street from the bus terminal. Several plainclothesmen were assigned to accompany them.

The time ticked by slowly. It was almost midnight before a car approached and parked in front of the terminal building. A burly man climbed out.

"That could be our man," Mr Hardy whispered.

"Trouble is, we don't know what Kurt looks like," Joe muttered.

Frank was struck with an idea. He stepped out of the shadows and nonchalantly walked towards their suspect. "Hi, Kurt!" he said.

The man whirled. "Hi! Er—who are you?" he responded with a startled expression.

"You're under arrest!" the young detective declared.

The man tried to make a break for it, but Frank seized him. Plainclothesmen closed in from all sides.

"What is this?" their captive shouted. "I ain't done nothin'."

"We know who you are!" Frank shot back.

"Where's the ransom money?" Mr Hardy demanded.

"What money?" Kurt sputtered.

"It's probably in his car," Joe put in. He quickly searched the vehicle and found a package stuffed underneath the front seat.

"That's it," Mr Hardy observed.

The prisoner was taken to police headquarters. There he was brought face to face with Dodson.

"Gosh, Boss," Kurt began, "I . . ."

"Shut up!" Dodson screamed. "Idiot! You walked straight into a trap!"

"But nobody warned me! How was I supposed to know?"

"As long as you're in the mood for talking," Frank spoke up, "suppose you answer a few questions."

"I told you before," Dodson retorted, "you're not getting anything out of me."

"Is there someone else in this with you?" Mr Hardy inquired.

A smirk spread across Dodson's face. "Why don't you ask Alden's son?"

·15·

Plea for Help

"WHAT do you mean by that remark?" Frank demanded.

"You guys think you're so smart," Dodson snapped. "Figure it out for yourselves."

After the prisoners were escorted to their cells, the Hardys went to a local hotel to spend the night. The next morning Mr Alden and Jack Wayne arrived just as the boys and their father were finishing breakfast.

"You've done a terrific job," Alden said. "And I'm glad to know that Topnotch is all right."

"We've recovered the ransom money too," Joe announced.

"What!" Alden exclaimed. "That's incredible."

After a pause Mr Hardy inquired, "How's your son?"

"Fine, thank you. It was just a minor car accident, and I was happy to hear it wasn't his fault. Fortunately Roger escaped injury and reported for work at the stable this morning."

Frank said quietly, "We're sorry that your cousin is one of the thieves."

Alden also expressed some remorse for Dodson. He hinted that he might drop the charges against him.

"But you can't let him go free," Mr Hardy objected. "We've reason to suspect that your cousin is involved with someone who is trying to steal your experimental motor. He might turn out to be our only link."

Alden finally agreed.

Then the detective said, "We're going to take another crack at questioning Dodson before we fly back to Bayport. You'd better come to headquarters with us. The police will want a statement."

"All right." Alden sighed. "But please don't ask me to be at the interrogation. You understand. Anyway, I want to arrange to take Topnotch home today."

When Dodson was grilled by the Hardys, he continued to be unco-operative.

"You were the one who fired the smoke grenade into our father's study, weren't you?" Frank said.

"I don't know what you're talking about," Dodson insisted.

"No use denying it," Joe interjected. "We have evidence to prove that the grenade was fired from your rifle."

The prisoner nervously gripped the arms of his chair. "You're lying!" he screamed.

"Who's trying to steal Mr Alden's experimental motor?" Mr Hardy demanded.

"I don't know anything about a motor!" Dodson shouted. He jumped to his feet. "I want to go back to my cell!"

Shortly he was ushered out of the room. The Hardys then questioned each of the other prisoners in turn. But they too refused to talk. Obviously Dodson had frightened the men into remaining silent.

After lunch Jack Wayne flew the Hardys back to Bayport. When they arrived, Frank suggested that they drive to the stable near Alden's plant and tell Roger about Dodson's remark.

"I'd like to see what his reaction will be," Frank added.

"You boys go ahead. I must get back to another case," Mr Hardy told them. "I'll take a taxi home."

The boys hurried to the airport car park and climbed into their car. Soon they were at the stable confronting Roger with Dodson's insinuation.

"I barely know my father's cousin," the young man yelled. "He's crazy!"

"Then what reason would Dodson have for trying to involve you?" Frank asked.

Roger grew pale. "Don't ask me!" he retorted. "Maybe he's trying to get back at my father through me."

"Then you've nothing to worry about—if you're not involved," Joe said.

"Leave me alone!" The young man nervously fumbled with a bucket he was carrying. "Get out of here! I have work to do!"

"Okay," Frank replied. "But don't forget this. When Dodson and his gang are put on trial, your name is likely to pop up again. If so, the prosecutor will have you subpoenaed."

When the boys returned home, Chet Morton was waiting in the driveway with his bicycle.

"Hi, fellows!" Their friend was bubbling with excitement. "Long time no see!"

"Hello, Chet!" Frank said. "Why the bicycle? Car break down?"

"No," the plump youth answered. "Remember the

rocket cycle I told you I was going to design? Well, this is it!"

Frank and Joe noticed a square canister attached underneath the seat of the bicycle. A long, funnel-shaped nozzle protruded from it.

"Don't tell us it works," Joe said.

"I don't know yet," Chet admitted. "I wanted to wait until you master minds could be on hand to witness the supreme test."

"Forget it," Frank advised. "That thing looks dangerous."

Chet shrugged off the warning. He leaped on to the seat of the bicycle and flicked a small toggle switch mounted on the handle bar. A crackling sound came from the canister. Then suddenly a long tongue of flame shot out from the nozzle. Chet was carried off with a roar. He manœuvred the bicycle through several wide circles as its speed rapidly increased.

"Cut off the motor!" Joe cried anxiously.

"I—I can't!" their friend stammered.

In the next instant Chet steered on a straight course and vanished down the street in a trail of smoke. The Hardys jumped into their car and took off in pursuit.

"Where did he go?" Joe said anxiously, after they had travelled about half a mile.

"Look! Over there!"

Frank pointed to a bicycle, minus its rider, turned over on a spacious lawn. The wheels were still spinning.

"There's no sign of Chet," Joe muttered worriedly.

"I see him!" Frank declared.

He led his brother to a thick hedge a short distance away. Chet's legs were protruding from the top.

"Are you all right?" Joe yelled.

"Yes, I'm okay! Get me out of here!"

The boys pulled their chum free of the hedge. He was badly shaken by his experience, but other than a few scratches he had suffered no injuries.

"Better stick to the old-fashioned way of propelling a bike," Frank urged.

"Guess you're right." Chet sighed. "It wasn't such a good idea, anyway."

The Hardys drove their friend and his rocket bike to the Morton farm. Then they returned home in time to enjoy a delicious dinner. The meal was interrupted by the telephone. Frank answered it.

"This is Roger," the caller announced. He seemed frightened. "I've got to see you right away. But I don't want to come to your home. Meet me at the municipal car park in Bayport."

The boys quickly finished eating, then drove off to their rendezvous with Alden's son. They found him seated in his car. At Roger's request the boys climbed into the rear seat.

"What's this all about?" Frank demanded.

"You must help me," the young man pleaded.

"Help you?" Joe snapped. "Why should we?"

"I'm in terrible trouble," Roger said shakily. "I *was* in on the theft of Topnotch. But I didn't know the horse was to be held for ransom."

"Then why did you get involved?" Frank asked.

"I wanted revenge for the way my father has been treating me."

"How did you get mixed up with Dodson?" Joe questioned.

Roger stated that he met his father's cousin one night in Clayton. "I realize now that it was not a chance meeting. He must have followed me there after work. Said he'd heard I wasn't on friendly terms with my father. I never thought to ask him how he knew that."

"Hm! Interesting," Frank muttered.

"Dodson then told me that he also had a grudge against my father," Roger continued, "and asked me if I would like to play a joke on him."

"Like stealing Topnotch?" Joe interjected.

"Yes. But Dodson promised that the horse would be returned in a few days. It wasn't until they attacked the groom the night we took Topnotch that I realized the theft was meant to be more than a joke."

"Why did you meet two of Dodson's henchmen in that restaurant in Clayton?" Frank inquired. "By then you knew they were crooks."

"I had to," Roger replied. "Dodson sent them to warn me not to talk; otherwise he'd see that I went to jail with them."

"What made you change your mind?" Joe asked.

"When you told me Dodson had mentioned my name, I thought it over and decided to tell you what I know. I would have before, but I was afraid."

"You made a wise decision," Frank assured him. "And if you continue to co-operate, we'll do everything in our power to see that you get a break."

"What should I do now?" Roger asked.

"I suggest you tell your father everything you've told us," Frank advised. "You're going to need his help as well as ours."

Roger thanked the Hardys and drove off.

"Roger's completely changed," Joe commented, as he and his brother returned to their car.

"He's scared," Frank said. "And it's a good thing. Maybe this will teach him a lesson."

When the boys arrived home, their father greeted them with alarming news.

"Dodson has escaped!" he announced.

·16·

Dilemma

FRANK and Joe were startled by the news.

"I can't believe it!" Joe exclaimed.

"How did he manage to get away?" Frank asked quickly.

"That's the most fantastic part of what I have to tell you," Mr Hardy replied.

He told his sons that Lieutenant Monroe of the Haversville police had telephoned. The officer had informed him that Dodson escaped while he and his men were being transferred to the county jail in Myles City.

"The prisoners were sent in a patrol car," Mr Hardy continued. "When they were about halfway to their destination, the windshield suddenly crazed. The driver lost control, skidded off the road, and turned over in a ditch."

"Leaping lizards!" Joe exclaimed. "That's exactly what caused Mr Alden's racing cars to crash!"

"Then what happened?" Frank asked.

"The occupants were badly shaken up," the detective replied. "But one of the officers faintly recalls seeing two masked men run towards the patrol car. They pulled Dodson out and disappeared. That's all he remembers."

"What about the men with him?" Frank inquired.

"They were left behind," Mr Hardy answered.

"That's strange," Joe muttered. "I wonder why."

"I don't know," their father admitted. "But I suggest we fly to Myles City tomorrow and have another talk with Dodson's pals."

At that moment Aunt Gertrude entered the room and began one of her tirades.

"Horse-thieves! Ransom money! It's all too horrible to imagine," she sputtered. "And to think those criminals were connected with that awful stable I inherited."

"It's not really as bad as all that," Mrs Hardy commented in a soft voice. "Horses are wonderful animals. Think how pleasant it must be for them to have a lovely place to retire."

"Fiddlesticks!" Aunt Gertrude retorted. "I'll have no part of it." She glanced at Mr Hardy. "Are you sure Mr Benson is doing his best to sell the stable?"

"Yes, he is," the detective assured her. "You'll probably be hearing from him any day now."

"I certainly hope so," his sister said. "The next thing you know, they'll be setting up public ticket booths and holding races in the paddock."

The others smiled, then Frank changed the subject.

Early the next morning Jack Wayne and the Hardys were streaking down the runway on take-off at the Bayport field. Less than three hours later, the boys and their father were at the county jail in Myles City. Lieutenant Monroe was there to greet them.

"We've checked on the prisoners," he said. "They all have police records a mile long."

"We'd like to question them one at a time," Mr Hardy requested.

"Okay," the lieutenant replied. "We can use the chief guard's office."

Beaver was the only one among the three prisoners willing to talk. "Dodson's left us holding the bag!" he growled. "That rat won't get away with this. Whatcha' want to know?"

"When did you first meet Dodson?" Mr Hardy asked.

"A couple of months ago in Maryland," Beaver answered. "I was on the lam at the time and came across the stable he was managin'. He was lookin' for workers and offered me a job. I took it 'cause I thought it would be a good place to lay low for a while."

"Was it his idea to steal Topnotch?" Frank questioned.

"Yes," the prisoner admitted. "I got to be on friendly terms with Dodson. Told 'im I had a police record. He said not to worry about it. Later he asked me if I would help his men steal a race horse, and get a couple o' my friends to come in on the deal. Needin' money, I jumped at the chance."

"Do you know if he was involved in any other shady activities?" Joe asked.

"Not that I know of," Beaver replied. "But he was away from the stable two and three days at a stretch sometimes. Maybe he *was* up to somethin' that he never told me about."

"Think hard," Mr Hardy urged. "Did Dodson ever

mention anything about experimental racing cars or motors?"

"Not to me he didn't," the prisoner answered.

When the interview was over, the boys and their father discussed the information.

"I believe he was telling the truth," Frank commented.

"So do I," Mr Hardy agreed. "And it explains why Beaver and the other two prisoners were left behind."

"What do you mean?" Joe queried.

"I'm convinced that Dodson is part of a gang that's trying to steal Mr Alden's experimental motor. The theft of Topnotch must have been his own private deal. As a result, the gang knew nothing about his horse-theft plans or the men who were helping him."

"Makes sense," Joe remarked. He thought for a moment. "But how did the guys who helped him escape know he was being taken to Myles City?"

Frank turned to Lieutenant Monroe, who was seated nearby. "Did Dodson have any visitors, or make any phone calls from Haversville?" he asked.

"He didn't have any visitors," the officer told him, "but he was permitted to make a call. When I informed him that we were taking him to Myles City, he demanded that he be allowed to contact his lawyer. I dialled the number for him."

"Did you check the number?" Frank asked.

"No," the lieutenant replied. "But I have a record of it back at headquarters. I'll call the desk sergeant and have him check it immediately."

Monroe picked up the phone. Twenty minutes went by before he obtained the information. "It's an unlisted number in Clayton," he said, "registered in the name of Barto Sigor."

"Barto!" Joe exclaimed. "Mr Alden's chief sheet-metal worker!"

Mr Hardy jumped to his feet. "There's no time to lose!" he told his sons. "We're flying back to Bayport immediately!"

Shortly Jack Wayne and his passengers were airborne. When they reached their destination, the Hardys drove at once to Alden's plant. They found the executive in his office. He was greatly upset.

"What's wrong?" Frank asked.

"Barto drove off in my experimental car!" Alden declared.

"When?"

"A few minutes ago! I've already notified the police."

"Have you any idea which way he went?" Joe asked.

"No."

"Your car has a bright silver finish and a distinctive shape," Frank commented. "We should be able to spot it from the air."

"Good idea!" Mr Hardy said. "You boys go aloft. I'll stay here with Mr Alden in case the police come up with anything."

Frank rushed to the phone and dialled the number of Jack Wayne's office at the Bayport field. Luckily he caught the pilot just as he was about to go home.

"Sorry to ask you to go up again," he said. "You've been doing so much flying the past couple of days you're likely to sprout wings. But this is an emergency!"

"I don't mind," the pilot assured him.

Frank glanced at Alden. "Is it okay if Jack lands the

plane on your private drag strip?" he asked. "It'll save time."

"By all means," the executive said.

Soon the boys and their pilot were cruising high above the plant.

"Where do we start searching?" Joe inquired.

"My guess is that Barto will stick to the back roads," Frank explained. "There are lots of them to the west."

Jack manœuvred the sleek aircraft in a westerly direction. Frank and Joe scanned the terrain below. Thin ribbons of secluded roads cut across the hills and through the heavy forests.

"I'll climb a bit higher so that you can take in more area," the pilot said, as he advanced the throttle.

More minutes passed. Then suddenly Joe pointed down towards a bright speck moving along one of the narrow roads. "Look!" he cried. "That might be the car!"

"I'll go down on the deck and make a head-on pass," Jack announced.

Descending to almost ground level, the pilot headed towards the oncoming vehicle. The tall trees that flanked the road seemed just inches away from the wing tips.

"It's Mr Alden's racing car all right!" Frank observed. "Barto is pulling it off to the side."

The plane swept by the vehicle at high speed. Then Jack pulled up into a climbing turn and came round for a second pass. As he did this, Frank saw a man run out on to the road. "Must be Barto!" he shouted.

As Jack flew closer, the boys noticed that the man was aiming a long, cylindrical object at them.

"Be careful!" Frank warned the pilot. "It might be a weapon of some kind!"

In the next instant the windows of the plane crazed completely. The occupants were unable to see through the milky whiteness.

"We're flying blind!" Jack cried, as he hauled back on the control wheel and soared skywards.

"How can we land?" Frank asked tensely.

17

Emergency Landing

THE Hardys sat frozen in their seats. They heard the loud, thudding sound of the treetops whipping against the underside of the wings.

"I veered off course slightly!" Jack cried. "We just managed to clear the trees!"

Seconds later a large, dark shadow flashed over the top of the plane's canopy. This was followed by a severe buffeting that rocked the craft violently.

"What was that?" Joe shouted.

"We almost collided with another plane!" the pilot declared nervously. "I must contact air traffic control. They'll have to handle us just as if we were flying in bad weather!"

Jack switched the radio transceiver to emergency frequency. "Mayday! Mayday! Mayday!" he declared. "Bayport Centre! Do you read me?"

There was an immediate reply as the radio's loudspeaker crackled to life. "This is Bayport Centre!" came a voice. "Aircraft calling Mayday! Give position, altitude, and identification!"

"This is Skyhawk One-One-Eight-Howe-Boscoe!" the pilot responded. "Now inbound on the two-eight-four-degree radial of Bayport Omni, approximately forty miles from the station! Present altitude, three thousand!" He then explained their predicament.

"Roger, Eight-Howe-Boscoe!" the air traffic operator replied. "Maintain present heading and altitude! Will advise when we have radar contact!"

It was several minutes before the air traffic controller informed Jack that the plane had been identified on the radar screens. He was also told that his craft would be brought down for a landing by means of a Ground Approach. Frank and Joe knew this meant radar operators would detect their aircraft's heading, descent, and distance from a landing runway. Jack Wayne would be literally "talked down".

The boys watched in admiration as he skilfully manœuvred the plane. When finally advised by the controller that he had just crossed the threshold of the runway, Jack chopped the power and settled to the ground.

"Whew!" Joe sighed, mopping his forehead. "I don't want to go through that again. For a while it was like driving in heavy traffic with your eyes shut."

Jack brought the plane to a stop. "We'll wait here until a tractor arrives to tow us back to the hangar."

After this was done, the Hardys and their pilot examined the windows of the plane curiously.

"I've never seen anything like it," Joe declared.

"It looks as if something had upset the molecular structure of the material in the windows," Jack said.

"Whatever caused the crazing," Frank concluded, must have had something to do with that gadget Barto was aiming at us."

"Let's search his apartment in Clayton," Joe suggested. "Maybe we'll find a clue."

"Just what I had in mind," Frank said. "I'll call Dad at Mr Alden's office and ask if he can arrange to get a search warrant."

"I almost forgot," Joe interjected. "Our car is at the plant."

"Use mine," Jack said, tossing a set of keys to the boys. "I'll stay here and see about getting the windows replaced."

The boys hurried off to meet their father at Alden's office.

"The warrant's all set," Mr Hardy said. "Clayton Police Station is sending a man to meet us at Barto's apartment."

They were greeted by a jolly, sturdily built policeman. "I got a master key from the superintendent," he informed them. "Makes it easier."

The Hardys were not surprised by what they saw when entering the apartment. A chest of drawers had been emptied of its contents and the closets were bare. The general untidiness of the rooms indiciated that the tenant had left in a hurry.

"Barto didn't waste any time getting out of here," Joe commented.

"Dodson's call from Haversville obviously scared him away," Frank concluded. "He knew the police might check his number."

"This proves one thing," Mr Hardy put in. "Barto must be in with the gang that's after Alden's motor. In fact, he might even be the leader."

Frank discovered a single fingerprint on the telephone. He lifted the print with his special tape and placed it in a celluloid container. "Must be Barto's," he remarked. "But I'll ask Chief Collig to check it just to be sure."

Meanwhile, Joe was rummaging through the waste-basket. He pulled out a crumpled, typewritten letter and two sheets of carbon paper. "I've found something," he called to his brother and father. They examined the letter together. It read:

Dear Barto:

I'm sorry to hear that your brother had trouble with his employer and moved on. Perhaps the strain of his labours was too much for him.

I wish you could visit me. I'm still operating my old mansion as a restaurant. One night I had forty customers. They came from miles around. However, I have competition about two miles north of my place. It is called the Claymore. Tonight I intend to go there to see how well they are doing. It is just off the main highway. I must go now, since it is getting late and I always make a point of retiring by twelve.

Write soon.

Your friend,
Eric

"I wonder who Eric is," Joe mused.

"Too bad we don't have the envelope the letter came in," Mr Hardy said. "It would tell us where it was mailed."

"What's written looks innocent enough," Frank observed. "Just the same, I want to examine it more carefully, and for luck I'll take these two sheets of carbon paper."

A further search of the rooms revealed nothing more. The Hardys thanked the Clayton policeman who had been assigned to accompany them and returned to Bayport. Frank stopped to give Chief Collig the fingerprint he had lifted from Barto's phone.

"I'll check it right away," the officer said.

"Thanks," Frank responded. "I'll be at home. Please call me there."

The boys and their father arrived home to find Aunt Gertrude in a jovial mood. "I have wonderful news!" she exclaimed. "Mr Benson telephoned. He's found a buyer. My stable is as good as sold."

"Glad to hear it," Mr Hardy told her. "That should put your mind at rest."

"Indeed it will," Aunt Gertrude agreed. "But I hope the new owner is an expert in caring for horses. I would dislike the thought of those poor animals being neglected."

"Do I detect a change of heart?" Joe asked, with a grin. "How come you're so fond of horses all of a sudden?"

"I always have been," Aunt Gertrude defended herself. "I just don't think they should be raced round a silly track for people's amusement."

Joe said, his eyes twinkling, "Someday I'm going to take you to a race!"

After supper the boys went to their crime lab and examined the letter they had found in Barto's apartment.

"Do you think it contains some kind of a code message?" Joe asked his brother.

"Not any more than the first letter I found in Barto's

wastebasket the day I took his fingerprints from the doorknob," Frank replied. "What about the sheets of carbon paper?"

"Haven't had a chance to examine them carefully yet," Joe said. "So far, it looks quite ordinary."

At that moment Chet Morton entered the lab. "Hi, master minds," he greeted the Hardys. "Got a few minutes to talk?"

"We always have time for you," Frank assured his friend, with a smile. "What's on your mind?"

"It's about my rocket cycle," Chet announced.

"Oh, no!" Joe exclaimed. "I thought you gave that up as a bad idea."

"I intended to," Chet replied. "But then I had a brainstorm."

Frank winked at his brother. "This ought to be good," he remarked.

"Okay!" Chet protested. "If you don't want to hear about my invention, just say so."

"I'm sorry," Frank said. "Go ahead."

The chubby youth took a rolled sheet of paper from his hip pocket and spread it out across the table. On it was the rough sketch of a bicycle. "See these tubes underneath the seat?" he began.

"Yes," Joe told him. "How could we forget? They're your rockets."

"Wrong!" Chet declared with a flourish of his hand. "What you see are jet engines. And I won't even have to build them myself. The hobby shop sells these units for model planes and boats. About four of them will produce enough thrust to propel my bike."

"If you insist on going ahead with the project,"

Frank warned, "just make sure that there are plenty of hedges around for you to fall into."

"Stow the comedy," Chet retorted. "The bike won't run away with me again. Since the jets are operated with liquid fuel, I'll be able to control the power."

"When do you plan to unveil this great invention of yours?" Joe inquired sceptically.

"In a couple of days," Chet announced proudly.

"This calls for a celebration," Frank said. "Aunt Gertrude baked an apple pie today. What say we go to the kitchen and have some?"

"Lead me to it!" their friend exclaimed.

As the boys were being served, Chief Collig telephoned. "I just got the results on the fingerprint you gave me," he said to Frank.

"I assume it's Barto's," Frank commented.

"No," the chief replied. "The print is from his brother Vilno!"

18

Night Chase

"THAT's incredible!" Frank declared.

He and Joe rushed to their father's study to tell him the news.

"Then Vilno was in his brother's apartment," Mr Hardy concluded. "But why?"

"To help Barto steal the experimental car," Joe suggested.

"If so," Frank argued, "why wasn't Vilno with his brother when we spotted the car from the air?"

"Maybe they decided to go their separate ways after the theft," Mr Hardy said.

Frank frowned. "I wonder," he muttered, "if Vilno has been posing as his brother all the time."

"Impossible!" Joe said. "Those were Barto's finger-prints you lifted off the doorknob the day you followed him to his apartment. And don't forget, Vilno is not a sheet-metal worker. How could he do his brother's job at the plant?"

"Guess you're right," Frank finally agreed. "But it's an interesting theory."

Mr Hardy rubbed his chin dubiously. "I'm going to try getting more background on those two," he said. "It may lead up a blind alley. Yet I might discover some useful information."

Their discussion was interrupted by a telephone call from Alden.

"The police have retrieved my experimental car," the executive told Mr Hardy. "Unfortunately Barto got away."

"What happened?" the detective asked.

Alden explained that a state trooper, who was patrolling the road indicated by the boys, had spotted the car travelling at great speed. He gave chase, but found that his motorcycle was not fast enough to close the gap.

"Then Barto blew a tyre and spun out of control," Alden continued. "By the time the officer reached the spot, Barto was gone."

"Was the car damaged?" Mr Hardy queried.

"A little," Alden answered. "But nothing that can't be repaired in a few hours. In fact, I had considered entering it in a road race that's scheduled near here a couple of days from now. However, I don't think I will."

After hanging up, the detective told his sons what Alden had said.

"I wonder where Barto was taking the car," Joe mused.

"Your guess is as good as mine," Mr Hardy admitted.

Frank thought for a moment. "I have an idea," he said finally. "Let's ask Mr Alden to enter his car in the road race. Then the night before the event Joe and I will inspect the route. We might spot one of those signposts."

"It's worth a try," their father agreed.

The following morning Frank telephoned Alden and told him his plan.

"I'll do anything to help clear up the mystery," Alden stated. He agreed to the plan, then described the route of the race.

After Frank put down the phone, Joe said, "I hope you don't plan on our using bicycles like the last time. If you do, I'm going to ask Chet to install a couple of his jet engines on mine."

Frank grinned. "We'll use our car."

"But if there are members of the gang around, they'll hear us coming," Joe objected.

"So far, the signposts have been set precisely beyond a sharp curve in the road. There'll be a full moon. We can cruise along with our lights out, and every time we come to a curve we'll stop and inspect it on foot."

It was clear and cool the night before the event. The boys waited until midnight before starting out for the race site, which was situated a few miles west of Clayton. When they arrived, Frank turned out the headlights and drove slowly along the route described by Alden.

"Maybe we're too early," Joe warned. "If the gang does intend putting up a signpost, we might finish our search before they get here."

"We'll keep patrolling the road till dawn," Frank said. "If they haven't set one up already, they'll have to do it before daylight."

The boys stared into the darkness. As they approached the first sharp bend in the road, Frank stopped the car. He and his brother edged their way around it on foot.

"Nothing there," Joe observed.

The Hardys returned to the car and continued on.

They had almost covered the entire route when another sharp bend appeared ahead of them. They climbed out of the vehicle and walked forward.

"Hold it!" Joe ordered in a low voice. "Do you hear something?"

Frank listened, then nodded. "Sounds like several men mumbling to one another," he whispered.

Crouching low, the boys cautiously worked their way around the bend. Then suddenly the Hardys came to a stop. The shadowy images of five men could be seen standing near a pickup truck a short distance down the road. A signpost stood nearby.

"Rotten luck," one of the men growled in a hushed voice. "This generator we brought doesn't work."

"We should've checked it out at the lab," another man added.

"I know those voices," Frank hissed. "It's Dodson and Barto!"

"I wonder if Vilno is with them," Joe whispered.

A couple of men lifted a heavy object on to the back of the truck.

"Slade! You and Tadlow go back and get another generator," Barto ordered. "But be quick about it. Everything has to be set up before it gets light."

Two men leaped into the truck and started off. The driver executed a U-turn and headed in the direction of the Hardys.

Frank pointed to a clump of brush a few feet away. "Take cover!"

The boys managed to conceal themselves just before the truck flashed by.

"They're bound to spot our car!" Joe said anxiously.

A moment later he and Frank were panic-stricken to hear the truck screech to a halt. Soon one of its occupants came running back to rejoin his companions.

"Barto!" the man exclaimed. "There's a car parked beyond the bend. It wasn't there before!"

"Maybe it's the police!" Dodson spluttered.

"I don't think so," Barto argued. "They would've driven up and asked us what we're doing here." He turned to his pals. "Spread out and start searching the area. There must be snoopers around."

The men took out flashlights and began walking down the road towards the Hardys.

"What'll we do?" Joe said.

"Our only chance is to make a break for it," Frank decided. "Head for the car. There'll be only one man to get past."

The boys leaped to their feet and sprinted down the road as fast as they could.

"Look!" Barto yelled, as he directed his beam of light towards the fleeing youths. "There go a couple of guys!"

"It's those Hardy kids!" Dodson shouted. "Don't let them get away!"

As Frank and Joe rounded the bend, they saw the driver of the truck standing beside their car. Joe crouched low, shot forward, and buried his right shoulder into the man's midriff. The fellow went crashing to the ground.

Frank leaped behind the steering wheel of the car and started the engine. Joe climbed in beside him just as Barto and his friends bore down on the boys.

"Stop them!" Dodson yelled.

"Don't let those Hardy kids get away!" shouted
Dodson

After making a quick U-turn, the boys sped along the road and away from their pursuers. Joe peered out of the rear window. "They're coming after us in the truck!"

Frank gave the convertible more power. "Are they gaining on us?"

"No!" Joe answered. "But we're not losing them either!"

After rounding another sharp bend in the road, Frank noticed a trail ahead which struck off to the right and into a wooded area. "Hang on!" he cried. "I'm going to try something!"

Swerving sharply, Frank turned on to the trail. After they had travelled a short distance, he switched off the engine and lights. A moment later their pursuers raced past and continued down the road.

"Your manœuvre worked!" Joe said with a grin.

"We're not out of this yet," Frank warned. "Barto and his men are sure to figure out what happened. We'll get back on the road and drive in the opposite direction."

He restarted the engine and rolled only a few feet when he brought the vehicle to a stop.

"What's wrong?" Joe queried.

"I'm afraid we have a flat!"

The boys climbed out of the car and were dismayed to see that the left front tyre had been punctured by a sharp rock.

"What a time to have this happen!" Joe muttered.

At that instant they heard the sound of a vehicle approaching in the distance.

"It must be Barto and the others!" Joe concluded.

"Quick! Let's hide!"

"Where?"

Frank glanced around. "We'll climb a tree. That one over there should be the easiest. Get going! I'll follow you!"

Soon the Hardys were pulling themselves up through the branches, high above the ground. A thick mass of leaves provided excellent cover. There was one small clear spot which permitted them to view the road.

"We made it just in time," Joe said. "There's the pickup truck. Barto and his men are turning in here!"

The boys' pulses quickened as they watched the truck come to a halt immediately behind their car.

"I told you those kids must've turned in here after we didn't see them on the road ahead!" Dodson declared. "Good trick. Lucky I remembered our passing this trail."

"But where are they?" Barto growled. He examined the damaged tyre. "I see they have a flat. Why didn't they try to fix it?"

"Probably heard us coming and ran off," Dodson replied. "Just the same, let's take a look around."

Frank and Joe were almost afraid to breathe as they watched their pursuers take out flashlights and search the area. At one point, a beam of light was directed towards the place in which the boys were hiding.

"That was close," Frank thought, as the beam was finally turned downwards.

"We'd better not waste any more time here!" Barto shouted. "Those snoopers may be on their way to call the police!"

"They've ruined everything," Dodson snarled.

447 THE SINISTER SIGNPOST

"We'll have to forget about using the signpost on Alden's car during the race. Let's pick it up and get out of here."

One of the men walked to the rear of the Hardys' car with a sharp-pointed tool. He proceeded to punch several holes in the fuel tank. Gasoline began to stream from it. "That'll stop 'em from usin' this in case they come back."

Barto and his henchmen climbed into the truck and drove off. The Hardys waited for a few minutes before leaving their hiding place.

"Here we are in the middle of nowhere without transportation," Joe said angrily.

"Won't help to complain about it." Frank sighed. "Must be five or six miles to the nearest telephone. Let's start walking."

They began trekking along the road. It had been daylight for more than an hour when they saw a saloon car approaching.

"Oh-oh," Joe remarked. "I hope none of Barto's men are in it."

As the car came to a stop, the boys were elated to see Alden behind the wheel and their father seated beside him.

"Am I glad to see you two!" Mr Hardy called out. "I became worried when I didn't hear from you. I decided to look for you and asked Mr Alden to come along." He peered at his sons curiously. "Why are you walking? Where's your car?"

The boys climbed into the rear seat of Alden's car and told the men what had happened. Then they drove to the spot where they had seen the signpost.

"This is where it was," Frank announced, pointing to a small hole on the shoulder of the road.

"The gang made certain that they didn't leave any clues behind," Mr Hardy observed.

"You boys have saved my experimental car from being wrecked," Alden interjected.

"You must be tired," Mr Hardy said to his sons.

"I insist you come to my house for breakfast and a few hours' sleep," Alden added.

The young detectives readily agreed. They rested until mid-afternoon, then returned to Alden's office. They had been there for only a few minutes when the phone rang. Alden picked up the receiver. He turned pale as he listened to what his caller had to say.

"What's the matter?" Mr Hardy asked after his client hung up.

"That—that was Barto's brother Vilno!" Alden stammered. "He has Roger! He said unless I give him my experimental motor, he'll harm my son. He's calling again in two hours for my answer."

·19·

Breaking the Code

THE Hardys were shocked by the news.

Alden was almost at the point of collapse. "If Vilno and his gang want my motor that badly, I'll give it to them."

The three detectives were angry. Mr Hardy exclaimed, "I'd like to get my hands on those scoundrels! They'll stop at nothing!"

"If only we had a lead to where their hideout is," Joe put in.

Frank frowned. "Maybe the lead is right in our files at home."

"What do you mean?" Joe asked.

"Maybe the letters we found in Barto's apartment do contain a code after all," Frank answered.

Mr Hardy nodded. "Why don't you boys go back to Bayport and work on that angle?" He handed them a set of keys. "Take my car. It's in the plant's car park. I'll stay here and be on hand when Vilno calls back."

"Meanwhile," Alden told the boys, "I'll send one of my tow trucks to pick up your car."

Frank and Joe hurried home, took Barto's letters from the file, then went to their crime lab to study them.

After an hour had passed, Joe sighed. "We're no closer to discovering a key than we were the last time we examined the letters."

"Looks hopeless," Frank agreed. "But let's keep at it a bit longer."

Shrugging, Joe turned his attention to the sheets of carbon paper found in Barto's apartment. He scrutinized them carefully and thought they looked a bit different from the usual carbon paper. Suspicious, Joe sandwiched a sheet between two sheets of white paper, picked up a pencil, and began scribbling on the upper one.

Suddenly he sat bolt upright. "This is odd! The carbon doesn't produce a copy except in a few isolated spots."

Frank jumped to his feet. "Joe! You may have discovered the key to the code!"

"I hope so. Fortunately our typewriter has pica type like Barto's machine. I'll type an exact copy of the first of his letters," Joe said. "If our hunch is correct . . ." His words trailed off as he inserted two clean sheets into the typewriter. Then he began tapping out the words.

Dear Eric:

Forgive me for taking so long to write you, but I've been so exhausted from work the last few days that I didn't feel I could write a coherent sentence. How I wish I had the stamina of two hard-working boys who have taken summer jobs at the plant. Any family would be proud to have sons like that.

As I already told you, my brother has left the Alden company . . .

When Joe finished typing the letter, he pulled out the sheets and quickly examined the carbon copy.

"That's it! We've broken the code!" he exclaimed. "Trick carbon paper!"

Joe showed Frank the copy. "Notice that the carbon has transferred only certain words and portions of words on to the copy sheet. First we have the word 'hard'. Next, the 'y' and 's' from the word 'boys'."

"Spelling out 'Hardys'!" Frank declared.

"And the next word is 'sons', and so on."

The boys observed that the complete message read:

Hardys, sons of detective, here. I'm sure they're investigating.

Tingling with excitement, Frank handed his brother the second of Barto's letters and the other sheet of carbon paper. "Quick! Make a copy of this!"

Joe repeated the procedure. The carbon copy revealed the following message:

moved lab to old mansion forty miles north of Clayton on route twelve.

"It must be the location of the gang's hideout!" Frank exclaimed.

He rushed to the telephone and dialled Alden's private office number. There was no answer.

"It's after office hours," Joe said. "Mr Alden's secretary must have left. Why don't you try the company's main number?"

Following his brother's suggestion, Frank finally got a response from the plant's chief watchman. "Sorry, I can't help you," the man told Frank. "Me and my men just came on duty. I haven't seen Mr Alden or anyone else."

Next, Frank tried the executive's home. Again there was no answer.

"I wonder where Dad and Mr Alden are," Frank muttered.

"Maybe they went to meet Vilno."

"Dad would have called us. I don't like this."

"If they're delivering the experimental motor to Vilno, he and his gang may try to make a getaway after they have it. Let's go to their hideout."

"Okay!" Frank agreed. "But since Mother and Aunt Gertrude won't get home from the theatre till late I'll ask Chet to stand by the phone here. He can tell Dad where we are if he should call."

Twenty minutes later Chet's ancient yellow car rumbled to a stop in front of the Hardy home. The boys noticed that their friend had his jet-propelled bicycle lashed to the rear bumper.

"I'm taking my bike to a secret spot early tomorrow morning," Chet announced. "It's ready for the supreme test."

"Lots of luck," Frank said. "I hope the job we're asking you to do isn't going to interfere with your plans."

"Not at all," the chubby youth replied grandly. "What is it you want me to tell your father if he calls?"

Frank handed him the message they had decoded revealing the location of the gang's hideout.

"I'd rather be going with you," Chet muttered, "instead of having to sit at the telephone."

"We wish you could too," Joe assured him. "But

your job is an important one. We'll check with you later."

It was already dusk when the Hardys drove off. Forty miles to the north of Clayton, Joe pointed to a dimly lighted building in the distance. "I think I've spotted the mansion! It's behind those trees over to the right."

Frank brought the car to a stop near the foot of a long wooded driveway. He and his brother continued on foot. The house was situated quite a distance from the main road.

"I don't see anybody or signs of activity," Joe whispered as they neared the building.

"Just the same, be careful. If this *is* Vilno's hideout he's sure to have one or more guards posted."

The boys crept forward towards the front of the house, keeping in the darkness of the trees. Suddenly Joe grabbed his brother's arm. "Look!" he whispered. "There's a man up ahead, seated on that big rock. He's armed!"

"It's a guard all right, Joe. He's Tadlow, one of the men we saw with Barto and Dodson at the sinister signpost!"

"Then we're at the right place. Let's nab him."

"Okay."

The Hardys stalked their quarry. When they were within arm's reach of the man, he jumped to his feet and whirled round to face them.

Quick as a flash Joe leaped and caught the man squarely on the jaw with a right uppercut. He tumbled to the ground unconscious. Nearby lay his rifle, which Frank flung into a clump of brush.

The boys dragged the man to a slim tree, put his arms around the trunk, and tied his wrists together with a belt. The placing of a handkerchief gag completed the job.

Moving cautiously, the boys continued towards the mansion. They kept a sharp lookout for other guards, but there were none. When the Hardys reached their goal, they detected a humming sound.

"What do you think that is?" Joe hissed.

"Offhand, I'd say it's some kind of machine," Frank answered. "Seems to be coming from the basement."

The boys started to creep round the outside of the mansion. Soon they discovered a metal air vent in the foundation. Frank peered through it in amazement.

"See anything?" Joe asked in a hushed voice.

"Yes. Looks like a physics or electronics laboratory."

Joe crouched just as three men came into Frank's view. They were Vilno, Barto, and Dodson. The boys pressed their ears against the vent in an effort to hear what the men were saying.

"This is a good set-up here," Barto remarked. "Too bad we have to leave it."

"Now that we have the experimental motor," Vilno put in, "there's no reason for us to stick around."

"What about the prisoners?" Dodson inquired. "Alden and his son don't worry me, but that detective Hardy can be dangerous to us."

Frank and Joe gasped. Their father had been captured together with Mr Alden and Roger!

"Forget it," Vilno told Dodson. "We'll be miles away before anyone finds Hardy."

Frank turned to his brother. "We must rescue them!"

"We can't do it alone! There are probably more members of the gang inside."

Suddenly the tall figure of a man loomed up behind the boys. "Who are you?" he demanded.

Frank and Joe leaped to defend themselves. A wild struggle followed. They crashed against the side of the house several times. Then Frank dealt the man a blow that sent him crumbling to the ground.

Suddenly the young detectives heard another, but louder, humming sound. In the next instant they were horror-stricken to find that they could not move.

"What's happening?" Joe exclaimed.

The boys were frozen in their tracks. Some powerful, invisible force was holding them!

·20·

Jet Action

"IT'S THE Hardy kids!" Dodson shouted as he, Barto, and two other men arrived on the scene.

"Don't get too close to them," Barto warned his pals, "or you'll get caught in the sonic trap yourselves. Tadlow! Go and tell my brother to turn it off."

Within a couple of minutes the boys were released from the mysterious force that had prevented them from moving. The after effects, however, caused Frank and Joe to fall to the ground, exhausted. Dodson and the others pounced on them and tied the boys' hands behind their backs.

"So! How do you like our little sonic trap?" Barto sneered.

"Sonic trap?" Frank said weakly.

"Yes," Barto replied. "It's another of Vilno's inventions. A device which encloses objects of our choosing within a solid shell of hypersonic vibrations. Your father also had the honour of experiencing its effects."

Frank and Joe were marched into the mansion, then down a flight of stairs leading to the basement. They were awed by what they saw. The area had been converted into a large laboratory, and was filled with various pieces of electronic equipment. In one corner of the room lay several signposts marked DANGER.

"Welcome! Welcome!" Vilno exclaimed with exaggerated politeness. "Looking for your father? Well, you've come to the right place."

"If you've harmed him," Joe began, "or . . ."

"He's perfectly fit," Vilno interrupted, "and is in our storage room with Alden and his son. You shall join them shortly."

For the first time the boys had an opportunity to see Vilno and Barto together. They were identical twins. Except for a difference in dress, it was difficult to tell who was who.

"Perhaps our guests would like to see some of the things we invented," Barto sneered.

"That *we* invented? You're forgetting it was my genius alone that made our devices possible!" his twin said boastfully.

"How did you manage to craze the windshields of Mr Alden's racing cars?" Frank interjected.

Vilno seemed pleased by the question. He led the Hardys to the signposts. "Inside each of these is a hypersonic generator of my own design. I found that I could disturb the molecular arrangement in some materials with the waves it produces. These are what crazed the windshields of Alden's cars."

"And the windows of our plane!" Joe said angrily.

"Ah yes," Vilno said. A sinister smile spread across his face. He walked to a table and picked up a long, cylindrical object. "Your plane was among the first objects on which I tried the portable version of the hypersonic generator."

"Then it was you, and not Barto, who stole Mr Alden's experimental car," Frank remarked.

"Precisely," Vilno replied.

At that moment Barto began to roar with laughter. "They still don't know," he told his brother, "that it was you who was working at the plant all the time, posing as me!"

"But how could you carry on the deception?" Joe spluttered. "You're not a sheet-metal worker."

"That's where you're wrong," Vilno shot back. "My brother and I were both trained in sheet-metal work as youths. But I never claimed it as one of my skills. My ambition was to become a scientist."

"Why are we standing around here talking?" Dodson said impatiently. "These snoopers might have told the police they were coming here!"

"Then where are they?" Vilno countered. "You worry too much."

"I don't care what you say!" Dodson retorted. "I . . ."

"Shut up!" Barto broke in. "We should've let you stay in jail for stealing Alden's race horse. Why did you do it? Aren't we paying you enough?"

"And your stupidity didn't end with the horse theft," Vilno added, with a touch of irritation. "You made the mistake of telephoning me at my apartment from Haversville Police Headquarters. Idiot! I knew the Hardys were bound to check the number."

Dodson grimaced but said, "You're not so smart. You started a fire in the experimental lab."

Frank broke in. "Vilno, you say you were posing as your brother all the time. Yet it was Barto's fingerprints

I found on the doorknob of your apartment the day I followed you home from the plant."

"Quite simple," Vilno answered proudly. "Barto and I were dressed exactly alike and switched places in the lobby. It was he you saw enter the apartment."

"But how did you know you were going to be followed that day?" Joe asked quickly.

"Your taking summer jobs at the plant didn't fool us," Barto put in. "We knew you were probably investigating the Alden case. Vilno guessed that he would be a suspect, and that you would undoubtedly shadow him. So, each day, we wore similar clothes in the event we had to switch places. The plan paid off. You followed the wrong one on the street in Clayton. Vilno pretended a friend was a tramp and shoved him away."

"We've told them enough," Vilno growled. "Put them in the storage room with the others."

Dodson and two men marched Frank and Joe out of the laboratory and down a narrow passageway. They came to a stop in front of a heavy metal door. Dodson pulled it open.

"Inside!" he ordered.

The boys entered a small, windowless room made of stone. Before the door was closed, they saw their father, Alden, and Roger.

"Dad!" Joe exclaimed.

"I see you two also had some bad luck," the detective said remorsefully.

The metal door clanged shut and the Hardys and their companions were in total darkness.

"We were surprised to learn that you and Mr Alden

had been captured, Dad," Frank remarked grimly.

"I walked into Vilno's sonic trap," Mr Hardy explained.

"How did you find the gang's hideout?" Joe asked.

"After you left Mr Alden's office, I went to Clayton Police Station in Mr Alden's car to tell them about the situation, and to arrange for help in case we needed it. I planned to return to the plant in time for Vilno's telephone call. When I was driving back, I saw Mr Alden go by me from the opposite direction in a truck."

"Sorry about that." The executive sighed. "This is how it happened, boys. Vilno called me again shortly after your father left. He told me he'd been watching the plant and saw Mr Hardy drive off. Vilno was worried he was going to the police and demanded I deliver the experimental motor to him immediately. For Roger's sake, I had no choice."

"What happened then?" Frank asked.

"Vilno ordered me to bring the motor to the Bryant crossroads north of Clayton," Mr Alden replied. "There, two of his men jumped into the truck with me and told me to drive on. We came here to the mansion."

"I followed the truck," Mr Hardy interjected. "Too bad I didn't have my own car, or I would have contacted you boys by radio. And unfortunately I couldn't stop to use a telephone."

"You people wouldn't be in this mess if it wasn't for me," Roger muttered.

Frank began to grope around their enclosure, hoping for a way of escape. His father said, "The walls are solid, and you couldn't budge that metal door with a bulldozer."

"The room is completely sealed," Mr Alden added, "except for an air vent. Thank goodness for that."

"Air vent," Frank repeated, looking for it.

"It's near the ceiling," Mr Hardy said. "But if you're thinking of an escape route, it's too small for any of us to crawl through."

"Let me try," Joe urged. "I've managed to squeeze through some pretty small spaces before."

Mr Hardy guided his sons to the rear wall of the room. "The vent should be directly above this spot."

Frank hoisted his brother on to his shoulders. Joe ran one hand along the upper portion of the wall. "I've found it! The vent is covered with a metal grating." There was a momentary pause. "I think I can pull it loose."

Joe tugged the grating hard. Finally it broke free of the wall. "The opening is small, but I'm sure I can manage to get through. Boost me up higher."

Frank grabbed his brother's feet with both hands and shoved him upward. An instant later Joe was gone.

"Be careful, son," Mr Hardy called.

But Joe was not free yet. He was in an air duct. His arms stretched out in front of him, Joe forced his way through the narrow passageway. Minutes seemed like hours. Finally he was elated to find that the vent led directly outside the mansion.

Another grating, however, barred his way. He grasped the bars with both hands and shoved with all his strength. The grating loosened and dropped outside to the ground.

After climbing out of the vent, Joe scanned his surroundings. Several yards away he saw Vilno and his henchmen preparing to depart in Alden's truck.

Stealthily, the young detective stalked towards the front door of the mansion. Luckily it was unlocked. He raced inside and ran down to the storage room to free his companions.

"Quick! Vilno and his men are getting ready to leave!"

The three Hardys and their friends rushed outside. They were crestfallen to see that the truck had already pulled away.

"We'll never catch them!" Frank declared.

"Look!" Joe yelled. "What's that glow?"

His companions were startled to see a bright ball of light approaching the truck head-on. Just as a collision seemed imminent, the vehicle veered off the lane. This was followed by a loud crunching sound.

"What's that?" Alden shouted.

They detected a roar as the glow grew closer. Then it suddenly vanished. Seconds later Chet Morton coasted out of the darkness on his jet-propelled bicycle.

"Hi, fellows! Am I glad to see you!"

"Chet! What are you doing here?" Frank exclaimed.

"I began to worry when I didn't hear from you," the chubby youth explained. "So did your mother and aunt. I decided to see what was going on. My car ran out of fuel about a mile from here, so I came the rest of the way on my jet bike." His eyes widened. "By the way, I almost ran into a truck! What happened to it?"

The Hardys hurried to the spot where they had seen the vehicle veer off the lane. They found it tightly wedged between two stout trees. Vilno and his pals were desperately trying to open the doors but without success.

Just then a State Police car arrived on the scene. One of the troopers got out. "Did any of you see a wild kid on a bicycle?" he questioned. "We think it turned in here. Looked as if it was on fire."

"I'm the one," Chet admitted sheepishly.

"What were you trying to do?" the officer demanded. "You went by us as if you'd been shot out of a cannon." His attention was attracted by the disabled truck. "What happened here? Accident?"

Mr Hardy stepped forward. "Let me explain," he said.

After hearing the story, the officer radioed for additional men, then the troopers took Vilno and his henchmen into custody.

"We'd have escaped if it hadn't been for that crazy friend of yours and his bicycle," the gang leader growled.

"That's your hard luck!" Joe told him.

Mr Hardy said, "We know that specifications of Mr Alden's motor were leaking out of the plant. How did you manage it?"

Vilno's egotism caused him to forget his predicament for a moment. "Easy! Alden's machinists worked from plans recorded on film slides. I just roamed around the plant and photographed the projected pictures with a spy camera in my wrist watch. Other components I committed to memory and put them down on paper later."

Soon more troopers arrived. The prisoners were herded into patrol cars. The case of *The Sinister Signpost* was over. Frank and Joe always regretted such a moment. They were not restless for long, however, because the mystery of the *Footprints Under the Window* soon came their way.

Before departing, one of the officers walked up to Chet. "I should give you a ticket for speeding," he announced, winking at the Hardys.

"I—I wish you wouldn't," Chet stammered. "It won't happen again."

"Well, under the circumstances, I think I can overlook it this time." The trooper sighed, trying not to grin. "Anyway, I wouldn't know how to describe your jet-propelled bike to the judge."

"We warned you about that invention of yours," Joe whispered, nudging his chum. "Lucky for us you didn't listen!"